THE KAWAI SCROLLS

THE
SCROLLS

A NOVEL

Louis Druehl

TIDEWATER PRESS

Copyright © 2018 Louis Druehl
All rights reserved. No part of this publication may be reproduced, stored in a retrieval system or transmitted in any form or by any means—electronic, mechanical, audio recording, or otherwise—without the written permission of the publisher.

Published by Tidewater Press
New Westminster, BC, Canada
www.tidewaterpress.ca

ISBN 978-1-7751659-2-7 (paperback)
ISBN 978-1-7751659-3-4 (html)

Cataloguing in Publication data available from Library and Archives Canada

Cover credits:
The Hell of Foxes and Wolves, Hell Scroll, 12th Century, Heian Period,
Nara National Museum, Japan
American flag: Can Stock Photo / stillfx

1 3 5 7 9 10 8 6 4 2

Printed in Canada

For four decades of Japanese camaraderie

My barred cell is cold. Outside, I hear the sounds of nature and I imagine the forests, fields and waterways, with their generous gifts of food, clothing and tranquility. Here my necessities are provided by my executioners, not God. The jailer has gone from taunting me to being openly curious. Why will I not denounce my religion to save my life? My vow is greater than my life. He asked if I had regrets and I told him the loss of Yezo wilderness, the loss of first friend Unacharo. I blessed him for providing me with this parchment, and for this brush and ink to write what I must. I pray my testament will find sympathetic eyes and that my words will live, as I will not.

Maple spirit whirls, lands, gods wait.
Owl sings, fox barks, aconite arrow stings.
Shiro now Ainu god.
The gods have spoken.

> Discovered with Shiro Kawai's testimonial, written on the eve of his martyrdom, September 22, 1670

John Fox leaned over the rusty railing holding a flapping toilet paper streamer.

On the dock below, a transvestite Amazonian pulled on her end of the bunting and shouted up, "I love only you. Come back soon. Johnny, don't forget your Lulu."

She looked gaudy, her makeup not quite hiding her morning shadow, her tight clothes wrinkled and not quite fitting right, and her smile slightly forced, like a dowdy mother more interested in booze than some kid. But John saw only his deliverer.

In twelve hours, she had guided him through Chinese and Thai foods, cable cars, escalators and underground parking, coke and the realization the world was not just inhabited by cowboys and Indians and corn pickers, but by a plethora of Asian races and blacks: Jamaican, African, Yankee. And sex: not guiltily, recklessly, and mostly joylessly screwing, but happy, ice-cube-explosive, wolf-howling, chow-mein-hungry copulation.

"Johnny, call it fornication. It's dirty, get-down-on-your-knees dirty. *Hoooowl.*"

As the ship slipped lines, the streamer stretched, breaking the bond between traveler and homebody. Goodbye, San Francisco.

The iron deck shuddered under his feet. Holding his Winnie the Pooh bear high, he filled his lungs with tangy sea air, his brain screaming, "I, John Fox, of Rolfe, Iowa, aspiring anthropologist, am liberated from the chains of Podunk academia and American mores. Japan, here I come."

And gulls wheeled and squawked and threatened above.

A lady spoke, "You're from Rolfe, Iowa? My grandfather, on my mother's side, was from Rolfe. I'm Betty. What's your name?"

She stood about five-foot-six, trim figure, no flab, pleasant swell of breast, taut skin slightly freckled, brown hair framing a carefully made-up face, and curiously spiky teeth.

Did she read minds, or had he spoken out loud? In any case, he wanted to be away to meet his cabin mate and steerage drinking buddies—a compatible band, to quote his travel agent. And he needed to digest the last few days events: his transformation from an Iowan hayseed to an academically clad associate of sophisticated septuagenarians and the lovely Cathy, all leading to his first Ainu encounter—Koro, the blind domino player. Then, last night: Lulu, and her spinning San Francisco tour, climaxing with a divergence from the not undelightful, desert-scent-driven—albeit conventional—First Nations' sex with Nursey, his Hopi bride. Ex-bride.

"Nice to meet you. I'm John Fox. Please excuse me, I've got to get down to my cabin."

She grasped his elbow in a manner that would become familiar and turned him toward her. "Dr. John Fox, let's go to my cabin and get acquainted. I want to know all about your fascinating Lulu."

Courted by a woman, probably his mother's age, and he hadn't even unpacked. Her nutmeg scent, a mulled wine memory, removed any dithering on his part. And the prospect of seeing a topside cabin also beckoned. According to his travel agent, his would be a second-class cabin, "below the waterline," while some perpetual guests of the ship had first-class cabins, "above the waterline."

Following Betty through the passageways, John puffed up: Dr. John Fox. Sounded right. Nursey would never consider him Professor Doctor and he would never have revealed this imminent academic accolade to Lulu, not smutty enough. But Betty? This encounter had potential.

John's mother, having just dowsed his dad with his evening scotch, turned to John and said, "Johnny, a botany lesson. Every seed has potential; to discover its potential you must water it and pray it's a good seed. I pray you're a good seed. I pray Mendel is wrong. I pray you have a natural leaning toward curling." As she turned to leave, she pretended to hurl the glass at his father.

He ducked; she laughed. "It's Waterford, dear, much too valuable to waste on you. Don't stay up for me. I expect we'll be playing extra ends in tonight's bonspiel. Kiss, kiss."

They entered her cabin; the scent of gardenias swirled about him. He plopped down on a pink brocaded love seat, facing her, as she settled on a matching sofa.

"So, you're joining us merry wanderers. I must say, new blood will be refreshing and you are interesting, John: scrawny, slouched and bearded, with brown mousy hair, but nicely coiffed. Hmm, I wonder: a Spartan or, better still, a Rasputin? But then, the Harris tweed with leather elbow patches, and you do smell nice. I think we should go with something semi-clerical: Rasputin fits. You're a little rough around the edges."

"I've been to two universities, you know," he blurted.

Betty grew distant, suggesting a reconsideration of options. John nervously flipped through magazines resting on a glass-topped coffee table, ignoring the *San Francisco Chronicle* with its blaring headline, "Timothy McVeigh, the Oklahoma Bomber, Defiant."

Betty sighed, "Don't be presumptuous, John. It's not becoming, not in our company."

"Our company" struck him as an insult, a challenge. In response, he was about to say ship's rules discouraged mingling of steerage and first-class passengers but, as the new Dr. Fox, he thought otherwise. He felt he had just passed a test.

"I'd like to meet your friends. Maybe I'll study differences between those living above the waterline and those below . . . an anthropological field trip."

"Oh, John, that's too easy. In a word: Grey Goose."

Vodka? He looked at her.

"And, John, who my friends are is more important than what they're named: 'the little lady behind the seat of power,' 'the heiress of a vast estate.' You get the idea."

"And who are you, Betty?"

"Me? I'm just the constant traveler."

The thought that the difference between those above the waterline and those below could be reduced to a drink and obscure epithets went against his training. Comparative anthropology was complex. Many factors had to be considered: religion, architecture, pottery bits and weaving and arrowheads; economics, and bone structure and skin color and hairstyles. He worried he had forgotten something. He would have to check his notes.

To begin his research, he asked, "How do you get fresh flowers and the latest magazines? And what's your destination?"

"My bridge mates and I have no destination. The *Golden Maru* is our home. We choose to live this way because in our earlier lives we were too well known. We cherish privacy. And money is no problem for us." She pointed to a cluster of silver-framed photos, each showing Betty in the company of some famous person: Glen Ford, Henry Kissinger, Saul Bellow, Pierre Trudeau, Louis Armstrong.

John stood for a closer look. From each frame, Betty smiled, her tongue resting on carnivorous teeth. And on every photograph, the salutation: "To Betty, with love," and a famous signature.

"Sit beside me." She had kicked off her shoes and tucked her feet under a duvet. Her hand crept up the back of his neck and she twirled his hair through her fingers. Not too gently, she pulled his head toward her and sniffed. "Curious smell. Maybe from your San Francisco *Freudenfest*? Now, Herr Professor, the naughty bits about our Lulu."

A collapsed marriage—hot and premature—and a failing doctoral research project—ill-conceived and gutless—had compelled John to escape New Mexico three days ago, with the plan to establish residency among Japan's northern aborigines, the white Ainu of Hokkaido, and the subject of his revised thesis.

Eighteen Greyhound-bus hours later he was in San Francisco. He found the Folsom Street bus depot hectic, erotic and just plain scary. A quick trip to the washroom, where head-spinning suggestions scribbled on the walls sent him reeling out into the vibrant, foggy city.

A booking agent found him a berth on a freighter of opportunity, the *Golden Maru*. "She's not pretty, but the old girl is tough and Captain Tveit is the best Norway has turned out."

The agent then told John that the *Golden Maru* contained a large quantity of cowhides, available to the highest bidder, and a variety of shipped items destined for Yokohama. Their route to Japan would be adjusted to accommodate the sale of the hides.

"So, you may arrive in Japan later than you expect. This doesn't bother the first-class passengers, as they will go anywhere, and the others don't care where they are going. Your trip will be like a step into the past; slow down and enjoy it."

The thought of not having a scheduled arrival in Japan bothered John, but deep down it brought relief: the prospect of entering the alien Japanese culture terrified him.

The night before sailing, John strolled through North Beach

hoping to pluck the fruits of his newly found liberation—his interpretation of being compelled to go abroad to study. He was ready to live on the edge of the best San Francisco had to offer.

Life in Iowa and New Mexico had been corn and sagebrush, suffocating and drab, and left no fond memories. His hot-cold marriage with Nursey, his Hopi princess, and the efforts of Sue, the university psychologist, to restructure his life now seemed so . . . ho-hum.

Lulu was spectacular. Mile-high heels propelling a grand pelvic thrust, seamed silk stockings directing one's gaze to an inverted heart-shaped butt and a perfect bust to match. This wonder was John's pickup date under the Golden Gate. They had fun, and she had an STD to share.

Lulu asked if he would like to do a line and he replied, "According to Dr. Baker, my professor, Margaret Mead had it all wrong."

"You really don't know what STD means, do you?" she hooted. "To the pharmacy with you, off now to purchase a French letter, a willie warmer, a gummy bear, a manhole-cover or no buggery for you."

John explained that Sue, his psychologist, the practitioner of Kama Sutra for mental health, had warned him bus travel brings on constipation. Lulu shrieked, "That's a new twist."

She was gentle, she was kind, and she brought John out of the desert into the Land of Vaseline. He, John Fox, had just stepped about as far away from Iowan, Methodist, apple-pied mores as possible without blowing a major circuit.

"Good heavens, what fun. So you're not a doctor, you're . . . ?"

"My wife, Nursey, screwed the chairman of the philosophy department, and the chairman of my anthropology department insisted I put some meat into my thesis—lists and diagrams, stuff to thicken it up, appendices. So, I'm a cuckolded academic failure."

Betty patted him on the head, hummed a little Gershwin—"It ain't necessarily so"—and aimed him toward the door.

"Now leave, it's time for my nap," she said, handing him the latest issue of *The New Yorker*. "And John, don't forget your Pooh bear."

John ducked out onto the deck, clutching his bear that he silently scolded. Passing under the Golden Gate, he tried to look beyond the city's skyline to the nooks and crannies where Lulu had exploded his previous existence. He sniffed his jacket, seeking an olfactory cue of last night's debauchery, but that improbable dream defied reliving.

Now, his future rested with this rusty hulk and its sheltered human cargo. Then it struck him: he was on the ocean. He'd only laid eyes on saltwater yesterday. Today this tin can was all there was between him and dark fathomless depths. His only previous encounter with the sea was from Bible study: Jonah and the whale.

Mrs. Carver, the minister's wife, knelt beside John, resting her hand on his knee, her talcum scent whirled about him. He fought not to peek down her blouse, not to will her hand to creep up his thigh.

"The message is, you can't run away from God, Johnny. God is everywhere; he knows everything."

Mrs. Carver stood, tugged her skirt and smiled.

"He even knows what you are thinking and so do I. But don't worry, no matter what you think or do, if you repent, like Jonah, you will be saved. 'And the Lord spake unto the fish, and it vomited out Jonah upon the dry land.'" She reached down and gave his knee a squeeze.

The memory of the apricot-scented Mrs. Carver—God's messenger, the devil's agent—made him consider what was going to keep him from a watery grave: lifeboats, life jackets, that sort of thing.

Relying on God would not do. He decided to explore his new home. John cautiously stepped onto the catwalk overlooking the cargo hold. A smell, a memory of a slaughterhouse, rushed over him. The vast hold was stacked with bundles of hides: Hereford, Angus, Brahma, Holstein. The effect was a sprawling quilt, but nothing to remind him of the moon-eyed, soft-muzzled Jessie he had reared as a 4-H project, the first of many, he had hoped, to bear the unique Fox brand. And like a first love, this bovine had bewitched John. Many the sultry afternoon he had joined her in the stable where she chewed cud and belched, gently rocking him as he rested his head on her undulating tummy, his mind on sweet girls, sweaty and grimy, de-smutting fields of corn.

"Congratulations, son, you won the blue ribbon. She'll fetch an additional four cents a pound for you at auction."

"Auction?" parroted John.

The kind man, a Gene Autry, reached for Jessie's halter. "Here, give her to me. John, you've done a great job. I'd be a lucky man to eat a steak from this little heifer. I bet it'll be perfectly marbled."

"Steak? Jessie a steak? Marbled?"

"Yes, sir, and a fine leather jacket and gelatin and glue and tripe, too."

Misty-eyed, John followed his freshly trimmed and shampooed and brushed Jessie from the auction house to the stockyard where she joined other terrorized cattle in a corral of shit and mud, reeking of death and betrayal. He last glimpsed her straining to see him, her eyes white with fear, and being electrically prodded for her effort.

Creaks and groans from the weeping, rusty hull interrupted John's Jessie reverie. The thought that these walls were all that separated him from miles-deep ocean sent him scurrying to his cabin and what little comfort he could extract from his steerage mates.

Below the waterline, John met Sugar Baby, a kindergarten teacher who only spoke in three-word sentences, a stuttering remittance man who insisted on being addressed as "Sir" and a foul-mouthed preacher, whose only hint of religion was his ecclesiastical collar. Sharing quarters with John was a self-deprecating Canuck, a cliché of all that was Canadian. His fellow steerage passengers didn't speak of their past and they didn't know where they were going. For them, the *Golden Maru* was like a lens, first gathering and then scattering them; unlike those above the waterline, for whom she was a sanctuary.

John looked in the cabin mirror and tried to relive the past two days. He patted his nicely barbered hair, considered his new jacket and relished the memory of the thrill of having met Koro, his first Ainu. And Lulu.

Walking up Market Street, surrounded by immaculately coiffed men and women wearing nice clothes—smart suits with phallic ties, pleated skirts with dark high heels and matching purses—*Oh Nursey, is this the life you wanted?*

John sat on a park bench in Union Square and ate a spicy hot dog with fried onions; his first meal since getting off the bus. The swish of pantyhose distracted him, resulting in the plopping of a delinquent glob of mustard on his shirtfront.

Across the road was a tailor's shop. John left the distractions and went inside.

"How might I help you, sir?"

"I'm passing through. I don't have time for custom-made, but I'd like a sports coat, pants, shirt and tie. What have you got?" said John.

"You strike me as an academic. Am I correct, sir?" The elderly tailor was as formal as his speech. John shrugged a modest shrug.

"If you don't have a preference, might I suggest a Harris tweed jacket with leather elbow patches? That would look very smart on you and you'll find it comfortable." The first jacket John tried on fit perfectly.

"Now for the slacks, sir."

John stood in front of the mirrored back wall, looking this way and that, exploring his profile, seeking academic features.

The clerk kneeled at his side, rolling the pant legs up just so. He extracted pins from his mouth to secure the adjusted cuffs. A little tablet of chalk scribed the exact bottom of each pant leg.

"You'd be surprised how few people have legs the same length."

The man kneeling there and fussing with his pants gave John a strange feeling: a supplicant? His father begging forgiveness?

"Your pants and jacket will be ready in an hour."

John thanked him and made for the door.

"The barbershop is across the street," the tailor suggested. "Ask for Antonio."

"I saw you getting fitted by Henri. You're a very lucky man."

Antonio pulled John's shirt collar back and inserted a scratchy tissue. He misted his head with cologne, combed his hair and asked how he wanted it cut.

John snorted, "Surprise me."

"Oh, you are a daring young man," Antonio said, tilting John's head this way and that. "This will take a few minutes. Might I have my friend, Joe, shine your shoes?"

"Precious Lord Take My Hand" alternated with "*Il mio tesoro intanto*" from the barber's boom box, accompanying the duo as they transformed John.

The swish of a soft talcumed brush around his ears and a final snap of cloth across the toes of his shoes brought him back to reality and the awareness that all this attention had left him slightly aroused.

Black and white, Joe and Antonio stood together grinning as John inspected the new him: Marlon Brando, in *A Streetcar Named Desire*. Gingerly, he patted the sleek pompadour, feeling its gelled resistance. John smiled, paid and left.

"How smart of you to get your shoes shined," said Henri, pressing a light blue shirt and subdued striped tie against John's chest. "Now, put these on and see what you think."

They stood side by side, John amazed and Henri basking in the glory of his creation.

"If sir is spending the night in the city, I recommend the Park Floral Hotel up on Yeats Street."

Once on the sidewalk, John glanced over at the barbershop to see Joe and Antonio, thumbs up, smiling at him.

Walking to Yeats Street, John had the feeling people noticed him. He stood a little straighter, his shoes clicked on the sidewalk; he liked the way he felt. The new John would experience San Francisco.

A discreet bronze plaque announced the hotel. The foyer was cool and subdued, lots of wood, leather-covered chairs, and a high ceiling with a slow-turning fan. A pretty Chinese girl, who stood behind the reception desk, smiled as he approached. John liked the place instantly.

"I'll see to this gentleman. Thank you, Miss Li," said a cheery, over-the-hill Caucasian, built like a sumo wrestler. "How might we help you, sir?"

John looked over at the retreating receptionist, catching her backward glance. He asked for a room with a bath.

"Certainly, sir. We can arrange that. Will you be needing assistance with your luggage?"

John said not and, taking his key, walked up the wide staircase to the first floor.

He soaked in the bathtub, taking care not to disturb his hair. He would rest for a bit and then put on his new clothes and invite San Francisco into his life.

As he dozed, he dreamed a beautiful woman approached him as he sat at a bar. She smelled of crushed sage and her familiar voice whispered naughtiness in his ear. He turned—it was Nursey, but she did not recognize him. John tried to explain who he was. She told him to grow up.

A knock at the door and a housemaid ended the dream.

"Oh, I'm sorry, sir, I just came to turn down your bedding. I'll come back later."

John hoped she hadn't seen his boner beneath the towel. In the shower, the chilly water lowered his blood pressure, but endorphins continued to circulate. Awake and refreshed, John decided a steak dinner was what he needed.

"Sir, if you would be so kind as to leave your key, we'll keep it safe for you."

Maybe they want to break into my room? No, they must have other keys. John deposited the key in the waiting hand and turned to leave the lobby.

"Sir, may we recommend the Tadich Grill? It is just around the corner at 240 California Street and the food is excellent. Gentlemen are well treated there."

He couldn't remember when he had last made a choice for himself. Maybe when he asked for a room with a bath? Well, tonight he was going to treat himself to a well-done T-bone steak.

The Tadich Grill was packed. John sidled up to the bar, ordered a Coors, and scanned the Wild West decor. Behind the scarred wooden bar several waiters, none it seemed under seventy, took orders and delivered food and drink.

"Sir, the gentlemen in the back booth would appreciate the pleasure of your company."

Henri, Joe and Antonio, all nattily dressed, stood as John approached. They seated him next to Joe. Their waiter poured him a Knob Creek bourbon over ice.

"Would sir like a twist with his drink?"

He felt himself slipping: Nursey, giving him that how-can-you-be-so-stupid look.

They invited John to join them in the topic of the evening: colonization of the Americas prior to the Wisconsin Ice Age. When John confirmed his profession, Henri stood, took a little bow, congratulating himself on selecting such an appropriate wardrobe.

"I think perhaps, upon reflection, Richard Burton in *Who's Afraid of Virginia Woolf* might have been more appropriate than Brando," murmured Antonio.

"According to my PhD supervisor, 'Only a fool would consider the possibility of primitives crossing the Pacific to our shores. Can you imagine some Asian paddling a fifth of the way around the globe on a pile of bamboo?'" said John, mimicking the smug tones of his professor. "But then the man also thinks Heyerdahl was a crackpot. In any case, it's accepted that Asian migrants crossed to North America on the Bering land-bridge. My own studies are focusing on the relationship of the Ainu, the Caucasian aboriginals of Japan, with other Pacific groups, but this is a little too complicated to go into here."

Antonio tapped on his glass, "Gentlemen, our knowledgeable friend has clarified what we thought was a confused issue. Thank you, sir. Now let me refill your glass, and let's order."

John could almost taste his steak, the fries, the red plonk.

Their ancient waiter came over, his disjointed movements resembling an Egyptian hieroglyphic dance. Everyone laughed.

"May I recommend the Halibut Florentine served with new

potatoes rolled in butter with fresh cilantro, and steamed artichokes. The fish was caught this morning, the artichoke snipped this afternoon and the potatoes would make Luther Burbank cry. What's your pleasure, gentlemen?"

"We'll have your halibut, a basket of sourdough bread, and another bottle of Knob Creek," said Joe. "Everyone agree? Good."

Their entire meal would consist of foods John had never heard of. Dessert would be different, he assured himself.

The fish flaked off with ease; each tender piece swam in a rich sauce and leaped into John's mouth, seeking refuge from the bourbon chaser. A pile of artichoke petals, each scarred by the impression of his uneven lower teeth—a gift from his father who felt orthodontics were a waste of money—replaced the disappearing cilantro-flaked spuds. Somehow, dessert had been ordered without his knowing: cheeses, fruits, port and cigars.

Henri leaned over, smoke slowly escaping his mouth, and looking him straight in the eye, asked, "Well, John, you seem to be a cosmopolitan chap. Tell us a little about your history."

John looked at his new acquaintances. They seemed sincere in their interest and he did not think they were mocking him.

Without any thought, John started, "I hope my history starts today. Thank you, gentlemen. You are very kind."

He knew that sounded strange, but it felt right. And his companions accepted it as a reasonable truth. He talked about the pains of growing up in dusty Iowa, his failing studies and marriage in New Mexico, and he talked about his feelings. When John had finished, they all laid their hands on his and shared a brief communion.

Joe broke the silence. "Up to a little gaming?"

John looked at his watch. He really didn't know why. "It's after one," he said.

They all nodded. Was this some test? "Sure, what the hell."

This seemed to please them. John knew this was going to cost him a bundle, the dinner alone . . .

Antonio grabbed the bill, "I'll settle this, boys. You go hail a taxi." John offered to leave the tip, wondering if he could get change for a fiver.

"No, no, you're our guest," said Antonio, to John's relief.

They piled into the taxi and there was room to spare. For the first time, John realized how frail they were; he was the only one weighing over a hundred pounds. Yet they seemed so big. Their lives were big and he loved them. He thought he might cry. *Oh, Dad . . . socks?*

The cabbie, a young Asian man, exchanged wisdoms and jokes with the erudite septuagenarians, while John, tongue-tied, felt like a bumpkin.

The taxi deposited them on Grant Avenue, in Chinatown. John tried to pay the fare, an offer that was quickly declined.

Joe guided them through a dim sum shop into a low-ceilinged room full of exotic smells.

"This used to be an opium den." The sound of a soft feminine voice, after listening to those of old men all evening, thrilled John. He turned to face this gorgeous girl, no, woman: Miss Li, the receptionist from the Park Floral Hotel. His eyes tracked her dark red Mandarin dress as it flowed over her soft curves from her chin to the floor. "You certainly get around, Mr. Fox."

"Please call me John," he replied, craning his head to glimpse the slit running down the side of her dress.

"And you, John, please call me Cathy. Once a week, I work as a hostess here at the Domino Club. It helps pay the bills and I meet the most interesting people."

As she spoke, her hands twiddled the little pearl buttons that marched from her tightly buttoned collar over her right breast.

"How long does it take to undo all those buttons?" John asked.

She laughed. "I see now why these gentlemen find you interesting. I like curiosity in a man."

A series of ancient wooden platforms, each with a wooden pillow, occupied one side of the room. Cathy explained that a single customer might have frequented one of these cribs over decades. "If you look closely, you'll see where someone has worn a groove, probably by running his forefinger back and forth those many years, while chasing opiate dreams."

From the dark recess of the room, a busy clicking rattled. "Come," said Cathy. "Join the domino game."

John followed her, taking care not to trip on the uneven floor. His friends, seated on wooden stools around a heavy plank table, smiled at him as he approached. Antonio indicated he should sit next to a gaunt, hairy old man who rhythmically clicked the bones. John looked askance at Cathy.

"That is Koro," she whispered. "He's a blind Ainu."

"My thesis is on the Ainu! I can't believe my luck! What an opportunity. Scholars speculate that the Ainu were driven from the Korean Peninsula to Kyushu, at the southern end of the Japanese Archipelago. The arrival of the aggressive Japanese forced the Ainu northward to their present homeland in Hokkaido."

Cathy, looking bored, adjusted her earrings. "Koro told me he's from Sakhalin Island, north of Hokkaido. John, take your seat. They're about to start play."

John sat next to Koro. *My first Ainu!*

The blind Ainu player emanated the sweet fragrance of marijuana. Koro ran his hand up John's leg, exploring and, feeling a slight erection, chortled.

"He's just learning about you: your sex, state of mind, strength of character, soundness of teeth," explained Joe.

John submitted, a thing he was good at. Koro squeezed his arms, his hands; stuck his finger in his gut; carefully sized out his

Adam's apple; fingered his eyes and ears; clicked his fingernail on John's front teeth; and gently patted his freshly coiffed hair. When finished, he gave thumbs up to Joe, Henri and Antonio. He was one tactile son of a bitch.

John excused himself and went to the men's room. As he washed his hands, he saw Koro's reflection in the mirror, then images of a tattooed woman bleeding, an ancient scroll and a dagger embossed with outlines of a fox and an owl. John shuddered. It must be the bourbon, he thought. Hadn't Dr. Baker told him visions only happen in the Old Testament? He splashed water on his face and returned to the game room and the waiting Koro.

John felt good. If there was any game he knew, it was dominos—thanks to his father for a childhood deprived of television, of sex instruction, of Boy Scout jubilees, of hugs.

Each player retrieved five bones from the boneyard. John had the highest double and slid it to table center. With the sound of clicking in the background, he studied his dominos. When he was familiar with the bones, he looked up to see what was stalling the play. Five dominos were arranged on the table. It was John's turn. He carefully studied the options, then matched a three. In turn, the other four played their bones immediately and again it was John's turn. He couldn't keep up; desperate, he looked around.

"Here, drink this," said Cathy. "It will relax you."

John tossed back a shooter of Knob Creek and, enjoying a warm glow, thanked her. "You must be a professional hostess."

Seeing the shocked look on Cathy's face, he realized he had worded that wrong, "I mean, you must have done this a long time, you're so good."

She laughed, "I only do this to help pay my tuition at Berkeley. I'm studying international relations."

Koro won every game. At about three in the morning, they each put ten dollars on the table, said good night and departed,

John to the Park Floral Hotel, after thanking the elderly trio for the memorable evening. One that was followed by an astonishing night with Lulu.

Once out of the harbor, the ship turned toward the Orient. By two days out, life onboard had fallen into a routine of eating and waiting for the next meal. Below deck, in steerage, quarters were cramped and the passengers started to snarl at each other.

"What is that?" asked Sugar Baby, pointing a carrot at a monogramed envelope, leaning against John's coffee mug.

"An invitation from a friend," he replied.

"A friend onboard?"

John excused himself, ducked into his cabin and put on his Iowa State tie—*Go, Cyclones, go.*

Above the waterline, little crust-less sandwiches, toothpick-impaled olives and pickles and doily-cradled cakes defied disturbance by the likes of John. But the ladies, with their lavender aromas and lilac hues and grandma-soft faces, put him at ease.

"We play bridge," said one.

"Sometimes we paint each other's nails," added another.

"We always enjoy company. Right, Betty?"

"John, don't let the ladies fool you; they're shrewd and not without lust. Now help yourself to a cake."

The remittance man suggested they play Monopoly. That way they'd get to know each other.

"Why are you crying?" John asked.

Sugar Baby stabbed her finger on Baltic Avenue. "I want it."

The remittance man reached into the bank and grabbed Baltic Avenue. This he sat on. "Say, please sir may I have it, and I'll give it to you."

"I hate you," she wailed and smacked the board on his head.

At first, he pulled back his fist. Then he laughed. "Little baby wants her silly Baltic Avenue, boohoo."

She stood, turned her back to him and lifted her skirt. "Bite my ass."

John retreated to the bulkhead bench where the preacher and the Canadian, both soused, competed to see who was most godless. He found this interesting and quoted from his notes on comparative religion, "The Ainu of northern Japan consider everything god."

"So what, pervert," snapped the preacher. The Canadian just shrugged.

Even though John bunked with the Canadian, they rarely spoke. The Canuck intimidated him; he had a swimmer's physique, bleached short curly hair, squinty eyes and soft, slurred speech, often studded with senseless apologies. His mutterings, laced with references to Céline, Vonnegut, Wilde and the like, accompanied spastic stabbings of arms and a bobbing head. His breath reeked of booze. The Canadian's conversation with His Darkness, the preacher, added to John's discomfort with his cabin mate.

The Fox family was not particularly religious, but in the tight community of Rolfe, everything was about appearances. Easter, Christmas, funerals and Sunday School concerts saw the gathering of families—many that laid claim to ancestors' pews—who conveyed condolences and exclaimed over rapidly sprouting children or wayward neighbors, while sizing up economic or amorous or political opportunities.

Post-service dalliances on the stoop of the Rolfe First Methodist Church: Reverend Carver, his nose dripping and his hands itching in the sanctuary of his robes for the tender flesh of little Mary or Rose and, on occasion, little Johnny Fox, encouraged his flock to deliver their children to the manse on Tuesdays for religious instruction. John's mother fumed in Carver's presence, but no one took her seriously as she always wore dark glasses and her voice was too husky.

Repulsed by scattered Monopoly pieces and talk of God, John decided to wander up to first class. At the door, he turned and said, "See you later."

"Yeah, later, gigolo," said Sugar Baby.

Everyone laughed.

Gentle breezes ruffled the calm seas off Hawaii and by the Aleutians, tiny ripples jostled each other and fused, creating chop: little spiky waves that seemed nowhere bound. Increasing winds harnessed the chop, creating swells that swiftly fled the gales.

A week out, the *Golden Maru* encountered heavy seas: waves originating from two storms collided, producing intimidating rollers, an unpredictable ocean.

Steerage life became hell. At first it was funny, bouncing around their cabins and the below-the-waterline mess. And then it got scary. Sugar Baby got sick first, "Mommy, it hurts."

Only the Canadian was unaffected. He seemed unaware of the smell and he moved about effortlessly, as if he was a human gyroscope.

John retreated up to the deck and tried to focus on the horizon but couldn't. His ribs ached from retching and he felt as if his teeth were dissolving. He was beyond frightened. He wished for death or worse: being back in New Mexico or Iowa.

"Well, what have we here?" asked Betty.

She had been strolling on the promenade deck, totally unconcerned with the ship's pitching and yawing. She might as well have been dallying in a country garden, bending to smell a rose, to pick a sweet pea.

He covered his mouth and bent over the ship's side, expressing no fear of the chaotic waves lunging up at him.

"John, you don't look good. I think I have a cure for you. Follow me." He relinquished the hold the sea had over him and pulled himself hand-over-hand along the ship's railing.

"Use my shower and then I'll serve you the magic potion," she said, her tongue tapping weasel teeth.

The hot water cleansed and soothed him and freed him from his *mal de mer* death wish. His mind turned to his body. He had never liked his body, much less given it a lot of thought. But the closeness of Betty, and the memory of her declaring him "scrawny and slouched," challenged him.

He could be described as scrawny: scrawny like an Ethiopian distance runner—that can't be bad. And slouched: Rodin's Thinker was hunched, a kind of slouching. Then the reality of his carcass, his white, soft, almost saggy flesh, the result of an academic existence without the benefit of achievement, disgusted him. He ran his hand over his poorly defined chest, feeling its rather impressive mat. His tummy lacked firmness. But Nursey and Lulu hadn't complained.

He could hear Betty puttering around the bathroom. She was humming a spiritual, something about crossing over. "Are you clean, John?"

John replied that he was and she reached through the shower curtain, her hand brushing his thigh, and turned off the hot tap.

"Oh my God, it's friggin' cold."

She laughed and handed him a towel. She stood close while he dressed; he could feel her heat and he became embarrassed. Briefly, he thought of Lulu, whose last traces had been washed off. But now there would always be his dream Lulu: Lulu the Indelible.

"You look better, John. Now drink this. One shot, dear."

He lifted the tumbler. It was very cold. The clear liquid slid smoothly down his throat. His stomach tightened, forcing an alcoholic belch up through his nasal passages. His eyes teared up and warmth spread through his limbs. Everything became clear and he looked about as if seeing things for the first time.

Betty grasped his elbow and steered him to the love seat. "Feel better?"

He nodded, yes. He couldn't remember when he had felt so good, so in tune with his surroundings. Betty laid her hand on his shoulder and gave him a toothy grin. "That's Grey Goose, darling."

A shudder vibrated the iron ship. Betty grabbed the vodka bottle, which threatened to spill. Then, for what seemed a lifetime, the *Golden Maru* drifted, powerless, pitching and yawing on the hostile sea. Betty crossed herself.

John imagined them spiraling down through the depths as the old ship creaked and moaned, its eggshell-thin rusty hull surrendering to the increasing pressure. Soon they'd lose the lights and the air would go stale. The *hssst* of air being forced from the cabin, only to be replaced by cold, oily water, would announce their doom. Finally, they would be compelled to stand on tiptoe, to grope for that last human contact, for that last pocket of oxygen.

For one moment, John considered shoving Betty aside and bolting for the deck, taking the only life jacket that hung on the back of the cabin door. He was young and had much to experience in life; she was old, washed up. Anthropological justification: Inuit cast their elderly, non-productive family members adrift on ice floes to ensure the survival of the young.

As if reading his mind, Betty grimaced and declared, "John, we need a plan."

I have a plan.

Again the ship lurched. One engine sputtered to life. Slowly, she turned into the surging seas. Her course through the waves became less violent and her bobbing on the seas became more regular, not so threatening. As the *Golden Maru* steadied, Betty pulled John down on the pink sofa and grasped his hands, "John, that was scary and you behaved well. But remember, two heads are better than one."

Betty poured two tumblers of vodka and raised her glass, "Here's to our captain, John, may he command our *Golden Maru* forever."

John couldn't look her in the eye. And, for a fleeting moment, he considered the plight of his mates below. But for the grace of God, or Betty, he could have been down there.

The squalid and rank steerage offered no comfort, even with power. He couldn't conceive how Sugar Baby, a kindergarten teacher usually surrounded by happy children with baby powder aromas—the smell of innocence—wafting about her, had coped. For the three male below-deck mates, knowing their egocentric nature or constant state of drunkenness made them immune to terror, he had no sympathy.

On the next morning, the passengers awoke to a calm sea, wondering where all the wickedness had gone. It was like going to bed with a mean drunk, only to awaken to a contrite, loving mate.

The passengers gathered in the library, where a weary Captain Tveit addressed them. "We have weathered a cruel storm. The *Golden Maru* faltered, but the problem has been fixed. We can now steam safely, but our trip to Yokohama will be delayed as I have been ordered to proceed to Vladivostok, where most of the hides have been purchased."

"To Russia," cheered one of Betty's bridge mates.

"Yes, to Russia, or wherever," chorused the other card players.

The Canuck, pasty from days below deck, approached John. "Where are you going, roomy?"

John explained he needed to be alone and was turning in.

"Come on down to the mess and let's drink. If you come, I'll tell you our next port of call."

"Vladivostok?"

"How did you guess? I'll get my Canadian Club—it's party time."

John followed his roommate through the low, oval hatch into the crew's gallery. The air reeked of wet woolens and garlic and cheap cigar smoke. The flickering of two light bulbs threatened to cast the mess into darkness.

His steerage companions, still high on life-after-near-disaster, jostled each other, spoke too loudly, and quickly finished off the Canadian rye.

"It was scary," said Sugar Baby, her fingers tapping on John's thigh.

"Not really, our captain had control . . . whoa," said John, resisting the spider's search.

Her tongue reamed his ear. "Is this real?"

The steerage mates came to feel a certain moral superiority over the upper-crust set: those with portholes; those who relished their vain existence; those for whom there was neither heaven nor hell but bridge, lavender toenails and idle chatter. Rebellion led the lowlifes to rechristen their rust bucket the *Honky Maru* and to begin fraternization with those "up there," the non-hoi polloi. Mostly, they were well received. But the Canadian, who accelerated his drinking, broke with his habit of being reticent and agonizingly shy. He became a boor.

"Antichrists," said the Canuck, his eyes red from booze-exploded blood vessels. He rubbed his aching kidneys. He stank.

"The perfect metaphor for heaven is hell and for God the Devil. We've been duped, John." He struck a papal-like poise, his hands crisscrossing his chest this way and that. "Heed ye, there are antichrists among us, they went from us but are not of us. Remain vigilant, John."

Later the captain approached John. It seemed his roommate had been hassling the older ladies. "Not that the ladies aren't interested in new company, but he insists on badgering them as they play bridge. His slobbering spoils the nut mix and his alcoholic breath challenges the air conditioner." Captain Tveit felt that, for the all the passengers' safety and Canuck's health, he should pull into the first available port for medical attention.

They would land on the west coast of North America, but where? The travelers rushed to the chart tacked to the library wall and tracked the most recent penciled-in course. A crush of la-de-da ladies and steerage bums tried to fathom their position and what exotic berth they might obtain.

"Port Alberni," said Betty. "Sounds Spanish."

The captain towered behind the throng studying the chart, seemingly unaware of Betty who appeared to be protected by the Norwegian's hulk. "We'll visit Port Alberni, and deposit our Canadian friend into the hands of the West Coast Hospital, an institution famous for treating hardened livers."

A moan passed through the ship's company.

"Yes, Canada is a cold, God-forsaken place. But then maple syrup, red-coated Mounties, real Monopoly money and a meek peasant population have their advantages, too."

While the other passengers dispersed, Betty turned to face the captain, who experienced her fragrance—suggestive of pickled herring?—and her inviting form. She smiled into his tired face, curiously not exposing her teeth. "Captain Tveit, you do know how much we appreciate your managing our voyage? We . . . I'd be less resolute in my quest if you weren't at the helm."

The *Golden Maru* passed through British Columbia fjords leading to Port Alberni. All aboard stared with wonderment at the giant cedars and firs growing in a continuous rainforest from the water's edge up the surrounding mountains. Here and there, it appeared as if a giant had shaved its forest beard.

John thought of Lulu, who had bitched about those damn prickly hairs. "John, I'm cursed with a scratchy crotch."

About halfway through the inland waterway, they encountered a vast area of chalky water. According to the captain, the cloudiness resulted from herring cum. "Once a year, on a full moon, herring concentrate here and spawn," he explained. "The herring attract all sorts of sea life and their sperm and eggs are eaten by little crabs and jellyfish."

The *Golden Maru* shuddered to a stop. The passengers, jarred from their lethargy, hurried to the railing and looked down. Big purse seiners, sixty-feet long, their coarse nets encircling balls of herring, blocked the way. Winch-driven pulleys strained to lift their catch onboard. These fish could sink the boat if they were to swim down in unison. A float plane approached one seiner and bought the unlanded fish for $5,000, cash. The transaction completed, the buyer's packer ship pulled alongside and sucked the herring into its hold.

In contrast, but no less serious, a native fisherman straddled a tipsy canoe, his muscular arms piercing the water with a severely spiked stick. Each pass impaled a dozen herring, which were shaken off into cedar baskets. Betty leaned against John, barely breathing. "Oh, John, he is beautiful. Lucky you for studying anthropology."

John settled in a deckchair facing the setting sun and considered what he had just learned about herring. The water mirrored the evening sky. Lively colors playing over the low ocean swell exploded as a sea lion broke through the surface in noisy pursuit of herring. A fish, temporarily stunned, lay on the surface only to be plucked by a passing eagle, which in turn dropped the morsel in response to a gull's harassment. John watched this little fish's fate unravel, hoping it had fulfilled its role.

Suddenly, the sea surface sparkled like champagne. Below, a humpback whale herded herring into a tight column with a curtain of bubbles. Moments later, the whale, its baleened-mouth agape, rocketed up through the herring ball into the air and, with a twist, plunged back into the nurturing sea, releasing a rainbow-laced spray.

John wondered if, as with the herring, some larger cosmic force was playing with him, his idle carcass perched on a rusty deck going from nowhere to nowhere, the unknown lurking below.

John hadn't left Iowa so much to go to graduate school as to get away from his dysfunctional family and the monotony of rural folk who, like the endless rows of corn, were totally predictable. Iowa, where smut was a disease of corn; where the Beatles conjured up images of insects and biblical plagues; and where a musical event was a Holy Rollers gospel night.

And anthropology: why had he chosen to study ancient cultures when he had no concept of his own identity? Professor Downforth, a tweedy scholar at Iowa State, had complimented John on an Anthropology 101 project. "Well, John, seems anthropology runs in your family. Your dad turned down an anthropology scholarship to the University of Chicago."

Dad? My dad an anthropologist? He makes socks for a living and resists mom for recreation.

John understood he was motivated for all the wrong reasons, but he would go along for the ride. Certainly, San Francisco had been a big plus, two plusses. And, for the next little while, the *Honky Maru* would determine his fate.

Turning the final bend, they saw Port Alberni. Roads leading from commercial wharves snaked over the surrounding hills, swerving to avoid thousand-year-old cedar stumps and tall gray snags. On one edge of the village, a pulp mill belched sulfurous smog into the salty air. Opposite, a fish plant churned out cans of salmon, their guts left on the beach for the crows and seagulls and eagles and stupid dogs. In the heart of this industrial sandwich rested a quaint cluster of pubs, cafés and used-clothing stores. There were things to do here, to explore, to savor.

The men, loitering in stoops and on street corners, looked natty in their plaid shirts, denim pants with wide braces, lace-up boots, and woolen toques with curious little burn holes. Their cheeks were ruddy, the result of weather and booze-ruptured veins; their teeth were crooked and stained from smoking unfiltered Players cigarettes; their eyes were shifty.

The women were in constant motion. Most were busty and all had hawk-like expressions. But one could see, once they had their way, they might be loving.

These were a people who could break into a jig, drink a dram and flatten your nose in the slap of a beaver tail, all the time apologizing. John couldn't imagine their ancestors burning Washington, his nation's capital, to the ground. But he would be careful.

He walked up Argyle Street pondering his Canadian money. Wasn't a US dollar a dollar and not ninety-three cents Canadian, as the bank had told him? And why these different colors, why not greenbacks?

The Somas Pub, a Tudor-style building whose stucco siding was variously discolored with swallow droppings and green patches of urine-loving algae, invoked the feeling of merry old England. He entered the door marked "Gentlemen"; the alternative, "Ladies & Escorts," seemed inappropriate.

In the foyer, a bulletin board advertised—in addition to offers of firewood and babysitting and eaves-trough cleaning—weekly bingo nights at the United Church, an upcoming mud wrestling match in the basement of Royal Canadian Legion, and laundry while you wait at a Swedish widows' retirement home with tea, polkas and company.

These alternatives to men-only drinking pleased him, especially after the ugly removal from the ship of his Canadian roommate: struggling in a straitjacket, the demons of sobriety whipping any rational thought from the Canuck's dissolving brain.

John pulled out a slick, padded chair and sat down. The air reeked of stale cigarette smoke and flat beer. The carpeted floor felt spongy.

"How many beers do you want, sonny?" asked the largest man he had ever seen.

John asked what kinds of ale they had.

"Don't get funny with me," was the reply. "Now, how many beers do you want? I ain't got all day."

Afraid he would look cheap, John said, "Two," for which he got a terrible scowl.

The waiter put the beers down and tapped on his tray, a signal that baffled John. The waiter cleared his throat. Not knowing what to do, John lifted his beer. The waiter extended his hand and said, "Two dollars, sonny."

Confused, John shuffled through his wallet, studying the strange bills.

"The orange one, sonny, like New York Place. *Deux dollars.*"

John's eyes adjusted to the darkness. The other patrons, mostly old men, snoozed over their beer-and-tomato-juice drinks, or carried on sprightly conversations with buddies—living and deceased—and a few stared beyond a forty-inch-high wainscoted wall to the Ladies & Escorts side: The Land of Promise. This wall dividing the spectators from the players—it wasn't clear who was who—bore obscene pictures and misspelled smut and, here and there, rusty brown claw marks.

Across the wall, their eyes met. She bobbed her head to one side, as one would with water in an ear; obviously an oblique social signal. John responded similarly, hopping on one leg. His years of studying primitive civilizations had prepared him for this, his first foreign encounter.

A heavy hand fell on his shoulder, forcing him back into the chair. The waiter slammed another beer on the soggy terrycloth table cover. "No drinking standing up, sonny."

John inched to the front of the chair and craned his neck in hopes of continuing the strange encounter. The lady caught his eye and commenced nodding and finger-stabbing in the direction of the nod. Her actions reminded him of Balinese temple dance moves, which he'd studied at Iowa State. He copied her as best he could; it was difficult. His neck stiffened and when John turned back to the table, he discovered several glasses of beer on its eighteen-inch diameter.

As he puzzled over this, a voice cut through the beery afternoon. "Hey, dough head. Yes, you, limp dick. Go outside."

When she started toward the door, John picked up the table of beer and stumbled for the door, his mind fuzzy with anticipation.

Again, the heavy hand. "Put it down, sonny."

As John tried to explain his problem, a tightening of the hand on his shoulder brought tears to his eyes. "The blue one, like Boardwalk. *Cinq dollars.*

John paid five dollars and exited empty-handed, having not touched a drop.

She sure didn't look the same in full daylight. Her large cow eyes searched John's face for signs of intelligence as he tried to guess her measurements. Roughly five-foot-five tall, her bottom half sported a tartan skirt that stood straight out; ham-like upper arms with little tufts of hair peeking out from her armpits, chorizo sausage fingers—nails painted pink—and magnificent breasts. *My Scottish Heather. A possible Canadian Ainu?*

"Buy me a beer, honey," she said, as she dragged him through the Ladies & Escorts' entrance. She pushed him into a chair, "Best seats in the house." The table immediately became a sea of glasses.

She laid her hand on his thigh and bent forward, examining the glasses in front of them. John was unfamiliar with this Canadian ritual and, admittedly, a little nervous.

"Son-o-bitch," she bellowed, "what the hell is this all about?" Her roar reminded him of the sea lions barking in the fjord. At first John thought she was commenting on the absence of life in his nether regions; then he saw her pointing at a glass in which the beer did not reach a small, etched white line. A flustered waiter replaced the delinquent beer with two overflowing glasses.

On the Gentlemen's side, the tables rapidly filled with a pasty group of American miners and some loggers, one of whom had a strong French accent. Both groups wore knotted muscles and nitroglycerine smiles. They did not mingle.

John leaned in close to his date, as much to determine her scent as to be heard. Concluding asparagus urine, he shouted, "Sure is noisy."

A sudden quiet settled and John's sweetie's hand vice-gripped his leg. Her breath came out in short bursts: a sour egg smell.

Then a twangy Texas-accented voice bellowed, "Hey, Frenchie," and all hell broke loose.

The white and the tan clashed in the center of the room; broken chairs and glasses slashing the air and the occasional head. The brawl seemed to follow certain rules: apparently you were only allowed to kick your fallen opponent three times in the ribs; a good thing as everyone was wearing steel-toed boots. On cue, John's burly waiter, who had been in the wings, slapping a baseball bat into his palm, stepped forward and delivered *coups de grâce* to the few standing combatants.

The big man bowed and did a little soft shoe shuttle, encouraging his audience. A ripple of applause from the Ladies & Escorts became loud cheers, punctuated by bravos: high Canadian theater.

John snorted and rooted in the valley of his Heather's breasts as they embraced. What a great icebreaker; what a great anthropological moment.

Three beers later, John's honeybunch had him demonstrating the Hopi snake dance to the accompaniment of the Beach Boys. He was clever. He was smart. Then he became sappy. "My ex was Hopi. Why did she leave me?"

His date looked at him as though she understood and ordered two more pickled eggs.

John's head bounced off the low cabin ceiling. "To the Rising Sun," he mumbled and collapsed back onto his bunk. Through foggy eyes, a carved wooden bear came into focus. His head hammered painfully. Then his Canadian adventures came back to him.

The pub had closed and John had joined his new friends wandering along the waterfront. They sang, they danced the conga, they howled.

"Let's duck in here, honey. I'm hungry." She parted the bamboo curtain and dragged him into a hot steamy room. "Hey, John, there're my crazy Indian friends. They're good for a hoot. Hi guys, mind if we join you?"

"Babe, anytime, you know it."

John and Heather slipped into the booth as an older man and three younger guys scrunched together. They could have been fishermen, like those John had seen on the seiner. He sneaked a peek at their jackets, looking for telltale fish scales. Nothing.

John's seatmate slapped him on the back.

"So, you're an anthropologist. Don't think I've had anthropologist before. Guys, do they have anthropologist on the menu?"

Everyone thought this was funny. These were big people and they grinned with bright teeth. John worried they might have cannibal blood. To make him feel better, Heather gave him a big hug.

"Hey, look," she said, digging her fingers into his ribs, "they have lamb chops." Then she grabbed at his tummy, "They have pot roast."

All around him people roared. "Do they have hot dogs?" someone shouted.

John lurched backwards as all these arms with feather and eagle tattoos reached for him. "Please don't eat me," he cried.

"Hey, we're Dog Salmon People, man. We don't eat professors, only missionaries and the occasional government bureaucrat," said one of the younger men. The silverware danced and the water glasses threatened to tip over as the whole table erupted with laughter. John was getting confused.

"It's okay, honey, they don't meet gentlemen like you very often," said Heather, squeezing his thigh. "Should I order for you? These Chinese-Canadian menus can be tricky."

Relieved, John nodded weakly. Anthropological protocol had not been his university strong point.

"He'll have liver and onions, sweet and sour pork ribs, chop suey, curried shrimp, and hash browns. Would you like anything else, honey?"

"Apple pie and a cup of tea," John replied. Then, as an afterthought, he added, "I'll help pay."

"Oh, no, tonight you're Mr. Herring's guest," said the older native.

Ten minutes passed in silence, with only the slurps of drinking, the chatter of cutlery on porcelain plates, and sighs of satisfaction. At first, John thought the peculiar way they used knives and forks was an aboriginal thing. Then he recalled seeing his Canadian steerage mate eating the same way: the knife in his right hand and fork in the left. John had been brought up to put his knife down after making a cut, transferring the fork to the right hand and delivering the morsel to his mouth. John wondered if he had just made an original anthropological observation, maybe a latitudinal effect? He would have to look it up.

John wiped his plate clean with a piece of white bread and sipped his tea, Twinings Earl Grey. Tea was apparently the beverage of choice in this Sino-Canadian-First Nations longhouse. Leaning back, enjoying his companions and listening to his happy stomach rumble gave him peace. The burp started with the half-dozen pickled sulfurous eggs, passed through a few quarts of beer, grew in strength in the Chinese-Canadian buffet and then burst with a glorious volcanic belch, a Vesuvian event. Silence fell over the restaurant. A few halfhearted burps from fellow diners were lost in the echo of John's granddaddy of all eruptions.

The man John took to be an elder stood. "My Dog Salmon brothers do not honor you enough. In the north, home of my people, the spirit bear is the totem of our clan. Through him, we can trace our ancestors to the time of the great ice. Yours is a special gift, and the white bear will be your protector. We will all respect you."

The others nodded their approval. "We want you to become a blood brother."

Heather gave John a big kiss on the cheek and everyone cheered.

He thought: a cut finger, a little exchange of blood, and then fulfillment of every anthropologist's desire—Indianhood. John stood and bowed, trying to look modest, but his heart swelled; his autobiography was picking up steam.

"Tomorrow, you will start three days in the sweat lodge with only water to drink. Then you will be taken to the top of Mount Arrowsmith, where you will remain without food or drink until your spiritual leader reveals itself." Too serious, the elder continued. "After that, you will be suspended by rawhide rope laced through your chest muscles over an alder fire, like our beloved smoked salmon. Then you will be a true brother."

Ouch, John thought.

"Yeah, man. Then you'll be a real brother," said one of the others, as they all nodded solemnly.

"Sorry, but I sail out tomorrow."

The fishermen, feigning disappointment, muttered dire consequences, but the elder shushed them. "You will always be welcome in our territory. Please take this, my clan's totem, and remember this night."

A calming coolness radiated from the elder's touch. For the first time, John took in his features, the clouded eyes and wrinkled face that spoke of many injustices. He saw a sincere, confident and compassionate person.

Sheepishly, John received the carved bear. This is a poor substitute for Indianhood, he thought. "Thank you," he said, embarrassed that he'd taken the elder's joke seriously and his gift too lightly. He cradled the crude, carved cedarwood bear. His childhood nightmare nemesis, the bear, was on his team now.

"Johnny, we're having a cocktail party. You really must go to sleep."

"But I'm not sleepy, Mommy."

"Now close your eyes and think sleepy thoughts."

"Can I come downstairs?"

"No, it's just for grown-ups. Here, let me help you."

Mother laid John's Winnie the Pooh bear over his face, "Sleep, Johnny. I must visit with my friends."

He couldn't breathe. He thrashed about, trying to heave his body away from her smothering weight, but she pressed down harder and harder. Everything got dark. It hurt.

"Ethyl, what the hell are you doing? Let him go."

"No, he . . . both of you are screwing up my life."

John took five aspirin and snuggled in with his newly acquired sacred wooden bear. He wondered if its too-large hind legs held significance. He felt surprisingly good. He had dwelled in the house of honest men, drank their beer, known their women. He would survive the Ainu.

After breakfast, he retreated to a deck chair. Behind closed eyelids, his retinas tracked the sun's passage through shearing flashes of orange, red and green. He tried to make sense out of his foreign encounters: the self-deprecating Canadians, the welcoming natives, the in-your-face Americans—"Hey, Frenchie!" And Japan . . . ? John thought of his Ainu thesis, how it would contribute to world knowledge and, more importantly, to his uniqueness.

After enduring Nursey's ridicule of his Hopi studies—"Well, sweetie, what did you learn about us today? Anything I can pass on to our elders?"—John just quit. Stopped his research, put down his thesis. Why was he studying the Hopi, anyway?

Why? Because Professor Downforth had advised him to make himself unique. "Become an expert in something obscure. That way, you will stand out. Anyone can be a neurosurgeon, an astrophysicist or a dishwasher. Give it the mirror test: look yourself in the mirror and say 'I, John Fox, in a world of a zillion people, am unique because I know more about (fill in the blank) than anyone,' and see how it feels. Maybe the Hopi, John?"

And the Hopi were a million miles away from Iowa.

After a period of doing nothing (playing solitaire, getting under Nursey's skin, hiding her Marlboro cigarettes—"You're ruining your health"—avoiding old friends and not making new ones) he got bored. Then he got hungry. Then he rejoined the treadmill of graduate studies.

His fellow students were occupied in that grand New Mexico tradition of creating lists of stuff and comparing them, hopefully to gain insight into anthropological questions. This was the key to academic success: a publishable thesis. One could only dream of *Nature* or *Science*. A particularly profitable comparison was between Southwest Native American and Eastern Asian languages, particularly those of a Siberian tribe, possibly Caucasian. Tonal aspects of these languages, which could be discerned by students illiterate in both, suggested a close affinity.

John had a eureka moment. Siberia, while being happily distanced from everywhere, was too hostile. However, the existence of a little-studied white aboriginal group on the Japanese island of Hokkaido, the Ainu, would be perfect. And the contrast of geishas and gulags settled it.

The Ainu would be his salvation, his ticket to academia, and they passed Downforth's mirror test. They're white, hairy and, perhaps most important, they live in faraway Japan. Ainu lesson number one: bear and Ainu are one. He had feared bears, but the Dog Salmon encounter had established *Ursus americanus* as his totem. This was a step forward.

A few brief stints in the university library and John felt confident, naively, to pursue his Ainu studies.

Steerage life after Port Alberni started to bore John. The Canuck, with his insufferable alcoholic ways, had at least been intellectually stimulating. The preacher and remittance man continued to be wrapped up in themselves, and Sugar Baby—well, she was just there. She was like an old terry-cloth bathrobe, comfortable and familiar, like a sister but without the incest.

On the other hand, the first-class crowd with their bridge and light chitchat seemed fine. He was curious as to their obscure greatness and they seemed to appreciate his philosophical contributions. And, actually, they weren't that old.

"John, could we pour you a glass of Amontillado? It's an extraordinarily complex sherry, goes great with olives," asked Betty.

John sipped his drink and winced. "We academics are a little more down to earth, you know. Could I have a beer?"

"Of course, John. Earlier, you mentioned your interest in studying the Ainu. The girls and I were wondering how you intend to pursue your studies. You know, the nitty-gritty of knowledge pursuit."

John strained to remember his notes from Anthropology 401, Anthropological Methods, but nothing came to mind. "Well, this is an interesting question. As you may know, I have attended two universities and taken many courses related to my studies. This makes me eminently qualified to conduct my researches."

"Yes, John, but when you first encounter Hokkaido Ainu, what will be your approach? Will you present them with a gift? I understand that it was customary to present North American Indians with tobacco. And how will you communicate with them?"

"Of course, I'll have to observe them and then act appropriately. And surely they can speak English."

"Don't you mean Japanese, John?"

John bashed about his cabin, alternately chastising Pooh bear and berating his spirit bear totem, "How could you let me down? You let me make a fool out of myself. Somehow I must show Betty I'm a normal guy, a human. Not a boor, but a qualified academic." He grabbed his bears and headed back to Betty's cabin.

"Hi Betty, may I come in? I want to show you something."

Betty opened the cabin door and indicated he should take a seat, "I'll just be a minute, John."

She fetched two beers and joined John on the couch. "Yes?"

John showed her the spirit bear totem and explained his near-Indianhood.

"Oh, John, how delightful. Thank you for sharing this with me. You're beginning to change and that can be good. But don't be big-headed. We girls have caught you making ridiculous statements, all with an air of unearned authority. While we appreciate you've been to two universities, you're no mental heavyweight . . . "

"Betty, let me explain. I wanted to impress you and your friends, to show you I belonged. This is all so new to me."

"Thank you, John, but do not despair, you do have something to offer," she said, laying her soft, well-manicured hand on his thigh. "Just don't be an asshole, dear."

The Violet and Lavender Girls were fun and good for his ego, too. Each, in her way, made it clear they considered John a potential physical, as well as conversational, distraction. The thought of "doing it" with them repulsed John but, after several days at sea and familiarity over sherry and pedicuring, he began to wonder, why not?

"John, what was your weirdest sex ever?" asked one bridge player in a quiet moment between rubbers. "I mean, hetero-sex."

Polite sniggers from East and West.

"Johnny, more shooters of tequila and baby oysters, please dear."

As he extracted the sleeping mollusks from their shells, taking care not to impale his palm with the shucking knife, he proposed Sue of the Kama Sutra moves.

"John, pull up a chair, pour yourself a tall one and tell us all about Sue. We've got the rest of our lives to listen. Maybe a little shoulder rub to get you started?"

Love was Nursey: passionate-of-body and kind-of-mouth, paying his way through graduate school. Until she left him for the chairman of the philosophy department.

Salvation was Sue Harris, the University of New Mexico's psychologist: green tea, a little grass and lots of me. Sex as a therapeutic tool. "John, relax," she would say, clinically, as she completed a Kama Sutra move called the helicopter. She was sweet; she was green-eyed; she had been the Yakima Peach Queen. Rolling on her side, she grasped John's jaw with her tough little fist, forcing his attention. "John, face it. You exploited her. You never loved her; she was your Indian trophy, for God's sake."

His hand crept forward to brush away the blond hair plastered to her brow.

"Stop it!" she snapped. "You're always avoiding reality. You've got to grow up. Now, help mommy paint her toenails." Sue nurtured him and he began to contemplate a life after Nursey.

During what turned out to be his last session, Sue had an unexpected caller. She moved John into her closet, tossing her discarded but still body-warm flannel pajamas in after him.

A woman's voice: Nursey. At first, he panicked—he wrapped his head in flannel, trying to block his ears. Then he felt an unfamiliar strength, an ability to cope and learn; peeling away the pajamas, he pressed his ear to the closet door.

Little licking and slurping sounds could be heard over low moaning. Finally, relative quiet, and then the smells of a Marlboro cigarette (Nursey) and freshly applied fingernail polish (Sue), punctuated by flesh-muffled "Johns" and titters.

The cabin boy paged John to attend the captain in his private office on the upper deck.

"Damn it, Mr. Fox, these are ladies of high station and deserve your respect." The captain didn't add that his job would be in jeopardy if he lost these valuable passengers, nor did he mention his particular attraction to one: Betty.

John felt ill done by. He had been the one seduced or, as Betty put it, liberated from his multigenarian-phobia. While applying chartreuse toenail polish to one of the shyer ladies later that same day, John mentioned his meeting with the captain.

The next day Captain Tveit came below decks. "Perhaps I spoke out of turn, Mr. Fox," he said, turning his hat in his hands. "You might consider working for our shipping line. You'd meet wonderful people and get paid for it. Think about it, if Japan doesn't work out for you."

"I'm no gigolo, Captain."

"Of course. Well, would you settle for a drink?" he asked.

"Do you have any Grey Goose?"

John had gotten into the habit of sitting on the deck, late at night after the others had turned in. Free of Sugar Baby's attentions, Betty's manipulations, the haunting and almost threatening presence of the remittance man and preacher, he could sort out his feelings, think about what he was leaving behind and what he would do once cast into an intimidating Japanese milieu.

Earlier, the captain had pointed out a blinking light passing overhead. "Mr. Fox, that is United Air Flight 762 out of San Francisco. In about two hours it will land at the Narita Airport, near Tokyo."

After that, John saw the lights of Flight 762 almost every night. The travel agent had said this voyage would be a step back in time; since he joined the *Golden Maru*, Flight 762 had completed the same trip about fourteen times. He thought about those people up there, rocketing between two cultures, their brains scrambled by jetlag, their bodies poisoned by stale, microbe-invested air, the vessels in their cramped legs threatening thrombosis, all the while maintaining their focus on the "lavatory occupied" sign, praying for green. These people shared the same anxieties, hopes and joys as his shipmates. But here on the *Golden Maru*, they were suspended, the throb of the ship's powerful engines thrusting them forward in slow motion.

Sometimes, while watching the blinking light cross the sky, he wondered if his observing them, spying on them, would somehow jinx the aircraft and cause its aluminum-foil skin to rupture, tossing one hundred, two hundred bodies into the frigid atmosphere where they would descend like so many human meteors into the black sea.

And he wondered if the Hopi and Ainu and Dog Salmon ancients had pondered life in the skies as they tracked the erratic passage of planets and stars through the seasons; seeing in meteors celestial beings invading their narrow worlds.

The air of the Vladivostok wharves reeked of exhaust and decay. Its citizenry—muscled pinheads, Dickens's waifs, harlots and saints, ax murderers and vegans, whores and pimps and priests—cruised, loitered, slunk, spit, hacked, sleazed, waiting for an opportunity to rip off, mutilate, lift, heist or otherwise express their illegitimate skills.

John and his fellow passengers viewed the scene from the relative safety of the deck. He wondered: did they sleep, have mothers, ever stop to smell the violets, think about death, have children, grandchildren, drink tea from bone china cups on translucent saucers?

"My dear passengers," said Captain Tveit to a ship's company already traumatized by their brief introduction to the port. "Tomorrow we will unload the hides and replenish supplies. I strongly advise you stay on board."

Sugar Baby sidled up to John. "It's party time."

Following her up out of steerage, John tapped her on the shoulder. "Hey, Baby, where are you going? You don't party with those people," he said, nodding up the staircase.

"Tonight we do," she replied. She was dressed in a flounced summer dress and carried a small boat hook, which she latched around his neck. "Come along, sheep."

John wasn't going to argue, her scent—some blend of bourbon and avocado—drew him on. Nice legs, he thought.

Halfway up, Sugar Baby stopped at the hatch to the cargo hold, turned and rested her hand on John's chest. "Are you ready?"

"Ready for what?" John asked, anticipating the stench beyond this door.

They stepped onto the catwalk above the hold and into a grand party, the captain's treat. Crêpe paper and balloons and Grey Goose and pickled herring greeted them. It was a mingling of the classes, those from steerage and those from above the waterline, all quite jolly.

"Bon voyage and good riddance," said Betty, toasting the hides with a glass of vodka. "Now we are free, John. No longer will these dictate our destiny."

"Drink up, sweetie," said Sugar Baby, shoving a bottle of Red Roses bourbon into his face.

He glimpsed Betty plying the remittance man, who was trying to explain the evils of his family, with precious Grey Goose. Elsewhere, he saw the Violet and Lavender Girls, dressed in bathing suits and at various stages of intoxication, approaching the preacher.

"Ladies of the Painted Toes," the preacher declared. "Come on to me and I will free you from inhibition."

"Amen," shouted the chartreuse-toed Violet-and-Lavender girl.

The drinks and silliness took their toll. The party stumbled, threatening to bomb, when the hatch flew open and the captain entered.

He saluted the gathering, "Welcome to the *Golden Maru* swimming club." Tveit grabbed the railing and dove into the quilt of hides. The others followed, arms flailing, legs kicking, booze sloshing.

Betty called over to John. "Observe the *te-waza,* dear," and proceeded to execute the hand-throwing judo move, tossing a breathless, exhilarated captain. She caught John's eye and he understood the message: she would have been the one with the life jacket.

"Johnny, catch me," shouted Sugar Baby. They landed in a tangled heap, her crook around his thigh; her bourbon smell and husky breathing rescued him from Betty's message. "Johnny, bite me." He succumbed to Sugar Baby's invitation. Exhausted, John rolled over and, to his horror, saw the Fox brand. His anguished "Jessie!" was the evening's death knell.

After breakfast, Betty approached the captain and gently grasped his elbow—John knew that touch and, as a Pavlovian response, wished it were he she clasped—"Captain," she said, "I have errands in Vladivostok this morning. Mr. Fox will accompany me."

The captain, resisting Betty's charm, replied, "I'd prefer you didn't go ashore; the waterfront isn't safe."

Her squeeze brought a flush to the captain's face. "Yes, of course, I understand," said Tveit. "But take care."

John, uncomfortable in his role of bodyguard—the captain had armed him with a sap—nervously kept an eye out for trouble, while an elegant Betty strolled as if on Park Avenue, casually looking through grimy shop windows, all the while avoiding human discharges and despicable riffraff, ignoring foul mutterings.

He recognized several languages, including Hopi. Everyone seemed to be doing business. They went into a coffee shop where the floor was littered with cigarette butts and bits of food. A stunning woman caught his eye and walked over to their table. John pulled back a chair for her. She was Romanian and did not speak English. Nina tapped her fingers on John's thigh, reminding him of Mrs. Carver, the minister's wife; as he willed her hand to creep up his leg, he thought he would explode.

"John, I don't think you could afford her," said Betty, as she paid for the ten-dollar coffees.

At the door, he turned back to wave goodbye but his Nina, her hand now caressing another customer's thigh, didn't notice.

The smell of Vladivostok's waterfront overwhelmed them: pee, decay, exhaust and fear. The passed a group of children, scarcely teenagers, openly drinking. Cocky, armed young men, wearing recycled Soviet-style uniforms embellished with gang insignias, were everywhere. The Kamchatka Peninsula, apparently the used car capital of the world, sported fume-belching ancient cars and new SUVs—both right- and left-hand drive—representing felonies committed on every continent.

"John, I want to make a few purchases. Be a dear and don't wait for me," said Betty, touching up her lipstick.

"Betty, the Captain told me to stay with you. It's my duty to protect you."

"John, dear, I'll be fine," she said, returning the Chanel red lipstick to her purse. "Now return to the ship. I'll see you later." She stopped in front of a shop with miscellaneous goods in the window. It could have been a pawn shop, but John couldn't read the Cyrillic script.

As Betty was about to enter, her way was barred by a burly guard. She pulled a letter from her bag and handed it to the thug. He snapped his heels and opened the shop door. John observed his animated, carnal pelvic thrust at her departing backside.

John slunk nervously, guiltily, through Vladivostok byways; he'd left Betty on her own. Back on the *Golden Maru*, he crashed on his bunk. Sometime later, he awoke and picked up his spirit bear. Its wooden lack of response pissed him off and he rolled over, grasping the little totem to his chest. "Say something or you're a toothpick."

John growled at it, tumbled off the bunk and onto the littered deck; beer cans, food trays and soiled underclothes flew about. He shoved the bear to his mouth and was about to chomp down on its ear when he saw a pair of golden sandals and ten purple toenails.

"John, what are you doing?"

His eyes followed up taut calves, firm thighs and a neat little sailor's jacket with fur trim, to a grimacing face. "Lost a sock."

"This place is a pigsty, you look ridiculous, and what's that in your mouth?"

He decided to ignore her. She'd know a lie and John couldn't believe the truth. "Been busy with my notes. You know, academic stuff, quite technical."

"Don't be presumptuous, John. Here, look at this." She held out a lovely icon, a small wooden panel with a Byzantine painting of Christ.

"Betty, where did you get that? You shouldn't have it. That looks antique. You might get in trouble."

"Yes, it is a valuable museum piece. I have rescued it from the lowlife scum from whom I just purchased it. And what about that special little spirit bear whose ear you are now gnawing? Don't lecture me." Turning on her golden heel, she exited with a parting, "This place stinks."

John had struck a chord not to Betty's liking.

Later that morning, John planned to visit the Museum of Eastern Russia Antiquities where, he had read, there might be documents important to his Ainu studies.

Escaping the dock on his first Russian solo outing, John discovered an elegant neighborhood of old colonial houses: paint peeling, shutters sagging, but Cuban proud. Passersby tipped their hats; little girls curtsied. He half expected to see children running, playing hoops. The warm summer air smelled of boiled turnips and day-old bread, and the people of talc and mushrooms. A lichen-encrusted stone wall guarded 17/19 Semenovskaja Street, the museum's home. Its cobblestone drive, lined with towering poplar trees and drooping willows, meandered through untended lawns and overgrown flowerbeds with discreetly placed wrought iron benches: John imagined a tragic Anna trysting with her lover, Alexei, while John, her cuckolded husband, whimpered at the loss of . . . Nursey.

The knocker on the massive wood door boomed. Its echo reverberated but brought no attention. Skirting the building, pushing aside brambles and ivy, John looked for signs of life: an open window, a burning light—nothing.

An ancient apricot tree, festooned with feathery moss and licorice fern, beckoned. He slumped against its trunk, closed his eyes and allowed the moment and the memories of apricot-scented pubescent illusions subdue him. A sharp rap on a nearby window exploded his reverie.

John leaned near the smudged window and peered into bespectacled, cold blue eyes. Bolts clicked and hasps slapped, and the heavy door opened.

"Do you speak English," John shouted.

The elderly gentleman held up a finger and pointed to his right ear. "Yes, my ear hears English quite well, thank you." Raking one hand through thin graying hair that needed cutting, the man gestured with the other, waving his visitor to enter.

"I want to talk with you," John said.

The old man said nothing and looked questioningly at John.

John reached into his pocket, wrapping fingers around the security of his spirit bear. "I mean, may we talk?"

The blue eyes softened, sparkled. "Of course, young man, please come in. I'm the curator here. So, tell me your name."

"John Fox, sir."

"John Fox. And what then is your father's name?"

"Chuck, his friends called him Chuck."

"Hmm, Charles Fox, John Fox. These names mean nothing to me."

"Dad runs a hosiery factory in Rolfe, Iowa. I'm an anthropology student. That's why I'm here, sir, to visit your museum."

The curator led the way through the musty display hall. John followed his trail of pipe-tobacco scent, noting his threadbare suit. Like a Hopi elder, he wore poor pride. Here and there, sunlight spotted specimens, a Tyndall effect in dust or light broken as through a stained-glass window. Heavy oak showcases with beveled glass displayed skins of birds, jaws of rodents, hooves of ungulates. Skeletons of marine mammals appeared to fly overhead and a stuffed Siberian tiger gnawed on a bloodied deer. Everything was labeled with the tight handwriting of the devoted curator: a Latin name, a date and some undecipherable Cyrillic script.

One diorama featured a marine manatee, the Steller sea cow. This docile herbivore owed its extinction to the naturalist whose name it bore. Elsewhere, a curved tusk, measuring about seven feet in length, rested on a marble altar. The wooly mammoths had also been hunted to extinction, but long, long ago and for meat, not sport.

Tea was served in a sunlit private drawing room. High pink walls, trimmed with white filigree and interrupted by windowed alcoves, spoke of an earlier eloquence, of Amadeus at a clavichord and of René dropping caviar into Catharine the Great's yearning mouth while filling her brain with self-awareness: "I think, therefore I am."

The curator deposited a tea tray on a gilded antique table. "It seems there is no time to make proper samovar tea, no time to be civilized."

On the tray rested two slightly off-white sugar cubes and a can of condensed milk. The old man positioned the can opener, covered the can with his grayed handkerchief and opened it. The curator's eyes glazed over as he sucked tea through the sugar cube clenched between his yellowed front teeth.

"Now, Mr. Fox, the specific purpose of your visit?"

"I'm on a stopover, on my way to Hokkaido, where I will study the white Japanese aboriginals known as Ainu. I read somewhere that you may house some related records here."

The old man straightened up, tugged at frayed cuffs and, clearing his throat, declared, "The Ainu are Russian."

Before John could argue, his host continued, "At the end of the last World War, we repatriated several Ainu children from Sakhalin, near the northern tip of Japan's Hokkaido Island. These children, once given a proper diet and a good education, developed into intelligent, healthy individuals, indistinguishable from us Russians."

He led John into his office where he cleared a chair of a stack of yellowing manuscripts. Squinting at a row of disintegrating red cardboard file boxes, he sought reports that supported his claim.

John scanned the shelves of the ancient library and spotted an icon—Betty's icon. *Strange! She had that this morning.*

How academic this room was, compared to the littered office of Dr. Baker, his New Mexico professor. John could still visualize his slouched body, behind a barren desk, waiting in boredom to demoralize another plebe. But here, surrounded by clutter—stacks of books, journals and loose papers tottering on stools, the floor and jerry-rigged shelves—stood a frail but confident scholar, a giant. A raspy cough brought John's attention back to the present.

Gleefully, it seemed, the curator charged on, supporting an Ainu Russo-genesis. He became impassioned, his voice rose as he addressed his foreign audience.

At one point, he sought verification, "Mr. Fox, does that not seem a reasonable hypothesis? And I am certain there is other evidence. There is a rumor Sakhalin Ainu passed long-harbored scrolls on to friendly Japanese when the Soviets occupied northern Japanese islands at the end of the last war, scrolls that proved Ainu claims of nationhood, claims that are ridiculous."

Scrolls, undiscovered ancient Ainu scrolls, thought John. Eureka, my thesis! A Nobel or at least a Pulitzer.

"Mr. Fox, in all fairness, while we espoused the Ainu, certain scholars among us feared they might achieve international recognition supporting their aboriginal claims. The prospect of Ainu nationhood alarmed us then. This remains true today, with the rise of our newly rich oligarchs whose survival depends on unlimited access to natural resources."

The old man pulled one old box from a shelf behind him and began pawing through yellowed papers. Triumphantly, he pulled out a few sheets and held them up. "See, here is a carbon copy of a memo, stating Stalin proclaimed that the Ainu were Soviet citizens with no aboriginal rights in the Soviet Union."

The curator, stimulated by the challenge of proving his thesis and his success at finding a long-misplaced memo, snatched more documents from files and shelves, and waved them in John's face.

John struggled to concentrate. There was something very significant being said here, but John was having trouble grasping what he was being told. This was his first major breakthrough into researching the world of the Ainu and he was blowing it. He pounded his forehead with his fist. *Focus, John, focus.*

"Here, Mr. Fox: evidence Imperial Russia recruited the Ainu to capture two forts on Yezo, their subversive rebellion resulting in the deaths of many Japanese." Seeing the bewildered look on John's face, the curator explained, "Yezo was the old name for Hokkaido. This was in the summer of 1457."

He continued pulling out papers, willy-nilly, and barking out episodes from the history of the "Russian" Ainu. "Ah-ha," he said, "here, this one suggests the Ainu sided with the Russian Empire against the Japanese in the war of 1904. Tsar Nicolas II lost that one—the first time an Asian nation defeated a European country. Unfortunately, this victory encouraged our Japanese neighbors in their expansionist aspirations."

Another document was the copy of an order directing Soviet soldiers to execute Japanese soldiers caught on Sakhalin following the retreat of the Japanese at the end of Second World War.

"Why would the Soviets do that?" John asked naively. "They won the war, didn't they? Hadn't enough people died already?"

The curator, deflated, confessed, "Mr. Fox, we academics often forget the human reality of the events we document. We are so clinical, cold. Have you seen 'Liberty Leading the People,' Delacroix's painting celebrating the French Revolution? His barebreasted Liberty carries high the French flag in one hand and a bayoneted rifle in the other, proclaiming the people's victory. Look closely and you will see the cost of that victory: Liberty walking on the corpses of the winners and the vanquished."

John hadn't considered the humanity that accompanied all those dates, places, and names that rattled around in his head: Stalingrad 1943, Gettysburg 1865, Hiroshima 1945. But now, standing in this old office, surrounded by packed bookshelves, threadbare upholstered chairs and oriental rugs, accouterments of a grander time, John experienced a moment of truth. And he knew the old man recognized it, too. "Sir, this is too much," said John, waving at the growing pile of papers. "These will be great for my studies. But I . . ."

The ringing telephone, an ancient sound reminding John of *The Honeymooners* reruns, snapped the curator back to his world of protecting Russian heritage from the surrounding lawlessness of Vladivostok, far from the joys of academic discovery and contemplation.

An angry exchange played out over the telephone line. "The

bastards," the curator exclaimed to John, holding his hand over the mouthpiece. "Mr. Fox, unfortunately we cannot continue our discussion. Please take these papers and go."

On the way out, John paused to examine the icon. Then he saw, next to the painted wood panel, a silver-framed photograph of the curator with Boris Pasternak and Betty. The inscription read, "Ivan, thank you for caring. Love, B."

As John left the museum, he stopped to pick up the remaining sugar cube from the tea tray. *No sense wasting good sugar.*

Laden with an armload of papers, manuscripts and government reports in both Russian and Japanese—which he had no idea how to translate—John returned to the ship. He deposited them in his cabin, then marched to Betty's room. She was dressing for a cocktail party and, before he could confront her, she turned her back to him, "Zip me up, John." He did.

"Do you like the perfume, darling? It's made from ambergris, not recent of course; I don't believe in exploiting endangered species, including Moby Dick, for vanity's sake."

"First icons, now endangered species," John said petulantly, trying to block the seductive fragrance. He had a momentary vision of a sperm whale, Earth's largest creature, diving hundreds of feet, grappling with a giant squid in the cold dark depths. Then he considered: Betty had saved the icon for the Russian people, possibly putting herself in the way of danger and certainly at great expense to herself.

"Professor, please don't lecture me now," said Betty, turning to face him. "I do what I do to make my life interesting and livable and to assist those who need help. Now, be a good little Johnny and escort me off the ship. I'm going to bring joy to some sweet orphans."

They were met at the foot of the gangplank by two goons who, after helping Betty into a waiting car, brushed John aside. He tried to record the license number as the black SUV whisked her away, but could only make out "Beehive State."

Back on deck, he was confronted by Captain Tveit. "The first mate saw you leave the ship with Betty. Where did she go?"

"Gone to bring joy to sweet orphans. I don't know."

The captain swore. "We sail soon, but such a valued passenger as Betty cannot be deserted."

John felt economics was not Tveit's only concern.

Lying in his bunk, John reviewed the day's events, eagerly imagining the accolades the haul of papers from the museum would bring him. A knock on the door interrupted his vision of international anthropologists applauding him as he concluded his seminar.

"A parcel and note from Miss Betty, sir," said the ship's purser.

The note said, "John, deliver this package to Ivan. And please give him my love, dear."

When John arrived at 17/19 Semenovskaja Street, he found the heavy door on its hinges and the curator on the stoop.

"What happened, sir?"

"They stole the mammoth tusk, just to make trinkets for tourists. This is not the first time this has happened," he said grimly.

"What about Betty's icon? The one she saved?"

"No, they did not take the icon. They only wanted the ivory."

John passed the old man Betty's package. "Betty asked me to give you this and she sends her love."

The old man perked up on hearing Betty's name and his eyes gleamed when he opened the box of sparkling sugar cubes.

"Sir, I'm really worried about Betty. She left the ship, saying she was on a mission. Something about sweet orphans. But I didn't like the look of the men who picked her up. They were in an American SUV, with Utah plates."

"This is not good, Mr. Fox. This is very, very bad," said Ivan, agitated, and putting the sugar cubes aside. "They are bastards. Let me make a call. I may have some idea of her whereabouts."

The curator retreated to his office, leaving John to explore the museum's galleries. Close to the Steller sea cow display was a petrograph of a human form being birthed by a manatee. A large lactating bear stood guard over the vulnerable pair. But for its threateningly large size, the protector looked comical: the baggy fur on its hind legs suggested pulled-down trousers; not unlike his spirit bear. This bear, the sacred bear of Kamchatka aboriginals, a god, was thought extinct. John knew of no mythology connecting human origins with the sea cow. Closer scrutiny showed the pain on the manatee's features as it suffered this unnatural birth.

"The birthing canal results from pliability of the female pelvic region," lamented Lulu. "There's no way. Watch."

She swung one leg over the metal railing running around the Presidio and hopped ever further away from that support. One excruciating split. "Squat down, you'll see."

John squatted and looked on in amazement. The earthbound foot, elevated by a spiked heel, quivered from the strain, its attendant calf taut, but the stocking seam remained straight; the thigh's muscles and sinew appeared exaggerated by the shadows cast by moonlight. And at the apex was Lulu's crotch, on a full midsummer moon. It was so beautiful.

"There's nothing I can do about it. No more can I have a baby than I . . ."

"Lulu, Lulu," said John, recalling legends in which ravens gave rise to worlds and clams belched civilizations, "history is full of stories of improbabilities. Hang in there."

A white SUV pulled up in front of the museum. No license plate. Two beefy, tattooed men climbed out, scanned the yard and lit up foul-smelling Gauloises cigarettes. Shortly, the curator appeared, wearing a greatcoat and carrying a gold-headed cane. "Igor. Igor," he bowed his head slightly to the men. "Thank you for coming so promptly."

Turning to John, he brushed the sleeve of his coat. "I wore this during the defense of Stalingrad, over fifty years ago. I slept in it; I ate in it; I marched in it. I never took it off for the whole siege, nearly a year. It served me well."

They climbed into the luxurious SUV, which included a minibar stocked with Grey Goose. The guards stubbed out their cigarettes and hunched into the front seats. An Amos and Andy video was playing. The curator said something in Russian and they replaced the video with a tape of the Vienna Choir Boys.

"Betty will be all right. Do not fret," he said, patting John on the knee.

But John wasn't fretting about Betty, he was enjoying the moment. Then it came to him, and he didn't like it. His every negative experience was opposed, superficially, by a pleasant distraction: Iowa and New Mexico, Nursey and Sue. On the *Honky Maru*, he'd been a hangdog academic, then a pompous know-it-all. And now, here he was, a hero on a mercy mission, being transported in luxury to God-knows-where... *God, I am shallow.*

They pulled up to the locked gate in a metal security fence that surrounded some sort of a factory. The Igors growled Russian threats at the man in the gatehouse and they were waved through. Pulling up to a side door to the windowless building, the four men exited the luxury of the SUV. Suddenly, John felt naked, vulnerable.

After vigorous pounding and more shouting from the Igors, the heavy door opened and John and the curator entered a cavernous, dimly lit room, while the Igors stood guard outside. A long trestle table in the center of the space, more brightly lit, supported the elbows of an army of waifs, each one carving a small block of ivory into the likeness of a bear reared up on its baggy-pants hind legs, head twisted to one side, mouth agape in rage.

An improbably large man stood at the head of the table, a Fourth-of-July political smile plastered on his pulpy face. He was arguing with Betty.

Noticing their arrival, Betty gestured to the curator.

"Ivan, help me convince this man that these children need proper care. This orphanage is very badly run, and these children need better nourishment, security and should not be working."

The curator looked at the big man with disgust. This was no orphanage, and these kids were slaves.

"You would destroy a wooly mammoth tusk to make these? These useless trinkets?" he said, coldly outraged.

Taking a piece of ivory from the nearest child, Ivan threw the carving at the large man.

"Ivan, whoa. Let me explain," said Mr. Improbable with a Midwestern twang. "How else am I to make money to support these sweet kids and keep the orphanage going?"

John guessed Iowa; he thought of his father. He thought of walking down endless rows of corn, tearing smut from the developing ears; he thought of a Methodist picnic with sweet girls shucking corn, exposing pearly cobs, and being enraptured.

"Betty," said the curator, "take the children and wait outside."

The children stood and followed Betty to the door. John followed, too.

"Mr. Fox, please stay here. Now, about these orphans, Harry. We will need, of course, some financial help from you to maintain them as they deserve to be. I suggest the proceeds from the sale of these ivory trinkets should be sufficient. Trinkets, I might add, carved from a mammoth tusk stolen from my museum."

Harry the Improbable shrugged and moved menacingly toward

the curator, his hand slipping inside his coat. "Ivan, you know I can't do that. Be reasonable. There are some pretty bad people who would be upset if this little operation was shut down."

The curator slashed at the man's hand with his cane, sending a Beretta M9 clattering to the floor. The slash was followed by several blows. "And this is for your destroying my tusk. And for mistreating Betty. And for messing with those children's lives." The big man retreated.

"Let us go, Mr. Fox. Our business here is finished. Thank you for standing by me."

Back in the car, Betty poured them vodkas. "He was a most objectionable man," she said. "I thought I could buy him off and set the children up in a proper orphanage, but he was Nebraskan stubborn."

The curator blew on the golden nob of his cane, which he rubbed vigorously with a handkerchief as if to banish some vile substance. "I'll arrange for a Danish group I know to look after the children. Maybe Vladivostok is not the best place for them, but they must stay in Russia."

"Can I see that cane, sir?" said John.

Hefting its impressive weight, John understood why Mr. Improbable had yielded. An inscription encircled the cane's head read, "Ivan, thank you for preserving our glorious past. Your Stalingrad Comrades, 1943."

Betty reached over and placed her hand on the curator's arm. "Ivan, dear, I don't know how to thank you."

"My dearest Betty, the sugar cubes are thanks enough."

"Ivan, the sugar was a gift from John." She turned to him. "Right, dear?"

He had to get this right. "No. Yes. Well, I brought them to you, but Betty gave them to me." John smiled and the others laughed. He was confused.

Back at the museum, the curator served them enormous "ten-thousand-year-old mastodon" steaks and they finished the Grey Goose.

As they said their goodbyes, Ivan pressed a hard object into John's hand. "A souvenir, Mr. Fox."

He opened his palm: a small ivory bear.

The Igors drove Betty and John through the nicer areas of Vladivostok, returning them to the *Golden Maru*.

"John," said Betty. "Ivan is anxious about loaning you those papers. He is a very sympathetic person and wants to see you succeed at your studies of the Ainu. But these are difficult times. There is concern over the international status of the Ainu, and some big industrial players want the Japanese Ainu to remain as they are: assumed assimilated in the Japanese population and holding no aboriginal rights."

John wasn't interested in this political talk. He was an academic, preparing for a cloistered life grubbing through musty manuscripts, seeking linking threads to support insignificant hypotheses. He tapped on the partition separating them from the Igors, indicating he wanted them to stop the car.

"Betty, let's get some candy. I've got a sweet tooth after that humongous steak."

They entered a Red October candy store. The chocolaty aroma reminded John of the See's shops, stateside, and had the same effect on his salivary glands. He pointed at a twisted confection, an Alvida Crème Brûlée, and the sales clerk indicated that he, John, had good taste. Betty paid and they returned to their SUV.

Betty, savoring her one bite of the chocolate, took John's elbow and commanded his attention.

"John, you did understand what I said about Ivan's papers? The point is, they may contain information critical to the present political situation. You must return them, and soon."

John, overwhelmed by the events of the evening, sprawled on his bunk, fondling his new bear, enjoying the coolness of the ivory. *Well, bear. An icon, lost scrolls, Russian documents and a quadrillion-year old mastodon steak. That's enough for today.*

A knock on the cabin door broke John's reverie. "Mr. Fox, the captain would like a word with you. Could you come to his cabin?"

"Well, John, it seems you have had quite the day. We sail in a few hours, but I feel you deserve to be introduced to an older, kinder Vladivostok. I understand from Betty that you have mostly experienced the less seemly parts of this city. What you have seen here is common to all the world's ports. It would be unfair to have you leave Russia without experiencing another aspect of its great culture."

John felt he might blow a fuse if he were to experience *more* Russia.

"I have some retired Russian navy friends here, and it is our custom to take a late-night sauna before I depart Vladivostok. Would you care to join us? It would be relaxing and I would enjoy getting to know you, away from all the prattle on—excuse my saying—this old rust bucket."

The sauna, once the pride of the Kamchatka Peninsula, was housed in a great hall, its large beams supporting a roof showed signs of decay. The place smelled musty.

Mosaics depicted the harsh life of the land and sea: whaling from skin boats, fishing among drift ice, women and children grubbing under snow in search of edible roots, forlorn families staring out at a callous sea, and a bleak burial.

What attracted John the most was a depiction of a man, wrapped in hides and armed with a knife, fighting a gigantic bear. This work could have been done by the same artist who had portrayed the lactating god bear in the museum.

Some small detached pieces of tile lay on the floor. John picked one up—an orange hexagon—and searched the murals for its home. It seemed to fit everywhere and nowhere.

"Any ideas, Captain?" he asked, holding up the hexagon for Tveit's inspection. Then it struck him: this was like trying to reconstruct the hanging gardens of Babylon, the shattered ruins of ancient Greece, his life. Maybe it couldn't, shouldn't be done. Excelsior!

An officer indicated they should bathe.

John placed his clothes in a wicker basket and headed for the sauna. Not-too-gentle hands redirected him to a pan of soapy water and a shower. He shuddered under the chilly water. The plumbing was rusty and made thumping noises. Coppery stains streaked the mildewed walls. Washed and rinsed, he entered a dark, crowded room and climbed the stepped wooden benches, facing a pile of red-glowing stones, pulsing with heat.

Sitting on the highest level, safely distanced from the heat source, he breathed in the warm dry air. The aroma of ancient wood, scalded birch leaves and thirty glistening bodies surrounded him. Someone closed the door and the men broke into robust song as they flung water on the stones.

Steam washed over John, invading every pore; his eyes felt like sandpaper, his hair threatened to ignite. A sizzling sound interrupted his hyperthermic state, as cold water flowed over him. Kinder hands led him to the lowest bench. "Thank you," he murmured.

John became comfortable in the company of men, perhaps for the first time. A primitive, childish camaraderie prevailed. The men sang a mesmerizing ditty and played a simple little game, involving hide-and-seek with a pebble. The pebble was passed from hand-to-hand and when the singing stopped, whoever was "it" guessed the location of the pebble. Failure to identify the hand holding the pebble resulted in a little knuckle blow to the upper arm.

"*Ooooo,*" John gasped, as they rushed from the sauna and into the lake.

The cool water sucked heat from his parboiled body; he produced electricity, his skin tingled, and his balls shrunk to normal size and then beyond. Sitting outdoors, their bodies equilibrated to the pleasant evening air. They could hear the women in their sauna; the sweet voices and giggles seemed so carefree.

Once he imagined he heard "John," followed by merriment.

Back in the sauna, their hosts made room for John in the hide-the-pebble game. He deftly passed the pebble from hand-to-hand, behind his ear, under his thighs, and pretended to pass it off until the singing stopped. He surrendered the pebble and immediately lost track of it.

"Ouch." A knuckle dug into his arm. And again, and again—how could they hit the exact same place?

During happy hour, following their departure from Vladivostok, Captain Tveit called for attention. "I have a favor to ask. Head office gave me permission to make a charity call at the Commander Islands, provided you agree. Please understand that traveling to these islands, at the western extreme of the Aleutians, will set us back about three days."

Upon hearing this, the Violet and Lavender ladies cheered.

The captain shook his head and went on to describe the plight of the Nikoslkoye villagers on Bering Island. "When the Soviet Union collapsed, the military, the only employer in these islands, pulled out. They simply packed up, boarded navy transport and departed."

The captain hesitated, as memories of earlier injustices swept over him. He took a deep breath and continued. "The natives, who for three generations worked for the military, are destitute. They have no source of income. The shelves in the abandoned stores have been picked clean and fuel tanks have been drained. Only vegetable gardens and limited wild foraging remain. Betty, through her many connections, has arranged to cover all expenses associated with this venture and to pay for food and supplies necessary for these people's survival."

As one, the passengers agreed. No one, including John, was anxious to get anywhere soon. And that the daunting specter of departing this floating womb for a frightening Japan would be delayed, pleased him. His Ainu research would be postponed, but this could be compensated for; this isolated place might reveal traces of early Asian migrants as they worked toward the Americas, bypassing the Bering land bridge.

"Land ho," sang out Betty, as she pierced the drizzle with pearled opera glasses.

Ahead, rising out of the gray sea were two islands, Bering and Medny, and a cluster of islets. Their profiles were reminiscent of docile volcanos, capped by low-lying clouds. Soon the drab cluster of army barracks, shacks and warehouses that made up the village of Nikoslkoye on Bering Island, came into view. The ship dropped anchor and the captain motored ashore to arrange for the transfer of goods.

"This is not enough," said Betty. "I want to participate. I want to nurture that great feeling of doing good. I want to meet the peasants and celebrate mankind with them. We can do more than feed their bodies; we can bring joy to their souls. I say we all go ashore, help move the supplies and put on a grand party. We could have a sleepover."

A flotilla of native boats tied up alongside the *Golden Maru*. The villagers wore clean but tattered clothing, with scrubbed skin and glistening hair, but a gauntness signaled their plight: they were poor and hungry. Politely, they shook hands and otherwise gestured welcome, but their eyes kept darting back to the heaps of goods that would soon relieve their struggle to survive.

John rowed towards shore in a launch that wove around dense patches of canopy kelp. The Commander Islands seemed a carousel ringed by marine mammals and birds. Sea otters, tethered to the seaweed, pivoted like wind vanes in the ocean currents as they basked in the high-latitude sun. Flocks of scoters dove for mussels as puffins bulleted by. Whales breached; sea lions barked.

"Get out, seal," screamed Sugar Baby at the pinniped that had flopped on board, taking refuge in their boat from a killer whale. A slicing dorsal tracked the circling leviathan's journey around the launch. The whale lifted its head; its emotionless eyes scanned the boat where the seal quivered. The seal looked at the humans, then at the predator; a splash, an anguished thrashing and bloodied froth ended the drama.

This brutality shocked John. He had rarely observed such a clear consequence of a dire decision. His had been a sheltered life, first in a sleepy Iowan town and then in academia. The choices that directed his life so far evolved from indecision or chance or blind stupidity, and the results of all were mostly inconsequential.

The launches crunched onto a pebble beach; all aboard leaped out, grabbed the gunnels and dragged the boats clear of the water.

John grabbed a case of Del Monte fruit salad and struggled up the beach over yielding pebbles to the waiting horse-drawn army truck. At the top of the beach, near high-water level, his way was further challenged by a wind-roll of rotting kelp. On his third trip, he collapsed into this wrack and slowly sank into the sordid mass. At first, he found the warm slimy plants, with their sweet smell of decay, repulsive. Then slowly he surrendered to its womb-like embrace.

"Oh, John, look at you," said Betty. She stood over him, calf-deep in the kelp, and offered him a hand. When almost upright he slipped, pulling Betty down with him. She laughed as they rolled and wrestled in the ooze. She sensed John's awkwardness, reached out and stroked his forehead. "Oh sweetness, let's rinse off in the sea. We have work to do and, tonight, a grand party."

The village was like nothing John could have expected. Instead of huts, there were drab, mostly deserted, army barracks; instead of a village square, there was a parade ground. What should have been a commercial area housed a former grocery store, now a community hall, and a gas station with creeping vegetation smothering the pumps. A very long runway, projecting like a tongue from gaping mouths of large, now door-less hangars, extended from the village to the west. On the eastern side was an abandoned mink farm: row upon row of little wire cages, stacked ten high. Beyond this hemorrhage of a defunct military compound, a few rural huts existed, surrounded by vast grassy stretches laced with pure streams.

Pollen from the tall dry grasses stung John's eyes. He couldn't see the villagers trekking ahead of him but he could hear the crackling vegetation as they plodded toward a fish trap. A softness surrounded him, no bright colors, just earthy browns and tranquil greens; no trees, just low-lying shrubs and grasses and, everywhere, lichens and mosses.

A goose, just a few feet ahead of him, stretched its wings and honked. Foxes approached out of curiosity, one with bloody feathers dangling from its mouth. After about an hour's hike, they reached the salmon weir. Their shadows panicked the trapped fish; some would not spawn. After gutting their dinner, John was pleased to see the remaining fish were released. They could swim upstream, come and conclude their life cycle.

Returning to the village, the troupe fanned out and searched the tall grass for boletes, quickly filling their sacks with this fleshy fungus. After three hours of being a hunter-gatherer, John succumbed to the buzzing of insects and the soft late afternoon light, lying down in the grass.

He shooed a squatting goose. "Hi, Mrs. Goose, mind if I nap by your nest?"

John signaled his buddies to stay low, to not startle the spawning salmon. Slowly he rose and launched his spear. The fish jerked and thrashed, trying to escape. A flick of the spear and a blow from his club ended the fish's life. Soon a dozen salmon hung over a low smoky fire while the hunters thanked them for their gift and prayed they would return.

Nearby, Sugar Baby scoured the earth with a deer antler, grubbing wild garlic and pigweed. Her linden bark bag grew heavy with mushrooms, rose hips and vegetation from the soil. She stood and looked about.

"John, wake up, we must push on."

John awoke in a panic, gasping for air. He had no idea how long he had slept. He stood, looking for his companions—no one, just vast reaches of waving grass, wedges of flying geese. Then he caught a whiff of harsh Russian cigarettes. Laughing, his mates, the hunter-gathers, revealed themselves and slapped him on the back.

Back in the community center, John acted as the facilitator for the distribution of supplies to the villagers. The almost Dr. Fox grew quite hoarse coordinating this international distribution of stores.

"Hey, you," John shouted at one man, "put all the canned goods in one place." When the man didn't respond, John stomped his foot in frustration. "Don't you understand English?"

"John," said Betty, "he's Aleut. All these people are Aleuts or abandoned Russians. No one here speaks English."

Dismayed and confused, John took a break. The idea that everyone didn't speak English seemed impossible and scary. Could it be the Japanese too didn't speak English? He tried to remember his Vladivostok encounters; the curator spoke English, as did the terrible Nebraskan. But the Red October chocolate shop, those nice people he encountered on his way to the museum, the sauna crowd, how had they communicated? Then he recalled his boasting exchange with the Violet and Lavender ladies that ended with his humiliation: "Don't you mean Japanese, John?"

The village shaman beckoned John to join him on the beach. They sat cross-legged and remained mute. At first his mind thrilled at the excitement of this unique anthropological moment . . . his first aboriginal group experience since the Port Alberni Chinese-Canadian café. He tossed stones into the water, trying to achieve tranquility. He concentrated on the lapping water, listening to the tinkling of small rocks as the waves washed over them. But still he remained restless. Then the Aleut shaman gently rubbed John's wrist while chanting simple sounds that echoed those of the waves flushing the beach. And John's mind flowed into an earlier time.

John soars high, a majestic Steller's sea eagle, and sees a large ancient sailboat anchored just off the fringe of kelp. Burly men row a scow laden with empty barrels and baskets to the virgin shore. Sea mammals, drawn by curiosity, approach the men, one of whom rests the barrel of his rifle on the forehead of a gigantic sea cow. The blast shatters the island's tranquility. The six-ton carcass is dragged to shore and butchered, and the flesh replenishes the ship's stores. Now, the sailors shoot the sea cows for sport. They laugh when they realize the mate of a slaughtered animal mourns its loss and makes no attempt to escape. Georg Wilhelm Steller stands by, witnessing the extinction of his namesake.

More boats come and shacks are built. Aleuts arrive to hunt and slaughter sea otters, fur seals and sea lions. The Russians build their airbase and runway. A Soviet Mig shoots down Korean Air Line flight 007, releasing 269 flaming souls. The Soviet military abandons its base, the civilians and the Aleuts. Collapse. Hunger.

"John, stop daydreaming You're missing a grand anthropological opportunity. Explore the village," said Betty.

A path beckoned and John followed it, allowing this unknown to seduce him. He leaned on a weathered wooden fence and let the sun warm his face. A shadow intruded. John raised his hand to block the glare and saw a young woman holding an armload of vegetables and melons that complemented her own honest curves. He shouted, "My name is John Fox."

Even though his voice cracked, he took care to enunciate each word carefully. She stepped forward, kissed her fingertip and placed it against his lips. Then, with a sweet smile, she led him to her porch where she gently settled him into a rocking chair.

She returned with a glass of water. As John rocked and sipped, she silently shelled peas. The firm little legumes went plunk, plunk and the pot slowly filled. He could live here forever and raise babies with this beautiful girl as the seasons rolled by. He would die first, of course, and people from all over the globe would come to pay homage to his brilliant contributions. John would be compared to Albert Schweitzer, Henry David Thoreau, and Mahatma Gandhi, and his father would donate ten dollars to the Salvation Army in his name.

A soft nudge brought him back. His Lady of the Garden handed him a carrot. It smelled sweet and looked perfect.

"Is this for me?" John croaked.

She didn't respond. She bit her own carrot and he matched her chomp for chomp until their carrots disappeared.

He fell asleep to her humming.

"John, a fox has taken our little Amanda. You must rescue her."

Beautiful Rosalinda stood over him, her peasant blouse askew from satisfying her baby's demand for milk.

He looked up from his slide rule, just one more calculation to validate Einstein's Relativity Theorem. Dare he break his train of thought? No.

"Rosa, sweet, we can make another Amanda as soon as I finish this. Could I have a drink of water?"

Rosalinda seemed a little put out and he could understand that. The fox, on the other hand, appeared happy, chomping on the child.

The not too gentle swishing of fresh beet greens across his face returned John to consciousness. He launched himself from the rocker and loaded up with cabbages, onions, leafy greens and carrots. As he entered the community hall with this beautiful woman at his side, John felt his shipmates were watching him with envy. A Violet and Lavender lady tutted, "That rascal."

Following grace, they all sat down to a table heavily laden with the bounty of the land. What a treat. Fresh salmon, mushrooms, vegetables, bowls of Del Monte fruit salad, and glasses of cool water.

Once all were served, an elder approached John with a silver platter held high. Soviet military discards hung loosely over his emaciated body, but he stood proud. A woven band of beach grass secured his long gray hair in a single plait. His gray eyes conveyed intelligence, strength and understanding. He could be the loving parent, the brother, the puppy John never had.

The elder lowered the platter to the table in front of John and, looking him in the eye, shouted, "Cutlet." All the villagers sighed.

Dumbfounded, John received this flesh as if it was a communion wafer. As he lifted the offering, a hundred eyes tracked its trajectory. He replaced the meat on the platter, stood in preparation for speaking, but couldn't think of anything to say. Also, no one was looking at him; all eyes remained on the cutlet.

"To the Cutlet Society," pronounced Betty, her water glass held high. "Let this meat symbolize our mutual respect and hope in a prosperous future."

Shouts of "Cutlet, Cutlet" rang through the hall. Holding his glass high in one hand, John shouted, "To mankind."

As the diners responded to the toast, he lifted the cutlet, smiled down on their intent faces and chomped. This was a sacred moment. John turned and bowed to the elder as he replaced some gnawed gristle on the platter.

As if on cue, the village ladies cleared the tables while the guests stood to one side. Their efficient and muted efforts, perhaps a reflection of their servitude to their earlier Soviet masters, caused all cutlery and crockery and remains of the feast to vanish, only to be replaced by a row of chilled Grey Goose bottles—courtesy of Betty—platters of garlic dill pickles, and steaming teapots resting on bases atop small candles. A tumbler, a cup and a fork defined each place to sit. The elder made an announcement and everyone settled at the table.

"My, it's dark in here; where do I sit?" said John. Betty shushed him.

A loamy, birchy presence sidled up to John and his Lady of the Garden rescued him. She seated him next to Betty, taking the place on his other side. Soft candlelight cast shadows from her gracious curves—a bust, a nose, a shoulder, slightly parted lips, a flickering tongue.

The elder stood and spoke. John couldn't understand a word but the voice was compelling. Often, the old man clutched his fists against his chest, looking toward the ceiling as if for the god who had long deserted his villagers. His speech ended and all eyes turned to John.

God! Does this have something to do with that tough cutlet?

His Lady of the Garden took his hand, placed it on a bottle and kissed him on the cheek. He stood and stepped toward the older man, who lifted his glass for John to fill. Taking the bottle from John, the elder then filled John's glass. They clinked glasses. John and the elder looked intently at each other, paused, then tossed back the rich liquor. John offered the old man a speared pickle and everyone cheered.

Betty moved around the table, pouring Grey Goose into glasses, and the guests and hosts exchanged toasts. Someone clinked a fork against a bottle, asking for silence and attention. A soft song arose from two little girls standing at the head of the table. Their voices seemed to come from a gentler time, neither Aleut nor Russian, that spoke of a pure land, an arctic Eden, now disemboweled by exploiting foreign masters. They evoked waving grasses, vast fur seal colonies, soaring birds and breaching whales and lulling sea cows: a harmonious nature, a time before Herr Dr. Steller and the acrid smell of burned gunpowder, the thud of a crude club.

The elder rose, clapped and said some words of thanks to the girls and everyone cheered. Quietly he directed the native women to serve tea.

Betty leaned over, "John, this is not your ordinary Earl Grey. Be prepared to flow."

After three sips of the bitter tea, his Lady of the Garden put her hands on John's cheeks and turned his face to hers. Her large black eyes looked frankly into his. Her pupils expanded until a pure void beckoned. Bewildered but curious, John entered this darkness, arms outstretched, feeling his way. A phosphorescent light lit a path paved in dominos.

Slowly, he shuffled down the bluish corridor. One branch led to an old man who traced figure eights on the surface of a pond. Upon hearing John's approach, he turned and, with a toothless grin, declared, "Someday sweet academe will be yours, John." He retreated to another path, only to stumble on a pox-ridden maiden who chanted over and over, "I wait by the Golden Gate, Johnny." Then a tweed-coated oaf bearing a gold-plated pork cutlet led him out of the maze into blinding light.

A scream filled the hall.

Betty gently placed her hand over John's mouth. His tablemates helped him to the door as the onlookers politely applauded.

"Come on, John, the villagers have prepared cots for us in the hangar."

Outdoors the air felt so good and John was so confused.

The next morning, still confused, John entered the community hall and joined Betty for a breakfast of more salmon and mushrooms. "What happened last night?"

"You had a bad trip, John. Last night's tea was derived from *Amanita muscaria*, the fly agaric, a hallucinogenic mushroom."

"Is that all?" asked John. "Why did it taste bitter?"

"The fly agaric is first eaten by a woman and its active ingredients are taken up in her urine. It is this urine that is in the tea."

"Yucky," said John, scrunching up his face. "I drank some old hag's pee?"

Betty nodded toward John's Lady of the Garden who was serving with the other village women. She smiled at John.

After breakfast, John approached her. "Last night's tea was interesting, but I think I'll stick to Earl Grey. And thank you for the meals. What a treat to eat fresh salmon and mushrooms for dinner and breakfast. You're so lucky."

She smiled, nodded but remained mute.

"John," said Betty, "while they only have mushrooms and salmon, and then only in season, they are a generous people. We have done them a fine service with our stores."

On the beach, the women villagers knelt facing the waiting boats, singing and praying for the passengers' safety. One by one, elders and villagers came to John and, standing a few inches away, shouted farewells, spit flying, in his face. Finally, the Lady of the Garden winked at John, before falling, wailing, into Betty's arms.

In the final days of the *Golden Maru*'s journey to Japan, the captain took an increasing interest in John, deciding to share some of his knowledge to prepare the neophyte scholar for what he might encounter. And John saw in the captain the strength and compassion he missed from his father.

As the ship sailed past northern Hokkaido, Tveit pointed out a few small islands. "During the last days of the Second World

War, the Soviets forced the Japanese from Sakhalin and the Kuril Islands. Most of the Japanese made it to Hokkaido but some, mostly young women radio operators, were trapped. Rather than be captured by the northern barbarians, they committed mass suicide." He flipped his half-smoked cigarette into the sea.

"Who was responsible for those lost lives? The Japanese propagandists, the Soviets? Who cares? In any case, the Communists made up for this loss by kidnapping several Ainu children. It's rumored they were interned in Soviet gulags."

Slowly, Japan's largest island, Honshu, slipped by. The shores of northern Honshu appeared as a green strip with an occasional village, seemingly unspoiled, inviting; they gave no hint of the centuries of social unrest and international conflict that made up the history of this archipelago nation.

"John," said the captain, "this is the same scene Paul Tibbets and the crew of the *Enola Gay* flew over before dropping Little Boy on Hiroshima."

Later, in his cabin, over Grey Goose, John listened to the captain's story. "I grew up on Norway's west coast. We were poor and we four kids wore only hand-me-downs. In the summer, I never wore shoes. We ate well, from what the sea could provide us, but no meat. Christmas treats were new hand-me-downs and a piece of chocolate. Our only luxury was a good education. This, along with love, was our parents' legacy to us.

"I was a teenager during the Second World War, and I worked on a fishing boat that plied the waters between Bergen and the Shetland Islands. We were part of Leif Larson's Shetland Bus. We smuggled arms and radios and spies into Norway, and downed Allied airmen and refugees out." Tveit's pale blue eyes grew teary, his fist tightened round his shot glass.

"Two of my brothers were also in the Shetland Bus. They died. Hundreds died. During the war, no one knew what we were doing and, after the war, nobody bloody cared. For every airman we saved, many Norwegians died and no one gave a damn."

John thought of his father. He'd been very young at the time and never spoke of the war. But John remembered seeing some civic medals for selling war bonds. And socks—they would have needed socks for the war effort. Someone had to make them. Not everyone could go marching gallantly off to war.

After four weeks on board the *Honky Maru*, John was more confident about his ability to cope with the alien culture that awaited him in Japan. He had partied in the Presidio with Lulu; achieved near-Indianhood; helped liberate Kamchatka children; brought Del Monte fruit salad to a desperate people; and shared visions with the Aleut. Now he was ready—he would flourish in Japan. And the curator's papers promised a successful thesis.

Banzai!

They docked in Yokohama harbor in the late afternoon.

After dinner, the passengers from below the waterline joined those from above at the captain's table, awkwardly anticipating the forthcoming fare-thee-wells and wishing to be done with it.

Captain Tveit tapped his glass and announced, "Those of you leaving us here will disembark first thing tomorrow morning. You will find the Japanese agents efficient and courteous."

He stood and, looking around the room, said, "I wish you well. You should get a good night's sleep. Tomorrow will be hectic."

As John stood to go, Betty took his elbow and led him to the deck. "Sit here with me for a moment. I have something to tell you." John settled into the deck chair. He was apprehensive.

"John, pay attention," said Betty. "I have arranged for a young lady, Aki Kawaguchi, to meet you in front of Yokohama Station. She'll be your guide and translator for the next few days."

Relieved and suspicious, he wondered if Betty would continue to script his life and why was she doing this . . . part of her do-gooder philosophy? But her help made him less terrified at being launched, rudderless, into a society where, to begin with, all forms of communication would be incomprehensible.

"How will I recognize her?" John asked.

"She's five-foot-four, slim, black hair and dark eyes. A neat dresser. Don't worry, she'll know you. Now it's late, I'm going to bed. Goodnight, John."

He sat up most of the night on the deck, listening to the sounds of the busy port: the cranking of cranes, lifting and pivoting; the whirring of electric vehicles, racing about, lifting crates from the dock and depositing them on waiting trucks; and human shouts, directing activities and warning of dangers. All superimposed on the soft motherly humming of the *Golden Maru*'s electric generators.

John would miss seeing United Flight 762 overhead and speculating on its occupants: Yokohama's lights made the night sky too bright, and he was too near Tokyo, the plane's destination. It would be flying low.

Everything about this journey was so vivid—the smells, the colors, the emotions—in contrast to Iowa and New Mexico, where things were drab and predictable and his actions puppet-like. John vowed to make his life one long voyage.

After breakfast, they all gathered near the gangway.

"John," said Sugar Baby, "I'm pregnant."

John looked startled, frightened.

The preacher and remittance man collapsed in laughter.

"John, just kidding." She gave him a big hug.

With kisses from the Violet and Lavender ladies, handshakes from the crew, and back thumpings from the preacher and the remittance man, John was ready to walk down the gangway. Tveit's ham-sized fist stopped him. Pulling John aside, he held out a black woolen turtleneck sweater.

"I want you to have this. I wore it when I was in the Norwegian underground navy. Think of me when you wear it. God's speed, son."

Son, thought John.

"John, Arne, let me take a picture." Betty snapped the pair.

"Just in case."

"You're going to New Mexico to study anthropology? You're going to throw away all that I've sacrificed to make Fox & Son Hosiery a great company and to assure your future. Are you stupid? Your poor mother will be heartbroken. Ethyl, talk some sense into your son."

"Not now, dear. I'm late for curling. John, if you're gone before I'm back, please be careful and write. Kiss, kiss."

His father looked resigned. John felt sorry for him.

"Well, if it's going to be, so be it. But I'll want my cardigan back."

John stepped off the gangplank, looked back at the *Golden Maru*, took a deep breath, threw back his shoulders and proclaimed, "I, John Fox of Rolfe, Iowa, an aspiring anthropologist, am liberated from the chains of Podunk academia and American mores. Japan, I am here."

The Great Hall of Customs and Immigration teemed with organized bedlam—a disturbed New Mexico ant's nest—Nursey's threat, if he wouldn't be this Hopi princess's love slave. Pigeons cooed on high rafters in the cavernous space and gritty windows failed to let in light.

Blue-uniformed young ladies and gray-clad men shepherded confused travelers. In clear but stilted English, John was instructed to find his luggage and if it was marked with chalk, to take it to a table along the nearest wall. If not marked, he could leave.

He found his bag in the section marked "F," but there would be no quick escape: it bore a white chalk checkmark. Customs was located on the opposite side of the hall.

A white-gloved elderly gentleman bowed to him. "Would you please open your luggage, sir?" John obliged.

"Please show me items that might be illegal, sir."

He uncovered four bottles of Grey Goose. "Good taste, sir. But I think you will like our whiskies—I prefer Black Nikka. May I reach into this side pocket?"

He extracted the carved wooden spirit bear, his memento of Port Alberni and of near-Indianhood.

Making a sucking noise, the agent said, "This is a national treasure. How did you come by this Higuma bear?"

He called over an inspector of antiquities and John tried to explain the bear's origin. The inspector turned it this way and that and then muttered something that included "Hong Kong." With a superior grunt, he handed it back to John. "Now, tell us why you're visiting Japan."

"I am a student of anthropology and I want to study your white aboriginals, the Ainu."

Abruptly, there were no more questions and his passport was stamped. So much for the joys of multiracialism, thought John. Admiral Perry may have opened Japan to the world in this very harbor, and the chocolate-dispensing, silk stocking-whoring Yankees, magnanimous from their vaporization of Hiroshima and Nagasaki may have brought Western culture, but Japan was still xenophobic.

He made his way along a row of twenty-story-high gantries that bowed, pivoted and swung like an army of discordant praying mantises. A series of pictographs suggesting a steam engine pointed the way to Yokohama Station. He focused on these, as he had sought the horizon on the storm-tossed Pacific. To be caught in the ebb and flow of this hectic Asian world, to try to make sense of the flashing signs, the blaring of speakers cajoling passersby, only invited vertigo.

Finally, this river of Japanese, half of whom were five-foot-four, black-haired beauties—little bees, thought John—funneled into the station.

"Aki! Aki!" he shouted and a dozen heads turned. Then a woman, just as Betty described, stood before him.

"Hello, I am Aki Kawaguchi. Welcome to Japan, John-*san*."

The press of the crowd scrunched John close to her, which he didn't resist. He sought reassuring human warmth, anything but the impersonal coldness he felt all about him. She tensed, pulled away, cocked her fist, her face locked into an expressionless mask. He backed off, giving this ninja doll space.

"Miss Kawaguchi, my name is John, not Johnson. I'm pleased to meet you. I was afraid you couldn't find me. How did you spot me in this crowd?"

Disarmed, she replied, "You are just as Betty described. *San* is Japanese for Mr., Mrs., Miss and Ms. So, I address you as John-san." Taking his elbow in a very Betty-like manner, Aki led him to a taxi stand. "I am taking you to a Japanese inn, a *ryokan*."

This, John assumed, would be like a Holiday Inn and he looked forward to a retreat from this morning's chaos.

The white-gloved, liveried taxi driver first polished the door handle and then stood at attention as they got in. John allowed Aki to enter first, enjoying the sweep of her little bee knees across the seat. He climbed in after her, feeling the heat of her glare. He tugged the door but it would not budge.

"It is automatic," she said, "the driver will close it."

The car moved smoothly from the curb as the driver flipped up the rear-view mirror. Aki scowled and then relaxed. Music softly flowed through the taxi. Vivaldi. "That is Yo-Yo Ma playing. Do you enjoy classical music, John-san?"

"No, I'm more into country and western music. I find it stimulating. I like the twangy sounds. Hank Thompson is my favorite."

A frown drifted across Aki's face and then, with resignation, retreated. "You will find more than enough stimulation here. We Japanese appreciate the subtleness of good music. It is our solace from city life."

They moved easily with the heavy traffic. Robot-like policemen controlled every intersection. Silver whistles clenched in their teeth, they directed traffic, miming the desired flow with white-gloved hands.

For John, this was *Alice in Wonderland* insanity: swirling, milling but never touching humanity; nameless streets, shining towers and gray wooden hovels; neon signs advertising Marlboro, Kleenex, Jack Daniels; and a million blue-curtained doorways leading to God-only-knows what. It was smothering, oppressive. John rested his head back on a lacy seat covering and tried to imagine the New Mexican desert, but no image came to mind.

Arriving at a gray wooden, one-story building with sliding doors and no Holiday Inn sign, the cabbie unloaded John's luggage, while an elderly mama-san and papa-san, looking formal in their kimonos, bowed and directed them to the entrance. "Thank you," John said, too loudly.

The old man jerked and stiffened. John wondered if he was suffering an angina attack.

Aki pulled him aside, her face red. "In Japan, we do not shout to make ourselves understood; we whisper." Then, very softly, she continued, "When you whisper. the other person must pay more attention. That way you have a better chance of being understood. And 'thank you' in this situation is *arigato*."

John turned to his hosts and bowed, "Arigato."

He signed in and surrendered his passport, which left him feeling vulnerable. But why? Was that little blue book like Aladdin's lamp, rub it and a steely-eyed Marine, bayoneted-rifle at the ready, would deflect a runaway semi-truck or destroy salmonella lurking in his sashimi?

Aki and John followed the mama-san to his quarters. He peered past the rice-paper sliding door into the small room. It appeared mostly empty, except for a futon and a small table with a lovely flower arrangement standing on the woven floor matting. One wall contained two closets and three large drawers. It smelled nice, like clean straw. For a moment, he thought of his first and only bovine, Jessie, on soft and itchy straw in the Iowa sun, and him resting on her ruminating belly. Before entering, he followed Aki's example and traded his shoes for slippers. "Aki, this room is beautiful, but where's the furniture?"

She knelt, indicating he should do the same. He could not kneel comfortably; he felt tipsy. He crawled to the wall where he could lean to keep his balance. *I'm going to miss chairs.*

"Everything you need is here. You will find many things different in Japan but you will quickly learn. Observe what other people do and copy them. Study this little book, *Easy Japanese*. It will give you insight into our customs and some Japanese phrases."

The book felt comfortable in his hands. As he flipped through it, he saw many penciled notations and understood that he wasn't Aki's first foreign pupil. He wondered who else Betty had sent to her for guidance.

Aki stood, "I must go now. I will see you in the morning after you have had your breakfast. But first, let me show you the water closet."

The tiled room was about four-feet square. The floor was a shallow depression with a drain in the center. Two pedestals were strategically positioned on either side of the drain. It didn't smell nice and John couldn't imagine reading in there. "This is a Japanese toilet, *benjo*. You squat with your feet on those two porcelain pedestals. Do not stand anywhere else."

To John, it looked like an Asian birthing room, maybe something that would make Lulu's life simpler. Further down the hall, they came to a tiled room with a little stool and enamel basin in the middle of the floor and a steaming tall wooden tub. "This room is the bath, Japanese *furo*. You sit on the stool and scrub yourself. Once you are clean, rinse off and then enjoy a hot soak."

He followed Aki to the foyer, trying to decide how to part. Bow, shake her hand, hug her? John expected his ninja princess would not like a hug. He would bow his farewell.

She reached into her pocketbook and pulled out a cell phone. "Do not go out, you could be easily lost. Later, when you do go out, always carry this with you, turned on. Do you understand?"

"Yes."

On tiptoes, she kissed his cheek. "John, I've asked the innkeeper to bring you an assortment of sushi and tea for your supper. We will have fun. Sayonara."

He returned to his room. A twist of the volume knob on a wall-mounted speaker released a haunting guitar rendition of Erik Satie's *Gymnopédie*. He lay back on the futon and let the image of naked dancing youths quell his first Nippon impressions.

"I am in Japan," he said over and over. "I, John Fox, from Iowa, am frightened."

After a brief nap, John decided he needed a bath. "Furo," he said to the mama-san who handed him a robe and a little kit, and pointed down the hall.

John squatted on a stool, his knees pressing his chin. He soaped and scrubbed, he pried dead skin from his heels, he reamed his ears and nostrils, he stood and dribbled hot water over his head.

The lid to the hot tub slid back exposing steamy water. Slowly he inched in, the pain giving way to a tingling sensation, the tingling to thoughtfulness: If it hadn't been for Aki—Betty?—he wouldn't have survived this long.

He sensed a presence. He wiped stinging sweat from his eyes and peered over the lip of the tub. Mama-san knelt below him, stoking the little wood fire under his perch. No wonder Aki insisted he scrub before soaking; he was being rendered into an exquisite Japanese broth. Mama-san stood, covered her mouth with her hand, and shuffling backward, bowed and departed.

John, now a pink prune, poured cold water over his head from a pitcher on the counter. Then he squatted on the low stool. A magnifying mirror revealed the craters of his pimply past. His little kit yielded a miniature toothbrush with a doll-size tube of toothpaste, a disposable hairbrush, comb and razor, and numerous little vials with incomprehensible labels. These he arranged on the floor and then began a journey of toiletry exploration. He sniffed, he daubed, he tasted, he probed, and he trimmed his modest chest hair into a heart.

I'm the John of Hearts, he thought.

Back in his room, he discovered a lovely lacquered tray with sushi and a pot of tea.

After a frightful morning benjo visit, mama-san delivered a bewildering breakfast to his room: a tray with about a dozen bowls and saucers each with a foreign food of assorted colors and shapes, and an egg, whole and uncooked. John toyed with the unappealing dishes and then set them aside. He would ask Aki about all these strange foods.

He opened *Easy Japanese* and saw on the title page that it was by Samuel Martin, published in 1957, by Charles E. Tuttle Co., Inc. Not very Japanese, he thought. "Lesson 1. Hello and Goodbye."

Aki hopped into his room, chirping like a sparrow. She pirouetted, sunk to her knees, and smoothed out her floral skirt: a hibiscus flower in full blossom and sensually scented.

"How was your breakfast? Ready to go shopping?" she asked.

John shrugged. "I expected bacon, eggs—over easy—toast, and coffee. But it was okay." He guessed mama-san would have told her otherwise.

"And how did you sleep?"

"Great, I loved the futon but the pillow was a bit hard." He didn't want to tell her that he'd mistaken the wooden block for a door-jamb at first. "And about breakfast, perhaps you could coach me? I'm afraid sushi is the only Japanese food I know, and," he added, "my total Japanese vocabulary."

It felt good to be open about his ignorance and she seemed delighted. "Futon is Japanese, John."

He excused himself, went to the bathroom and dashed cold water onto his face. Frightened eyes stared out from the mirror. His eyes. He couldn't make his eyes lie. Aki would know; everyone would know.

"Breathe deeply and slowly," Sue had said. "Define that which frightens you."

Being lost, unable to communicate; for all purposes invisible to those around him: these were his worries.

"Arm yourself against these anxieties," Sue had advised.

He patted the cell phone and the little phrase book and his spirit bear totem; these would assure his survival, and John returned to his room and Aki.

John was surprised how close Tokyo's shopping core, with its modern buildings and hustle, was to his soothing, wooden ryokan.

"Well John, we will start here," said Aki, swinging the heavy glass door open.

The shop was long and narrow, with tall bookshelves lining the walls. Deep-piled, blue carpet absorbed any sound. The bookseller, a man in his fifties, wearing a western suit, approached and welcomed them and wondered if they would like tea. He seemed most courteous but lacked that cardigan air John associated with booksellers in the States.

"May we look around?" asked Aki

"Of course," he replied. "Maybe I could direct you. What are you looking for?"

"Actually, anything on the Ainu," said Aki.

The man's demeanor turned cold. "I am sorry, we do not carry that kind of material here. Now, if you will excuse me, I must go. I will have my assistant help you if there is anything else you want."

They visited two other bookstores, with the same result. At both shops, the book dealers denied having any such material. At first, John and Aki took them at their word and moved on, but then Aki became suspicious and challenged a proprietor.

"Sir," said Aki, "I find it hard to believe you have no material on the Ainu. They are Japan's second largest indigenous population, next to the Okinawans."

The dealer switched to Japanese, speaking angrily to Aki.

John thought Aki looked even angrier when he was finished. Ignoring John as if he were one of the books on the shelves, she spoke to the bookseller in English, her voice more guttural but her words widely spaced and sharply enunciated.

"Sir, you would not want this international scholar to think you and your establishment could hold such bigoted views. I suggest you find something for him."

The man spun about, said something about *gaijin* and walked into the back room.

Aki, still furious, explained to John, "What he said to me was, 'Madam, those cannibals, those baby-bear torturers, are filthy animals. They are a blight on the Japanese people. Why would I, anyone, handle material on them, when really they should just disappear?'"

A clerk, really a kid, brought John a parcel. "My superior said that this is for you and he thanks you for visiting this shop."

John pulled out his wallet, but the clerk waved him off.

Standing on the street, John unwrapped his prize: a catalog of Ainu-inspired clothing, marketed by a Taiwanese firm.

"Aki, one more shop, that's all. I'm woozy from looking at all those Japanese letters and hearing all that chatter. And then lunch?"

"*Kanji*, not letters, John-san, and hopefully, someday, you will understand that chatter. What is woozy?"

Their final stop, a shop not more than eight feet wide, bulged with books and sheaths of papers secured with lengths of dried grass. The air smelled ancient. Aki called out, "*Konnichi wa.* Anybody here?"

A bass voice responded as its elderly owner wheeled his legless hulk out from behind the counter. John balked. He always avoided anyone handicapped, walking an Iowan country mile to sidestep such an encounter. Even a gimpy dog gave him the willies. The owner smiled toothlessly and said something to John.

"John, he wants you to reposition him on his trolley; he has slipped a little and is uncomfortable."

John was repulsed. He looked pitifully at Aki, who just shrugged. John had to do this thing. Kneeling, he explored the worn leather straps and brass buckles binding the old man to this oversized roller-skate. *A slipped buckle, that's all.*

Gingerly, he wrapped his arms around the man, whose skin was firmer and smoother than John would have guessed. And his breath smelled sweet, gingery. With a grunt, John lifted the man up and repositioned him, much as he might a fallen playground chess piece, and refastened the buckles. "Is that tight enough?" John asked. Aki translated John's question.

"*Hai, arigato,*" replied the man.

"He says, yes, thank you."

The two, a kneeling John and a relieved amputee, smiled and bowed to each other. The old man grasped John's hands, lifting and dropping them on his legless lap, over and over, all the while speaking.

"He is very thankful; he would like to be of assistance to you. He asks, would you like a book, an ancient scroll, anything?" Aki translated.

Ancient scrolls, John thought. He looked at the cripple, now seeing him not as an embarrassment, but as the potential savior of his studies and his thesis. John stood, brushed off his knees, turned to Aki who mouthed at him, "Ar-i-ga-to." He bowed—as deeply as to royalty—and said, "*Mucho* arigato."

Both the bookseller and Aki laughed. As she explained their mission, the old man lit up.

He beckoned John to lean over and then, tugging on John's beard, he said in English, "I love Ainu. I will get tea. We can talk. I am Kei-ichi Matsuyama." He wheeled over to a hanging string and tugged on it three times.

When Aki asked him the significance of the string, he responded, "It rings a bell next door. One ring is for beer, two for bathroom and three for tea."

"And four?" asked Aki.

Blushing, he said, "Even old cripples need company."

The tapping of a white cane announced the arrival of tea. The skinny old man was nearly bent double at the waist and his eyes were clouded, but there was something about his demeanor that suggested a great sense of humor, like he was about to spin around and say, "Gotcha!" He set the tea basket on the counter and waited expectantly.

"This is my friend and neighbor. He repairs wicker furniture." Turning to Aki, Matsuyama continued in Japanese.

"He says that together, they almost make one whole person," she translated. "They combine their incomes and army pensions, which barely suffice to keep them in weekly beer."

The blind man responded in Japanese and Aki translated, "He says, 'Well, what do you expect, we lost the war, you know.'"

The bookseller said something quickly to his friend and waved him away. They settled for tea on the floor. Aki, comfortable with her legs tucked under her, the old man secure on his trolley, and John, leaning against a bookshelf, not quite knowing where to put his legs.

"Now, tell me of your interest in the Ainu."

John could hardly say he switched to studying the Ainu because his Hopi princess ex-wife had ridiculed him for being so pretentious as to think he could add anything to Hopi knowledge. Nor could he explain that, according to Professor Downforth, one had to become an expert in the unique and the obscure to achieve academic prestige: translation, a professorship. The fact is, he stumbled on the idea of studying Asian white aboriginals and their affinities with other groups from fellow students, and the Ainu were accessible and distant to his New Mexico failures. So he kept his response short, simple and truthful.

"I'm a student, trying to understand everything Ainu. Soon, I will go to Hokkaido to continue my studies. Your interest in the Ainu seems unusual to me, sir. The Japanese I've met so far don't want to talk about them."

The bookseller cuddled his warm tea mug, his eyes looking inward to memories. He began to speak, in Japanese, and Aki translated his words as he related his Ainu experiences.

"I was trapped behind enemy lines on Sakhalin Island at the end of the Second World War. I must have stepped on a landmine. When I regained consciousness, I was in a primitive hut: dirt floor, no windows or furniture, and only a rag fluttering where a door should be. Alone, in pain and scared, I tried to stand. I had no legs. The stumps were bound with skins. Nearby rested a dish of some pulpy substance and a cup of tea. Famished, I ate and drank. Immediately I experienced a profound sense of well-being. For what seemed days, I dozed, awoke, ate, dozed, never seeing anyone.

"I was beginning to feel normal and didn't need so much rest. At one meal, I poured the tea on the ground and feigned sleep. To my horror, I discovered my benefactors were the hairy Ainu—evil cannibals, child molesters, thieves, animals, not humans. What would be my fate? They explained to me that the Japanese army had been routed and that only a few like me remained behind. The Soviets were keen to find survivors.

"I remained with them for the better part of a year. They were a superstitious people, and held the bear in awe."

The bookseller stopped talking and, with a pair of telescoping tongs, retrieved a book of etchings from the top shelf. This he opened and showed John a series of images: the Ainu fighting bears, bears protecting human babies, bears providing salmon.

"I witnessed a bear fight, which, being a soldier, astonished me. An Ainu warrior, wrapped in thick hides, allowed a bear to grab him into a bear hug. As the beast attempted to bite his attacker's neck, the man calmly drove his knife into the bear's heart.

"On the occasion of the first autumn full moon, the Ainu built a sweat lodge of hides. No sooner had they heated the lodge than a troop of Soviet soldiers burst into the camp. They quickly buried me under skins and threw dung on the fire. The smell was overwhelming and the soldiers refused to enter. The commander, suspicious of the Ainu, threatened to take the chief's son as hostage. A great roar from the forest sent the soldiers scurrying away. The soldiers took no hostage, and the Ainu saved my life for the second time.

"I later learned they created that fearsome roar by projecting their voice through a thin-walled clay pipe. Eventually the Ainu transported me to Wakkanai on Hokkaido Island. There are very few of us who know and respect the Ainu. They really are a fun people, full of jokes and cheery even in adversity, but fierce fighters if need be."

He stopped, suddenly distressed. He wheeled himself behind the counter, returning a few minutes later, in better humor and with a whiff of whiskey on his breath.

"We did lose the war and a lot more. But I have good memories.

On Hokkaido, I was cared for by an Ainu, Oma. We married and had a son we named Kru. When the Japanese authorities discovered me, they moved me to a miserable military hospital, fit me out with this contraption, pensioned me and shipped me off to Tokyo, never to see my family again. The authorities couldn't imagine a Japanese marrying an Ainu."

Aki knelt beside him and rested her head next to his. "I am so sorry," she said, "it must have been one big mistake. You were not cared for in the Japanese way. Is there anything we can do for you?"

"I ask two favors. When you go north to Hokkaido, I want you to seek out my son and my wife. I want Kru to know I love him and I want him to know of me. He would be forty-eight now, old for an Ainu. And I want my love, Oma, to know she was my one and only wife. Now, let me see what I can find for you."

The old man paddled here and there, extracted books and manuscripts with a caliper-like device he manipulated from floor level. He muttered, he cursed, he spun around the small shop—a whirling dervish—all the while insisting he had more, something special that John needed.

The bookseller reached up and squeezed John's hands. "*Gomen nasai.*" He said more in Japanese, his anxiety clear, as he pushed bundles of paper towards John.

Aki translated, "He is sorry. He's certain there is an old scroll here, a unique item, somewhere. His old man's memory is weak, but he will track the scroll down. He will find it, and you will find his son."

John bowed, "Hai."

They left the shop, John laden with manuscripts, a promise and the profound impression of the shopkeeper, an amputee relegated to living on the floor, a pauper scraping by on a meager army pension, who had shared his joy of his books and love of the Ainu, and who held the hope of reuniting with his son.

"Aki, let's have lunch and then call it a day. I need to rest and sort out my impressions and these papers."

After a simple meal of soba noodles and beer and a final cup of tea, John asked Aki about a word he'd repeatedly heard that day, *gaijin*.

"Gaijin means foreigner, usually a white foreigner. It can be derogatory and implies a low status."

At the gate of the ryokan, she gave him a hug.

"That was very brave of you, John, to help that old man. I could see your discomfort. I am proud of you."

She turned away, stopped, and added, "I will join you for tomorrow's Japanese breakfast. Sayonara."

In his sparse, grass-scented room, John contemplated the possibilities of the misplaced scroll, perhaps his ticket to professorial success, to fame, to his silver-framed photograph, signed with love, hanging on Betty's cabin wall . . . just in case? And he wondered how the miserable bookseller could have such feelings for a son he didn't know. He thought about his dad, the father who failed.

"Hi, Dad, where's Mom? She said she would help me with my math."

John's father put the newspaper down and looked at his son. He seemed at a loss. His undeclared role had always been that of the silent parent, to be ridiculed by son and wife. He paid the bills, repaired the broken stairs, and provided some normalcy in social settings, like church, curling dinners, and such. Although he frequently said he hoped John would go into the family business of making socks, he rarely interacted with his son.

"Maybe I could help, Johnny. In school, I was quite good at math. Did I ever tell you I almost won the State championship in accounting? Why don't you get your books and let's have a go at it."

John's mother barged in, breathless. "Sorry I'm late, Johnny." His father picked up his newspaper.

Too much newness, too many thoughts, impressions. John left the inn; just a walk around the block. No signs in English and nothing in Japanese that looked like street names or house numbers. The wooden buildings, one- and two-storied, all seemed the same. He splintered off a small piece of gray wood and recalled Captain Tveit's description of the fire bombings of Tokyo: no escaping the tsunami of hot poisonous air, the buildings so tightly packed, the streets so narrow.

At one point, three little kids followed him, singing some ditty. Did he hear the word gaijin? The sidewalk meandered around some multisided non-geometric shape. He became confused. Maybe he had been distracted by the lady who was wiping her dog with a tissue after it had peed. Having transited what should have been a whole block, he couldn't find the inn. Every doorway sported a banner bearing Japanese characters. Timidly, he peeked behind some, hoping to see the familiar foyer. No luck.

He found a small park and sat down.

"Well, Mr. Almost PhD, you're lost," he muttered. "How are you going to find your way out of this Iowan cornfield maze?"

He opened *Easy Japanese* and looked for the appropriate phrase—*Doko* my inn?—but he didn't know the name of the inn.

"Johnny, where have you been?" his mother asked. "You scared me to death. I told you to stay by the shoe store. You could get lost in this mall."

John hung on to two kind ladies. With their oversized pocketbooks, print dresses and tidy hats, they could have been the grandmothers he didn't know.

"You're the mother of this little boy?" one asked.

His mother nodded.

"Do you know where we found him?" Not waiting for an answer, she said, "He was behind a trash bin, terrified, crying."

His mother cringed.

John had heard his dad talk to her that way but she just brushed him off.

"He just seems to wander off. I don't know what to do."

The ladies pointedly looked at the liquor store parcel. His mother opened her purse and handed them a picture of him hugging his Winnie the Pooh bear.

"There, are you satisfied?" she asked and dragged John back to the car.

John's cell phone rang. He fumbled with the unfamiliar device, trying to answer it, fearful it would stop.

"John, when you answer a telephone say *moshi moshi*. How are you? Everything okay?"

"Sure, I'm just out for a little walk."

"Good, I was worried about you. The people at the inn said you had been gone for almost two hours. I will ring off now."

"For God's sake no, wait. Aki, I'm lost."

A long silence and then a deep sigh.

"Any hint where you are, John?"

"I'm in a little park with a big Buddha," he hesitated, "and a dumb *gaijin*."

"Leave your telephone on and don't move. I'm on my way."

A rattled John settled under a Japanese maple, its rustling plumage soothing him and protecting him from the summer sun. Cracks in the pavement, Japanese graffiti on the park bench, windblown litter caught in some flowering hollyhocks: the same as any park, but no gray splotches of fossilized gum. Comforted by these minutiae and knowing rescue was on its way, he opened

Easy Japanese to "Lesson 2. Excuse Me, Thank You, and Please."

"Paul, you got chocolate for pretty girl?"

Expecting Aki, he turned and saw an old lady peeking over a tattered fan. Not five-feet tall, she wore a flowered pillbox hat, a lavender shawl and canvas army boots. She sidled up as he searched his pockets, her eyes looking through his breastbone to another time.

"You've been gone too long, Paul," she said, reaching out for the lapel of his jacket. "Why you name your bomber after your mother? Your mother!"

Aki stepped between the old lady and John. "Go take care of your grandchildren, leave this man alone," scolded Aki. "John, please forgive her. The fire-bombings, Little Boy, the American occupation prey on the minds of some of our old people. Foolishness. We young Japanese create our own destiny and live beyond our past."

He glanced at Aki, then quickly diverted his eyes.

"John, why aren't you looking at me?"

"Here, read this." He handed her *Easy Japanese*, opened to Lesson 1.

She read, "Tips. Try not to stare at a Japanese when you talk to him. If the person has an ugly face, he will feel uncomfortable." Aki looked up at him. "John, that is so silly. The book was written by an American."

Aki settled the breakfast tray on the tatami and knelt down beside John. "Break the egg into the cup. Now add a dash of soy sauce and whip."

Aki took John's chopsticks—"we call these *hashi*"—and whisked. She dipped a greenish sheet of dried seaweed, nori, in the cup. "Here, open up."

John hesitantly opened his mouth and she teasingly waved the morsel under his nose. "Come on, bite it. Pretend it is a potato chip."

He snapped but she jerked it away. He snapped again and she surrendered the nori with a giggle.

Breakfast instruction continued with Aki moving around him on her knees, brushing against his shoulder, her hair swishing lilac scent. John resisted and remained committed to the task at hand: mastering the Japanese breakfast. He poked a grayish spongy square.

"Tofu, a challenge for amateur hashi users," said Aki. "Now eat up."

He resisted and she picked up a piece, pinched his nose and, when he gasped for air, flipped it into his mouth.

"John-san, here is your reward," she said, handing him a piece of toast. "Do you like grape jelly?"

He'd be her slave for life.

Aki watched John wrestle with his tie. "Here, let me."

She grabbed the tie, settling it this way and that, making it comfortable against his Adam's apple. He looked down into her smile and lay his hand on her cheek. She winced. Then he noticed the bruise, the blue and purple beneath a dusting of powder.

"It is nothing," she said, "let us go."

They walked toward the city center, a place where cement and glass buildings and wide, straight streets replaced flimsy wooden structures and narrow roads. At one point, some children shadowed them. They sang the same ditty he heard last evening. Aki spun around, shook her finger in disapproval and berated them. When finished, the children, looking sheepish, chorused, "Gomen nasai."

"Those children were rude and now ask to be pardoned."

Ueno Park surrounded them with rural serenity and boisterous

Tokyo was lost in century-old deciduous foliage. John skipped a rock across a large pond, causing the reflection of the ancient Honkan building, Tokyo's Japanese Gallery/Museum, to wobble as it might have during the 1923 earthquake.

Aki just shook her head.

Their heels clicked on the marble floor as they passed guards as dead as the exhibits. They whispered.

One hall featured samurai, Japan's privileged warriors. Their armor and weapons bulked normal physiques into terrifying hulks. John, intrigued by the elaborate gear, asked Aki if he could learn to be a samurai.

She laughed, "You are late, John. The samurai class was dissolved and steel swords prohibited in the 1860s. I think all those samurai, looking for employment, introduced kendo, using bamboo swords, to the general public. John, once you are settled in Sapporo, you might consider learning kendo. It is manly and very Japanese."

"Aki, really, do you think I could look like one of those?" he asked, pointing at a cluster of particularly intimidating mannequins.

"Now you can. At the end of the war, your General McArthur halted kendo, deeming it too warlike. Once Japan regained its independence in 1952, kendo was restored."

They wandered through the great halls and John began to lose focus. "Aki, do you think they might have some old scrolls?"

"Unfortunately, the collection of Ainu artifacts is poor," replied Aki.

White-faced mannequins, modeling kimonos, knelt pouring sake and serving rice, their faces shyly diverted. John looked at Aki and tried to imagine her kneeling near him, a supplicant. He could be her samurai, he could be her protector, defending her purity against evil warlords. But how? He had placed second in his high school's chicken judging competition; but no wrestling or boxing.

As if reading his thoughts, Aki said, "Modern Japanese girls usually do not serve, but if we do, we expect a good foot rub."

One alcove was dedicated to models of Shinto temples. "*Kami* is the spiritual driving force of Shinto. Kami represents the mythical forces of good, evil and nature," she explained.

John found it hard to concentrate. Aki's lilac smell propagated futonic fantasies through his mind.

A little fist plowed into his ribs. "John, pay attention. If you want to understand Japan you must try to understand Shinto. Shinto represents a three-dimensional world. This world is vertically arranged with the Plain of High Heaven, Kami's World, on top. Middle World is the present World, the one where you get your earthly joys, John, and pains," she added, jabbing him in the ribs for emphasis. "The lowest, Hades or the Death World, is, I like to think, the World of Myths."

His ribs ached, just like his arm had when he played that silly kid's pebble game in the Kamchatka sauna. What was Aki saying?

She stepped back, tilted her head and studied him. "John, we should eat."

They entered a little hole-in-the-wall eatery and took counter seats. The other patrons were engrossed, alternately in their food and a newspaper or paperback. Everything was rushed, so unlike his ryokan. Their server stared at John as if he were a movie star, paying no attention to Aki. She reminded John of a pimply teenager in Rolfe at the Dairy Queen drive-through window. She said something in Japanese. For a moment, John felt he could handle this. He smiled and patted his stomach.

Aki laughed, "John-san, back to *Easy Japanese*. You have much to learn and not much time. Just two days and then Sapporo, solo, John, solo."

Aki spoke to the awestruck waitress. "I told her you are new to Japan and that you appreciate her attention but that you are very occupied. And I told her grabbing your beard is off limits. Also, I ordered us curry rice and tea."

Bending over his steaming bowl, John tried to mimic Aki's rapid and efficient use of hashi.

"Very good hashi work, John. When you can play kendo for five minutes, when you can pick up one grain of rice with your hashi, you can have any girl in the Kingdom of the Rising Sun," Aki teased.

Inspired, he stabbed at his rice and held up his hashi: one grain remained between the two sticks.

Aki let out a little gasp and suggested they go shopping, "*Kaimono shimasu.*"

John thought they were entering some little shop. But no, it was the entrance to a Japanese department store, a Pandora's Box of everything one could conceive of selling.

"Aki, which World does the Japanese department store belong to? Hades?"

She grabbed his tie and dragged him to yet another escalator. A river of glistening black-haired shoppers swirled around him: a waterfall of humanity. They wandered through a three-dimensional maze of seaweed shops, a Birkenstock shop, Cartier, travel agents, florists, book dealers—contemporary and rare editions, but nothing on the Ainu—Tiffany, golf shops, and a driving range on the roof, Ivy League Universities' recruiters, noodle shops, a Frommer's guide distributor, McDonald's, funeral accessories, herbalists, tattoo parlors.

"Aki, let's go into this music store. I want to buy a CD."

John hummed to the shop girl, whose face lit up, and she pulled a disc from the shelf.

John joined Aki and they continued through the mall.

"Well, Cowboy John, let me guess, how about Johnny Cash and his *Ring of Fire*?"

"Nope, Vivaldi's *Four Seasons*."

Aki smiled and squeezed his arm. "John, now for clothes. You will need clothing for a Siberian winter and a Congo summer; the weather in Hokkaido is harsh."

Like a chicken in a field of mealworms, Aki darted from shelf to rack, pecking at shirts and sweaters and jackets, her ponytail swishing. She stretched a measuring tape around his waist, releasing a wave of domestication and arousal in his challenged brain.

"John!" Aki gave him a push.

Fleeting thoughts of Lulu as John browsed haberdashery; he held up some garters and looked questioningly at Aki.

"Those are to hold up your elastic-free socks. You do not want to impede your circulation, John. Might lower your sperm count. What do you think of these Speedos for public bathing?" she said.

"I hope these are large enough." Giggling behind her raised hand, she was transformed from ninja to geisha.

Aki held up a blue satin housecoat that just reached his knees. An emblazoned American eagle, clutching arrows and feathers, screeched over a map of Okinawa and the words "US Navy." Honky Japanese. "Mr. Fox, my treat. It is a Japanese happi coat."

Sherpa John, laden with parcels, watched Aki slip into the taxi. She does have nice knees, he thought.

Pleasantly cocooned, isolated from the city hubbub, Aki rested her head lightly on John's shoulder. Their taxi labored through Tokyo traffic. Impressions ricocheted around his skull: the exotic foods and sights and shopping; the pleasant domesticity of being with this delicate woman, her teasing, her desirability. Suddenly, Japan seemed doable; he could cope. And now, New Mexico, not Japan, seemed distant, and Iowa didn't even register.

An ambulance, its siren blaring and lights flashing, crept

through an intersection. The driver and attendant bowed to all the inconvenienced cars. "Aki, shouldn't they be racing instead of bowing?"

She explained that the medics were being polite and practical. "They cannot go much faster and your western 'life or death urgency' is not so strong with us. For us, the difference between life and death is like a piece of tissue, easy to transcend."

Back at the ryokan, Aki whispered to mama-san who hissed at her and then scuffled off, but not before appraising John, as she would a two-hundred-pound tuna.

"Open the door, John," Aki said.

She kicked off her shoes, dumped the parcels, and undid her ponytail, allowing her hair to cascade. "Come on, off with the tie. Relax."

Aki, the ninja princess, the karate kid, the pusher of little old ladies, the barterer who shamed shop girls into ridiculous price reductions— now made happy little sounds as she unbuttoned his cuffs and his shirt's top button. Mama-san brought in a red lacquered tray, muttering something that John guessed was "Slow down, girl, you're scaring the shit out of him," and quietly backed out of the room.

"Next lesson, John, proper drinking etiquette." She poured him a cup of sake. "*Dozo*. Now, I have said please accept this drink. Your reply is *domo*: thank you, I will. Dozo, please; domo, thank you. Now, before you drink, you offer me one."

A star student, he poured her a cup, reciting this new litany. Aki lifted her sake, looked him in the eye.

"*Kampai*, John. Welcome to the flowers of Japan." The fragrant fluid slipped over John's tongue and down his throat, warming. She gently pushed him back, removed his socks, ran her hand up his leg to his chest where she undid his shirt buttons. "Oh, what a nice little rug you have, but why a heart?'"

Then, without waiting for an explanation, Aki delivered a bevy of butterfly kisses to his nipples. John's eyes glazed over. She removed her shirt, exposing small breasts, one with an enticing mole. John reached for her but she pushed his hands away. "It is lesson time, John-san. First, vocabulary." Her finger touched his nose, "*Hana*, hana-banana;" his ear, "*Mi mi*, my little mouse;" his mouth, "*Kuchi*, my kuchi meets your kuchi."

John felt he should be taking notes.

"That is enough words." She straightened up. "Oh, one more: *heso*," and she plunged her face into his bellybutton and blew.

Little Aki, a lioness, self-indulgent in sex; her eyes challenging, slapped, scratched and bit, and then with a moan and "gomen nasai," she cuddled into him.

Aki lay dying in a cherry orchard, cherry blossoms kissing her breasts. He was here, her samurai, to save her from the wicked warlord but she waved him off, saying, "I am here, John, just a death away, just a tissue away."

"John, darling, wake up, our taxi is waiting. Your Hokkaido is waiting." He opened his eyes to see Aki standing over him. She wore a little yellow dress he had purchased for her, and a straw hat sitting jauntily on her pretty head. He ran his hand up her bare leg. "Aki, you're alive!"

In the cab, she laid her hand on John's cheek. "I hope I didn't hurt you. I get quite stimulated with sex, John. It's a chemical thing."

Lulu, lubricants; Nursey, sage; Sue, introspection. Now chemicals: sexual derivatives, a new fruit of anthropology for the picking? This could be John's post-Ainu research opportunity.

"John, I will be guiding Chinese travel agents through the best destinations in Japan. The hot spots. Great job, yes? Sapporo is a hot spot and will be on my itinerary. It will be nice to know you will be there. Maybe you could show me around? That would be fun," Aki said, her fingers tapping teasingly on his thigh."

The cab arrived at the downtown depot for All Nippon Airways, where travelers were quickly separated from those seeing them off. The scene reminded John of Yokohama Station: surrounded by all those people swirling about him as if he were an inanimate object, engrossed in their Japanese lives, parting, meeting, worrying about work, the kids, school. That first meeting already seemed so long ago.

Aki, standing on tiptoe, lightly kissed John on the cheek. "John-san, you are smart and sharp. You have come far in just three days. Sapporo will be yours. Sayonara!"

John slipped his hand into his pocket for the comfort of his spirit bear totem.

John stepped on the tarmac, feeling the slap of hot, humid June air. Signs in English and the flow of fellow passengers delivered him to the baggage claim area. Now what, he wondered?

The airport announcing system blared in broken English, "Paging Fox-san, please come to the All Nippon Airways information counter."

A surge of relief passed through John. He had a Sapporo connection; he would survive. And he wondered if somehow Betty had set this up.

At the information counter, a small man waited for him. He stood about five-foot-six, weighing around 110 pounds, his Emperor Hirohito-style wire-rim glasses askew. "Mr. Fox, sir, I am to be your translator. I work for the Hokkaido Ministry of Antiquities," he said in English with a peculiar BBC accent.

"Thank you for picking me up. Please call me John."

The translator sniffed the air, like a pup checking out a new territory; he seemed openly curious about John's beard. John wondered if he should sniff back: some northern Japanese courtesy?

"Fox-san, Boss, I am pleased to meet you. I am called Ike. We will take a taxi to the university. Normally I would take the train, but today, the ministry is paying."

"What's your last name, Ike?" John asked.

"I prefer just to go by Ike, Fox-san," the small man replied.

The long ride was tedious. John felt awkward conversing with this odd stranger. He was surprised by Ike's reluctance to give his full name. He wanted to pursue this discussion but the translator appeared lost in the passing scenery. And this was fine with John, as the rolling hills, expansive fields of corn and the occasional cattle ranch made him feel at home. Finally, they arrived at the University of Hokkaido. It could have been Iowa State with its open lawns and its fine ivy-covered buildings. There were few students about, which John assumed was because of summer break.

The taxi drew up in front of the university's museum. They got out and Ike paid the fare. The driver muttered something about gaijin, slammed the cab door and roared off, wheels squealing.

"Ike, what was that all about?"

"He expected a tip. We Japanese do not tip. He assumed, you being a foreigner, he would receive one. Let us go to your office. Then I will introduce you to the director."

The building, an annex to the museum, could have been a shed for garden tools. The windows were slits through thick concrete and the door was made of heavy wooden planks held together by iron strapping.

"This was a bomb shelter during the war. The university has not bothered to tear it down. It serves as useful storage."

"What are these?" asked Join, pointing at several chips in the concrete.

"Shrapnel scars. Your B-52 bombers."

Ike opened the door and John looked around at the peeling plaster, the moldy window sashes, the worn linoleum.

"Nice office," John said, "reminds me of home." He opened an interior door, which revealed a small water closet with an American Standard toilet. John was ecstatic.

Sitting down at the desk, a heavy steel contraption with a gray linoleum top and chrome trim, John indicated Ike should sit in the room's only other chair, a wood kitchen chair with half the back missing. His office, his hovel: an ex-bomb shelter. "Well, Ike, it does have privacy and a real toilet in the bathroom. And I love the high ceiling."

Checking his watch, Ike stood up. "Let us go meet the director. Then I will take you to your new home."

They walked across a small parking lot and entered an old brick building. The air was stale, the lighting weak, and there was no one walking around the exhibits. As they passed the glass display cases, John caught a glimpse of a hippopotamus skull. It seemed out of place, John thought, and lonely. At the director's door Ike hesitated. "He is always very busy. We rarely see him. He is responsible for my assisting you. Fox-san, please thank him."

Ike cautiously opened the door. "Excuse me, Dr. Yotsukura. I would like to introduce Mr. Fox. He is your visiting anthropology student."

"Ah, Mr. Fox, welcome. Please excuse my poor English. Your Professor Baker is a fine man. If there is anything we can do for you, let Ike know. Nice meeting you. Goodbye."

Backing into the hallway, Ike congratulated John. "That was the longest interview I have ever heard him give."

John looked down the long, bleak corridor. The numerous windowed doors were all darkened. "Are there other anthropology students here, Ike?"

"No, there are not. Sapporo University has an active anthropology program, under Dr. Kawasaki. There was a political embarrassment here, some time ago. An incident with mislabeled skulls. The University of Hokkaido's program was shut down. The director hopes you will be the beginning of a refreshed program."

Why me, John wondered, but didn't ask.

Nothing about the director was memorable, but the image of the lonely hippopotamus stayed with him.

Ike carried John's bags to his university-provided lodging, a simple room in a foreign students' residence located a short distance from the bomb shelter, on the edge of the campus.

"This is a very good room, an easy walk to your work," said Ike. "You can eat in the cafeteria. There is no reason for you to ever leave the university."

John inhaled the sweet summer scent of the crisp tatami mats. He ran his hand over the woven bamboo wallcoverings and looked out on the university's densely treed, deciduous forest. He felt restless. The room's sole adornment, an earth-colored scroll depicting a perfect sparrow sitting on a pine branch, its nervous energy frozen in brush strokes, mirrored John's frustration. The lethargy of the transpacific *Golden Maru* voyage had left him hungry for action, not meditation. He couldn't stay here—inertia would set in, would finish him.

"Ike," said John, thinking of Aki's hot-spot Sapporo, "this will not do. I need to live Japanese life to the fullest. To get among the people. But Ike, I'm curious, are foreign students . . . " Here John felt awkward, he didn't want to insult his translator, " . . . normally confined to campus?"

Ike looked at John, as if seeing him for the first time. "You should ask Dr. Yotsukura about that. I am not the best person to answer. Now, I think Little Ginza could be what you are looking for. It is reasonably close to the university. It has everything you might need."

Taking a taxi, Ike toured John around Little Ginza, a mini-city carved out of mega-Sapporo. The numerous shops and bars served the local urban dwellers and the Hokkaido University community. Big establishments—department stores, sports centers, malls—were located a subway ride away near Sapporo Station and the grand Ōdōri Park.

John's Tokyo-induced anxiety receded in the almost western

city of Sapporo. Wide streets in understandable grids, pedestrian and car traffic manageable—bicycles less so—and the country air, rolling in from surrounding farms and forest, refreshed, unlike the stifling Tokyo air.

"Ike, Little Ginza is just fine. I can manage this neighborhood. Now let's find a place for me."

"There are many places to rent here, Mr. Fox. That sign over there is for a vacant room," said Ike pointing at a gray wooded building, not unlike his Tokyo ryokan.

John was not certain where to knock. The rice paper and wood door seemed too fragile. He rapped on the door frame and nothing happened. Ike pointed at a bell. John rang it. They could hear scurrying inside. The door slid open and a middle-aged woman looked questioningly at John and smiled. Quickly Ike explained Mr. Fox, an American, was looking for a room to rent. The lady squinted at Ike and slammed the door.

This same scene was repeated a few times, only once with the landlord saying, "Gomen nasai." Ike suggested John approach the next place alone.

"Ike, I'd scare them off. You are my Japanese translator. How would I communicate?"

"Mr. Fox, I can give you the phrases. The problem is not you. It is me. I am what is preventing the landlords from giving you a place. They do not want to rent to anyone associated with me. Look at my face."

John looked at his translator closely. He saw skewed glasses, a fair complexion and a clean-shaven face, not unlike the faces of New Mexico's aboriginals. "You don't look Japanese, Ike."

"Do I look like you, your university teachers, your father, any white person?"

"Well, no. I don't get your point."

"I look Ainu. Maybe not the hairy Ainu you have read about

and studied. That is what these fine Japanese see when we stand in their doorway. An Ainu."

John was stunned. How had he not noticed this? "Ike, let's get coffees."

They entered a little shop, the Egg Coffee Shop, and a lady, maybe the owner, politely asked them to please be seated and would they like coffees? No one looked at them oddly. John looked around and saw some foreign students among the young working folk.

Hunched over coffees with little wafers, they sipped and ate their biscuits in silence. Feeling uncomfortable, John ventured, "Ike, who are you? I mean, the you you think you are?"

Ike leaned back, adjusted his glasses, and sighed, "An Ainu or a Japanese bastard. My mother wanted her son to do well and so she deprived me of everything Ainu. I think she sold her Ainu soul to educate me, but she did it well. I have a better education than most Japanese. They call me Ike Kobayashi; by law, the Ainu must have a Japanese name, but the law does not say we must have two names. So I go by just Ike. It is my small protest.

"My mother's disjointed tribe did not know what to do with me—I did not understand the Ainu way. I had no place with them. Japanese bureaucrats saw me as an opportunity; they would showcase me as an assimilated Ainu. Now the Hokkaido Ministry of Antiquities boasts a beardless, Japanese and English-speaking Ainu. One who is mostly Japanese, but slightly off-color."

"But your tribal experiences must have influenced you."

"Fox-san, we were an urban tribe. We lived diluted by the dominating society around us. Is that not the same for your American aboriginals? Those Hopi you studied in New Mexico? Your Indians are red and Japanese Indians are white."

"Why do the Japanese look down on the Ainu, Ike? Ever since I've been in Japan, whenever I mention the Ainu, I get shut out."

Ike took a sip of his coffee before answering, "Japanese legend says the Land of the Rising Sun was first peopled by gods. These gods become the Japanese. So the Ainu, who were here before the Japanese, could not be people. Just savages, dogs."

"What about your father, Ike?"

"Enough, Fox-san. Now you must find your Little Ginza home, solo."

Trying not to let his anxiety spiral into panic, *Easy Japanese* at the ready, John knocked on a door. It slid open.

"Hello, I would like to rent a room."

The lady smiled.

"I am an American."

More smiles and her hand gesture invited him to enter. A deep sigh acknowledged the removal of his shoes. She slid open a door.

John peered in expecting to see a typical Japanese sleeping room, but no, instead a thing of beauty: a white porcelain throne, American Standard, with toilet paper bearing images of cherry blossoms. The water closet was bright and the air smelled of pine.

"I'll take it," he whispered.

Office and home secured, now to connect the two.

"Boss, this is the Sapporo you want to experience," said Ike, holding up a map half the size of a Ping-Pong table. "Here is where you live, on the edge of Little Ginza. Over here is your office at the university."

The map of Sapporo reminded John of the patterns his father chose for his hosiery designs: symmetrical. He had read that an American laid out the plans for the city after the Japanese had invited foreigners to Hokkaido in the late nineteenth century.

Looking at the map more closely, John saw unintelligible kanji, and Sapporo became a jumble of streets and bus and tram and subway routes for a city of two million. Only Ike's two red Xs, joined by a line stretching from "home" to "work," connected the subway stations, indicated by "ST".

Subway. The word struck horror in the heart of this recent inhabitant of New Mexico—population two people per square mile—this guy who slept with his Winnie the Pooh bear until the age of twenty-two: "It's bear or me," whispered Nursey from behind a fan of eagle feathers.

"Ike, can you walk me through it? I've ridden a bus but never a subway. We could go early in the morning, say six o'clock."

"Boss, you can do it. This will be your solo challenge. And the subway instructions are in English. Besides, I am not supposed to leave the compound before seven."

Six am. The subway station was not crowded, perfect for his inaugural excursion, and he would beat Ike to work. The ticket vending machine's cream-colored panel of many buttons smiled at him. John smiled back.

From behind him, a hand reached around and pressed the button marked "English."

John's finger hovered. Push another button? What's the worst thing they could do? Shoot him, tie him down on an ant hill—Nursey's threat?

He stabbed, numbers appeared. Fares? He fumbled in his coin purse, inserted two hundred-yen coins—*kachunk*; the money disappeared. Nothing.

The hand returned and pushed another button, "¥200," and out popped a ticket. At the turnstile, the machine sucked up his ticket and spit it out, just ahead of him, luring him like a worm-baited hook through the gate onto the North 24th Street ST platform, the first of Ike's two Xs.

The train was there, waiting for him. He looked around, got his bearings, and cautiously approached only to watch the doors snap shut and the train disappear, leaving behind a great sucking sound. Having no idea when the next train would come, John decided to explore.

No time, another train. He settled in. The benches were comfortable and there were lots of advertisements to ponder. He would get off at the North 12th Street station—the second X—that abutted Hokkaido University.

Four minutes later, the train pulled out of Sapporo Station and John realized he had missed his stop. The train rocketed on toward the end of the line, to Makomanai. John hoped if he just stayed on board it would eventually return to North 12th.

He envisioned being forever lost in subterranean Sapporo. Headline: "Beware Hairy Gaijin, Haunter of Sapporo Underworld." John would join the Flying Dutchman of forlorn seas, the Phantom of the Opera, the giant alligators of New York sewers.

Racing back from Makomanai, the train was now packed. John stood and looked down the crowded, undulating tube, a snake slithering through desert sand, hundreds of freshly shampooed heads bobbing in half-sleep, reading comic books, waiting for their new day. His sour odor of fear clashed with the early morning freshness—soap, aftershave, sun-dried shirts—surrounding him.

Finally, his stop. The turnstile refused him passage. A hand reached around from behind him and gently plucked the ticket from his shirt pocket, fed it into the ticket sucker and John pranced free, the Kingdom of the Underworld subdued.

At the bomb shelter: "Boss, it looks like you had quite the night."

Aki had suggested John should frequent the same shops once he settled in; "This way you become a member of many little families."

That evening, he set out to discover compatible oases.

He didn't recognize Little Ginza at night. Gone was the sleepy ambience of little shops and coffee houses. This Little Ginza sparkled, laughter spilling from the numerous bars as boisterous crowds of nine-to-niners escaped from the drudgery of their cooped-up office jobs.

Walking down the narrow streets, John felt he was in another world: a nomad moon shone down on a thousand tents, each marked by cryptic kanji on blue curtains covering doorways. He hesitantly parted a less daunting pair and, in *Easy Japanese*, squeaked out his longest Japanese sentence to date: "What food here is?" Blank faces turned to him.

Someone said something that he interpreted as, "Buzz off, gaijin." John was backing out through the curtain when a tough-looking man, smoke from his cigarette dribbling out of his nose, grabbed his elbow and pointed to a display case of modeled entrees: perfect epoxy replicas of curry and rice, noodles, shrimp and greens floating in a clear broth, stew-like concoctions, possibly a hamburger patty. John pointed, muttered something in Hopi—*God, why?*—and perched on a bar stool.

After a couple of evenings, exploring his new neighborhood in search of food and drink, John recognized a pattern. Once he was settled on a stool, a pleasant, usually tipsy Sapporite would sidle up to him and say, "Please excuse my English," and proceed to ask him three questions—always the same questions—to which John would provide the same answers: American, one year, Hokkaido University Museum.

Many dozos and domos and kampais would follow, then a declaration of everlasting friendship—"You are my tomodachi"—followed by amnesia and a hangover. His little family grew.

During the day, he leafed through the various papers he had accumulated from Vladivostok and the legless bookseller. Mostly these were incomprehensible, but some had dates he could decipher and organizing them chronologically gave him some sense of achievement. Occasionally, he would wander through the museum looking for inspiration among the exhibits. He always concluded these excursions by acknowledging his comrade-in-exile, the hippopotamus skull that so impressed him when he first met the museum director.

"Well, Mr. Hippopotamus, it seems we have survived another day in this alien place. Take care."

In Little Ginza, John discovered an American bar, where he often finished his days. This burger hangout was frequented by university students, American wannabes, seeking escape from their highly regimented academic lives. It was rowdy and loud, numbing his senses as much as did drinking.

However, he preferred to close his days with a scotch and water at Yaseragi, which translated as "Place of Rest." This was a somber bar, with old-fashioned service—hostesses proffered snacks, lit cigarettes and poured drinks, while engaging the clientele in light conversation. John was their tame gaijin, and the regulars and servers accepted him.

"Boss, purchase a bottle from your bar," Ike advised him. "Your drinking will not cost so much."

So John's bottle of Black Nikka scotch, a hand-drawn outline of a fish on the label marking it as his, rested behind the bar and entitled him to free hors d'oeuvres. His Yaseragi name was thus acquired: Sakana-san to the bartender, Sakana-*chan* to the geisha-like bar girls.

"Do you drink, Ike?" asked John.

"The Japanese discourage our drinking alcohol. But, as the Ainu are assimilated into the Japanese population, we must share their deficiencies," said Ike. "Our bodies are cursed, like those of Caucasians, with the enzyme alcohol dehydrogenase, the substance that breaks down alcohol. This deprives us of the civilized Japanese symptoms of proper drunkenness: a red face, cold sweat, incoherence, loss of ambulatory function, early kidney failure. Rather, we Ainu are subjected to silliness, followed by melancholy."

Looking sheepish, Ike excused his pontification, "I do not have a beard, but I do like Nikka whiskey."

Ike had arranged for a second, smaller desk in John's office. John didn't object. The more activity, human warmth, the less depressing his bunker suite became and the less isolated he felt. This morning he was busy copying drawings from a musty sketch pad, perhaps belonging to an early explorer, that the legless bookseller had given John.

"Good morning, Boss. New plans for today. The museum director thinks you should meet Hokkaido's leading anthropologist, Dr. Kawasaki. He has made an appointment for you at one this afternoon. Dr. Kawasaki is at Sapporo University."

This would throw off John's routine of avoiding new challenges. Maybe a quick visit with Mr. Hippopotamus, but no, not enough time. He would tough this one out: two subway lines to complete a seamless flow from his office to Sapporo University. He could do it.

"Boss, do not think I am a snob, but Sapporo University is just a junior college. It was established in 1968 to meet the demands of an expanding middle class. But it is the home of the only functioning anthropology department in Hokkaido."

Somehow, John found himself at the campus gate. Sapporo University was a monolithic building of no architectural or historic interest. But it was surrounded by a lovely treed expanse and populated by many students. Apparently, middle-class students were under greater pressure to continue their studies through the summer.

The concierge directed John to the fourth floor where the Humanities Faculty was housed. He wandered down a warren of narrow halls, the walls plastered with posters of ancient conferences and dire warnings to delinquent students.

John peered into Room 472 and saw a pleasant-looking woman rinsing out tea mugs.

"I'm here to see Dr. Kawasaki, the anthropologist."

She straightened up and brushed some stray hair from her cherubic face, then, in perfect English, the accent slightly North American, replied, "I'm Dr. Kawasaki. And you are?"

John was in a daze; perhaps his blood sugar was low. He tried to remember what he had for breakfast. It was Wednesday; he must have had Quaker Oats, or perhaps just a piece of toast.

"Sorry. I'm John Fox. I was expecting you to be a man, but you're a woman."

She looked down at herself, raised her hands, twisting them back and forth, and then placing her finger on her nose, nodded in agreement, as if making a sound scientific decision, not hastily but thoughtfully.

The office featured the expected academic clutter—stacks of papers, tipsy piles of books, most of them appearing ancient—and, here and there, a personal touch: a photograph of Dr. Kawasaki and an older man standing in front of an Ainu dwelling, a Navajo rug tossed over a mountain of correspondence, a pair of baby shoes—her child's?—a jar of licorice sticks.

She offered him a chair and sat across from him at a little table, her cluttered desk remaining unoccupied, and extended her hand.

"Please call me Moko, John. And I was expecting a Jan, not a John," she chuckled. "You see, in my little universe, I deal mostly with confident women."

He caught his breath at her touch: her hand was cool and her grip firm.

She cocked her head, further softened her face, smiled, revealing squarish, gapped teeth, a pretty Stonehenge.

A confident woman, a confident anthropologist: what a contrast to Dr. Baker, his self-abusing, egotistical PhD advisor, surrounded in his office by unsold copies of his fraudulent thesis and his beloved hash pipe.

"So, John, what may I do for you?"

"Talk to me in complete English sentences, tell me about the status of Ainu anthropological studies in Japan, and keep smiling just like that."

She blushed, "John, I'm happily married. And, yes, my English is exceptional. I was a professional translator before attending graduate school in Saskatchewan." That explained the accent—born of dry summers and bone-brittling cold winters.

She reached for the photograph of her and the older man.

"This was my professor, my mentor, Dr. Featherstone. A genius. He taught me to respect the cultures I would study, to distance myself from politics, to be objective and open, and, above all, to love life. He died last spring of prostate cancer, just after this picture was taken. I didn't even know he was ill. His wife wrote me."

John watched as a shadow of sadness drifted across her face, only to be replaced with a look of warm cordiality.

"You asked about the status of Ainu studies in Japan. In the 1970s, it was all the rage to investigate our indigenous peoples. Detailed analyses of cranial and other skeletal features were published. What really caught the world's attention were the large sample sizes. The Japanese had a gold mine of material to measure. Anthropologists everywhere were jealous, but a few were concerned."

She rose, walked to a wall of bookshelves, and extracted a thick volume. "This is an example."

He flipped through the pages, illustration after illustration, all annotated with measurements and Japanese notes: an impressive catalog of skeletal dimensions.

"Hell broke loose after an Ainu stumbled on a cache of skulls and other bones, all clearly labeled Ainu. Everyone assumed Ainu were illiterate and never would one venture into the University of Hokkaido museum archives. Those assumptions were dead wrong. Tea?" she asked, fanning her flushed face, her voice cracking.

Her breath became even as she bustled about preparing tea. Everything had to be just right: the sugar bowl in the center of the table, seedless lemon wedges arranged into a five-armed star, highly polished teaspoons resting on crisp linen napkins.

She leaned close to John, concentrating on her pouring.

He could feel her heat and her smell reminded him of watermelon. For an instant, his mind flashed back to the perfect picnic: sitting with Nursey in the stingy shade of a desert juniper, gobbling succulent bits of a smashed watermelon, its juices drooling down their faces onto their naked torsos.

"Are you all right, John?" she asked. "You look hot."

He returned to his academic skin.

"The Ainu elders held a news conference. They explained how they had been praying over empty graves, burning food so that their ancestors might eat where there were no ancestors. Instructing their children on Ainu afterlife, while all the time, unknown to them, their ancestors tossed restlessly in the musty catacombs of academia. The elders demanded to know who sanctioned those burgled graves. They wondered, out loud, about their status in Japan, about the uncaring nature of the Japanese people. 'Rest in peace. Where?' they said."

Dr. Kawasaki stood up. "It's stuffy in here, let's walk."

She directed them to a small Italian restaurant where they had a light pasta meal with water and then coffees. She talked about her early experiences as a woman professor in a male-dominated environment.

"Our student body used to be comprised of mostly males. Often they would appear disappointed when they discovered their teacher was of the opposite sex. They quickly discarded that view," she concluded, with what John thought was a flourish of masculine pride. "And you, John, what has been the highlight of your academic journey?"

"This discussion," he blurted. John felt his face turn red. When had he started being so honest?

Dr. Kawasaki waved him off. "Now, let's go back to my office."

John spotted an ST sign and felt relieved he could find his way back, if only he could remember which side of the track would put him on the train to his university and not some distant, as yet unexplored, part of the city.

Back in the office, she placed a file in front of John: newspaper clippings. The first one showed a delegation of proud Ainu elders and contrite government and university officials at a newly constructed cenotaph commemorating dishonored Ainu ancestors.

Leaning over his shoulder, her seductive fragrance enveloping him, she pointed at the photograph, "What's missing, John?"

He shrugged.

"There's no anthropologist in that picture. The Ainu vowed to never again associate with those academics."

John looked at Dr. Kawasaki, questioningly.

"I was a new face, and from Sapporo University, which did not have a bad reputation among the Ainu. Turn the page, John."

He flipped to the next clipping. A large man, wearing a businessman's suit and an Ainu beard, stood in front of a Shinto shrine.

"That gentleman, a true Ainu, had accepted Shintoism and, in a gesture of appreciation, contributed significantly to the construction of that shrine. This event coincided with the revelations of the anthropology scandal. The Ainu believed they would finally be listened to."

She straightened up, rested a hand on John's shoulder and asked him to turn the page.

"After all that had happened—the repenting university, the goodwill expressed by Ainu to their Japanese oppressors—this is still what the public think, when and if they think of Ainu at all." The pictured bear head, impaled on a stake and surrounded by offering bowls, left John cold. She sensed John's reaction and translated the headline: "Heartless Ainu Kill Baby Bear."

She rubbed the heels of her hands into her eyes and sighed, "John, Ainu don't kill bears, they don't kill anything. According to their beliefs, they send animals and plants and things to heaven to become gods. They send them with respect so that they might return. An Ainu village is no slaughterhouse for Kobe beef."

Dr. Kawasaki pulled a metal film canister from a filing cabinet.

"John, this might give you some insight into the Ainu's relationship with bears. It was reportedly shot by a Methodist missionary sometime in the 1930s."

"Excuse me, professor," said a firm but young voice. "I did not realize you had a visitor."

"John, this is Abe-san, he is one of my graduate students. He represents the future for studies of Japanese aboriginals."

The young man bowed his head. John thought he could have been Ike's brother: the same build, clean-shaven, but no cockeyed glasses and more self-assured. Then he realized this student, this Ainu, was like all graduate students, grubbing data to support a thesis, coping with a demanding home life, ignorant of what lay ahead. Maybe there was a Nursey in Abe-san's life.

"I have a hard time imagining myself as aboriginal," Abe-san laughed. "And my professor gives me a hard time to finish my studies." He gave Dr. Kawasaki a little bow and an Ainu palm rub and turned to John.

"It is important we know about our past, but we do not trust the old guard that desecrated our ancestors' graves. We turn to Dr. Kawasaki and a few like her, who, with integrity and skilled research, help to answer our questions. I have been seduced by this wonder—may the gods of trowel, quadrate and calipers protect me."

Dr. Kawasaki clapped. "I don't think seduced is the correct word, Abe-san. Please explain your studies to Mr. Fox. Try to keep it short and not expand in your usual Ainu way . . . if that is possible."

"Well, sir, I am interested in forces that differentiated Hokkaido and Kuril Ainu. As you well know, we Ainu have been resisting outsiders since the first millennium AD. But around 1300, Hokkaido Ainu were overrun by the Mongolian dynasty that ruled China. Trade between Hokkaido and China introduced iron into our culture. This benefit of being under foreign rule was not extended to the Kurils or Sakhalin Island. Is that brief enough, Dr. Kawasaki?"

John was flummoxed. This Ainu had dates, places and facts, and an interesting thesis, one that could be published in *Nature* or *Science*.

As he prepared to leave, his mind already mapping out the circuitous route home, he handed Dr. Kawasaki a box of cookies he had purchased from the university's gift shop.

She looked at the wrapping and then at John. "You are a sensitive person, John."

He glanced at the wrapping, with its singular phrase, the motto of Hokkaido University: "Boys Be Ambitious."

She stood and gave John a generous hug, and he dreamed, what if . . .

Back at Hokkaido University, the air felt light and smelled full of spring. Some tourists were taking their pictures with the bust of Dr. William S. Clark, the university founder.

"Excuse me," John said in rehearsed Japanese, "I you together photo."

They stared at him. A little girl, all pink, hair in tight braids, flapped her mouth open and shut, like a starved guppy.

John smiled at her. She started to whimper.

He wiggled his ears and she burst into tears.

Resolute, he repeated the phrase, this time pantomiming, pointing at objects, running from them to the bust and back: a new language, John-speak.

Nervously, the family examined each other, looking at teeth, nose hairs, invisible bits of fluff on perfectly clean and pressed shirts and blouses. Who knows, this gaijin may be a photographer for *Time* magazine.

"Say cheese."

"*Chizu.*"

Through the viewfinder, John read, "Boys Be Ambitious."

In 1876, Dr. Clark made this pronouncement at the opening of Sapporo Agriculture College, now the University of Hokkaido. Clark was one of several Americans brought in by the Japanese to Americanize Hokkaido, while at the same time the Japanese were Japanizing the hairy Ainu. The American West, with its savages, was a perfect model for the Japanese. Clark resided in Hokkaido eight months. It remains an open question whether American Clark with his university or the German brewers with their Sapporo beer had the greatest impact on Hokkaido.

"Gomen nasai," John said, "say cheese again."

"Chizu again."

Snap.

And there was not a spot of bird poo on Dr. Clark.

John knew he was going to enjoy his ESL teaching duties. They would be a refreshing escape from his plodding researches and would expose him to young, ambitious Japanese. And, of course, they were going to provide valuable cash.

His classroom, located in the Social Sciences building, across campus from the museum, had been a back corridor to a few faculty offices, perhaps an escape route for professors prone to dalliances. Now, it housed a small desk, three chairs, a blackboard, for which there was no chalk, two doors, but no windows.

She stood in the doorway, looking very prim: simple purse and matching shoes, white frilly blouse and deep blue pleated skirt.

"Are you Mr. Fox?"

For a moment, he was speechless. He had a premonition. This was Nursey, standing on the New Mexico highway hitchhiking, this was Nursey filling his life until . . .

She gave a little cough, waiting.

"Excuse me. Yes, I am Mr. Fox. Please come in, Miss . . ."

"Miss Murata. Would you like to see my résumé, Mr. Fox?" Her voice was uncompromising, and her English diction near perfect. He tried to imagine having a friendly—no, intimate—conversation with her. It didn't work. No Aki vocabulary lessons here; no heso, no kuchi.

He scanned the papers she had handed him, hardly able to focus. "So why do you want to join our ESL program, Miss Murata? Your English seems very good."

She sat in a straight-backed chair, her knees tightly clenched, ankles crossed, and her white-gloved hands folded on her lap. She didn't respond.

"I see you've graduated from the Keio University with honors in sociology and Russian. Are you thinking of graduate school or a government job?"

"Mr. Fox, are these questions important to my getting into your program?"

John felt uncomfortable. A strange feeling of power coursed through him. The taste of authority? Heady stuff, but he had known the downside, the ground-under-the-heel side.

He made a little temple of his hands, cleared his throat, and, in what he hoped was a scholarly way, said, "No, and you will be my first ESL student. So, when would you like to attend?"

Miss Murata scanned her appointment book. "Monday, Wednesday and Friday mornings I have piano lessons, afternoons cooking; Tuesday mornings, flower arranging. Are you familiar with ikebana, Mr. Fox? Afternoons origami or kendo. I work in the University of Hokkaido library Thursday evenings, a community service." They agreed on Thursday afternoons.

Miss Murata stood and gave John a look he could not interpret before turning sharply toward the door, her silky black ponytail swishing. A panther, thought John, and smart.

"Ike, I've got an ESL student. She's spectacular and intelligent. And she seems to have every hour of her time scheduled: ikebana, origami, kendo."

"Boss, she is not like the Japanese girls at the American bar or the ladies at your Resting Place. She is not different, either." Ike patiently explained, in his maddeningly, BBC-accented way, "Miss Murata is clearly a lady of good breeding, being groomed for matrimony. She will be gaining the qualifications of a clever, gracious hostess, one who would propel her husband to great achievements. Cooking lessons, for example . . ."

"Enough," John barked, "enough, I understand. And please straighten your glasses."

"Moshi, moshi."

"Very good, John, we will convert you into a proper Japanese in no time," said Aki over the phone. "I am flying into Sapporo on Saturday. Can you meet me? We could go to the Konbu Hot Springs near Niseko for a nice soak and to work on your vocabulary."

John hung up, his future secure: Aki was his anchor. Subway sweats, ticket-eating turnstiles, plastic model food and chirping bar girls retreated. He usually didn't know what he was eating, but it tasted good; Aki would explain it all.

John's continuing illiteracy had its drawbacks: he had yet to learn the kanji for push and pull, and men and women on doors, and his progress through *Easy Japanese*, was frozen at "Lesson 14: Did You?"

"Ike, do you know anything about Konbu Spa?" asked John.

"The rich sulfurous waters of Konbu Spa were discovered by my Ainu ancestors. Different hot springs address different complaints. Those at Konbu Spa cure weaknesses of the mind. The Ainu purportedly parboiled the occasional missionary and prospector in hot springs. By the way, many Japanese words are derived from the Ainu language. Sapporo, for example . . ."

"Ike, stop. You are babbling."

John knew he had stepped out of line and been rude to the only Ainu in his life. "Ike, I'm sorry, I didn't mean to be so sharp with you. I had a bad night last night. A new bar with some not too friendly people. Please excuse me."

"You are excused, Boss. But I feel I am your lackey. Why do you oppress me just as I am gaining confidence about my culture? Working with you, I am learning more about my mother's people, and myself. You are an anthropologist and study other peoples. So here is a lesson: the Ainu love stories, long stories, and they—we—love to talk."

John's life developed a cadence; things were not so frantic. He breakfasted each morning at the Egg Coffee Shop, where he and Ike had first discussed the modern day's Ainu position in society. The people there were his age, and the café was where they gathered to bitch about their work and classes, and connive to steal an evening from their routine by going bowling. John was invited to join them, and this crowd was a refreshing contrast to his drinking buddies at Yaseragi and the raunchy customers at the American bar.

Mid-mornings, before he met with ESL students, John continued to work through the various manuscripts he had acquired from Vladivostok and the legless bookseller. He was frustrated by his linguistic ignorance: most were in Japanese and the remainder in Russian. But he persisted, remembering his New Mexico co-graduate students had achieved success comparing the tonal qualities of languages in which they were totally illiterate: Navajo and that of a Siberian tribe, for example. Those studies had opened the door for John to Hokkaido and its Ainu.

Slowly, his study of sketches and photographs gave him a feel for the reality of Ainu life. Most of the illustrations were dated with Arabic numerals, which allowed him to superimpose these printed images on his book-learned history of the Ainu.

"Ike, look at this," said John, holding up a sketch showing an Ainu holding out what looked like a bundle of large pressed leaves to a seated shogun. "From the date, 1887, it seems this would be in the beginning of the Meiji Period. Is this some kind of a tax or tribute?"

Ike leaned in close, adjusted his glasses and studied the picture. "Boss, that is the Ainu's greatest gift to the warring Japanese: konbu, a large brown seaweed that makes wonderful soup stock, which the Japanese call *dashi*. It became very popular. Its use was restricted to royalty. This offering might be thanks for some short-lived truce. I will make us some tea."

John spread the legless bookseller's Ainu papers on the floor and, for effect, placed his wooden spirit bear in their midst.

Ike returned, carrying a tray and knelt next to John.

"Oh, master, let me your geisha be," he joked.

Absentmindedly, John nodded in agreement.

"See, you really do see me as your serf." Ike leaned back on his haunches and stared at the wooden figure. He gasped, "Where did you get that?"

"Port Alberni, Canada. It was the gift from a First Nations elder, for my almost Indianhood."

"That is impossible. The twisted head, the baggy hind legs—that is the sacred Ainu Hokkaido Higuma bear."

"And this?" asked John, handing Ike the ivory Vladivostok bear.

Ike studied both figures from all angles; he scratched his head; he hacked an awkward cough and said, "They all have baggy back legs. Boss, tell me if I am mistaken. Does this shared presentation suggest an ancestor common to the Ainu and those who populated the Americas and eastern Russia?"

"Ike, I was about to have the same thought. Hot diggety damn, you're right, I'm right. Arigato, Ike. This common depiction of the bear gives physical support confirming my thesis. And I bet they came by water and not over some land bridge."

Ike looked through the documents spread across the floor, with the intensity of a not-yet-jaded graduate student. When he looked up at John, it was with a hint of respect.

"Boss, what is it like to be a professor? I mean, to make great discoveries? To travel internationally and give speeches? To help young lady students understand complex matters?"

"Ike, I'm only an almost-professor so I can't really answer your questions. But I have known professors," he said, not wanting to let the ego-enhancing magic of the moment slip by.

"Fox-san, please tell me about the professor who impressed you the most. Do not leave out any details. We Ainu love long stories."

Suddenly John realized that, after all those years of undergraduate and graduate studies, he'd never got close to any of his professors. He wished he had known Dr. Downforth, his Anthropology 101 professor, better. He was left with Dr. Baker, his PhD advisor.

"John, you're over your head with this Ainu stuff. Nobody in their right mind would portray hairy Korean tribes as progenitors of our fine North American aboriginals."

"Japanese tribes," John inserted.

Oblivious, Dr. Baker continued, "You're swimming against the current of established anthropological theory. That's dangerous. Do you want to be in the turmoil of cutting-edge research or do you want a PhD and a great career? You have to decide."

This from a defunct academic, relegated to this Podunk Department of Anthropology, who wrote an entire treatise based on a discarded hash pipe he found in the Mojave Desert.

"Look, John, I once went out on a limb and promoted an unpopular theory. But I was lucky; the public endorsed my ideas. Why, even the governor of this great state publicly pronounced more academics should come down and talk to the little people as I had."

Everyone knew of this charlatan's spiral to success: his discredited thesis became an almost bestseller. But he was published. And now he was chairman of John's department with the power to throttle or boost his career.

"Tweak your thesis," he said. "John, you have almost promise. We'll help you. We know you have had some hard times."

John could almost hear mocking laughter roaring around Baker's empty skull: *This dickhead lost his wife to that fat, balding, philosopher, ho ho ho.*

He wanted to choke the bastard, see his face turn purple, his tongue swell and hang out, his eyes bulge and explode.

"Thank you," John said, "I appreciate your confidence. How do you suggest I strengthen my thesis?"

"To the Land of the Rising Sun, John. There you must go and live among the savages, learn to think Ainu, grasp their world. I see your thesis as a grand list, contrasting and comparing Ainu and Hopi, and concluding that the Hopi hopped over some ancient land bridge and didn't drift to our North American shores aboard a tatami mat. And John, that Heyerdahl with his ocean transport ideas was a crackpot."

John would obtain an ESL certificate with which to support himself in Japan. And he would find his way to boosting the university's collection of aboriginal artifacts, for which the department would compensate him.

"We'll become the leading center in the study of Ainu social anthropology. Therein rests your future, John."

John collapsed against the chairman's door. The secretary watched with a curious smile as John composed himself. A faint moan escaped from the inner sanctum. She put her finger to her lips and beckoned him to a gilded oval mirror, mounted by a cross-section of a corncob bearing the Future Farmers of America motto: Learning to Do, Doing to Learn, Earning to Live, Living to Serve. This she swung aside revealing a peephole.

"To serve"—John had a fleeting vision of Jessie being led to slaughter, followed by the more disturbing sight of Dr. Baker caressing his beloved hash pipe.

Ike stroked the bundle of ancient papers. He sniffed them, ran his hand around their rugged margins, walked over to John and held out his hand. "Boss, congratulations. I will follow in your footsteps."

John considered the extended hand; he hadn't touched many non-whites. He was from Iowa. Well, he had touched Nursey.

In Japan, in spite of being bumped around in crowds, he had only really touched Aki and, he recalled with a shudder, the legless bookseller. He cherished his bears, carved and teddy, considered himself touchable and loveable, but here he faced a dilemma: Ike's extended hand. John's mind flashed to the old photos and engravings of the Ainu, "the hairiest inhabitants of planet Earth."

John backed off and bowed, but not too low.

Ike bowed low enough to be deferential, but not as low as the proprietors of John's Tokyo ryokan. He shriveled a little.

"Boss, may I borrow these papers?"

"They should stay here. You can look them over, but they are too important to my studies to go missing. You do understand, don't you, Ike?"

"Yes, Boss. Is there anything I can do for you, beyond my translation duties?"

"Yes, there is." John told Ike about the legless book dealer who'd been the source of much of this valuable resource material. "Do you know of an Ainu called Oma? She'd be an old woman now. And what about Kru? Does that name mean anything to you?"

"Kru?" Ike repeated. "There's a shaman named Kru."

After Ike had left, John enjoyed the lingering feeling of professorial superiority, of having Ike as an admiring protégé. Then he felt bad about the way he treated Ike, the Ike who, in all honesty, had almost beaten him to today's great anthropological discovery.

He didn't want to be a phony like Dr. Baker with his hash pipe. He shuddered, imagining himself with some disease, perhaps a brain tumor, bringing on arcane language, the compulsion to dwell on inconsequential matters, the belief in his own self-delusions. John caressed the leather elbow patches on his tweed jacket; he saw Ike's dangling hand and he felt guilty.

John stood on a small dais with a clear view of the arrivals door and the giant All Nippon Airline aquarium.

Silently the fish, maybe groupers, effortlessly swam in graceful little circles. A particularly large fish with an ugly, fungus-infested wound demanded attention. Its fins slowly fanned the water, keeping its head facing John. Their eyes locked and he felt compelled to open his mind to any ichthyic communiqué. He cringed at the imagined stab of pain as a small tiger fish ripped off a piece of his correspondent's festered flesh.

"John, how sweet of you to think of flowers. Hollyhocks, so unique."

His heart jumped; there she was, his Japanese lotus blossom. He glanced back at the aquarium, at his now slightly diminished colleague, and flinched.

"You seem distracted," said Aki, as she guided him to the luggage carousel.

He breathed in her fragrance—jasmine—and tried to focus on her. "Aki, you're so perfect."

"Not really, darling. Now let us see if you have learned your lessons. What's this?" she asked, poking his navel.

"Heso," he wheezed, and received a cherry-flavored kiss as a reward.

They sat at the rear of the bus. As the hilly countryside slid by, Aki alternately snuggled close, her hand slipping under his shirt, her teeth nibbling his ear and then, when he thought he would detonate, she would search her purse for gum or a hairbrush. After about an hour, they reached Niseko.

The rural village, featuring the Konbu Spa and Hot Springs, was a nesting of inns and motels, gaudy stores selling trinkets, and eateries featuring Hokkaido fare: corn and lamb, as well as seafood from the coast.

The innkeeper showed them to their room, in reality a dormitory, their home for the next three days. John kicked off his shoes, launched into a somersault that ended in a teetering handstand.

Aki grabbed him about his knees.

"John, you will fall through the wall."

They tumbled on the matted floor. Her legs were bare and smooth against his face.

"Gomen nasai." They looked up to see a red-faced maid bearing a tray of cups.

"My friend suffers from vertigo," explained Aki, tugging her skirt.

John placed the luggage against the wall with the suitcases and backpacks of other guests and looked questioningly at Aki. She stepped up close, cupped his ear, and whispered, "John, it is time you discovered a Japanese love hotel. But first the spa."

Aki went to the wall and pulled out robes from a hidden drawer.

As John waddled down the cobbled street, elevated by the high wooden sandals, *geta*, foreign drafts invaded his robed body. At the spa gate, he and Aki parted.

He ventured into the men's changing room, stood by an empty locker, and casually looked around to see what he should do. *Mimic, John, mimic.*

He removed the robe tie, carefully folded it, and placed it in the locker. The strap between his toes chafed and he struggled to keep his balance as he hopped about trying to adjust it. He glanced at the men about him, searching for a clue; they were doing nothing.

Off came the robe, off came the geta. He grabbed the small basin, squatted on a low stool, soaped up and rinsed off. As he stood a great *ahhh* arose from the half-dozen men squatting around him. John raised his arms above his head, pivoted, bent over, and rinsed each glistening cheek. The solid and smooth, mostly hairless men let out a cheer and escorted him into the steamy hot springs.

He rested his butt on the coarse rock edge that surrounded the pool as his toes tested the water. Hot but tolerable.

Nearby, the men slipped in and out of the pool's hotspots like bronze seals, fountains of water arching from their mouths. Occasionally one would approach, and place a quizzical finger on John's nipple, or tug on the mat of his chest hair or beard.

Their intense curiosity and strange behavior made John nervous. Then he remembered Ike's remark about the hot springs being good for curing the mentally incompetent.

One bather in particular seemed drawn to John; his eyes sought contact briefly before flitting off, only to shyly return. John felt attracted to this silent person whose smooth body expressed as little as did his large head. He began to see him as an alien, a bringer of wisdom.

They performed a slow dance, their bodies moving through the hot waters. John's mind emptied, his senses poised, ready to receive whatever it was he was lacking.

An attendant's whistle shattered the moment and the troupe of human pinnipeds dispersed. John looked around for Aki. He saw a few ladies modestly crouching in the water, but no Aki.

Someone grabbed his foot, flipping him. He panicked and screeched. "Shush," a feminine voice demanded.

"Aki, you scared me."

Taking John's hand, she pulled him to a submerged step. They sat side by side, the heat and sulfurous fumes penetrated their bodies.

"John, I think you could use this," said Aki, as she draped a little handkerchief over his head. It felt cool and intercepted the copious sweat that stung his eyes. After a few minutes, she led him on a watery promenade seeking out hot spots and cool retreats. Occasionally, their elbows or thighs brushed; his nerve endings tingled.

"Shower, and I will meet you out front," said Aki from the shallow valley of John's breastbone.

"I don't have a towel."

She reached up, patted the silk handkerchief on his head, "Use this to wipe off the water, that is the Japanese way. I prefer big fluffy western towels."

After showering, John encountered the seal herd dressing in the men's changing room. None of them betrayed themselves as being his water nymph. They all had on robes similar to John's except theirs had very long sleeves.

John faced the band of loonies and, tilting his head back and forth, did a little jig; his wooden geta made pleasant splashy sounds on the slimy floor. Trying to mimic him, they hooted and hollered.

Then John glimpsed a matron, accompanied by two uniformed men, cautiously approaching him, and he realized that she thought he, John, was menacing her patients.

"Oh, John what have you done?" asked Aki, as he flew past her to the cobbled street, two attendants in hot pursuit. Aki called something to them about gaijin, made a little whirling motion with her finger around her temple and followed John. The posse stopped, the guards bowed. "Gomen nasai."

Flushed from the spa's heat and the chase, John's knees quaked. Aki led him by the sash of his robe, clomp, clomp, clomp, down the cobbled street—a goat to slaughter, little Timmy to his Christmas goose, Old MacDonald to his farm?—and it felt good.

A small building off the main street bore a blinking pink neon sign: kanji alternated with "Dream Hotel."

Backlit pictures of the various rooms were displayed. A Japanese character he interpreted to mean "occupied" flashed on some of the pictures.

"John, pick a room."

He pushed a button, a price was shown and Aki swiped her credit card. *Kachunk*: a key descended; *kachunk*, and a pack of condoms followed. In their room, it was cool, quiet and comforting.

"We have two hours, John." Aki took his head in her lap and rubbed his temples, relaxing him. He thought about not touching Ike and he slept.

John stood straight, threw his shoulders back, and reached for Ike's hand. "Shake."

"Boss, first we must play rock, paper, scissors."

Ike's paper covered John's rock, his rock broke John's scissors, his scissors cut John's paper.

"Boss, you are truly sensitive. Intuitive to the feelings of inferiors. Thank you for allowing this lowly creature to win, to feel comfort in the presence of greatness."

John bowed.

"Lower."

"Okay, but who do you think you are, the Emperor of Japan?"

Ike grabbed John's head and tucked it under his arm.

"Ah-ha, gotcha!" said Ike, giving John a knuckle rub. "So, Fox-san, now you have experienced full armpit contact with an Ainu."

"John, wake up." He sat up, finding himself tangled in the loose folds of her robe. Beside them, resting on a lacquered table, sat a porcelain sake server, two little cups and a plate of sliced daikon, the peppery white Japanese radish.

"Hai, dozo," she said, filling his cup.

"Hai, domo?" She smiled.

Lifting his cup and looking her in the eye, he said, "Kampai."

"Kampai, John. To our little sleepovers."

The icy fluid slithered down his throat into his stomach where it released a warm fog of well-being. A familiar cloud of alcoholic vapor rose, invading his nasal passages. Tears came to his eyes.

Aki held up the plate of radishes. "Grey Goose, darling."

John rolled over and recognized in the mirrored ceiling a very pleasant place. He remembered their love-making, rehearsed new Japanese anatomical phrases and touched the mean bruise on his ribs.

Aki laughed, "You are ready for Japanese 102."

Back at their dormitory inn, John and Aki joined the nine other couples sharing their room: honeymooners. Twenty purple robes kneeling around a row of tables, careful not to invade their neighbors' space, they chatted gaily; nuptial consummation waiting in the wings.

Beer, sake and whiskey bottles stood guard over bowls of rice and kelp consommé, platters of tempura, sushi, sashimi and little roasted fishes, skewered chicken. They ate and drank; the brides blushed and giggled.

John, the bearded gaijin who struggled to keep his balance, to excise charley horses, to not kick over the table, felt fraudulent.

The evening passed quickly with many dozos and domos and kampais. Everyone was impressed with John's hashi skills, but when he stabbed a little bride in the belly button saying, "Heso," a chorus of sucked-in breaths and muttered gaijins awkwardly filled the room.

John bowed. "Gomen nasai."

Flushed faces, slurred speech, spilled drinks; then the magic moment when, as the fairy of twenty-minutes-before-the-hour drifted by, a flurry of maids invaded the party, raining apologies over the guests and, after assuring the bottles were empty, cleared all evidence of the feast.

Aki and John joined the others in dragging bedding from secret cabinets for their communal sleep. Caught breaths followed little giggles.

Sleep evaded John, his arm numb from cradling Aki.

Cautiously, he shifted her head and felt hot tears running on her face. "Aki, what's the matter?"

"Gomen nasai, John." She sobbed, kissed his bruise and nestled into him.

He dreamed of Miss Murata, the flawless mate—Chopin, bouillabaisse, a thousand cranes, reptilian guile, nice butt—Miss Murata would not be celebrating her matrimonial conquest here. That wasn't her style.

After a shared breakfast with their dorm mates, John and Aki wandered through the village.

"John, have the man take your picture. With your beard, one would think you were Ainu."

He positioned his face on top of the gaudy plywood cutout of an Ainu warrior. The horsehair beard scratched and thoughts of a menagerie of coots and lice leaping into his beard repulsed him. At the photographer's prompting, John scrunched a brow, hooked his lips down into a scowl and lifted one nostril, causing its adjacent eye to squint, and snarled.

Aki gasped, "John you do look like the real thing."

A small crowd gathered, including yesterday's loony seals, tittering with amazement, and a little fear.

Aki gently pulled him across the street. "John, those security guards might think you are a renegade Ainu."

Mistaken for an aborigine—Caucasian almost-professor John Fox—ridiculous. He felt the need to add to this farce. Stepping away from Aki, he pivoted and postured like his spirit bear, raising both hands in claws, twisted his head, curled back his lips and roared.

The two uniformed guards pinned him to the ground.

"He is really quite harmless," Aki said.

They let him up when she explained he suffered from delusions of being Ainu and that his doctor had suggested the waters of

Konbu Spa might cure him. "Gomen nasai," said the guards as they brushed imagined impurities from their white gloves.

At the inn, the manager took Aki aside, speaking earnestly and throwing an embarrassed glance at John.

"The manager is concerned about your behavior last night, John. I told him you were an American student. He said he understood, but that you have upset the other guests. Your Ainu-ness offended them and they refuse to spend another night with you."

"I'm American, not Ainu. And even if I were, what's their problem?"

"John, many Japanese look upon the Ainu as a national shame. I do not share this view but I do resent their refusal to join in with modern Japan."

John felt confused; he wasn't being treated fairly. "Aki, we have two hours before the bus leaves. I'd like to walk around and think about the innkeeper's comments, and the way people react to me."

"You will be all right? If you want me, I will be in the pachinko parlor."

Disturbed, John climbed a cobbled street past tidy shops with pennants and balloons and T-shirts and bears (wooden, plaster-of-Paris, stuffed, authentic, gaudy, Hong Kong) and street vendor carts (roasted octopus, skewered lamb, broiled sole with clouded wobbly eyes, eggplant and carrots, shrimp tempura). Cooking smells, the sounds of happy children, the banter of flag-waving travel guides swirled about him.

He imagined raising a family with Aki here. They could cater to English-speaking tourists in the summer and make love in the winter. It seemed so perfect, but so un-Aki. Feeling guilty, he purchased a pair of pewter Yezo maple leaf earrings.

Leaving the village's commercial core, the setting quickly became rural. Little patches of rice, vegetable gardens and orchards occupied every inch of arable land. Where the pitch was too steep or the land too rocky, the native deciduous forest thrived. John wandered off the road into an inviting copse and lay down on the dry brown grass. A warm, gentle breeze and the rustling of oak leaves calmed him and the peaceful moment lulled him to sleep, to dreams.

John reached up, slipping his hand under Aki's shift. "Heso, baby. Come to daddy. Kiss, kiss, kuchi, kuchi."

She swatted his hand away.

"I'll do more than kiss your foul mouth, you worthless gaijin. Here is a new word for you: shigoto. Work, baby. Get a real job. Anthropologist, ha!"

He looked at her, seeing his mother heaping disdain on his father, and poisoning their son against him. His gaze shifted to scrunched papers littering the floor, a battered typewriter, soiled diapers, a mangled life, a mangled thesis, all bathed in the cheap pink light of a blinking love hotel neon sign.

She jiggled the baby on her hip.

"Daddy is silly, my little darling. He knows all these worthless words and the only thing he can do is make boring gaijin sex."

"Aki, please . . ."

He awoke to voices, not Japanese. John rolled over, half fearing he would see a demonized Aki or an angry farmer, and stared at two pairs of bare feet: broken toenails, dirt encrusted. Looking up he saw skirts of a coarse canvas-like material bearing strange symbols. Grass rope cinched the skirts up to the crotch. Black-bearded faces with pirate-white teeth grinned.

"Hello," John whispered.

They bowed slightly, rubbed their palms and then their beards. Then one held out an apple. His hand was rough, his fingernails dirty. He smelled of the earth, a farmer's smell. He said something, but John shrugged his shoulders. The other one pointed at the earth and said, "Ainu Land."

John said, "Dirt."

The buzz of Aki's cell phone interrupted the conversation. "John, the bus leaves in twenty minutes. You must hurry."

He hung up and saw he was alone. On the ground lay the apple and a wooden carving of a bear.

Walking back to the road, he came across a recently cleared area with little darts of whittled willow branches, the shavings still attached, standing at its four corners. John put one in his pocket, a souvenir of his Ainu encounter.

Aki was waiting for him on the bus. "Where were you, John? I worried about you. Nice apple." She lifted his hand. Aki took a loud bite from the fruit and then held the apple for him. John chomped.

"I found it on the ground in a little orchard."

She looked at him and shook her head, "Not here. These apples are precious and the farmers guard them."

Caught out in his Japanese lie, John smiled and presented Aki with the earrings. She sighed and put them on.

"What do you think?" John asked.

"Tacky."

Settling back into the bus seat, she asked John to put his arm around her shoulders. He patted the wooden bear in his pocket and pulled lovely Aki to him. She smelled of a man's cheap cologne.

"Ainu Land," repeated Ike. "Where did you hear that?"

John related his Ainu encounter near Konbu Spa and showed Ike the carved bear.

"Boss, you should stay away from those wild Ainu. The university does not want to be involved in any politics associated with the Ainu cause. Stick with the papers you have got and museum archival materials. Maybe you should spend more time pulling these together."

When John told of his encounter at the photographer's stall and the tourists' reaction, Ike collapsed into the broken chair. "They thought you were Ainu?"

"That's what Aki said. And I think the two Ainu in the field mistook me for one too. An Ainu in a tweed jacket."

"Boss, I am Ainu. Not you."

John inspected his fingernails, patted his beard. He liked being Ainu, he liked his souvenir Ainu photo. "Ike, Ainu Land. What is its significance?"

"Ainu Land is what we call Hokkaido, Sakhalin and the Kurils. It is our homeland. The Japanese fear a unified Ainu nation. They fear the reclamation of stolen lands. They fear retribution for oppressing us for centuries. They have gone to great extremes not to return our lands or compensate us."

"Us, Ike?"

John watched the startled look of realization sweep over the Ainu's face.

"Yes, us, Boss. Do you know that, by definition of my heritage, I am entitled to an esteemed salary one-third lower than a Japanese would get?"

"Sakana-san, kampai." Another night in the Place of Rest, ice cubes slowly melting, diluting John's Black Nikka scotch. He smiled a smile he didn't feel; his eye twitched. His tooth ached. He rubbed his jaw.

"Ah," said his companion, "a tooth matter. Open wide."

"You're a dentist?" John asked.

"Hai. Does this hurt?"

The swizzle stick bounced off his throbbing molar. Tears rolled down his cheeks. "Kampai," he moaned and drained his glass.

John felt shallow. He'd been in Sapporo for a little over a month and what did he have to show for it? His life was cluttered with trivia. Nights carousing new bars, sometimes bowling or playing Ping-Pong, sometimes staring at a Go board or mahjong tiles, but constantly retreating to his home bar, Yaseragi. Weekends with Aki, always with less to say, less to explore, distracted, impatient. And now a toothache.

"Hey, Boss, you look terrible. Another hot bar night?"

John collapsed into his chair, opened his mouth and pointed.

John loved teaching. ESL instruction was proving to be an honest interaction with the Japanese. Miss Murata topped the class, but she remained uptight, an explosive-laden Fabergé egg. Today, she was the only student, the hot summer weather having seduced the others to less stuffy quarters.

"Miss Murata, please explain the idiom, 'short fuse.'"

She glared at him. John wondered if she suspected he was Ainu, or just a run-of-the-mill white enemy.

After teaching he returned to his room. This home, with its scattered dirty laundry, unwashed crockery, smutty Japanese comics he couldn't read, the twisted, yellowing bed sheets, a CD player continuously delivering Vivaldi's *Four Seasons* and a one-burner propane stove for hot snacks and terrible coffee, was the joy of his life. And always his best friend, the American Standard, was close by.

He was on page 83 of the *Easy Japanese* book, "Lesson 20: Please do." Thanks to Aki, his comprehension of anatomical terms would qualify him to translate *Gray*'s *Anatomy*. And a few hours of nightly bar-time were advancing his comfortable, lowlife vocabulary.

"Hey, John-chan," said a little wannabe-American chick, "let us talk Japanese. Now repeat after me: *chotto matte, kudasi.* That

is 'please wait.' *Omoshiroi des ne* means, 'Interesting, isn't it.'"
Following John's nasal repetitions, everyone cheered.

"Have another whiskey, my American scholar."

Proud to show off his newly acquired language skills, John concocted excuses to visit the museum's employees. At first, they tolerated his trashy Japanese, thought it was cute. Often on these excursions, he would discover a little insignificant Ainu artifact, mislabeled or damaged: a new addition to his shipments to New Mexico.

"Boss, you sound like a Japanese whore. You should spend more time with men," said Ike. "Kendo that will take you to the core of every male Japanese dream: Bushido—the way of the samurai warrior. It will give your speaking a manliness."

Ike suggested the Kitano Kendo Club in Sapporo's Susukino district, "at night this is a hot spot, but during the day, it is quite respectable. Hokkaido All Japan Kendo Association is located nearby."

"Is that your club?" John asked.

Ike looked at him as if he were crazy. "An Ainu doing kendo? You do know I am not Japanese? You know Japanese and Ainu are not friends?"

"Ike, you sound like you're reconciled to being Ainu."

"Boss, you have an infuriating way of changing topics."

"Ike, please straighten your glasses."

He felt confident taking the subway from his home to the university. This trip would challenge him, but he had done it earlier when visiting Sapporo University. He would need to change trains, but this time on a different system. Everything would happen so quickly, announcements would be blurred, signs unintelligible, and he would feel strung-out. But the membership officer at the kendo club had insisted he visit this particular shop. He, John, was a resident of Sapporo, this was his city, and he was an almost PhD.

John squeezed on the subway at Little Ginza. Toe-to-toe, butt-to-butt with pretty bees and preoccupied men, his head among the noose-shaped plastic handholds. The train rocked and squeaked and slithered through its worm tube.

One of John's hands held a dangling loop, while the other hung dangerously unoccupied at his side. He considered putting his hand in his pocket, but that might be misconstrued. Reaching behind him, he used the wayward paw to tuck in his shirt: a perfectly innocent act.

An outraged shout and a violent jerking shattered the tranquility of the subway car as a middle-aged lady freed her skirt from his trousers. Comic books snapped shut, lip glosses were pocketed, hair brushed away from weary faces, fists tightened, chests puffed out. John imagined the next day's *Hokkaido Shimbun* newspaper headline: "Mob Brutalizes Makomanai Subway Gaijin Groper."

John stood frozen on the platform of Sapporo Station. Like a rock, he parted a river of people—they paid him no heed. Looking over their heads, he searched for a pattern. He saw thousands of tiny birds banking, swirling and settling in unison, all orchestrated by some primitive, yet-to-be defined force. John looked for exit No. 9.

His goal, the little shop, smelled of leather and sweat and featured mannequins dressed in protective kendo garb. They looked every bit as menacing as the samurai in the Tokyo museum. Most impressive were the face guards: wire cages mounted on leather ovals with an articulated leather flap as a throat guard.

A wizened old man looked in his direction with nearly white eyes.

"My name is John Fox," he said softly, "and I'd like to purchase kendo equipment."

The old man smiled and, running his hand along a tether, left the room. He could have been Koro's twin. A schoolboy returned, bearing a bundle of clothes and a bamboo stave.

"No, there's some mistake," John said. "I'm going to train in kendo and need a sword, not a bamboo stick."

"Sir, kendo, the Way of the Sword, is performed with bamboo staves. Many students were severely injured while training with steel. Now let me show you what you will need for kendo."

John wondered if this man-child was the vocal extension of the blind proprietor; he seemed so worldly, in spite of his rosy cheeks.

The lad laid out the bamboo sword and the uniform consisting of a thick woven top and pleated, skirt-like trousers.

"I need these in black," John said. "I was told everyone in the club wears black, not white."

The boy disappeared into the backroom where John thought he overheard the word "gaijin."

Returning, the boy bowed. "Gomen nasai, but your kendo club requests that we provide you with white clothing. White suits you. Besides, these are a gift from the club."

John couldn't believe this kid, this jerk. He seemed so authoritative, so sure of himself. But a gift . . . ?

John arrived at the next Thursday ESL class laden with some of the Russian curator's and the legless bookseller's papers.

"Miss Murata, could you help me with some translations?" John asked.

She looked up from her textbook and waited. She seemed to always be waiting for him to say something, to complete a thought. He found it exasperating.

"I have texts in Russian and Japanese, nineteenth- and twentieth-century documents about the Ainu that I need to understand and compare . . ."

Miss Murata cocked her head and looked out from beneath

perfect black bangs; her eyebrows, nose and mouth formed a question mark.

". . . to complete my PhD dissertation," John concluded.

She closed her book, rested her chin on her hands and looked inscrutable.

"I need to finish so I can join academia . . ."

She didn't move.

He thought of his mentor, the idiot chairman of his discredited department, and his promise of an academic nirvana.

". . . or just get on with my life."

She stood and seemed to soften. Her face took on a look of understanding. "Where?" she asked.

"We could meet at my place, where we would not be disturbed."

Instantly, she hardened, any sense of goodwill disappeared. Only the fragrance of her freshly shampooed hair that reminded him of Nursey after a midnight desert swim remained.

"By my place, I mean my office," John retreated, hoping she would return to being at least a neutral, if distant, Murata.

"Your office will be fine. Yes, I will trade you translations for ESL. Now, give me some idea of where your research is going, Mr. Fox."

He described the bears' common baggy hind legs and then demonstrated the similarities in posture of the Port Alberni, Vladivostok and Konbu Spa bear carvings.

Murata looked at him with astonishment; a brief hint of amusement flitted across her face as John uncurled his lips, de-gnarled his hands, and untwisted his spine.

"I want to trace these images and others to their origins."

He then showed her the papers.

She quickly shuffled through the pile, loudly exhaled, stood and gathered them into her satchel as she prepared to leave.

"Miss Murata, I can't allow you take those away. They're irreplaceable."

The look she gave him said, "So, Mr. Fox, you do know your mind, at least sometimes."

"I will be able to work from copies, but will need to refer to the originals from time to time."

She placed the papers back on the desk and rested her hand on the pile. "This seems to be a worthy project, Mr. Fox."

Before his first kendo lesson, John tested the heft of his bamboo sword, which dictated action. He sighted down the taut string that ran from the handle along the top slat to the sword's tip. He was a Japanese peasant about to fight Godzilla for the hand of lovely Murata. He twirled about his small room slashing the sword at imaginary ninja. Relentlessly, he pummeled a bag of dirty laundry, each blow releasing a sharp crack as the bamboo slats collided. The skirt-like culottes of his kendo outfit billowed out introducing unfamiliar drafts and giving his legs an exciting freedom. John gathered its canvas cloth to his face and breathed in the aroma of hemp. The thick-matted blouse felt sensuous. A sharp rapping from the room below brought reprieve to his imagined foes.

Then he saw his mangled Pooh bear. "Gomen nasai."

Self-consciously, John entered the North Sapporo High School gym, his sneakers scrunching across the waxed floor. The students, none of whom seemed over ten, were kneeling, facing the instructor who made gruff noises.

"Fox-san, *ohayō gozaimasu*," he said, indicating John should kneel.

John looked at the instructor. He was slight, of medium height, not the imposing figure John had imagined, not the protector of Japanese maidens, the slayer of rampaging Godzillas. He seemed quite ordinary, but with a confident bearing and a hint of humor.

The students breathed deeply together and John's anklebones crushed into the cold floor. He suspected the children were snickering at his discomfort but, when he glanced around, he saw in each face concentration and beatification. When it came time to stand, John couldn't. The instructor, expressing no emotion, helped him to his feet.

Embarrassed, John would have quit then, but for the thought of having to face Ike with failure. It was like being caught in the silent war between his parents, when John struggled to distract them—"Hey, Dad, I'll race you to the float," or "Don't worry, Mom, the ice is thick"—often to his peril.

His sense of obligation had led him to hurtful, self-depriving situations; being bonked by a bamboo stave seemed harmless compared to drowning or hypothermia. Besides, his way of speaking Japanese could use some manliness and he fancied the concept of Bushido.

Nursey interpreted his self-destructiveness as masochistic and hurtful to her.

"Johnny, close that book. Look, I'm a rattlesnake wiggling up your pant leg."

He looked down on her shiny black hair, cascading over his lap, and grasped her hand, halting its exploration of his growing erection. "Princess, don't. I've got to study."

In an attempt to cure John of his self-denial and salve her frustration, Nursey dragged him into an abandoned Navajo hogan. They spent two days naked, with tequila for drink, mescaline for drugs and antelope testicle-tartar for sustenance. She danced around the fire, slowly burning pages of his professor's thesis, the library's only copy. She tickled him with eagle feathers, whipped him with sequoia cactus, threatened to dip his penis into an ant colony. She sang ancient songs pleading with the gods of passion.

She conjured up images of fabulous sex, mountain-moving orgies, spent and whipped and satiated bodies.

Still nothing.

"Boss, your kendo instructor left a message. He said he would be available to work with you privately, just give him a call. He likes your spirit and thinks you have much to gain from kendo. You must have impressed him."

"He's like a father figure, Ike. Stern but concerned. I wanted to quit but I didn't want to disappoint him. Even though I blundered about, he didn't make me feel wrong. He's not large, but he emanated a great strength. And his hands, they're like a pianist's, but his arms are powerful. He's an ageless Achilles, a compassionate Japanese warrior."

Ike looked surprised. "I have not heard you talk like that before, Boss. You *are* a scholar. I did not think you noticed anything outside of your own preoccupations. I am proud to be in your presence."

John didn't know how to interpret this backhanded compliment. And he didn't want to admit that he'd stayed in the kendo class because he didn't want to disappoint Ike.

"Also, your student Miss Murata called, but she did not leave a message. She has an upper-class way of speaking. When she heard my voice, she tensed up. She is probably above conversing with an Ainu."

John decided to ignore this dig at the girl of his dreams. "How are you getting on with the search for Oma and Kru?"

"And when would I have time for that?" Ike asked. "I am your secretary, valet, guide and translator. Do not you think I have a life? How many children do I have? How many wives? You do not know anything about me. You do not care."

Ike's unexpected tirade upset John. He'd thought they were

growing close, becoming buddies even. John thought that Ike was benefiting from being around him, the almost-PhD, and the translator's interest made him, John, feel important. But what did he know, how many friends had he ever had? Really?

John sat at his desk in the bomb shelter, unhappy and introspective. He knew he couldn't survive without this Ainu's help.

"Ike, let's go out tomorrow night."

The office phone rang.

"John, you are forgetting your Japanese manners. Moshi, moshi, remember?" Aki sounded annoyed.

"Do not answer. I will be in Sapporo tomorrow. We can get together."

"Aki-chan, I can't. I've promised my assistant a night on the town."

"Aki-chan," she mimicked. "John, you are learning our Japanese ways, darling, and I am not even your favorite barmaid. So, you will be spending time with an Ainu man while I go to a pachinko bar. Impress him with your medical vocabulary."

She hung up.

A waitress led John and Ike through the noisy Sapporo Beer Hall and they joined several flushed Japanese at a crude trestle table.

Ike signaled they wanted beers and pointed to a picture of grilled lamb and vegetables.

"This one," Ike ordered in his BBC English.

She bent over, exposing fragrant lace falsies, and pointed to a bowl of rice. John and Ike nodded.

The waitress returned with what looked like a giant iron orange juicer—the kind you twist half a grapefruit on—that she placed on a propane burner. She then brought a platter of sliced lamb and chopped vegetables. John looked askance at this uncooked food and began to fumble with his chopsticks.

"Hai, dozo," said one of their tablemates.

Someone put a large piece of lamb fat on the top of the cooker and then the others arranged the vegetables and thin slices of lamb around the corrugated cone, like so many sacrifices to a god on an Aztec temple. The meal progressed famously, as their new tomodachi led them through the etiquette of eating Genghis Khan, a famous Hokkaido dish.

"Is this an Ainu dish?" asked John.

They did not understand the question but recognized the word "Ainu." A dark cloud threatened rain.

Ike started singing the Cherry Blossom song, "*Sakura, Sakura . . .*" and then hesitated, feigning ignorance. The lyrics were in their blood, the compulsion irresistible: everyone joined in and another round of beers appeared.

Following their authentic Hokkaido meal, John and Ike retreated to Yaseragi, the Place of Rest.

John pivoted on the small bar stool, hesitated, and then draped an arm around his assistant, now his drinking buddy, and asked, "So, how many wives do you have?"

Ike belched, assaulting John with the aroma of beer, whiskey, and ginger; trying to focus on John's face, he sobbed, "None. I have always hated my heritage. Then I met you. Now I understand the Ainu could be considered an advanced, if not superior, race. Now I am Ainu."

Ike said this with a straight face, but John knew he was joking. He waited for the translator to laugh or wink.

"The more I study your documents, the prouder I am to be Ainu," Ike continued. "I weep now, knowing that I should have been bedding many Ainu wives. I should be creating sons and daughters to advance the cause."

Ike sighed and then rested his hand on John's shoulder. "John, may I call you John now, you have given my life a new focus. Now tell me, what you would have been if you had not become what you are? Please, the full story. Remember, I am Ainu."

"Johnny, you sit on this stool and see how we, we of Fox & Son Hosiery, make socks," said his father with an irritating har-har-har and a not-too-gentle slap on the back.

He sat facing a long, tall table where four women perched on high stools. Their torsos and chattering machines saw to the making of stockings above, while below, restless feet tapped to imagined music or scratched itchy calves or patiently waited for the day's-end whistle.

John looked up and saw a bevy of bobbins spinning, each spiraling lint through a lonely shaft of sunlight, a galaxy forming. Descending from the spools, threads of many colors rocketed through metal eyes, around soft corners, downward in a dazzling cyclone. And the knitting machines—thousands of little mechanical bits pushing and shoving and knotting—pumped out socks. Human hands snipped them free and, with deflating tedium, tossed the newborns into a bin.

Quickly John became bored and shifted his attention to the women. One smiled at him and he shouted, "Hello, what's your name?"

She looked at him, shrugged her shoulders and snipped another sock. At first, he assumed she had not understood, possibly a Mexican laborer his father had smuggled in. Then John saw she was mouthing something. The din made it impossible to hear. Her lips projected short words, made emphatic by shaping each letter.

He blushed. She snipped another sock, slipped her hand under the table, and pulled up her skirt. John's eyes followed the hand.

"Well, son, soon this will all be yours."

The next morning, John arrived at the office to find a refreshed Ike studiously making notes on the manuscripts. He wished John a good morning, "Ohayō," and handed over two letters. John's heart jumped: Nursey? Sue? Lulu?

July 2, 1995
Golden Maru,
Somewhere between Japan and England and where I do not care

Dearest John,
    I hope this note finds you happy and in good health. Was Aki helpful? I found her fastidious, a great one for detail, the nitty-gritty, but maybe a little too intense and aggressive. Don't be shy about asking her for whatever assistance.
    After we unloaded the last of the San Francisco cargo, we took on a consignment of used Toyotas. The assumed market for these is England, but then you never know. Right?
    The reason I'm writing is that Ivan cabled me to say that he had made a grave mistake in loaning you those documents and papers and needs them back. You must respect the curator. He said you could copy them if you liked.
    I have enclosed an international postage voucher to cover expenses. I miss you.
    Love, Betty
    P.S. Grey Goose tastes flat now that you are gone.
    P.P.S. Arne says hello.

On the way to the photocopy shop, John offered to buy Ike lunch.
    Lovely waitresses, dressed in Tyrolean lederhosen and white fluffy blouses, bowed, exposing the gentlest of cleavages. John studied a slot machine with a portfolio of pictured meals, each labeled in Japanese. In frustration, he inserted four one-hundred yen coins and randomly pressed a button.

Their waitress exchanged their meal tickets for frothy glasses of Sapporo beer and disappeared. A burst of laughter erupted from the kitchen.

"John, you could have asked me to help you choose."

"I did just fine, thank you."

The flushed waitress approached their table, followed by a gaggle of kitchen staff. The platter was placed before John and he was surrounded by polite applause. The pink and tubular mound pulsated lightly: a living noodle? John picked up one end and a sticky substance dripped on his hand. It tasted sweet and smelled vaguely familiar. He stuck the end in his mouth and sucked it in. It was endless. Finally, the waitress leaned in and snipped the thing with a pair of scissors. It did not want him to swallow; it slithered around his tongue; it flossed his teeth; it tied itself in knots. He thought it would climb out his nose. At last he gulped and it was gone and everyone cheered.

In answer to John's unasked question, Ike explained that he had just eaten *shirako*: about three feet of codfish sperm sacs. John excused himself and, in the privacy of the washroom, contemplated the contents of his stomach. A rumbling of his bowels directed him to sit on the toilet. He realized his butt was warming. A small control panel, its buttons labeled in kanji, drew his attention. A pink button looked promising and John pushed it in hopes of cooling his posterior. A water jet zeroed in on his rear end. At first, he thought the toilet was back-flushing and, in a panic, he pushed a blue button only to gyrate the geyser. The yellow button shut the whole thing down.

Leaving the restaurant, Ike took John to an ST sign but, instead of passing through a subway turnstile, they turned into a gigantic hall of shops: a subterranean Sapporo shopping world, kaimono, kaimono, to which John had previously been oblivious. Shinto's Death World, peopled with dead perpetual shoppers, he wondered?

Centurion-like, Ike formed the prow of the two-man phalanx that tacked across the river of lost souls to Happy Times Photocopy. En route, John saw an unusual manhole cover and hesitated. His protective prow got ahead of him and he was in danger of being swept away.

Halfway through photocopying a mountain of Russian papers, they came upon a contemporary memo, in Russian, dated 1976; the other documents were dated between 1850 and 1930.

"We should get Murata to translate this first," John suggested.

As they rode the subway back to the university, John opened his second letter. It was from his father, the first he had ever received.

June 28, 1995
Rolfe, Iowa.

Dear John,
Your mother, Ethyl, has run off. I don't mind her skedaddling, but I don't like having to make my own coffee. I haven't told our friends, but it was with Mavis, her curling team's skip.
Now that you know of your mother's propensity, you might have insight into your failures.
As always,
Your Father

John decided to play hooky from his usual routine of Egg Coffee Shop, museum office, and bar carousing, and pursue his new obsession: Sapporo manhole covers. He'd begin rubbings of the more interesting ones he found around Little Ginza. Their markings didn't look like any script he was familiar with: Egyptian hieroglyphics, Babylonian cuneiform, Aztec pictograms, Navajo petroglyphs, Folsom Street bus depot smut. Was some ancient society secretly communicating among themselves? John thought he might be onto something with his new hobby. *There is more than one way to a Nobel prize.*

"Moshi, moshi," said John. No response. Again, "Moshi, moshi."
Husky laughter pealed from the telephone. Maybe he had dialed the wrong number. "Miss Murata?" he queried.
"No, Mr. Fox, this is her mother. She is away. May I take a message?"
"Mrs. Murata, how did you know who I was?"
"From my daughter's description, it had to be you."
"Oh," John replied, "please have her call me when she gets in."
"Certainly, Mr. Fox, I'll tell her. And you need not call here again."
Mrs. Murata's response puzzled John. Had she been rude, a very un-Japanese act, or had he misunderstood? That happened to him a lot.
Ike entered the office. He pulled up the broken chair and sat opposite John.
"John, we have a problem. There has been another theft at the museum. A guard was seriously hurt. Several valuable pieces were ignored, but some small artifacts and a few old manuscripts were taken. I have heard that there is a new black market for aboriginal artifacts. Perhaps this explains the recent disappearance of items from the collection. But this is the first time there has been violence. The police believe that gangsters are becoming involved."
John glanced over at his pile of documents, heaped haphazardly on a chair.
"Ike, maybe we'll keep these out of sight."
"That is smart, John, but that is not the problem. After the theft was reported in the newspaper, Happy Times Photocopy contacted the police. They said they saw two suspicious-looking characters photocopying what looked like old papers."

John had never considered how others saw the two of them. Surely, they were just your normal beardless Ainu and normal bearded white guy? "Ike, we're not under suspicion, are we?"

"The director thinks not. But he wants to know exactly what it is you are working on. And whether it might endanger the museum's reputation."

"The director knows I'm a visiting anthropology graduate student, studying Ainu culture. I just assumed he didn't want me to bother him. My New Mexico professor happily ignored me. Maybe a demonstration of my bears' baggy pants similarities would enlighten him. What do you think, Ike?"

"John, he is a very busy man."

John grabbed a thermos of instant coffee and a doggie bag of tempura, and rode the subway past bustling Sapporo and Ōdōri stations to the end of the line, Makomanai. From there a short walk brought him to the rural countryside.

Everywhere, fields of corn, tall corn, much taller than the corn grown in New Mexico, but not Iowa. The sight of this familiar crop, the rustling of its leaves and the warm dusty air lulled John's confused brain as he penetrated a field seeking solace, seeking respite from the constant flood of incomprehensible spoken Japanese, of new ideas. At one point, he thought he heard a voice, a voice speaking his name. The soft, convincing voice reminded him of Professor Downforth.

"Hi, Corn," he said to the waving foliage.

"And hi to you, John. Welcome to my home."

John wasn't superstitious but he suspected coincidences, particularly serendipitous ones, might be mediated by something out there. Bears with baggy trousers, lovely, domineering women, the promise that was Murata. Why not a god of corn?

He shuddered and decided he needed rest. He wandered deeper

into the field to a small area devoid of stalks. He sat down, had his meal of deep fried shrimp and surrendered to the dusty dryness.

He awoke, with a start, soaked. Nearby a sprinkler pissed water in a great arch. He had no idea how long he had slept nor any idea how to exit the field. After striking out in several directions he gave up. He shouted but the sound of his voice disappeared down the long rows of corn.

Once, he thought he heard, "Go to your right, John," but discounted it. Ridiculous, he thought. He waved a flag made from his handkerchief attached to a cornstalk.

"Next time, listen to me. I am your friend."

John surrendered. "Okay, Mr . . . ?"

"Formally, Mr. Maize, John, but you may call me Corn."

Soon he heard shouts of little children. There they were, just a few feet away, gibbering and pointing. John reached into his pocket and distributed Chiclets. "Gomen nasai."

He never ceased being amazed by the ability of little kids to speak Japanese. Just as he was astonished by the ability dogs have of running up and down stairs, and with four legs.

That night, refreshed and confused from his fieldtrip, John decided to explore a bar in a less savory part of his Little Ginza. He watched some attractive matrons, reminiscent of the *Golden Maru*'s Violet and Lavender Girls, entering a stairwell and felt compelled to follow.

There was a brief encounter at the entrance with three gentlemen dressed as crows, apparently on loan from the local mortuary, who, when they saw John's complexion, hopped off.

The dark stairwell smelled of urine.

Images of Japanese comic book gangsters and pimps, conducting nefarious acts on innocent maidens and naïve foreigners ran through John's mind as he cautiously advanced upward, step after step. On the fourth floor, a pink light shone gaily under a door hanging, and the richly perfumed air spoke of sophisticated women, the likes of Betty and Aki. The establishment had a bar and a dozen small oval tables, each supporting a zinc ice bucket with a bottle of cheap sparkling wine and a pink telephone.

He sat at the bar, ordered a beer, and waited for his eyes to adjust to the dark. The telephone in front of him started flashing; he looked closely and saw the number five was lit up. The bartender indicated he should pick up the phone.

"Moshi, moshi. Mr. Fox here."

The bartender indicated he should join the ladies at Table No. 5.

"So, you are from America," said a matron. "Tell us why you are in Sapporo, so far from your sophisticated homeland."

John had learned, in these situations, not to mention the Ainu.

"I am in your lovely city to study anthropology at the university."

"Well," asked another, testing the firmness of his thigh, "that's a big field. Could you be more specific?"

His mind flashed back to his tactile communications with his sweet Heather in the Port Alberni pub: the synchronized creaking of necks and stabbings of fingers.

"My present project is to determine the influence of music on non-verbal communication. Different cultures respond to music in different ways, but, on close analysis, it all boils down the pelvic movement."

They insisted he demonstrate. He stood and performed ancient Egyptian moves, reminiscent of the hieroglyphic postures of the septuagenarian waiter at the Tadich Grill. He started to return to their table, but they wouldn't have it.

"More," the three chorused, "encore."

John asked the bartender to put on some Beach Boys' tunes, with the idea of demonstrating the Hopi rattlesnake dance. When the surfing song came on, the ladies jumped behind him and formed a conga line. Da da, da da, da da: a fine pelvic grind. Exhausted, they collapsed at their table. "Mr. Fox, we need to have a serious discussion," said one lady, opening her purse.

Two hours, three magnums and a lot of hasty promises later, John stumbled out with three calling cards and a ten thousand yen note, an advance for services to be rendered.

Back on the street, he approached one of the crows and gave him five hundred yen, "It's from the ladies at Table No. 5."

The next day, when John came into his office, Murata was there, working on the translations. "Miss Murata, what a pleasant surprise. I didn't expect to find you here."

"Mr. Fox, your assistant, Mr. Ike, let me in. I needed to check some papers. But I do not see how you get anything done. Your phone keeps ringing. I just intercepted two telephone calls for you from some ladies wanting a rendezvous."

John explained his nightclub research, adding he could be a professional, citing the sophisticated crowd on the *Golden Maru* and Captain Tveit's offer of employment.

"Mr. Fox, you should return the money to the nightclub so the gigolo you displaced can get his due."

John tried to protest but Murata shushed him, "It is not a good idea to give out your phone number."

A defeated John collapsed at his desk and asked, "Anything else, Miss Murata?"

"Yes, Mr. Fox, I need to talk to you about this Ainu project. My mother is upset. She feels it is below my station to have anything to do with those primitives. I cannot do anything that might spoil my chances of marrying well. That would disappoint her."

"Primitives?" John asked. "And what about Ike?"

Murata seemed to shrink a little.

"Mr. Fox, I did not say that correctly. I respect the Ainu. Gomen nasai."

John was taken aback by her apology, so unlike the clear-eyed, controlled Murata he'd seen so far. Looking at her sitting stiffly in the broken chair, in her schoolgirl-style clothes and with her haired pulled back in an adolescent ponytail, he saw her lack of confidence. She needed more support than he had understood, and his heart went out to her.

"It's okay, Miss Murata. I understand. We all have our priorities and yours is to marry well. You'll give wonderful dinner parties, contribute to the arts, and forgive your husband any infidelities associated with successful business."

She took a deep breath, held it, and then slowly exhaled, "Mr. Fox, I will continue with the Ainu papers. I only ask your discretion. Please do not call my mother again."

"Thank you, Miss Murata. You are very important to the project."

John handed her the Russian memo he and Ike had flagged for early translation, and asked her to work on it.

"Now, if I'm not mistaken, you're late for flower-arranging class."

Her expression, which had softened under his compliments, became closed once again, and she left the room briskly, her ponytail swishing.

The next day, John was draped over his desk like a rag doll. He ached. He was bruised. He was humiliated.

"So, how did the kendo go, John?" Ike asked.

"Ike, my instructor is a good man. I respect him. But he is hard on me."

"John, your instructor is a strong samurai and to be respected. He is your *sensei*, your esteemed teacher, and you should address him as such."

John explained he had knelt on a hard, cold floor for one hour, repeating incomprehensible Japanese phrases. He explained mimicking the sensei's feinting, fleeting, fighting movements, sword held just so, leaping forward and backward, swinging to the right to the left and jabbing to the center. John told Ike about fighting a little boy who stood four feet tall, who attacked John's arms, ribs, the top of his head. "So I picked him up and threw him across the floor."

And how his sensei used him to demonstrate some new skills, and disarmed him by slashing his wrist that protruded too far from the shaft of his sword. "Then when I tried to copy him, I ended up with my sword tip on the floor and the sensei beating my ribs and bonking me on the head, saying 'Gomen nasai' the whole time.

"At the end of the lesson, a reporter arrived and interviewed me. I didn't completely understand the questions but I threw out a few gems, a little American color."

John's dentist friend from Yaseragi advised him, "Go to the Hamacho Arcade in Muroran. It is fun, cheap and nobody will know you."

Muroran, with its deep-sea port, was a short train ride from Sapporo, where Ike and John were just two gaijin passing through the anonymous crowds of dock workers and sailors and orthodontists.

Hamacho Arcade turned out to be a warren of pachinko joints—you could tell them from a mile away by the noisy rattling of ball-bearings—holes-in-the-wall eateries, and "authentic" Swedish massage parlors.

"Hey, handsome guys, want pretty girls, cheap whiskey?" heckled a Korean mama-san standing at the curtained doorway of her bar. "Come on, not shy. My girls clean, old fashioned geisha. They bring plenty joy."

Ike and John ignored her—Aki had warned John about these dives— and ducked into a soba noodle shop, where they chased slurped noodles with quarts of watered-down Sapporo beer.

At the door, on the way out, Ike scooped up a weeks' old copy of the English edition of the *Tokyo Shimbun* and read the headline, "Wolfman Jack Dies at Age 57."

In his best BBC-accented English, he said to John, "Pity, I enjoyed *Midnight Special*."

"You are English?" asked the cashier.

John laughed. "No, no, but my friend wants to be. Could you tell us where the Hanoi Social Club is?"

"You seem nice boys. It is there, across the street. Show them this card," she said, handing them an embossed red and gold square. "They will treat you real good."

It was the Korean mama-san's place. "Ah, I knew you very smart boys, you come back. Welcome."

She led them to a table where two little bees, dressed as schoolgirls, waited.

"American chocolates?" asked one little geisha-wannabe as she stroked John's thigh. He looked over at Ike, who was similarly occupied.

The Korean mama-san gleefully placed four glasses of whiskey, a bottle of soda water, and a zinc tub of ice on the table. Their hostesses grabbed their drinks, giggled and kampai-ed their marks for the evening.

"Are from American?" John's date asked, as she plunked a salty, sour plum into his mouth.

He nodded and then laid a plum on her extended tongue. This she pivoted with her tongue to her lips, her front teeth nibbling the flesh from the pit in a way that reminded John of his childhood hamster. She gracefully propelled the denuded seed, the expired lover, from her puckered lips into Ike's drink. "Gomen nasai."

They laughed and, salt-thirsty, they downed more drinks. This was the life. Mama-san brought more whiskey and peanuts.

Ike's date swung her leg over his lap and was energetically

pumping a wad of chewing gum into a large pink bubble. The bubble exploded. Somehow this seemed funny.

"You our American boyfriends. We go have plenty much joy."

John waved mama-san over and asked for the bill.

She returned to her adding machine and with flourish punched in numbers. This went on for a long time.

The *kaching-kaching* sobered Ike and he looked panicked.

"Do you feel all right, Ike?" John asked.

"No, John."

Ike looked ill, clammy, and, removing his date's leg from his lap, he bolted for the door. A neckless Korean with fingerless hands the size of Ping-Pong paddles intercepted him.

"What's the trouble?" John asked as he approached the bouncer who had his paddles firmly around Ike's neck.

"Freeloaders, thieves, molesters of little girls," the mama-san screamed. "You no sneak out of here."

"My American friend has been poisoned by your rancid peanuts and if I don't get him to a doctor quickly he could die, and then the American Embassy will be involved."

"You owe twenty-thousand yen, asshole."

"Do you take Visa?" John asked.

"Where you think you fucking are, Outer Mongolia?"

With one hand she snatched his extended credit card, while with the other, now shaped like a turkey claw, she grabbed his nuts and squeezed.

"You fuck with mama and you fuck no more, asshole."

John signed the bill. *Arigato. Sayonara.*

John and Ike hastened to the train station.

"Wait, wait! You my American lover. I die for you."

It was the bubble-blowing bar girl. Mascara ran down her cheeks and, in the harsh street light, her skin looked purplish. She was clearly not the schoolgirl she was dressed to be: older, maybe twenty-five, skinny, pallid, and probably undernourished. But, standing there, challenging Ike, she had a determined, don't-you-dare-fuck-with-me defiance. Clearly, she had been around. She knew her man.

Ike tried to push her away, but she stayed put. "You are a slut. Fuck off."

John could not believe his ears.

She backed off, spit her wad of gum in Ike's face, threw John's signed Visa bill on the ground and, as she turned to go, indicated she would probably be killed by the introduction of toxic substances into her nether regions.

"Wait," said Ike. "You can't stay here now. I will find you a safe place. Then you are on your own. I am not your American lover. I am Ainu. We eat little girls like you."

"Ha! Ainu, what is your name?"

"Deciduous Leaf Falling. And yours?"

She straightened up, pulled her hair back from her face. "Miura, soon-to-be wife of Deciduous Leaf Falling."

Dumbfounded, Ike muttered something about druggies and took her elbow.

The three of them traveled silently back to Sapporo. At Sapporo Station, they had tea. John could see his friend softening, as Miura joked with him. Her intense focus on Ike signaled a growing resolution in the girl. John feared for his friend and, at the same time, felt jealous.

"I'll take you to Niseko. My friends will be good to you," Ike said, taking her hand.

Leaving the station, Miura put her arm through Ike's and said to John, "You have a very nice friend, John-san. Goodbye for now."

Aki, pissed off, was kneeling on the tatami mat in John's room, conducting some form of Japanese voodoo that involved his battered Pooh bear. "Looks like you are in the habit of having nice Japanese gentlemen's evenings, John."

"Aki-chan, gomen nasai."

He told her about their Hamacho Arcade adventure, the Hanoi Social Club, the Korean mama-san and their little American tourist ruse.

"John, you are courting trouble when you mess with a Korean mama-san. You could be hurt, badly, if they come looking for you." She grabbed his crotch with one hand for emphasis, while she wagged her finger under his nose. "Now, I am going to give you a good washing."

Aki scrubbed him, applying the stiff brush like a punishment. His skin, rubbed raw, felt surprisingly alive.

"I can still smell that cheap perfume. I guess I will have to play dumb slut bar girl tonight. No new words for you, gaijin."

John laid his hand on the side of her face.

"Did you bite your lip, Aki?"

She bent over the side of the bed, holding her head between her hands. "No, John. Now cuddle me."

When he woke, Aki was gone. With toast and a hard-boiled egg from the Egg Coffee Shop, he entered his office looking forward to some humdrum activity. He was surprised to find Ike was already there.

"Are you now, or have you ever been, a virgin," John joked.

Ike shook his head, sighed. "John, I am in love."

"Holy Jesus, she's a bar girl, not the future mother of your Deciduous Leaf Falling Dynasty."

"She is the victim of being born at the wrong place, at the wrong time, of the wrong parents. Mama-san was enslaving her, making her dependent on drugs. She is smart, sensitive, streetwise and, yes, that too," said Ike, blushing.

Ike had lost his virginity and his heart.

John's first thought was, what about my research? But he looked at his love-struck friend and felt ashamed. He had to look beyond himself, to take Ike's feelings into account. Besides, he'd been the one to set this tryst up, and maybe, like the bar girl, he, John, too had been born at the wrong time and place.

"John, get off your knees," Sue said, tugging to free her skirt. "Today we're going to play a little word game. You know the routine."

He nodded, and slumped onto her office couch.

"Ideal parents?"

"Musicians, farmers, not academics, not manufacturers, I don't know, Bushmen?"

"Ideal place to grow up, John?"

"Iceland, poverty, Texas, not Iowa, I don't know."

"John, you're not trying. Now focus. The ideal era to grow up in?"

"Not now, maybe jazz, maybe early Cambrian, I don't know. Hug me!"

The telephone rang. John picked it up.

Ike mouthed, "Moshi, moshi," and John repeated, "Moshi, moshi. Fox here."

"Mr. Fox, it's important to our project that I see the original Russian papers before you return them. Could I come to your office this weekend?" Murata said.

"Our project." John liked the sound of that.

In the past month, Ike had spent every weekend away with his bar girl at Niseko, so John suggested she come in on Saturday, "or does that conflict with your piano lessons?"

She said something in Japanese John couldn't understand that contained guttural sounds. "I will come in around one o'clock."

Murata showed up exactly at one o'clock. Impeccably dressed in tan pants, a loose white shirt and brown shoes with a matching pocketbook, she waited at the door to be asked in.

John offered her his good chair. "Would you like some tea?"

"No thank you, Mr. Fox. Sorry to inconvenience you on a weekend, but I had some spare time and wanted to work on the manuscripts."

"Here are the originals. We keep them out of sight since the thefts from the museum archives."

As she poured over the documents, John bent over a blank notepad, pencil poised to write: what, he had no idea. As he watched her, a feeling of longing filled him. He recalled having similar feelings long ago in New Mexico when Nursey was taking a blood sample for his doctor. She was cool, professional, stand-offish, but that didn't block some mutual affinity. Once she had the sample, she snapped the rubber tourniquet smartly against his upper arm as if punishing him for ruining the rest of her life.

A commotion at the door announced the arrival of Ike and Miura, carefree lovers—he wearing a white T-shirt, brown shorts that exposed bow legs and sandals, and she wearing a short yellow sundress that accentuated her cute knock knees and turquoise sandals decorated with yellow plastic flowers. Ike and Miura were the same height and seemed to fit hand-in-glove.

"Sorry, John," Ike stuttered. "I wanted to show Miura pictures of my Ainu ancestors."

Murata blushed, and John could feel heat radiate from her.

"Miss Murata, may I introduce my fiancée, Miss Miura?"

Miura beamed. Her little pigtails flapped like butterfly wings, a perfect match for Ike's spiky cowlick and crooked glasses. John saw such happiness; he looked at Ike and smiled. Ike smiled back.

"What do you do, Miss Miura?" asked Murata politely, regaining her composure.

"I make Ainu babies," she squealed, hanging on to blushing Ike's arm. "Give me your hand."

Miura placed Murata's hand on her tummy, "Say hello to first-born of Deciduous Falling Leaf clan."

They watched Miura as she slowly sank to her knees, placed her hands gently on her abdomen and gave the room a smile of pure joy. Ike helped her up.

"I really must go," Murata said. "I have piano lessons. I am very pleased to have met you and I wish you a Cherry Blossom baby. Mr. Fox, I will come in next Saturday if that is all right with you." Like a robot, she moved stiffly to the door, paused as if she wanted to say something more, and left.

"We need to celebrate. Could I buy us all ice cream sodas?"

"That would be nice, John," said Ike.

John, remembering the twenty thousand yen she had saved him, said, "Or maybe a restaurant with a fat piece of Kobe beef."

Ike beamed. He had a princess warrior and he was one proud Ainu.

The Old Oak Restaurant, on the edge of the campus, featured patio tables, shaded by Suntory whiskey umbrellas. Miura was enchanted by the oak grove, the leaves just starting to show fall colors. She hugged Ike's arm.

The waitress took their orders with a coolness John had not experienced in Japan. Finally served, they enjoyed the autumn sun and their ice cream. Miura became preoccupied with the fearless sparrows, flipping them crumbs from her wafer, and Ike fidgeted.

"Well, Miura, tell me about your new home. Ike keeps going on about his village without telling me anything."

Miura looked at Ike, who nodded. "It is a sweet place. Everyday more Ainu come. Do I say more, Ike-chan?"

"John," said Ike, "My friends and I are creating a new Ainu village at Konbu Spa. It is actually hidden behind the Japanese

'Authentic Ainu Village' created for tourists. We want our pride back. We have to keep it hidden, because proud Ainu can be the target of violent gangs. Soon, I will bring you there."

John was distracted by hostile stares from a couple at a nearby table. Defiantly, he stared back, but they dropped their eyes, whispering to each other. John was angry.

These were not rude and curious children, chanting ditties; they were xenophobic racists, the products of blind nationalism. Why could they not see the beauty of this couple? Just over a month ago, Miura was a wasted bar girl and Ike a lost soul. Now they reflected a new future, not just for themselves but for all of Japan.

As they departed, Ike pulled John aside, "John, we do not want to expose our unborn child to these vile prejudices. Miura will remain in the new village. Of course, I will continue assisting you during the week."

"Good morning, John," beamed Ike. John wanted to pinch him on the cheek, hug him. This sensation of somehow being responsible for Ike and Miura's coming together might have been what Betty felt when she launched him off the *Golden Maru* at Yokohama, into Aki's care. But he shivered. A premonition of tragedy seemed to overshadow Ike's joy.

"Your kendo sensei called. He wants you to meet him tomorrow morning in front of the university's Shinto temple." Then Ike gleefully added, "At sunrise and in your full kendo regalia."

"Ike, take that look off your face. My doing kendo is important to me. Now, on another matter, may I review my findings on the Ainu's weapon of choice, the alkaloid aconite, with you?"

John explained that he had read in Murata's Russian translations that the Ainu used aconite-tipped arrows in hunting deer and as a weapon.

"Ike, I visited the Miyabe Botanical Gardens on the far side of the campus to check out the monkshood plant. It's a member of the buttercup family. The leaves are deeply dissected, shaped like your hand, and its purple flowers are reminiscent of a monk's hood. It is beautiful and deadly; the poison is concentrated in the root. Here, read this: it's from *A Modern Herbal*, by Mrs. M. Grieve, published in 1931."

Ike took the notebook and read, "The symptoms of poisoning are tingling and numbness of tongue and mouth and a sensation of ants crawling over the body, nausea and vomiting with epigastric pain, labored breathing, pulse irregular and weak, skin cold and clammy, features bloodless, giddiness, staggering, mind remains clear."

"Ike, what she didn't add is that death is by asphyxiation. I must say, your ancestors were to be feared."

"Strike!" shouted John's Egg Coffee Shop mates as the pins ricocheted against each other. This was going to be John's break from his usual carousing. A wholesome night of bowling.

The sweet bees tittered and blushed; the young men relaxed, free from the pressures of mate-finding, boss-gratifying, megasociety surviving. Congratulations on strikes were heaped upon opponents and modestly accepted. Soft drinks, little fishy snacks, and some exercise. John achieved the prize for the lowest score and everyone cheered.

As he walked home along the darkened street, he looked up and saw a blinking light: United Air Flight 762, inward bound from San Francisco? He remembered the nights on the *Golden Maru*, how amazed he'd been at how that plane had zipped back and forth over the Pacific, while he slowly crossed the sea, living in an older, slower time, as his travel agent had predicted. John knew if things got too hard here in Japan, if he couldn't cope, there would be a Flight 762 to zip him away. But tonight, life was good.

He awoke the next morning, lacking the usual dullness, and with a better understanding of his mother's fixation on curling. John had spent a booze-less evening with a group of young Japanese he hardly knew. Despite his weak Japanese, they had managed to connect, to communicate.

The cell phone rang. "Moshi moshi."

"John, I am very sorry," Aki said. "Our friend, Kei-ichi Matsuyama, has died. I stopped by his shop this morning and discovered his shop was empty. The landlord told me of his death. All of his books and papers have been sold to compensate for past rents due. It is so sad, John. He was a nice man. That scroll he promised you—if it was there, it is gone now. There is not much point in continuing to look for his son."

John's contented little world collapsed. The ancient scroll, the Rosetta Stone for his Nobel Prize, was now beyond reach. Bears in baggy britches, accompanied by detailed lists and padded appendices, would have to carry the day: another ho-hum Podunk University PhD.

He was surprised at how much the loss of scrolls that he'd never seen, that may not even have existed, hurt him. When Nursey left him, he felt resentment, but not this ache, this emptiness. Sue nailed it: "You're in pain because you've been rejected. Not because you've lost Nursey."

Nursey, his apricot fantasy, his anthropological coup, his trophy, was less real to him than those nonexistent scrolls.

"We should find out who the landlord sold the papers and books to. There must be other Ainu manuscripts, not just the scroll," said Ike when John told him the bad news.

"No, Ike. What's gone, is gone."

"I would like to keep looking. I still need to find Kru, to talk to him, and perhaps he knows something of this scroll."

"Only on your own time, Ike," John answered, then he wondered, how could he say that? Ike wasn't his employee; he worked for the Hokkaido Ministry of Antiquities.

Normally, Ike would pounce on that statement quicker than a dog on a flea. Instead, distracted, he said, "John, remember Miss Murata is coming tomorrow to check the Russian originals."

"Could you meet her? Miss Kawaguchi is flying in for the weekend."

"No, John, I cannot. Our elders will be conducting a cleansing ceremony this weekend at our village. This is very important to our unborn child."

John watched Aki walk across the tarmac. Looked down on from the observatory, she seemed vulnerable, fragile. He waited next to the aquarium. The big infested fish was gone; sashimi, thought John.

She came through the arrivals gate and, seeing John, leaped into his arms, gasping, "Hotel time, John. Oh, God, it is hotel time."

"You bet, Aki. But I need to stop by the office first. A student is coming by to look over the originals of some papers she's been translating for me."

A shadow briefly visited her face and then Aki smiled and led him to the airport's rail station.

On the ride in, John looked at her carefully. She was picture perfect. Not a blemish, her hair coifed to frame her oval face, clothes neatly pressed. He breathed in her favorite perfume—Chanel No. 5—thinking how very lucky he was. From Sapporo Station, they hailed a cab and she treated John to an exaggerated knee show as she slid in.

"There's Miss Murata, sitting on the stoop," John said, not believing his eyes.

Murata stood as they climbed out of the cab, more of her slight frame exposed than John had ever seen. The curvature of her little butt showed beneath pink shorts and the shirt tied high on her stomach outlined her breasts.

"Miss Murata, you look sporty today. This is my friend, Miss Kawaguchi. She's visiting for the weekend. Aki, Miss Murata is helping me with Russian translations."

The two ladies coolly bowed.

John didn't know whether to be proud or terrified. But he did feel a tinge of excitement. "Aki, I'll let Miss Murata into my office and then we can continue on to . . ."

Aki turned and watched him try to end the sentence. So did Murata. He couldn't.

Murata followed John into the building and settled in at his desk. As he turned to go, Murata said, "Excuse me, Mr. Fox, but wouldn't it be easier, if I am to research these papers, if I had a key to your office?" John couldn't be more agreeable.

"More Grey Goose, darling?" asked Aki as they relaxed in their Aurora Borealis Inn room, a Sapporo love hotel. "John, you are becoming quite Japanese and I do not mean that as a compliment. Your student, Miss Murata, is very attractive. It seems students dress differently since I was in college."

Lying on his back, watching the mirrored image of flickering candlelight playing on Aki's hip as she nibbled and cooed on his chest, he felt disembodied. He looked up, seeing two lovers, and felt nothing, even though he had an erection.

"John, are you okay?"

He didn't answer.

"John," she whispered, "Have you returned those papers to the curator, as Betty asked?"

He rolled on his side and rest his hand on Aki's shoulder. She looked so innocent lying there. He wondered about her relationship with Betty, and Betty's relationship with Ivan. The papers, the documents, the manuscripts—did they represent a danger to him, to the Ainu? "Aki, let's talk later. I need a snooze."

Later, over tea, he tried to explain to Aki the importance of having access to the original Russian documents, not just photocopies. "Much information can be gleaned from little pencil marks, smudges, dog-eared corners, anything that indicates the focus of earlier scholars and readers. It's not just the printed word. Miss Murata can translate the Russian, but she needs to handle the actual documents to learn as much as she can."

"John, Betty insists you return those papers immediately. And I don't want to hear your student's name again. Now, hand me my robe, darling."

John felt too much was not being said. There was an invitation here to take control, just as his sensei was teaching him. How much did he really know about Aki?

"No," he said. "Don't get dressed yet. I want to know what makes you tick."

Aki looked at him as if seeing him for the first time: her eyebrows arched, her jaw dropped, but she said nothing. She moved back onto the futon, jamming herself tight to him and her fingernails scratched his back and shoulders. A forest of goose-bumps raised itself on John's skin. Aki would not be denied and they hurtled voicelessly to a thoughtless climax. Her face was twisted, ugly, and she trembled.

"John, I am dirty. Please forgive me. Gomen nasai."

John put his hand on the side of her face, gently.

"Aki..."

"Shush, John."

Refreshed and confused by the Aki weekend, John entered his office to find Ike reading a newspaper.

"John, look at this," Ike said, handing him a copy of *Tokyo*

Shimbun. John took the newspaper. The photograph on the front page of the newspaper showed a smoldering ruin, inset with a photo of Kei-ichi Matsuyama, the legless bookseller. Ike translated the article: fire destroyed a bookstore; as the fire was being fought, the legless proprietor propelled his trolley into the inferno; he could be heard screaming, "The scrolls, the scrolls." The dead man was an honored war veteran; he had no known living relatives; arson was not suspected.

The picture of the charred ruins made Matsuyama's death all the more shocking. It added pain to the old man's passing. It also added deceit: Aki had lied. Now, John mourned the loss of the potential scrolls, his trust in Aki, and the loss of a friend: a generous person with humor who had introduced the Ainu to John.

John stood and turned to the door, "I need to get some air, some space."

The train to Makomanai had few passengers. In this less crowded space and in his anonymity, John relaxed and contemplated his visit to the cornfield. Would Mr. Maize, his god of corn, be there to offer wisdom? John would be disappointed if he was not.

John wandered into the field. The ears of corn had been plucked and the canes mostly broken.

"Mr. Maize, a good man died trying to save something for me. I didn't have the opportunity to explain to him what our encounter meant to me . . . my thesis, my humanity."

"Now, where did you get this idea, John? A brainstorm, some lower deity's revelation, perhaps?" asked the Downforth-voiced corn god.

"God, a little reverence: the man died."

"Okay, I'm sorry, but it's hard to take you seriously. I'm also the god of incipient idiots."

John chose to ignore that.

"John, remember, you don't have to speak to be understood. Mutual feelings, respect—both evoke understanding; in a word, empathy. He would have known your feelings."

"Thank you, god."

"John, Kei-ichi Matsuyama died for you, for his faith that you would bring his life story to his son, Kru."

John shuffled some soil, dislodging a corn kernel, frustrating its future quest for plant-hood.

"Bad move, John."

The storm hit.

Totally drenched, a half-blinded John handed over a double dose of Chiclets to the children who'd appeared in the field.

A drizzle cooled John's morning walk to the Shinto temple; soon there would be snow. He found these kendo sessions purifying. John bowed to his sensei and knelt in preparation for the incantations. They went through the ritual, the exercises. After three months, these felt more natural and he moved less awkwardly. Then the sensei challenged him. Unlike the previous lessons, the sensei didn't demonstrate patterns of encounter, he launched straight into an attack. John tried to resist but the sensei was relentless, slashing and beating his student with the bamboo sword. After what seemed an eternity to the thrashed John, the sensei stopped, bowed and walked away.

John staggered to a bench and sat, holding his head in his hands. What was the purpose of this, he wondered. He didn't enjoy being beaten up. But he knew he was learning an important lesson. Kendo was teaching him to be more direct, his interactions with others more consequential. The way he interpreted others, not just by their spoken word, but by their body language, had improved. Nursing his aching ribs and bruises, John felt more whole, significant and at peace.

Back at his office, he found Ike and Murata poring over the original Russian documents. They looked at him and gasped.

"John, did you get run over?"

"Something like that." John pulled up his shirt, exposing a series of diagonal welts running across his ribs.

Murata came over and placed her hand on his side. "Kendo. How Japanese of you, Mr. Fox." She gave him an inquisitive look and turned to the papers spread out on the floor. "You might find this interesting," she said, handing him her translation of the Russian memo from 1976.

John read aloud, "It is in our best interest that we cooperate with the Japanese and transfer all Ainu, particularly the shamans, from the Soviet Union to Hokkaido. The 1875 Russian-Japanese Treaty of St. Petersburg separated the Ainu into the two countries. The existence of Ainu in both the USSR and Japan could allow them access to international courts to pursue land claims and other alleged grievances. Our great leader, Comrade Stalin, declared the Ainu to be Russians, thus refuting any aboriginal rights. This ruling has been challenged by several so-called indigenous groups. We should maintain the non-aboriginal status of the Ainu and we must remove any historical references or records that support Ainu claims to be recognized legally as aboriginals in Japan and the USSR. Certain favors from Japanese conglomerates may be expected in return."

The original bore no fold marks and the paper was pristine, showing no evidence of having been frequently read or studied.

"I suspect this memo was never sent, possibly it was misplaced. It might have been used as a bookmark, forgotten," said Murata. "Its original location in the documents given by the curator might give us further insights into its significance."

"What does this memo have to do with understanding Ainu migrations?" John asked. "We must keep things in focus."

"But, John, think. We may be dealing with a conspiracy to undermine legitimate Ainu claims. Do not you believe it is our responsibility to follow up on this lead?" Ike asked.

"I see your point. But I have to give the migration study top priority. It's vital for my dissertation."

"John, I am Ainu and I find this memo very disturbing. I think we must pursue Miss Murata's suggestion."

Looking at Ike's earnest face, John understood, for the first time, that perhaps his thesis wasn't the most important thing about this research.

"Right, of course," said John. "The theory the memo may have been used as a bookmark should be checked out. The marks and notes on the documents around it might provide valuable clues."

John felt proud of himself. He had just reversed his opinion, had said what needed to be said, and that made him feel good.

Murata and Ike, who had been preparing to argue their case, to insist that they must pursue what could be an injustice, gawked at John. He smirked, enjoying his little coup.

Murata composed herself, tugged her skirt, and, gave a little cough. "The photocopies you gave me included the memo and I assumed you did not shuffle any papers when you were copying them. The memo's position in the photocopies should reflect its position in the original papers."

Giddy with the progress they had made, John offered to buy sodas but Ike declined. "For social reasons," he said.

"And I have an American cooking lesson," Murata added.

"Miss Murata, before you go, could I ask you a favor?" John explained his dilemma of not knowing how to defend himself properly against a kendo attack. "Could you write a note to my sensei for me, explaining this?"

Murata knelt, her hair splaying over her shoulders. With the sheet of stationery positioned just so, she contemplated the task at hand. Her pen swept and sliced above the paper—a baton directing an orchestra—carefully rehearsing the required strokes. Then, slowly and thoughtfully, she calligraphed the note. She removed a lipstick-shaped chop, the little stamp of her legally registered signature, from her purse and pressed it to the bottom right corner.

She handed John the note. "This should do, Mr. Fox."

"Thank you. That was very elaborate for a simple note," John said.

"Mr. Fox, your sensei is a famous samurai and he is giving much to you. You must honor him."

"Your chop, Miss Murata, what does it mean?"

Her smile was relaxed, and John saw not an armored porcelain doll, but the promise of a warm, loving woman.

Murata answered with a soft voice and her eyes modestly downcast, "The promise of an unopened flower."

Oh, my. An explosion in John's brain. Murata's promise beckoned like Nursey's mirage on a hot New Mexico morning. The thrill of what could be, the concern of how to nurture, to water that flower, pushed aside thoughts of Ainu, of kendo, of everything. He loved her hair worn loose.

"What a lovely name, Miss Murata. Look at us: a Promising Flower, a Deciduous Leaf Falling and a Fox, all right here."

Ike led John to the Authentic Ainu Village, an establishment where tourists were fleeced as they shuddered at the ugly stereotype of unsavory Ainu. The Curio Shop, which featured rip-off Ainu carvings (Hong Kong), T-shirts emblazoned with images of fearful warriors (China), and authentic Ainu snacks—smoked berries (Taiwan) and whale kebabs (Norway)—was closing.

Ike said something to an attendant. John understood only one word: gaijin. The attendant smiled, bowed and received Ike's lower bow. Then John and Ike made their way past the littered little park to an obscure trail that passed through a copse of mostly leafless birch and oak. As John stumbled along in the fading light, he heard sounds of village life: dogs barking, babies crying, the ring of an ax. A bear's roar caused his neck hairs to spike.

There stood Miura, tummy slightly rounded, with her now usual merriment. She held a cylindrical glass cover for a kerosene lamp. She tried to roar—a gruff ruff—and laughed. Then, walking towards John, she put the glass to her mouth and roared again. This time he leaped back, tripping on an exposed root.

"John, my ancestors used that trick to scare off invaders," said Ike, catching his elbow.

As they walked through the dark, John told Ike and Miura the story of how the legless bookseller had been saved by Ainu, using this same deception on Soviet soldiers. Arriving at a clearing, John saw six adults and four children waiting.

"John, what we are doing here is considered illegal. Our lives are governed by the Hokkaido Former Aborigines Protection Act of 1899," Ike said. "The word 'Former' implies that we have been thoroughly Japanized—haircuts and all. We want to have this stupid act rescinded. That is our goal."

Miura translated Ike's speech to the Ainu gathered in the clearing. When she'd finished, one man strutted about, brandishing an imaginary sword. Another mimed unrolling a proclamation, while the others bunched their hair into cockscombs, exposing their foreheads.

John looked around and recognized the architecture and many artifacts from illustrations in his reference books and papers: thatched huts with doorways facing east, stacked deer antlers, stretched hides. And, most curious, a caged bear that Ike explained was a pet for the children.

"We are striving to recreate our lost past here. This is from the memories of our elders, and from what I have learned by reading your papers, by helping with your research. This is not like that fairground back there," Ike said, indicating the path they had just walked down. "You are invited here because this small tribe believes you to be a friend."

Two men approached John, rubbed their palms and then their beards, and bowed. They could have been the two in the orchard. He bowed back, deeper.

They led John into the gathering house created of rough beams and poles and walled with thick-thatched mats. Raised earth created seating around the central fire pit, where iron hooks and a heavy wooden pivot for cooking hung overhead.

More men from the tribe entered, wearing robes made from elm bark fiber. The edges of the sleeves, the neckband, and hem were appliquéd with geometric designs. John recognized these designs from old photos and books: they were to ward off evil where it is most likely to gain access to the wearer.

An old man, perhaps an elder, brought a salmon on a wood plank. This he placed to John's right, its head facing the fire, and then he sat facing John. Once the men were seated, the women and children entered and formed an outer circle. Miura entered last, her eyes cast down.

"John, this is the Salmon Festival," explained Ike.

The lead man bowed deeply and spoke to the salmon. Ike translated. "Salmon, you are the first caught this year. I thank you for honoring us today. You will feed us humans, our gods, and little children."

The elder then cut the salmon into chunks and the women came forward to drop the pieces into an iron pot of boiling water, adding leeks and shredded kelp from other platters. A few chunks of salmon were held back, and these were placed on the fire.

Ike whispered to John, "The burned flesh is now smoke. It will be consumed by the gods. Once the gods are fed, the stew will be ladled into lacquered bowls for us mortals."

"Why lacquered?" John whispered.

"They are the one Japanese thing we treasure," replied Ike, his finger on his lips.

Following the feast, the women swept the hearth and arranged sleeping mats around the fire for the men. As the women and children left, Miura stopped in front of Ike, pressed her palms together, ran her right forefinger under her nose, and bowed.

"John, the elders expect us to spend the night in our assigned house," Ike explained. "I want to stay with Miura, and the women will make it appear that I am where I should be. You will be on your own tonight."

Sleep came slow. John lay on his back, watching the firelight dance on the walls and the steep thatched roof. Drowsy, he nodded off just before sunrise.

The gods made themselves known. The god of fire, the god of home, of each human, of all household items; gods of wildlife, trees, volcanoes, clouds, smoke, everything. And his god, the god of corn, was lost among the lesser gods. The gods had a hierarchy and were jealous of their positions. There were disputes among them. The gods of fire and water dominated, they fed first on the fumes of spilled drink and smoke of charred food.

"John, wake up. We must go before the Authentic Ainu Village opens."

"Ike, I saw gods. I saw your gods," John babbled, trying to explain his dreams, to make Ike understand about the gods who had visited him during the night, when each flicker of firelight brought another deity. Now John understood that these gods, unlike God, were accountable. If a woman failed to conceive or a warring tribe bettered the village, other gods chastised those gods responsible. "Ike, last night, with the sounds of barking foxes, hooting owls, and crackling coals, it all made sense, but now . . ."

"John, you scare me. Sometimes you seem Japanese. Now I think you are becoming Ainu. Maybe you should lose your beard."

John caught the early train to Sapporo and went directly to the university. The campus was quiet. The early morning light gave the surroundings an eerie golden glow. He sensed the gods of everything were gathering. Spooked, he went into the bomb shelter and shut and bolted the heavy wooden door. He looked at the books on the shelves, the bundles of documents, the stacks of photos. These are my gods for success, he thought.

His work had new meaning now; what he was doing might strengthen the Ainu's position, advance their cause politically. Heady stuff for an aspiring social anthropology academic.

He gathered his three carved bears and gave them marching

orders: "We need to know if, historically, the Russians or Japanese had any authentic claim, other than that extracted by them with force, over ancestral Ainu territories."

John had a mission, and that gave him a new sense of belonging; things did not seem so foreign, so alien. He could cope. He slumped on his desk and sleep released him.

The patrons of the yakitori shop looked up and smiled as John entered. "Hey, did the Hokkaido Fighters kick butt last night or what?" A cheer went up and someone put a glass of shochu in his hand. In his early days, John had refused to drink this, which he considered an alcoholic joke, a scam perpetuated by Hokkaido potato farmers: half-assed, 25 percent vodka. He, John Fox, connoisseur, imbiber of Grey Goose, would not stoop so low. But now it tasted good, and he bowed to his tomodachi. And they settled in for a serious boys' night.

"You know, you Japanese should not be surprised the North Koreans don't like you. You raped and pillaged the Korean Peninsula more than once. The South Koreans feel the same . . ." and here he made an obscene gesture, ". . . South Korea, like Japan sleeps with mama-chan America."

His audience's indrawn breath was a great sucking noise, like the first stanza of a snore. There was a moment of awkward silence, and then they forgave his shochu-fueled rant.

"Kampai, Fox-san!"

His glass was filled to overflowing, the excess spilling into the deep saucer in which the glass sat: a drinker's bonus. John panicked.

Everyone laughed.

John stood, bowed, and saluted all present.

"Let's have a good night," he said, repeating his earlier sign language.

"Tell us about your lovers, Fox-san." This drinking companion had stuffed two oranges under his shirt, his shit-faced manner common

to male drinkers around the world. His tongue flicked in and out, and he fought to stay on his stool and not go cross-eyed from squinting.

Again, everyone cheered. But John suddenly felt ill at ease. It would be a betrayal—Nursey and her erotic sage rituals, psychologist Sue and her Kama Sutra moves, Betty and her perfumed illusions, even Lulu and her sweet buggery.

Red fireworks blossomed in his shochu. John looked horrified at his severed pinkie resting at the bottom of his glass.

The bartender, a new fellow with disheveled hair and one walleye, wiped off his cleaver, then leaned over to apply a bandage to the stub on John's left hand. With a conspiratorial wink, he whispered, "It's worth it, son. Now you can understand all that chatter on game shows, the thousands upon thousands of motormouths you encounter every day, on the subway, on the streets . . ."

The bartender could not go on, and the tears of laughter gushing down his cheeks turned to steam.

John, screaming "Gomen nasai," ran out to the street, his hands over his ears.

"Mr. Fox, wake up." John untwisted his neck, saw a puddle of drool on his desk, and looked up into Murata's lovely face. "Isn't this your kendo morning?"

"Miss Murata, are you speaking Japanese?"

John arrived two hours late for kendo. The master stood and bowed, showing no irritation at John's arrival. John bowed deeply back, "Gomen nasai, sensei", and the morning ritual began as always. When it came time to face off in combat, instead the sensei knelt before John and grasped, in turn, the five pleats of John's skirt. He named each pleat, indicating the Japanese character on a sheet he gave to John. At the end of the lesson, John handed Murata's note to his sensei. "Please. Gomen nasai."

Back at the office, Murata was sitting at his desk. She did not say anything.

"He was still kneeling," John said, expecting her to scold him. "He took the note you wrote."

Silence.

"We didn't fight today, he just handled my skirt and gave me this." John passed her the sheet and she read the words: "Mercy, Righteousness, Etiquette, Intelligence, Trust." She turned back to the Ainu papers spread in front of her.

Agitated, Ike burst into the office, "What is this?" he exclaimed, waving a copy of *Tokyo Shimbun*. "Blue-Eyed Ainu Scholar Japanese Swordsman."

He threw the newspaper down on the desk and John saw what he thought was a rather nice photo of himself on the front page. Unfortunately, the picture also showed John facing off with a kid barely out of diapers.

"John, we do not need this kind of attention. The whole world is not your fan club. Remember Muroran?"

"Relax, Ike. 'Blue-eyed' is obviously a metaphor for handsome, and I'm definitely both a scholar and a swordsman." John tacked the article to the wall and winked at Murata, who was tracking a spider's progress across the ceiling.

"And the reporter was impressed with my mastery of the Japanese language as well as my fighting skills."

Murata cleared her throat; John thought of clerics and academics about to pronounce a significant pontification.

"Mr. Fox, the Russian memo was inserted in a treatise comparing Hokkaido Ainu decorative designs with those of other aboriginal groups in the northwest Pacific, particularly in the Kamchatka and Siberia regions." She stopped and looked to see if he was paying attention. "From the condition of the original, it seems this topic had been the focus of several scholars."

John looked over her shoulder and wondered what her scent was; it smelled peachy, reminiscent of his sessions with Sue. The papers rattled in front of him, directing his focus to the displayed pages that were smudged from handling and covered with lightly penciled lines connecting design elements.

Retiring lascivious thoughts, John forced himself to consider the carefully drawn designs. Obviously, the scholar who had studied these was sensitive to subtle differences. But the designs in their intricacies held no significance.

"There's no rhyme or reason to these drawings. I get no sense of a pictography, no timeline, no connection to deities," John said. "These are just pretty artifacts."

Ike sat, his head in his hands, slowly rocking back and forth. He could have been in mourning or suffering from a migraine or lost in a labyrinth of ancestral memories.

"John, each of these drawings tells a complete and detailed story. Some are mythical and others depict a real series of events or relationships. I'll show these to our elders. They may be able to give a detailed description."

John decided it was not the right moment to share his theory about the symbols on Sapporo's manhole covers: that they were the lost written language of some pre-Ainu civilization. He was convinced someone at the manhole cover foundry was genetically linked to that civilization and, by casting these ancient symbols in iron, he was keeping his lost language alive.

That night, in his room, John called Aki. "Moshi moshi, Aki."

"John, the person who answers the phone says moshi moshi. Not the person making the call. But thank you for calling."

Normally, the sound of her voice would send ripples of endorphin precursors through his blood system. But he remembered how she hadn't told him the truth about how the legless bookseller had died or about the fire. He couldn't trust her as he had before.

"Are you still there?"

"Sorry, something's caught between my teeth," John fibbed.

"John, Betty is upset. It is imperative you return the curator's papers now. He is in trouble for letting them out of the country. Betty is a valuable friend of those who wish to protect antiquities and the curator is her main Russian contact."

"Aki, the papers are now organized for shipping and will be posted within the week," John lied. This seemed to appease her.

"I can come to Sapporo this weekend. We can visit the Aurora Borealis Inn."

John hesitated for too long as images of their love motel encounters collided with the view of Murata, her hair flooding over slight shoulders, as she crafted the note for his sensei.

Aki hung up.

John dialed the university library, where Murata volunteered, waited and, after hearing "moshi moshi," asked for Miss Murata.

"This is Miss Murata, Mr. Fox. What may I do for you?"

He explained about the need to return the papers and asked if she could do a crash translation of those that remained.

"Of course. My schedule is nothing when the fate of a hopeful academic is at stake. I hope your head does not hurt too much after last night's Ping-Pong match. I will be in first thing tomorrow."

"Miss Murata, Ping-Pong is Ping-Pong, nothing else." John felt he should say something more, but his mind was muddled. "I'll be waiting for you. Thanks . . . Miss Murata."

Confused and in need of air, he decided to go home early. He stopped for a snack at the American bar, where sullen boys and bored girls played the role of disenfranchised US adolescents perfectly.

John superimposed the faces of his shallow loves—Nursey, Sue,

Lulu, Aki—over the bar's posters of Brando, Elvis, Chaplin and the Emperor.

"Which one will the fountain bless?" crooned the ancient Wurlitzer. Leonard Cohen walked to the river with Suzanne, reminding John of eating spaghetti out of a can after a long night studying, while Nursey twirled and dipped, an eagle feather fan teasing, first hiding, then revealing her Hopi body.

John felt his life would have been different if she had not chosen Emmanuel Kant over Margaret Mead, chess over Frisbee, sherry over all-night booze-ups, the chairman of the philosophy department over him. But he doubted it would be better.

Nursey leaned into John, forcing him to look her in the eye. "John, your obsession with Indian artifacts bores me; I'm just your kachina doll. You don't know me. Anyway, there's something about older, intelligent men. Try to understand, won't you? He drives a Mercedes; he's rich, for Christ's sake. Need I say more?"

He stammered something about vigorous youth, which she rejected. She patted him on the head when he asked if they couldn't try again.

John ordered a soda and a whale burger, medium rare, and forced his mind to concentrate on matters at hand. He would continue to be friendly with Aki; she might have misled him but she had helped him to settle into Japan. Perhaps a skiing weekend? And he would treat Murata with respect. She was his student and assistant, not some wayward cousin or—he could hardly think it, how could he say it—the future mother of his children.

His order came and with it the fragrance of Betty, and the vision of a gigantic sperm whale facing extinction, diving hundreds of feet, grappling with a giant squid as it had done for millennia. He retreated homeward, hungry.

North 24th Street wrestled with its usual kamikaze bicyclists, shriveled and moldy hollyhocks, luxuriated in moon shadows cast by monolithic apartment buildings, and led John home. A glimpse of what was possibly United Air 762, blinking overhead, reminded him that he could always bail.

His room seemed desolate. He decided to succumb to NHK television and a North American snack: his final can of Vienna sausages, smoke flavor added, the last of his hoard smuggled into Japan; ersatz mustard, *wasabi*; one quarter of a one-dollar apple, sliced; precious bread, spread with mayonnaise; and one bottle of scotch, aged.

He flipped the set on. Hello, bigger world.

The news: a plane has crashed somewhere, if he could only make out a license plate or street sign; a model plane is depicted landing in a storm; it crashes and toy passengers and crew are shown hurtling here and there. The segment is repeated three times, while the grim-faced announcer might be saying, "United Airlines Flight 235, in route from Nashville to Graceland, has crashed, killing all aboard. Fortunately, there were no Japanese on this flight." Or perhaps, "Godzilla has once again taken revenge against America for vaporizing Hiroshima."

Miscellaneous firefights, some in a desert region and one among houses, perhaps in Africa, interspersed with scenes of mobs wailing and running with corpses held high. Announcer: "If we give these creeps more money, maybe they would side with us on whaling issues."

The weather: a white swirl is approaching or has passed Japan; the baton-wielding weatherman indicates where this system will be at some other time.

John peered out the window and assured himself that the cottonwoods were okay. He studied the weather chart on the TV screen, searching for what he thought was kanji for Sapporo:

a tree, an umbrella and a squid. The map with lightning strokes, clouds, and suns was easy.

"Miss Murata, thank you for coming in." She stepped forward, bowed her head slightly. "Mr. Fox, I understand the importance of our studies, not just for your dissertation but for the Ainu people as well. Gomen nasai. I apologize."

John glimpsed Ike, who appeared to be praying to some god to make him invisible.

John wanted to lift the tension that filled the room.

"It's okay, Miss Murata, I understand you are under a lot of pressure to get a . . ." He stopped. He should not comment on such a personal matter, but both Ike and Murata stared at him, waiting in silence for him to complete his sentence. John glanced at his desk and saw a square brown envelope with his name crudely printed on the front. Reprieved, he handed the envelope to Murata. The back flap was sealed with red wax imprinted with three vertical Japanese characters.

"It was leaning against the office door," said Ike.

Murata looked at the seal, walked to the center of the room, knelt, and placed the large envelope just so on the floor.

John looked at her as she knelt, a perfect curve from the exposed soles of her feet to the flood of hair shadowing the package. He wanted to brush that hair, an act that had melted Nursey.

Ike and John knelt beside her and restrained their Ainu/gaijin selves, trying to experience this Japanese moment.

Murata picked up the envelope and presented it for their inspection. "This seal belongs to your sensei, Mr. Fox. These kanji mean 'the ever-changing river delta at the ocean's edge reflecting all that has gone on before.'"

John took the package, broke the seal, unwound the silk string from the bobbin and pried the flap open. A ten-inch square of rigid paper framed with a narrow gold band bore one sweeping Japanese character and a red signature chop. He placed the card on the floor.

Murata said, "Mr. Fox, the answer to your question about kendo defense is attack."

"Then we'll attack," John said. "Miss Murata, just complete the translations quickly, don't worry about grammatical details, just get the spirit of these documents. When you've finished we may be able to determine the relationships of various Ainu tribes and their ancestors and any political implications."

"Mr. Fox, some of the documents from the curator are in old Japanese. Our modern written language was simplified after the war, and I am not familiar with all of the old characters," she explained. "I will need some key phrases to help me identify promising sections."

"Miss Murata, my extensive anthropological training should help: look for bears, arrowheads, pottery shards, woven basket remains, as well as the decorative motifs on Ainu robes."

Ike rolled his eyes. "John, pottery played an insignificant role in my ancestors' lives. Early trade with the Japanese and Chinese brought us such things. We expressed ourselves through drawings and carvings. Willow wands, mustache lifters, and shaman's cloaks are the terms that should be hunted for and compared."

John protested, "But Ike, I don't know enough about these things yet."

"Ike is Ainu, Mr. Fox. You should be guided by his understanding. But then, Ike might not be Ainu. He does not seem that hairy." Murata smiled.

"I wax," said Ike.

John knelt on the office floor, comparing various sketches from his collected manuscripts. Some were labeled in Russian and others in Japanese. This was frustrating and he felt the need to break out . . . the cornfield, a new bar, but not United Air Flight 762, not yet.

"Good morning, John," said Ike. "I was just speaking to the director. He is concerned about how hard you have been working. He feels that you need to take some time off. He has asked a visiting American entomology professor to invite you for drinks. He was only too happy to, and he has invited you tonight. I will take you."

"Why would I want to meet Dr. Bug? I'm happy with the present company."

"John. You must. It is the director's suggestion and you would dishonor him if you did not go."

John quaked. What if this guy spoke better Japanese than he? What if he came from Harvard? What if he was tanned, muscular, and constantly tossed a baseball, one autographed by Babe Ruth, from hand to hand? Ike would see what a fake John was.

John thought of the white guys he'd seen strolling around Ōdōri Park. In the early evening, they strutted; they had the spit and polish of a sailor on shore leave. But later, after circling the park several times, invisible to the natives, they trudged like haggard zombies. John, on the other hand, drank and ate and partied with the natives, his new tomodachi. But it felt shallow: no real conversations resulted, just repetitions of meaningless clichés.

"Ike, on second thought, I'd love to meet this guy."

Dr. Bug was big, he was blond, and he spoke horrible Japanese. He could drink, he laughed too loud, and he used the force of his hand on John's shoulder to punctuate important points. They met in the American bar near the university.

Dr. Bug updated John on American sports: college football, NBA, women's professional mud wrestling, ten-pin bowling. On important political issues: the governor of Louisiana's mouthy mistress, blacks jamming the ballot box at a recent ARA meeting. And on global warming: "It's bullshit. It's no worse now than during the Cambrian."

John asked who was skipping the women's US curling team. Inquired about the status of the Mongolian pine tree gypsy moth invasion. Asked if the current American stance was that gay marriage would lead to sheep-man-pony *ménage à trois*?

"Of course, it would. Now let's have another double and then I'm going to take you home to meet the little missus. Georgette loves company."

"I'd love to, but I've got a lot to do. Better take a rain check."

Ike looked disappointed. He whispered, "She is a flight attendant for American Airlines."

Spending the evening in the company of an American woman, a stewardess, suddenly appealed to John.

As they departed, he realized that the usually noisy bar had been subdued. Dr. Bug's loud, overbearing exuberance and his own matching responses had quelled the room. John knew that was why he'd been reluctant to meet Dr. Bug. After four months in Japan, he felt alienated from his own kind. Alienated to the point of paranoia, of crossing the street or slipping into a doorway to avoid a white encounter.

They walked to the modern apartment block, reserved for visiting faculty. His apartment door was locked and Dr. Bug didn't have a key. He knocked and they waited. He called her name and they waited. "Goddamn it, Georgette, open this door. We have visitors."

The door flew open. "Welcome to Bugsy's wasp nest, gentlémen." With a theatrical bow, followed by a little stumble, Georgette ushered them in. This same bow revealed she was bra-less, reminding John of the buxomness of American women: the result of a diet of corn-fed beef and homogenized milk from hormone-treated cows.

"May I pour you scotches? I'm having my first of the day."

She looked down and saw there the splotch of yellow paste—mustard?— on her blouse.

"Oh my," she said, "I was just creating a Jackson Pollock-inspired garment when you knocked. Let me finish, then drinkies." With this she walked to the table, retrieved squeeze bottles of mustard and catsup and proceeded to paint what looked like the Japanese character for detour on her blouse.

Ike and John looked on, stunned.

Dr. Bug was reaching for the scotch when, in a sober moment, Georgette said, "Please excuse me, I need to dress for company. Bugsy, be a pussy and run out and get our guests some KFC. Boys, help yourselves to drinks."

Ike and John sat on the sofa. Ike would not meet John's eye. And John was at a loss for words.

Finally, Ike whispered, "Who is afraid of Virginia Woolf?"

John shrugged and cruised around the apartment. The living room was large and comfortable and dirty. The walls were bare, except for last year's calendar featuring Shinto temples. A very expensive-looking, glassed-in bookcase covered one wall; it was full of empty Suntory whiskey bottles.

"We're not drinking, are we?"

John could not believe it: she was striking. She wore a full peasant skirt, bare-legged and barefooted, and her long-sleeved white blouse was buttoned up to her chin. Georgette had twisted her blond hair into a severe bun, exposing a lovely neck.

"That won't do. Let's drink up before the praying mantis of Utah returns."

Ike handed John a watered-down scotch and they toasted their Queen of Hospitality.

A loud knock took Georgette to the door. She returned, clutching the elbow of her KFC-laden husband, while sniffing his jacket.

"This is our joke, isn't it, my little horny grasshopper? I try to guess the class of cunt that has marked our little chirper from its smell." She looked at Ike and John's astonished faces. "Excuse us, we are delaying your dinner with our silly games."

With a grand sweep of her arm, Georgette cleared the table: some magazines and a Harlequin novel fell on the floor. A glass shattered. Their hostess walked around the table, pointing, "Boy, girl, boy, girl," seemingly unaware she was treading on shattered glass.

Ike sat across from Dr. Bug. Georgette threw a roll of paper towels on the table and plopped down opposite John with a sigh. She slouched and her face traded its exuberance for wrinkled weariness, a deflating balloon.

John reached into the bucket and picked up a thigh. "Are you enjoying Japan, Mrs. Bug?" he asked politely, smiling.

"Mr. Fox, do you have a television in your apartment?"

He nodded.

"Do you have a radio, a DVD player, a little duck you wind up to make quacking noises?"

Before he could answer, she said, "Well, I don't. I don't have anything to amuse me except this . . ." she hesitated, searching for the right descriptive. Then she stabbed an accusing finger at Dr. Bug and sobbed, "I'm a prisoner. I don't know how to take the bus. I don't know how to shop; their goddamn money confuses me. And when I try to talk to someone they giggle, cover their mouths, bow and dash off. Or, if they're *his* friends, they just stare at my boobs. And this prick flits off to work in the morning, like he has something to do and returns fourteen hours later, mumbling excuses while pouring my douche all over himself and gargling toilet cleaner."

"Mrs. Bug, may I call you Georgette?"

Georgette looked at John as if seeing him for the first time. She reached under the table, grabbed his foot, removed his sock, and crammed his tootsie between her legs.

John looked at Ike, who was concentrating on retrieving the last bit of flesh from a wing. He looked at Dr. Bug, who was rotating his head like a helicopter wanting to take off. He looked at Georgette, who looked serious.

"Mr. Fox, I don't recall having done anthropology before. Please do call me Georgette," she said. She squeezed her thighs together. "What's a broad like me to do? If I leave him, I'd only end up with another asshole. Like you, sweetie."

A thousand possible responses lined up behind his teeth, but Mr. Big Toe distracted him.

"Georgette, do you know what a host bar is?"

Ike dropped his wing and Dr. Bug coughed.

"Hey, guys, it's getting late. Maybe you should go now."

"One minute, my sweet little arthropod. I want to hear about these bars."

As John explained these women-only bars, Georgette became ever more attentive and her face took on its earlier animation. His big toe flexed. Georgette moved forward on her chair, gobbling up his every word. Her posture became rigid and she seemed to stop breathing.

Then she leaned back with a sigh, "Thank you, John, that was very interesting."

At the door, all was lovey-dovey. They ignored the trail of bloody footprints: Georgette's march out of Bhutan, out of her matrimonial enslavement. She gave John a little peck on the cheek and slipped his sock into his pants' pocket.

"John, I hope you will further enlighten me in Japanese ways. Goodnight."

Ike and John walked to the Toho subway station under a full moon, the Hunters Moon. The same moon that was now looking down on some wretched Iowan kid, freezing to death in a blind with his rum-reeking father, waiting for a flock of south-bound snow geese that would mark his entrance into American manhood, into dames, into zit-free mirrors, and away from hot chocolates, mummy tuckings-in, jerkings-off in the apricot tree. John had not thought of being American for a long time.

"John, you are going to wash your foot, are you not?"

John shrugged. "Some American customs may seem bizarre to you, but believe me they are rational in context. Ike, I'd forgotten how charming American women could be."

The moon had slipped behind some cottonwood trees, casting shadow spears across the sidewalk.

Ike stumbled, trying not to step on John's moon shadow, while John bent, ducked and side-stepped.

Ike stopped, "I did not think Americans were superstitious."

Before John could respond, Ike moved up-moon from him. "How do you know about host bars, John."

"I live in Little Ginza, Ike. I explore." John went on to explain that his Little Ginza was multi-dimensional, like the Shinto view of the world.

"I live on street level, the Middle World, the present world of earthly joys and pains. In Little Ginza there are higher levels—the Plains of High Heaven—exactly four floors up." John laughed. "And Hades is the Happy Times Photocopy shop mall."

Another day in the Middle World, John arrived at his office to be greeted by Miss Murata.

"Mr. Fox, your kendo instructor called. He has invited you to participate in a tournament. The competition starts Saturday afternoon. He will pick you up here at eleven."

John's first fight outside of lessons. He felt weak. He remembered being on the stage at Rolfe High School, staring dumbly at Catherine who had just asked him a question, the answer to which explained the moral of the play, *Lost Horizon*. The audience cringed with embarrassment for him, his father tried to disappear and the prompter whispered louder and louder, but John remained mute. And he peed.

What if he forgot the kendo moves, what if his muscles turned to jelly?

Murata, head cocked, gave John a look of sympathy. "This is a big step, Mr. Fox. A test of the trust your sensei has given you."

This was not what John wanted to hear.

John entered the Sapporo Athletic club's gym with his teammates. All about him fighters leaped, lunged, grunted, and the air filled with the sound of whooshing bamboo swords. A sea of black warriors swirled about him, the white knight.

John tried to mimic the other fighters but only tripped over himself and his hands were all thumbs. He had to pull himself together. He hadn't been excelling recently, but he hadn't been failing either, at least not completely. *I can do this.*

A wizened patriarch grunted a command and all the competitors knelt in a circle, repeating incantations. Names were drawn from a lacquered bowl to pair the combatants. John's name was not called; he felt both disappointed and relieved. Then the elder announced a special bout, one for two aspiring samurai: John-san and Hirome-san.

John scanned the auditorium, looking for a Hirome: large, small, everyone looked the same.

The matches began and he withered. Such intensity. Airborne contestants collided, regrouped and collided again. The judge awarded a point for a winning stroke, and the fighters bowed and charged again.

John's name was called and he walked to the center of the gym. His knees wanted to buckle; he doubted his body could perform any act as complicated as walking, much less do kendo. There, opposite, stood his opponent, dressed in black. This face-guarded foe looked as fierce as the samurai mannequins in the Tokyo museum but smaller. For a fleeting moment, he assumed that, with his advantage in size, victory would be his. If only he stopped quaking; if only his teeth stopped chattering.

On command, John bowed to the judge, then to his team, the opposing team and lastly his opponent.

Hirome met him in the center of the fighting ring, they touched swords and stepped back two steps. The judge dropped his sword and his opponent lunged. John felt like a rag doll, hardly able to lift his sword, hardly able to breathe. In desperation, he looked for an escape. What he saw was his sensei, whose eyes willed him to fight.

A smart bonk on the head cured John, who then turned on his opponent. They circled, feigned thrusts and circled again. Then Hirome, a screaming menace, was on him. He parried blows from each side and from over his head, all the time backing away from the pressure. John tripped and the judge restarted the match.

Again his opponent attacked. They crossed swords and leaned into each other. But this time John used his weight and his opponent was down, but for only a moment, and then up again, flailing at him. The judge declared a point and they started again.

Around the room, the other fighters were silent.

Another collision, but John held his ground and then pursued the attack. They both attacked, over and over. Cheers arose from the sidelines. Sweat stung his eyes, his mouth was dry, he struggled for breath. Still they fought on. Calm settled over John and time froze—he remembered his lines—and then the judge pulled them apart. But John had tasted blood and wanted more.

They rejoined in combat until the spectators swarmed to the center of the hall, smothering the pair. Facing each other, John and Hirome sheathed their swords and bowed.

Their teammates lifted them high and, cheering, paraded the two combatants around the gym. As they passed, his opponent removed her mask: Miss Murata. Her face was flushed, her hair plastered to her brow. She smiled and called, "Well done, John."

Never, upon hearing his name, had he felt such a rush.

Following the tournament, John's team went to a city spa—men only—for a soak. His teammates smacked his back, laughed and John heard "tomodachi" a lot. John could hardly converse with them, but he was part of a team. He didn't even know who had won. John felt great. The heat was sulfurous.

Hirome. Will our parents get along? What will we name our children?

He dreamed of Hirome, their kids playing on a dirt floor with a rusting typewriter.

On Monday morning, John painfully settled at his desk.

"John, you look terrible."

He grimaced, "Thank you, Ike."

Murata stood in the doorway, her arms held uncomfortably tight against her ribs. "Good morning, John."

He had practiced for this moment. "Good morning, Hirome. I hope you're feeling better than I am."

Ike stared at them.

"We had a fight."

"Kendo," said Murata.

"Who won?" Ike asked.

They answered with silly grins.

John tried not to be distracted, but it seemed each day Hirome's skirts got shorter, and the shorter they got the more she fidgeted with the hem. "John, you are not paying attention. I asked you if you will go to a baseball game with me."

"A high school baseball game?" he said. "Are you kidding? Me sit cramped on a wooden bench for hours watching midgets egged on by my-boy-play-American-big-league-ball wishful parents? Besides, it's late in the year for baseball."

Hirome pouted—another newly acquired affectation.

"This is the final match of the All Nippon Junior Baseball competition. I must go. It is a matter of family pride. My brother will be playing. Baseball is an important part of our culture. I doubt Miss Kawaguchi has introduced you to this sport."

John raised his hands in defense.

"Do not say anything, John. We will go to the ballgame."

This was a dragon John would have to slay to win his princess. He would go to the game.

Working their way to their seats, John froze. Never had he encountered so many people in one place. This made the subway at rush hour look like an Iowan country hayride.

Then it struck him. "Oxygen," he said.

Hirome looked up at him, smiled and said something he couldn't hear.

John mouthed again, "Oxygen, what if we run out?"

She squeezed his hand with that eternal promise of hers.

A great roar went up from the orange section, answered by anguished shouts from the blue mob. Two bands, each with hundreds of bee-kneed cheerleaders and thousands of bullhorners, could compete with a fleet of Boeing 747s for the greatest noise ever.

Hirome touched John's shoulder, "There he is, over there."

He looked, there were no players on the field.

"No, over there." She pulled John to his feet; he extracted his knees from between the shoulder blades of the chickadee sitting in front of him.

Vertigo: John felt like a tumbleweed being blown across an endless New Mexico landscape. Dizzy, he reached out his hands and planted them on two dark shiny scalps in front of him. Stabilized, he removed them. Gomen nasai, gomen nasai.
"Look at the orange band."
John did. He nodded.
"My brother is the clarinet player, third row up and second in. Do you see him?"
John lied. He nodded, sat down, knees back among shoulder blades. "Gomen nasai."
The game began. To preserve his sanity, John retreated into scientific analysis. How much oxygen was being consumed by this hyperventilating mass? He calculated and the results were not pretty. John slowed his breathing to conserve air, his mind wandering to his mother.

John's mother leaned over his father's shoulders, her hands resting on his chest as he watched baseball on TV.
He ignored her. She began to sing, "... and with crotch dictated call the catcher beckoned."
She reached down and grabbed his crotch. His father roared and shoved her off. Two minutes later she was perched on a kitchen stool, chatting and laughing with a neighbor on the telephone.
Weekday baseball, their life a record playing over and over. Ditty, crotch-grab, roar.
"Mavis, I'm coming over for a drink..."

All about John the crowd groaned or cheered or fell into deep silence, choreographed by tribal forces, confident the Divine Wind, their kamikaze, would not fail them.
John, on the other hand, had dark thoughts. He saw this mass

of black heads as atoms of uranium, perfectly spaced, vibrating in exacting atomic harmony and he, John, an unstable isotope, threatening to turn them into a Little Boy.

Fifty-thousand cheers and fifty-thousand groans, and the game was over.

Hirome moaned. "We lost. Oh, my poor brother, my poor family." Climbing down through the bleachers, she dragged him onto the playing field—"Gaijin privileges," she said.

The losers, on their knees, scooped dirt into little Bags of Shame; the winners, ever humble, raced about the field, bowing to their fans and families, smiles revealing decades of parental bondage for their orthodontics.

The stadium cleared: files of ants streaming out the tunneled exits. Hirome's brother fell into his sister's arms. His life was over. He would become a subway conductor. A few feet away, an oboist, bowing her head in shame, sneaked a peek at Hirome's brother.

"Let's go, Hirome. He'll live."

An assemblage of dry cornstalks, complete with tassels and cobs, stood in the corner of the office, surrounded by John's bears and lacquered bowls of treats. A stack of his Sapporo manhole cover rubbings and the pilfered willow wand completed the display.

Hirome looked askance.

"It's Halloween, an American custom," John explained.

"And the carved bears?" Ike asked.

"They represent dead saints."

"And the bowl of candies?" asked Hirome.

"Trick or treat."

"What is this?" asked Hirome, pointing at a concoction of pulped bulbs and raspberries.

"Hirome, that is my attempt to reproduce an Ainu dessert from a recipe you translated," replied John, feeling proud.

Hirome held up the willow wand. "And this?"

Ike glared at John. "What are you doing with an Ainu willow fetish? They are sacred."

"Ike, I didn't know. I found it in near Konbu Spa. I meant to tell you, but . . ." Words failed him. God, how could he plummet from the heights of near engagement to the delicious Hirome—he considered their new first-name relationship the foundation for future intimacy—to deceiving and disappointing his friend in five minutes?

Then, in desperation, "Ike, museums are full of primitive gods, artifacts; this is important for science, for understanding the human condition." John could not believe he had said that. And then he thought guiltily of the ancient Ainu trinkets he'd shipped to New Mexico. At least Hirome and Ike hadn't noticed the Ainu arrowhead, which he had discovered in the museum archives, misplaced and mislabeled.

Ike promised John an ethnic treat on the next visit to his village, "Something that would make your anthropology colleagues jealous and hopefully give you deeper insight into our symbolism."

Yezo maple leaves littered the path to the village, which sat under a light dusting of the first snow. John kicked them skyward, reveling in their crunchy sound and musty smell.

Ike made a bouquet of perfect specimens.

Leaves flew as Miura bound from the undergrowth like a hare and leaped into Ike's arms. Her pregnancy was showing and her wholesomeness attracted John like a magnet. He could not superimpose the pathetic, mascara-streaked face of the Muroran bar girl onto that of this glowing mother-to-be. Taking Ike's hand, Miura led them into the village.

In the center of the square, men and women stood in a ring around a bonfire, its light dancing over their robes. They blew on their hands and stamped on the earth, as much to appease their anxiousness as to dispel the autumn chill.

An announcement, by an unseen elder, directed the group's attention to the bear's cage. The yearling gave an anguished roar as it was dragged to the edge of the fire: the same cub John had seen children feeding on his first visit.

A hunter with a short bow approached the animal.

"Ike," whispered John, "they can't do this." He started to move forward.

Ike grabbed John's arm, restraining him, and focused on the scene before them.

The arrow flew, the cub cried and collapsed. The hunter approached with a skinning knife. An elder poured oil on the flames. The sudden blast from the bonfire knocked John back and he stumbled, fell.

The bobbins spun out socks, the women scratched lint from their crotches, his father rode his Mexican whore, and his mother pressed Winnie the Pooh across his face.

John cleared dust from his eyes to see the hunter offering meat to the sky. A bear skin lay in the dirt. The Ainu were cheering.

The bear had been properly released back to the land of the gods from which it came, assuring the villagers it will visit again.

This promised a prosperous year.

Feeling sick, John rushed towards the brush.

Ike caught up with him.

"John, the bear was shot with an arrow tipped with a monkshood extract. It was just enough to tranquilize it. The meat offering is dog and the hide a relic from when we sacrificed bears. The cub will have a hangover. Then another year of dried fruits and pampering. It is not a bad life."

John felt deceived and told him so.

"Ainu do not lie, cannot lie," Ike said. "This necessary deception does create a moral dilemma. We must compromise our ways if we are to survive."

Back at the bonfire, the elders bowed, rubbed their palms and then their beards. Each flicked three drops of beer onto the fire. The men hefted heavy beer-filled bowls with one hand and used their mustache lifters with the other to clear the way for a draught. After everyone had drunk and toasted, an elder carefully formed a rectangle of willow darts around the "deceased" bear's pelt.

John threaded Dr. Kawasaki's film into the museum's projector. "Ike, make yourself comfortable. This should be interesting."

John dimmed the lights and turned on the projector. It started up with a rattle, the frames jumping on the screen. It was black and white and without sound. Slowly the scene resolved.

A bonfire cast flickering light over a small village. Elegantly dressed men and women, all wearing galoshes, stood awkwardly in front of a thatched house. The camera scanned their faces and then focused on their feet as they stomped on the slushy snow. The men looked severe in dark suits, dark overcoats and gray fedoras. The women wore fur stoles over long, black overcoats; patterned dresses showed below. The camera returned to the face of one woman who stood taller than the rest. A fine black veil, hanging from a pillbox hat, shadowed her face.

The camera slowly moved to the right where a second group stood. These men and women wore coarse bark robes: the men's had elaborate designs along the hems, while the women's were plain. Their feet were shod in skin boots and the men sported woven bark headbands. Snow speckled the men's wooly beards and the women's shiny hair. Jerkily the camera approached this group, focusing on faces. They were heavily lined and weary and, in many, vacuous eyes stared unseeingly into the lens.

A woman stepped forward, her head bowed as if paying homage. She carried a plank with what appeared to be cubes of frozen salmon, which she distributed to the city folk. In response, the well-dressed men rubbed their palms and then their beardless faces and their wives rubbed their palms and then drew their right index finger under their noses from left to right. These Ainu gestures of greeting were returned by the villagers. Then, slowly they embraced, some stiffly, others with emotion.

Now there was one group. Most everyone was caught up in lively discussion. Some presents were exchanged. As one, everyone turned, and the camera followed their direction. There stood a crude log corral, housing a bear of moderate size, perhaps in its second year. The bear poked its head between two poles and seemed anxious to join the festivities.

Children ran to the bear, petted it and gave it candies. The bear liked this and stuck its paw through an opening, moving it as if to shake hands. The delighted children streaked back to their parents.

Men approached the bear and secured two ropes to its collar. Others joined them and began to dismantle the enclosure. Out came the bear: a big happy puppy. The camera panned on the now broken cage. The ground was muddy and covered with food scraps and excrement. About three feet above the ground there was a straw-covered platform where the bear slept; tufts of fur were snagged on the corral fence.

Everyone formed a circle around the leashed bear. They sang and danced and drank. Some children shot the bear with blunt arrows, which fell harmlessly to the ground. The bear did not like this and started running this way and that, only to be reined in by those holding its leashes. Two men then taunted the bear with long sticks that bore tufts of wood shavings. The agitated bear appeared to be growling. The goading became more intense and a look of terror came to the bear's eyes. The bear lunged harder, trying to escape its now mostly ecstatic tormentors; puffs of steam escaped its nostrils and its tongue lolled in exhaustion. In final desperation, the bear bit at the restraining ropes.

The men holding the reins and those taunting the bear with sticks backed off. The bear gasped for air; it shuddered; it seemed to relax. Quickly, four robe-clad men rushed in and secured loops of rope around the animal's four legs. Everyone grabbed these and yanked them tight, spread-eagling the animal on its front in the muddy snow. A long log was laid across the bear's neck and then . . .

Clackity clackity, the film broke.

Ike stared straight ahead as a stunned John spliced the film, having to discard some. He dimmed the lights for a second time and turned the projector on.

The camera focused on the bear's head. Irregular puffs of steam escaped its nostrils, its eyes were glazed, and slushy mud invaded its mouth. The camera backed off showing about eight men, some suited and some in robes, sitting on the log, laughing and drinking beer, as they slowly squeezed out the bear's life. Women and children danced and sang to the ascending bear spirit. When it was clear the bear was heaven bound, everyone took turns to caress their friend, their new god; some poured beer into its lifeless mouth. The tall woman approached and the others fell back. She knelt in the sludge, lifted her veil and kissed the cooling head; she was crying.

An elder advanced and greeted the bear by rubbing his palms and then his beard. He unsheathed a short ceremonial sword that he passed to a townsman who might have been the tall woman's brother. This person received the sword with a bow. The camera panned on the now solemn spectators, all of whom were rubbing their palms, and then returned to the sword-wielding man. He seemed comfortable with the weapon, which he held, unwavering, at shoulder height. The sword flashed in a perfect arc and cleanly severed the bear's head. The body twitched, perhaps an involuntary muscular spasm, and then lay still. Blood darkened the slushy snow.

The elder lifted the head, closed its eyes, wiped mud from its chin and nostrils, and mounted it on a forked pole. Other villagers peeled the pelt from the carcass, releasing steam into the cold night air. The elder then wrapped the freshly skinned hide around the pole as if to reunite head to body. The tall woman stepped up to the totem and fussed with the bearskin, much as she might have done with her husband's coat, seemingly to give dignity to the deceased.

The tasseled sticks, earlier used to taunt the animal, were placed as fetishes to protect the new god. An elder dropped hunks of still warm bear flesh into a boiling cauldron for the bear festival feast. Gifts of beer, food and sweets were arranged around the totem. Dribbles of beer and bits of bear were thrown onto the fire: nourishment to appease the gods of fire, home, water, everything. When all seemed in order, an elder poured oil on the fire and a great light filled the village. The congregation ate and danced and drank and sang.

With streaks of light announcing night's end, the Ainu, villagers and townspeople together, posed with their new god. A photographer, bobbing in and out of his small black tent, cajoled his subjects into the perfect composition. Gone were the listless eyes and heavily lined faces: one sensed a rebirth. A flash signaled the end of the celebration.

The town-dwelling Ainu, now revitalized, now reminded of their origins, now no longer sullied by the oppressive Japanese, palmed, bowed and embraced their village cousins. Snow was wiped from Model T Ford windshields, a cheery blink of headlights retraced the two muddy ruts back to town.

The projector slapped the loose end of the film around and around, and the two, the Ainu and the anthropologist, stared at the blank screen. Neither had been prepared for this stark presentation.

John remembered the look of distress on Dr. Kawasaki's face as she pointed at the newspaper clipping—"Heartless Ainu Kill Baby Bear." And he felt the same revulsion now as he did then. But Dr. Kawasaki understood the Ainu perspective; she didn't let her culture distort what was true for the Ainu.

John sighed, "Deciduous Leaf Falling, I want to understand Ainu. You make everything god and you sacrifice everything so that it will return. I guess that's not so different from our crucifying Christ and waiting for his return."

"John, everyone lives with myths. The Japanese farm boy believes that his Kobe cow will have a good life. He has lovingly massaged and shared beer with that cow."

"Ike, I have lived that myth."

John and Aki had not seen each other for about two months. Each time they talked on the phone, he made excuses: work demands, teaching commitments, dental problems. The awkwardness that had developed between them and, though he would not admit it, his attraction to Hirome, made meeting difficult.

Aki had misled him about the old bookseller's death, and John had to face his growing lack of trust in her. He invited her for a ski weekend in early December.

The cold felt good. The snow on the Sapporo Teine run had been powdery, fortunately cushioning John's many falls. Aki proved to be an excellent skier, and she was constantly passing him as he painfully made his way down the mountain.

The short bus ride from the ski resort to their inn in Otaru had been agonizing. Both Aki and John couldn't seem to relax, to be their old selves.

John knelt and removed Aki's snow boots, knocked them together and they retreated to the warmth of their inn.

"John, something is the matter. You seem so distant."

Confronting Aki in the flesh, seeing the person who soothed his way into the chaos that is Japan—and provided great sex along the way—John decided against bringing up Kei-ichi Matsuyama. Instead, he let the greater truth prevail.

"Aki, there is someone else."

"Pink shorts, translator?"

"Yes, Miss Murata. Hirome."

Aki, the ninja maiden, crumbled for a moment, then with a shrug said, "That's fine, John. Now one last lesson."

For the moment, John saw her once again, not as a deceiver, but as the object of his lust. Wordlessly, he peeled off her blouse and ran his hands over her body. They made love; John to draw some last satisfaction from her body and she to feed her demons.

They parted at the Sapporo train station.

Ike bowed and John shook his hand. "John, we do not have a best man at weddings. Some god fills in. However, because you are the one who took me to that Korean bar, I am obliged."

The Ainu village, bathed in fresh snow, glowed. John stopped at the gathering house and knocked snow from his shoes. A cheery Ainu, a man of about forty years, dressed in a traditional robe, indicated where he should be sit.

The bride and groom entered, dressed in white birch robes, Ike's trimmed with symbols and Miura's plain. Ike wore a short, ceremonial sword at his side, while Miura carried a small bow. John was shocked to see the traditional tattoos of Ainu women around Miura's mouth, which he had only seen in old photographs. The couple was followed by a sinister-looking man who was draped with a heavy, black robe.

The black-robed man approached John. The carved bear's head on his elm-bark headband appeared to be snarling. Feathers, antlers, beaks, bits of rusted iron hung from his robe, suggesting these were his gods to beckon.

"My name is Kru. I am a shaman and I am here to witness this wedding. Deciduous Leaf Falling has told me that my Japanese father asked you to contact me. I hold him no evil, but I wish no dealings with that man."

Kru turned and faded into the shadows of the large room.

John was taken aback. This man might want nothing to do with his father, but John was determined to fulfill his promise to the deceased legless man, scrolls or not.

Ike and Miura knelt facing the eastern window; firelight cast wavering shadows on their faces as a white-haired elder recited incantations to the twanging of a bamboo mouth harp.

Across the room, John saw the shaman squatting in a dark corner: a sinister figure at a joyous occasion.

The elder passed Ike a crude wooden bowl filled with rice. When he had eaten half the rice, the elder took the bowl and offered it to Miura.

The elder offered prayers to many wedding deities. "I declare this woman, who came to us when the white swans returned from heaven, deserving of marriage to Deciduous Leaf Falling, our lost son, now at home. May the marriage gods grant them fecundity, long life and happiness. Should these gods fail, I will strip away their feathers and beaks and claws, and send them to hell."

Everyone cheered as Ike and Miura bowed their heads, receiving the benediction. The villagers crowded around the couple, offering their congratulations, touching Miura's belly and Ike's head.

Suddenly, Kru was beside them, his manner threatening. He shook a finger at Miura.

"Your Japanese blood dilutes pure Ainu blood. Your baby will be a half-breed, not Ainu."

He was a shaman, his presence defied response: he represented all deities. Kru's robe flared out, its evil creatures struggling to attack and rusted bits of iron became daggers.

Ike broke the shocked silence, "And your blood, Kru, how pure is it?"

Miura hissed. "My baby will be an Ainu warrior."

Everyone turned to her determined voice.

Miura's little bow was taut, an arrow pointing at Kru's throat. Her stance and the crescent tattoo over her mouth signaled the strength of ancient Ainu maidens: the strength that helped preserve the Ainu through centuries of foreign oppression.

Kru stepped back and bowed. Studying her face, her posture, her naked feet solid on the earth, he saw an Ainu as in times past.

"Miura, your intentions are pure," he conceded. "May you and your clan have strength for what lies ahead."

The arrow flew, creased the shaman's cheek and thudded into a wooden post.

Miura patted her belly and bowed to Kru. She then raised her arms and smiled at the onlookers, a smile that was at once hideous and beautiful.

Again, patting the yet-to-be-born, she spoke, "For Ainu Land, for the Deciduous Leaf Falling Dynasty."

Everyone cheered.

John, as honorary best man, was given the duty of distributing the gifts: a ceremonial quiver, missing one arrow, a ceremonial sword from the villagers, a set of lacquered bowls. And a case of toilet paper.

"John, how thoughtful of you," said Ike.

As John bent forward to kiss the petite bride, she rose on tiptoe and softly bit his cheek and neck, and nibbled on his ear. John bolted upright, smacking his head against a heavy wood cooking hook.

The ladies giggled behind shy hands.

For one moment, there were only Ainu; this was Yezo, ancient Hokkaido, there were many pleased gods and the Japanese invaders quaked.

Later that night, fighting insomnia, John slipped out of his sleeping hut and made his way along a narrow path toward a flickering light. It was dark and he had to shuffle his feet to feel the way. Leafless branches touched his face and the air smelled of wood smoke. For a moment he froze, fearing what he might encounter.

The path broke into a small opening and there was Miura hunched over a little fire. She did not see John, and he, not wanting to intrude, hunkered down.

She fed the fire birch chips whose smoke charred an iron pot suspended from above. In horror, he watched as she gashed the skin of her cheek near her tattooed lips with an obsidian knife. She tamped birch soot into the fresh gashes, completing the traditional face decorations that ringed her mouth.

The sight of this little woman, alone in the bare deciduous forest, enduring momentary pain and permanent disfigurement, overwhelmed him.

Miura rose and turned to John. She splayed her hands indicating no ring. Then she drew her forefinger around her tattooed mouth.

Hirome hung her coat by the door, a million miles away across John's office. She smiled politely, said good morning, and walked over to a pile of maple leaves in the corner that rested on his manhole cover rubbings. She picked up a leaf, held it in front of her mouth, and lowered her eyes.

"How was the skiing weekend, John?"

Was she asking about skiing or Aki or their future? Should he answer, the snow was great, or Aki is no more, or I love you?

Ike's entrance reprieved John.

"Good morning, Miss Murata," he said and then bowed to the corn and maple corners. "They are gods. For Ainu everything is god," he added.

Hirome looked at John as if to ask, and who are you?

John wanted to tell her he was a free spirit, that his heart desired only her. But this did not seem to be the time. Instead, he put on a professorial air, the façade he had fine-tuned to duck awkward situations.

The wedding encounter with the shaman had inspired John. "I think the instruments of shamanism might be a good avenue to explore. It's a new angle for comparative social anthropology and would be a great addition to my thesis."

Hirome smoothed her skirt and twirled a loose lock of hair around her finger.

Ike was stroking his fledgling beard, his eyes glazed.

Hirome sighed, "It would make more sense if we first compared the shaman's role in local Ainu culture with their roles in other aboriginal cultures."

"Ike," said John with a wink, "I'm wondering if there are any practicing shamans still in existence."

Ike left him hanging.

Hirome started to speak but John ignored her. He glared at Ike.

Hirome moved between them, put her hands on her hips and asked, "May I talk?"

John slouched down in his chair. "Go ahead."

She lifted a stack of Ivan's documents, and said, "The Soviet anthropologists wrote their findings in the past indefinite, possibly to protect living sources from Party officials who would—how would you say it, John?—sell their mothers for a Cuban banana."

John smiled and nodded. *Good girl.* Hirome glared back.

"From these documents, it is not possible to know if they had firsthand experience with shamans or if they were merely perpetuating unsubstantiated myths. What is clear is that they thought all shamans, from many places, posed a threat."

Hirome returned to her chair and continued, "John, you know shamans exist. I resent that you and Mr. BBC are playing sneaky games at my expense. We are supposed to be a team. And please, stop playing with that wooden bear."

The office building was gray and squatty, typical of those thrown up at the end of the war, and surrounded by warehouses. Not a nice neighborhood. In the lobby, white plastic letters spelled out the occupants: Pan Pacific Oil Explorations, Toshida & Sons Financial Group, Eurasian Labor Contractors and Northern Development Expediency Services—12th Floor.

"Kru at your service," said the shaman, now nicely dressed in a dark blue suit with a patterned tie depicting an abstract volcanic eruption. His cologne smelled of lime and cedar, not the elm smoke John had expected.

John and Kru shook hands, and Kru reluctantly traded a palm and face-rubbing greeting with Ike.

Ike and John had been apprehensive about this meeting. Nothing in their encounter at the wedding signaled they would be welcomed. A shaman, like a minister or a priest or a mullah, was above normal civility, isolated by his lofty calling.

"Can I offer you coffee, cakes?" asked Kru, indicating they should sit on the leather chairs placed around a low teak table. Kru sat behind his desk.

Ainu art adorned the dark wood walls along with several framed photographs of Kru in the company of corporation presidents, political leaders, and other luminaries. John half expected to see Betty, beaming, "With Love, B." and he wondered what Northern Development Expediency Services was about.

"This," said Kru, pointing at a row of locked, beveled-glass cabinets, "is one of the finest collections of Ainu religious paraphernalia in existence."

Bone, ivory and wooden carvings of bears, woodpeckers, foxes and other deities filled the shelves, some ancient and gray and others gaudy with modern paints. The same motifs decorated tobacco pouches, mustache lifters, drinking vessels and, of course, willow wands.

Most striking was the shaman's robe, the same one they had seen Kru wear at the wedding. Hanging on a stand, its arms askew, it hovered, facing a solid glass wall with a twelfth-story view of snowy Moiwayama.

"Mr. Owl guides me," said Kru, a twinkle in his eyes. "When Mr. Big Money has an aboriginal problem, he comes to me. Quid pro quo and voilà, Ainu artifacts and artworks saved from the Guggenheims, Louvres and Smithsonians of the world, not to mention the Gettys, Roosevelts, Jacksons and Gates. And you," he said, pointing at John, "and your anthropology buddies can just go on wondering what makes us primitives tick. Of course, a particularly generous benefactor could receive an heirloom."

For a second time in as many minutes, John thought of Betty, the rescued icon, the orphans. People using their influence to help others, but why? To absolve some earlier misdeed, to demonstrate power, or to sincerely do good?

Ike stared at Kru. "You are a shyster."

Kru leaned his elbows on his glass-topped desk and contemplated Ike.

"At the wedding, you asked about my blood. Well, my blood is as your son's will be: mixed." He chuckled, "That is, if your father was Ainu and not the descendant of some Japanese convict sent to build roads for the invading colonists and prospectors."

A sad smile came over Ike's face.

"That is my fear. My mother raised me away from the Ainu, and it is only in the past year that I have begun to explore my heritage. I do not know who my father was. I am trapped by Japanese customs and my Japanese education. My pure Japanese wife has more Ainu spirit than I do."

John looked at his friend, understanding at that moment the terrible forces that could destroy the promise that was Deciduous Leaf Falling.

A slight Japanese woman, dressed in traditional kimono, entered the office. She seemed to glide rather than walk; she did nothing to call attention to herself, but her ethereal presence dominated the room. After serving their coffees, she silently retired, but her fragrance of jasmine lingered.

A calling card rested on the rim of his saucer. John glanced at it and then slipped it into his shirt pocket.

"Mr. Fox, share your secret with us."

John looked up and saw Kru and Ike looking at him: Kru with a snicker, Ike suspiciously.

John extracted the card, sniffed it and read, "Would gentleman like discrete company visiting our strange city. I linger your call every-time. Solicitations, Junko Miyabe, 090-9528-6797." The business card featured two red cherries dangling from a Yezo maple leaf.

"Your first encounter with a business geisha, Mr. Fox? Most of my clients are lonely in our fair city. You would be surprised how many stay in their expensive hotel rooms, watching endless TV baseball and eating lousy room-service steaks, while outside sexy Sapporo nights beckon."

Kru, sensing Ike's discomfort, shifted his attention to the Ainu.

"Mr. Ike, we both use only one Japanese name; this meets the meddling requirements of Japanese bureaucrats and allows us the satisfaction of a small rebellion. But a bigger battle is required to give the Ainu the power, dignity and prosperity to achieve the greater victory: our own homeland, Ainu Land. For you, the way is through strengthening Ainu's pride of culture and an understanding of the real Ainu way of life."

The shaman hesitated, "I would join you in a moment if I thought our people had half the guts of your little bar girl."

"Do not insult my wife."

"I meant that as a compliment, and she was a bar girl, was she not? And I do admire her," said Kru, gingerly tapping the mark on his cheek.

Kru swiveled in his chair, locked his hands behind his head, and stared out at towering Moiwayama.

"Let me continue. Did you know that the biggest enemy of the Ainu was disease? But disease brought on by forced labor and the breaking up of Ainu families, a destruction of morale and spirit. Smallpox, measles, consumption and venereal diseases killed half of all Ainu during the mid-1800s. Much like your North American aborigines, Mr. Fox. Because of these injustices and because I am Ainu at heart, I will support you. I find your little insurgency ineffective, Mr. Ike, but the knowledge you are gaining with the assistance of this esteemed scholar from New Mexico is valuable."

Kru turned to John, "Mr. Fox, I hope you will enjoy our hospitality."

John's hand slid over the card in his pocket as he savored the compliment.

"Thank you, sir. We scholars are only interested in truth. My present line of investigation relates to bears..."

"Please, Mr. Fox, this is all too complicated for me." The shaman continued, "My way is to buy influence, friends, people who make things happen. They don't give a damn about the Ainu, but they like a souvenir, a little willow wand, perhaps" he said, laughing. "We can all use a guardian spirit, right professor? What they do want is no hassle from us. Yes, Mr. Ike, us, you and me, the hairy Ainu."

Kru walked to the stand and lifted off the shaman's cloak.

"Would you help me put this on, Mr. Fox?"

John stepped into an aura of elm smoke, smoked salmon, and stale beer. He held the cloak; its weight almost dragged him to the floor.

"Do you have any idea how old this is? No theories now, Mr. Fox."

John recalled Dr. Kawasaki's graduate student saying the Chinese had influenced the Ainu since the first millennium AD and had brought iron to Hokkaido around the thirteenth century. But this told him nothing. "Sir, I have no idea."

"Would you like to try it on?"

Ike protested, "Mr. Kru, this is most inappropriate."

"I agree, Mr. Ike. Only the true of heart should be allowed to wear this. Now, Mr. Fox, please hold it up for me."

Kru slipped his arms through the coarse sleeves, his shoulders comfortable with its weight. With his back to them, he placed the shaman's headband on and walked to the window. Slowly he turned.

He was all shadows and his cloak seemed alive. Birds and bats, salamanders and lizards, rodents and fish, and inanimate objects competed for attention, cluttered the room with noisy chaos. He raised his hand and a silence fell over them.

"Oma, my mother, gave me this strength. She sent me on my soul journey, exposing me to agonizing dismemberment. I observed from above my every organ, muscle, nerve, fingernail: every inch and bit of me, being crudely clawed free and scattered by the demons of envy and lust. Monster Bird retrieved my bloodied fragmented corpse—if he missed a piece, I would be doomed to purgatory—boiled and then reassembled my purified flesh, muscle by tendon by bone. Now I am a shaman. Do not doubt it."

Evening descended beyond the large windows, and the array of electronic totems that topped Moiwayama, blinking shafts of red and white light, mingled with the twilight clouds, pulsing geometric designs. Kru's cloak absorbed the night energy.

John recalled the Kamchatka sauna with its mosaic of a man, wrapped in a pelt, fighting a bear.

"Sir," said John, "were those scratch marks made by a bear?"

The shaman turned and pointed at a rusty red stain on the cloak's front. "Mr. Fox, there was a time an Ainu had to fight a bear to become a warrior. This cloak protected me as I released a bear to heaven with my knife."

"Mr. Ike, we will make war together. You will expose the world to our culture and the mistreatment we have suffered. This you will do with knowledge and rebellion and theater. I will guide you and provide money and friends. However, sir, we must compromise, as your son and I are compromised. Take this as your task; it is your bear to manhood."

"Thank you, Mr. Kru," Ike said, showing his admiration and pride.

Kru replaced the cloak and turned to John. "But I have talked too much. Mr. Fox, please explain what you want from me," he said, absentmindedly flipping through his appointment book.

"Excuse me, sir," said John. "I accidentally took a willow wand from a sacred place near Konbu Spa. I didn't understand its significance then. I do now. I do not want to upset your gods or the Ainu. Could you help me make amends?"

Pulling on his suit jacket, Kru, turned to John, "Mr. Fox, our gods are your gods and your God is our God. Are you superstitious?"

Before John could respond, he added, "I am. We must replace the wand with proper dignity. We Ainu believe that without fetishes the gods will send evil and not favors. Perhaps you could arrange to have it delivered here. Now, if you gentlemen will excuse me."

Miss Miyabe escorted John and Ike out of the office. "I like tweed," she said softly, as she brushed the fabric on his shoulders. She gave his elbow a little squeeze, and her floral scent weakened John's knees. She bowed as if inviting him to join her on the floor.

John started to sweat; he had no idea of how to cope with a kimono.

Ike tugged John's elbow, "Come on, John. Miss Murata is waiting."

As they stepped onto the busy street, John felt as if he had been released from an enchanted forest, an enchanted time, visited by an improbable shaman who was a trickster. And all these people in this tired neighborhood, hurrying from here to there, had no idea that, on the twelfth floor of this concrete and glass building, primitive forces prevailed. John tried to rationalize, apply anthropological discipline to the experience.

"Ike, he knew about the wand before I told him. There is no way he could have known. Did you tell him?"

Ike shook his head.

"Then that whole thing happened, the barking of foxes, the hooting of owls, the menacing bits of iron, everything?"

"John, think beyond your books. Think Ainu."

And John thought; he thought of his conversation with the god of corn, and he thought of what Monster Bird would do with his, John's, flesh for depriving the gods of their fetish protection.

On the subway back to the university, Ike asked John what he thought of Kru's plan.

"He seems sincere and he sure can put on a good shaman show."

Ike looked at John for the longest time.

John became uncomfortable. It reminded him of the look Nursey gave him when she explained why she was leaving; it was Sue's look when John would not focus on his problems; it was Hirome's look when he failed to explain himself. This look was not a good omen.

"I guess 'good show' was a bad choice of words," John said, pleased to see Ike nod in agreement.

John wondered at how he could make such a ridiculous statement; he knew this shaman was real, as real as a Hopi elder dancing with rattlesnakes, as real as his unjustified expectation of Hirome's love.

"So, your firstborn will be a boy. Congratulations, Ike."

Having dinner, with Hirome, she caught him fondling the Dragon Lady's card.

She looked at him speculatively, "May I see the card, John?"

He shrugged. "I don't know what you're talking about."

"You cannot have it both ways, John. In fact, you may not have *it* either way."

John knew the *it* of which she spoke, and he wanted *it* both ways.

Hirome turned her attention to a large bowl of ramen. Her head bent down and met chopsticks laden with lengthy noodles. She sucked and slurped and the ramen raced into her puckered mouth.

John squirmed, he fidgeted, and he then he threw the card down on the table in front of her.

"Did you make a copy, John? A note of the telephone number?"

"No."

She picked the card up by one corner as one would a dirty diaper. "Tacky," she said. "But I believe it would appeal to ignorant tourists and businessmen."

She then tucked the card back in John's shirt pocket. "Shall we go for a walk in the park," she said, daintily dabbing the corners of her mouth.

The cashier and Hirome laughed as John tried to count out the correct change to pay their bill. In exasperation, he opened his coin purse and stammered, "Take what is rightfully yours."

"John, how did you meet your first wife?" asked Hirome, straightening her skirt as they settled in a gazebo. She seemed to constantly be tugging, pulling, smoothing, or fiddling with her skirt, all twelve inches of it.

"I really don't want to talk about it."

Hirome settled back, gently rocking, and little frosty breaths punctuated the silence.

The rolled-down windows flooded John's van with sweet desert air.

Freed from domineering parents, he would make his mark as an anthropologist.

The blacktop drew him through towering mesas into the morning sun, where shimmering purple light alternately semaphored "Fox & Son Hosiery," then "Glorious Academia."

Far ahead a stick figure elongated, divided, and stood head-to-head, warped by rising vapors.

"Where are you going?"

She kept walking.

John drove slowly beside her. "Are you lost?"

No response. If he knew some Navajo, perhaps they could communicate.

"Do you speak English?" he shouted.

"Are you offering me a ride or just shouting stupid questions?" she asked.

She craned her neck, peering into the car, taking in his twenty-two years of accumulated goods. "What's in those boxes?"

As simply as possible, John explained they held the "Great Books" that contained the thoughts of all the great thinkers. She looked at him. Admiration, thought John.

"Oh," she said. "Where are you going?"

"To graduate school, where I will study anthropology: the study of ancient man. I want to understand ancient Hopi culture. Then, perhaps someday, I'll be able to explain their history to their people."

"Oh," she said.

"But enough about me, what about you? Are you Navajo?"

When she smiled, her dark eyes sparkled. "Do I look Navajo? Just kidding. I know you'd need cranial measurements to answer that. I'm Hopi."

She leaned back and closed her eyes, the wind swishing her hair about her face.

"I'm tired of dancing with snakes and cornstalks and loaves of bread, of listening to endless transformation stories, of walking in hot summer dust and cold winter mud." She spoke softly, demanding attention. Her voice surrounded him like a seductive perfume. She went on to explain how she had done well in residential school, achieving a nurse's aide certificate, and how it would be foolish not to follow a career off the reservation.

"Not that I like white people," she said, giving his arm a little punch, "but that's where my future is."

John melted.

They married two months later.

Neither of their families attended. Only a few curious anthropology graduate school colleagues, perhaps in hope of gleaning some Hopi insight, joined the celebration. Their Justice of Peace stammered through the ceremony, scarcely hiding her disgust.

That night, Nursey—she wouldn't tell John her Hopi name and she refused to be called by her government roll name—disclosed an ancient Hopi honeymoon ritual, as promised.

They parked in front of a liquor store, and she pointed, "Honey, go in there and buy an expensive bottle of tequila."

"You come with me."

Nursey yelped, "I'm Indian!"

They drove beyond the lights and sounds of civilization to rarified desert air. Barefoot, they walked far from the road to a small clearing in the sage and cactus. Nursey uncoiled a horsehair rope, shaping a circle around a shallow depression.

John watched as she scoured the sand for twigs with hooked fingers, her butt swaying seductively.

Sitting on her spread-out skirt, they exchanged slugs of tequila, each swallow a communion with the Great Creator.

"John, unbraid my hair."

Her hair unfolded, a fragrant silky cascade of sensual pleasure, over his hands. He buried his face in its dreamy essence.

Nursey smiled and pulled away from him. Her voice came

to him as if from the stars. "When I was a little girl, I prayed to the moon. I prayed that I might become a great Hopi princess. Tonight, the moon will be my judge."

She gently pushed him back on her skirt and straddled him. She chanted as John watched the moon shadows of her breasts play on her belly. She rubbed pungent sage into his chest.

In the morning three rattlesnakes observed them from outside the horsehair rope circle.

Hirome looked at John, wide-eyed, "She appears to be a nice person."

"Yes, a nice person," John agreed, while memories bashed about in his brain like moths in granny's linen closet upon seeing light for the first time. Tequila nights, bare-ass swimming in desert pools, and of course, the climax: "You've been screwing the chairman of the philosophy department?!"

"It must have been difficult in an interracial marriage."

"I hadn't thought about that. I mean, yes, she was Hopi and I was white, but I always thought of myself as the underdog. She was so self-confident."

John blushed at his revelations.

As they departed the gazebo, Hirome asked, "John, do you still have the horsehair rope?"

Everyone had looked festive, shuttling along the street: scarves wrapped around throats, beanies with silly little bobbles, galoshes, rosy cheeks. Red and green bunting, and the occasional Christmas tree brightening store windows. And there had been lots of kaimono: Christmas in Sapporo.

But the day itself was one of the dreariest John had experienced in Japan. The museum director had sent him a Christmas greeting on a card featuring pressed seaweed. Ike and Hirome had been avoiding him for the past few days, not knowing how to approach their Christian friend at this time of year. Only his Pooh bear kept him company.

The snow came in windblown bursts, inverting his third ¥100 umbrella. And the once proud hollyhocks that had brightened the street to the subway station still stood, but faded, moldy and broken, the victims of winter, of aging, of late night urinations.

John entered his office, expecting, well, expecting nothing. But no, there was good old Ike and Hirome, the new Hirome.

"Like it?" she asked, as she twirled around the debris-strewn office.

John's glance took in her smart open-toed black shoes, then her long legs, flat tummy, perky breasts, slender neck and smiling face.

"The sundress, Mr. Fox."

"But it is winter!" protested Ike.

"Mr. Ainu, soon-to-be father of the glorious heir of the Deciduous Leaf Falling clan, take brightness where you can find it, for soon sleepless nights will cloud your days."

Hirome turned to John. "Your thoughts?"

"Parboil me in a fumarole, Ike, I need to cool down," John said, taking in her essence of freshly snapped sweet peas.

Ike tapped him on his shoulder. "John, we have company."

"Tell them to go away."

The glamorous Japanese woman standing in the doorway was a looker.

"Mother, what a surprise," said Hirome, backing away from John. "May I introduce my employer, Mr. Fox, and his assistant, Mr. Ike?"

John bowed—this boded well for the future Mrs. Fox. "Mrs. Murata, indeed what a pleasant surprise. We were just rehearsing what we think was a pre-encounter Ainu ritual honoring the elm tree."

Mommy was neither amused nor convinced.

Mrs. Murata spoke to her daughter, "Hirome, you are not to involve yourself in anything Ainu. No proper husband would associate with an Ainu sympathizer."

Having sorted out her daughter, Mrs. Murata turned to John.

"I would appreciate it if you restricted your contact with my daughter to her ESL instruction."

John muttered something that he hoped would be interpreted as compliance.

"Come, Hirome. I'm taking you home."

"Mrs. Murata, before you go, may I have a word with you?" said Ike in his best BBC English.

She turned, "Yes, Mr. Ike?"

"Madam, Ike is my Japanese name. In my village, in Ainu Land, I am Deciduous Leaf Falling. That is the name I would like to be known as all the time, but the Former Aborigines Protection Act of 1899 forced us all to be Japanese. That is changing now. Deciduous Leaf Falling is the name I would like to give my son. Mrs. Murata, can you see anything wrong with that?"

"Young man, I will not engage in your silly political debate. Now, Hirome, shall we go?"

"Mother, I am a twenty-three-year-old woman. You gave me a good education. Let me use it. We have much work to do here, so I will be home late. Please give father a hug for me. Goodbye."

Mrs. Murata seemed to shrink. If she could, she would have started this whole conversation differently, thought John. Hirome's mother took a furtive look around the office and turned to go.

John hopped to the door. "Mrs. Murata, please come by anytime. You're always welcome."

She rested her hand on his chest and looked hard into his eyes. Then with a smile, she said, "Thank you, Mr. Fox."

The door shut behind her.

The three stood staring at the cluttered room for a long time. Then, in as cheery a voice as John could muster, he asked, "Sodas?" Ike declined.

Hirome positioned herself in front of John, hands on hips, and asked, "John, what do you think of my mother?"

He stammered, "She seems a nice person, Hirome."

She placed her hand on his forehead and glanced at Ike.

"Look, he is blushing," she teased. Turning back to John she said, "I do not think I like the way you looked at my mother when she arrived. But you did make her smile and I cannot remember last time I saw her smile at a man, even my father."

"Hirome," John said, "I enjoy meeting your family. You're very lucky. They're lovely people."

John balanced the boiled egg on a spoon, waiting for it to cool. The toast was dangerously near full combustion as the blue propane flames licked its edges. All that remained was for him to make a blah cup of instant coffee, turn on the television for Sunday morning baseball and settle down to a rare moment alone.

He would shout, let yolk dribble onto his naked chest where it could mingle with toast crumbs, scratch his balls, pick his nose; in other words, have a non-Japanese, delicious morning.

The telephone interrupted his reverie.

"John, Aki here. Have you given up on moshi moshi?" Her voice was cool.

"Nice to hear from you, Aki. What can I do for you?"

Instantly, John felt guilty. Aki had shepherded him, with all his naivety and insecurity, from the overly protective womb of the *Golden Maru* through the bustling insanity of Tokyo to a manageable Sapporo. Of course, she had a right to feel ill done by. Had she fallen in love with him? Now he was ignoring her. They had had great moments, hot moments, and he could not deny he owed his vocabulary to her—all those words he hoped to use to woo Hirome. And Aki was one hell of a great sex coach.

"I would like to visit you. I have some papers that might prove interesting," Aki paused, "and it would be fun seeing you again."

John agreed to meet her the following weekend in Ōdōri Park, close to the clock tower, 2:00 pm sharp.

He poured a little Suntory whiskey into his morning coffee, something he rarely did, and collapsed in front of the television. The breakfast party was over.

John was wrapping his monthly delivery of contraband for shipment to his professor when Hirome came into his office.

"What are you doing, John?"

He clumsily stuffed a broken mustache lifter under his desk.

"I'm putting together a shipment of my manhole rubbings. The folks in New Mexico are quite taken with them."

John didn't go on to say that he had sent an essay, exploring his ideas as to the origin of the Sapporo manhole symbols to his New Mexico professor. He had not shared his theory with Ike and Hirome, partly because he knew they would ridicule him, and partly because he felt they didn't need to know everything, like the occasional Ainu artifact he included in the shipments.

Hirome sat on the good chair, crossed her little bee knees, and watched him move about, stealing glimpses of her beckoning legs.

"I translated an unaddressed letter, apparently by a Soviet bureaucrat, John. It is dated 1954, but no month."

John looked at her perfect face . . . the face he would trace with his fingertips as she slept, cuddled on his chest.

"It requires your attention, John."

He wondered if she would moan when they joined, or maybe she would bite, Ainu style.

"John, do you want to say something?"

"You mentioned a letter?"

"Oh, thank you for reminding me," she said, shaking her head.

John watched her ponytail swish back and forth and imagined her hair whipping him in cadence with their lovemaking.

Hirome read:

Comrade, it would appear the Ainu adversaries are concealing their attempts to forge an international front, with what they call a Congress of Northern Spiritual Leaders. The Ainu are superstitious and within their culture their shamans occupy the same esteemed rank as our glorious Soviet leaders. It is crucial we halt these activities. The Ainu must not have a place on the international stage. We must discredit their shamans.

All Ainu should be shipped to Japan where our new allies will ensure their retraining and forced assimilation. All historical records giving credence to international Ainu claims should either be destroyed or revised. Revisionism, as we have seen, is very effective.

A long silence. "John, are you all right?"

"Hirome, this could still be happening now."

"This is an old letter, John, from the 1950s. Do not worry."

He reached for her, but she backed away.

"John, maybe you should visit the Dragon Lady."

"Oh, John, you do look good," said Aki as she stood on her tiptoes and kissed his cheek, her hand slipping between his coat buttons, her Chanel No. 5 stirring fond memories.

Then, as if realizing she had trespassed, she stepped back, nervously twisting a rolled magazine, and said, "Gomen nasai."

Arm in arm they walked to the fountain in the center of the park. All about them, groups of youngsters, tethered like linked sausages to their teachers, pointed at foreigners and giggled.

These many-hued visitors smiled at the children, then returned to their incomprehensible Sapporo street maps.

John found it strange that these chain-ganged, uniformed bundles of pure energy seemed to ignore him. Could it be he had changed in appearance, manner, smell?

"Let's sit," Aki said.

John brushed snow off the park bench and they sat side by side, she resting her head on his shoulder, he wondering where this visit was leading.

"Well, Aki, how is the travel business?"

"Boring."

She scooted forward on the bench, straightened her spine, and looked him full in the face. "John, I want you to know I'm sorry about my little deceit but I did it to protect you. After our ski trip, I had time to think, and now I want to make amends. And I understand about Miss Murata."

She took his hands in hers. "When they found Matsuyama's body, his charred body, in the ruins of the bookshop, it was wrapped around a box of scrolls. I deceived you about how he died. But I also deceived you about the scrolls. My contacts through Betty allowed me to convince the authorities to give them to me to pass on to the next of kin. They were only too happy to get rid of the papers. They smelled of burned hair and flesh, and the fire was not under criminal investigation."

At first, John was thrilled; finally something substantive—the scrolls could be his ticket to academic fame and success. But then he was suspicious. Why was Aki doing this for him now? Was she setting him up? He had seen her mood changes from coy to romantic to officious to enraged. He'd learned of an international conspiracy to suppress Ainu aspirations. He'd learned of Ainu artifacts and treasure being traded for favors. And, somewhere in there, there was Betty.

"Let's have lunch, then go to my office. Ike will want to see these." They ate at a little hole-in-the-wall place John knew and sat at the counter. He didn't need Aki to translate the menu anymore; sashimi, tempura and bonito were all familiar to him now.

Their trays arrived with a colorful assortment of sashimi and little bowls of misoshiru soup, rice, shaved dry fish on greens, and yellowed radish. They ate in silence, and then John reminded her of her one-rice-grain challenge, and she laughed. He told her of his kendo lessons with the sensei and the tournament.

Aki listened thoughtfully. She showed him her chopsticks; they were made of silver. "These were my grandmother's. I use them for special occasions," Aki said, laying her hand on his.

He felt comfortable sitting here with this lovely woman, thinking of earlier times, hot times, and sad.

"John, I need to explain something so you will understand what..." she faltered, poured more green tea, and leaned back, her hand sliding up and down his wrist.

"John, I was not always like this. I was groomed, much like Murata-san, to be an educated woman, to marry well, to make my family proud. I excelled at the piano. But I rebelled and my parents could not restrain me. If there was something I should not do, I did it. And, I admit, I enjoyed much of it. I became hooked on the bad."

She turned to John, gave his wrist a hard squeeze, "John, I was a slut. I could not get enough; it could not be too rough."

The cheap cologne, the talcumed bruises, the split lip, her pachinko visits—now they made sense.

Aki looked at him, and he could see she sensed the chilling that ran through his veins.

"I used to be worse, John, a lot worse. Betty rescued me; she is a kind soul. She told me about you, how handsome you were, about your sweet naivety. I did fall in love with you but I could not give up the other. Then you left. It hurt, John. But I will get over it."

She kissed his cheek and looked sadly into his eyes. "Now, shall we go to your office and drop off these precious scrolls?"

John's office was chaotic. Miura was clucking her tongue as she swept up months of trash from the floor, dead leaves and cornstalks. Ike was trimming his growing beard, further adding to the litter.

"What is she doing here?" Aki gasped.

"Don't they make a nice couple? The Japanese should be proud to count them citizens."

At that moment, a very un-collegiate commotion erupted through John's office door.

"Ah-ha, blue-eyed kendo asshole, I got you by the balls now." It was the Korean mama-san. "You took my best girl, you stole my money. Now you pay, asshole."

Her Korean Meatball pushed into the office, and one of his Ping-Pong paddle fists smashed John in the face, catapulting him against the wall.

"What's this? Hot girl Miura now gaijin's maid?" Mama-san grabbed Miura by the hair and yanked her to her feet. Mama-san spat in Miura's face and Miura spat back, her tattooed face defying the intruders.

Meatball moved toward Miura, only to be tackled by Ike. With a laugh, Meatball threw Ike against the wall, knocking the small man out.

Turning to John, mama-san said, "You owe me twenty thousand yen, asshole, and I take girl back."

Meatball wrapped his arms around Miura, lifting her off the ground. She thrashed and screamed.

Mama-san looked at Miura's swollen belly. She laughed and put her hand out to John, "The money, scholar asshole."

Painfully he climbed to his feet, moved behind his desk, straightened up, and looking mama-san in the eye said, "Fuck off, you blood-sucking corn smut. If you're not out of here with that piece of whale shit in one minute I'll call campus security."

Meatball dropped Miura and stepped toward him.

John spat in his face and he roared, raising a fingerless hammy fist above his head. John could see it coming a mile away: a really mean concussion.

Fascinated by Meatball's clothes—a nice Hawaiian shirt, featuring two chrysanthemums, the Emperor's flower, each mounting a blubbery breast; a garland of pink plastic flowers and a tiny Panama hat too small for his head—John failed to duck. Surprisingly, it didn't seem to hurt, but he had lost the ability to focus.

"Oh, you should not have done that. Now it's my turn."

"Kill him," shouted mama-san, her skinny varicose-veined legs quaking.

As Meatball moved forward, Aki stepped in front of him and laid her hand on his chest. "No. I'll finish this."

She grabbed John and slammed him into the broken chair. Bending over him, she hissed, "I'm not one of your little bees, John. They die when they sting."

She turned to the hag, "Mama-san, enough. Take your boy home. Your business is finished here. John, pay the good lady her money."

A warm wind blew over Sapporo, releasing the forces of spring. The cottonwood trees outside John's window mobilized sap stored in their roots. Soon their buds would swell, initiating the production of cotton seeds that would snow on sunny summer Hokkaido.

John made his way down the path between soot-stained snow banks to his office. He almost felt normal: his arms and legs generally obeyed commands, but chirping and ringing sounds still visited his head. John pushed the door open and shuddered at its screech; that same sound had heralded the Korean mama-san and Meatball.

Ike rushed forward, solicitous.

"What's this?" John asked, pointing at a new chair.

"It is a gift from Kru and the Ainu Sovereignty Movement. We kept the broken chair. It is a potential god."

Ike laughed, "From what Miura said, I missed a great show while I was knocked out. Miura was impressed by your Aki. She thinks we should introduce her to Kru. They would make a great couple."

"Enough, Ike. Aki was just reacting to her tragic loss . . . me."

Ike plopped into the new chair. "This chair does not feel right, John. I am glad we are keeping the broken one."

He swiveled this way and that, rested his elbows on the desk, cradled his head in a Kru-like manner, and asked, "Did you pay the twenty thousand dollars?"

"Yen. We shouldn't have run out on our bill. And you got a good deal on that skinny bar girl. Quid pro quo."

Ike grimaced. Then John noticed.

"Where are your glasses?"

"The mama-san's Meatball must have been an optometrist. His knockout appears to have corrected my vision."

Slowly the door opened and Hirome cautiously peeked in.

Joy flooded John's body. It had been two weeks since he had seen her, fourteen long days of absence.

She wore a purple angora sweater that showed off her curves. Her white pleated skirt fell to her ankles.

At first, John was disappointed with the change in skirt style, but then he saw her purple-colored toenails, peeking out of black sandals, beckoning.

"What happened here?" Hirome asked. "New chair, dents in the wall, clean floor?"

"Hirome, it's an old Hopi custom to flip a sagging mattress to bring a new spring to your life," John said, distracted by the vision of purple little doggies nibbling on his calves.

"And this?" she asked, pointing at the box of singed scrolls.

"A gift from Miss Kawaguchi," Ike and John said together.

"Scented with the essence of one charred legless man," John added.

"Are we a team? Do we share the same goals? Do I need to translate this for you?" she said, shaking her tight little fist in John's face.

The thought of another face hit brought tears to his eyes.

"Ike, your people revel in flesh and fire. Why don't you select which scroll we should work on first?"

The university's library offered curatorial expertise and the paraphernalia for properly handling ancient scrolls, but it was overheated and the white knit gloves and gauze face masks— " . . . to protect these historic relics"—added to the team's discomfort.

Ike and Hirome stood on opposite sides of the long, velvet-covered table and slowly folded out the scroll.

The nearby library staff, pretending to be occupied with mundane tasks, twisted themselves into Gordian knots to catch a glimpse of the ancient parchment.

When fully unfolded, the scroll consisted of eight feet of rectangular panels, two feet wide. The charred edges were the manuscript's only damage. It was well preserved; no whirling dervish of pestilence had disturbed the kanjis' centuries-long sleep.

Hirome reverently tracked the lines of text, savoring the beauty of the characters.

John looked at her profile, her slightly bowed head, as she read down each line. He thought she should wear her hair up, exposing that beautiful neck. She looked up at him, briefly rested her forehead on her hands, sighed, took a deep breath and, with her eyes filling with tears, she started the translation.

> I am Shiro, son of Kawai.
> Tomorrow I burn.
> Christian God my soul.
> Please, my last testament.
> Written on the eve of my crucifixion
> 22 September 1670.
> I blacksmith.
> I Wise Owl.
> My village Shizunai.
> Ainu Unacharo first friend.
> He Clever Fox.
> We shot blunt arrows at sacred bear.
> We forge friendship dagger.
> Father say Ainu Christian friend.
> Tokugawa Shogunate say Ainu dogs.
> Ainu say Yezo and islands beyond, Ainu Land
> Shogunate say no Ainu Land, Beast Land.
> Yezo Ainu trade with northern brothers.
> Tokugawa Shogunate close Ainu trade.
> Tokugawa Shogunate deny Ainu iron.
> Shogun samurai rape, murder, enslave Ainu.
> Samurai burn forests for settlers.
> Samurai kill deer and waterfowl.
> Ainu lose Land Spirit.
> Ainu starve.
> Settler rapes Unacharo's sister.
> Samurai kill her for impurity.
> Unacharo protests.
> Beaten, Fox flees.

Unacharo joins Samkusaynu's forces.
Samkusaynu victorious over Shogunate.
Samkusaynu murdered at peace talks.
Shogun samurai crucify Japanese Christians.
Now I die.
My age twenty-seven.
Sayonara.

Stunned silence, then Ike laid his hand on the scroll. He looked up, tears in his eyes. "There will be revenge. The world will know this martyr."

He went to bunch up the panels, but an apoplectic librarian raced over, pushing Ike away, and then she and Hirome carefully refolded the scroll.

John stared at the librarian's feet. She had lost her slippers in the scuffle. Each of her toes occupied its own little tube. He was about to ask her how she managed to put those socks on when he noticed another square of parchment lying on the floor.

"What's this?" he asked.

Hirome picked it up and placed it carefully on the table. Slowly, she translated:

I, Unacharo, killed Owl.
My first friend.
A poisoned arrow saved him from fire.
Maple spirit whirls, lands, gods wait.
Owl sings, fox barks, aconite arrow stings.
Shiro now Ainu god.
The gods have spoken.

Drained, the scroll properly folded, the threesome returned to John's office. Ike could not settle; his hands alternately explored his filling beard, tugged on his braided birch bark belt and patted his happi coat, decorated with Ainu symbols.

John imagined Hirome moving in and out of the firelight, shadows caressing her bare legs, as the short canvas robe yielded to her form and movement. She glided about him as he sipped on his bowl of beer. She stood near, he untied her birch bark belt and her robe fell open. She yielded to him as demanded by the gods.

Hirome jabbed his arm. "John, Ike is talking. Pay attention."

But Ike had stopped talking. His eyes lids flickered and little animal-like barks and hoots rolled from his curled lips. A sheepish look came over his face as opened his eyes and collected his thoughts.

"We must translate all the scrolls and establish their authenticity. Then we can prepare a campaign—the press, television, pamphlets. These scrolls will help us advance the Ainu cause, our nationhood, our Ainu Land. In Japan, in Russia."

John thought how envious his anthropology colleagues would be, the prestige these discoveries would bring. But somehow the importance of his PhD paled in the light Ike's fervor.

"Let's contact Kru. He'll know what to do and he has the contacts to help," John suggested.

Ike looked skeptical.

"We can trust him, Ike," John said. "He's one powerful Ainu."

"How do you know Kru is trustworthy?" Hirome asked. "From what you and Ike told me, he might use the scrolls for his own benefit."

She went over to Ivan's papers, "In the 1954 letter, the Party official advises the Politburo that Ainu shaman can cause them grief. For the security of the Soviet Union, they needed to be discredited or neutralized."

"I think Kru has been compromised. He is an Ainu shaman, but he is also a Japanese businessman. I don't trust him," Ike said.

"That letter is from a long time ago," said John. "Kru helped me with my willow wand problem and he offered to support your project, Ike. I say we go to him."

Ike tugged on his full Ainu beard. "John, conspiracies can last a long time. I propose a test. Let us go to where you stole the willow wand. Let us see if Kru did replace it as promised. If your wand is there, I am willing to share the scrolls and the other papers with Kru. If it is not there, I will demand an explanation from the shaman."

John plugged his transit pass into the turnstile, passed through the gate and, with a flourish, retrieved the pass on the other side. Hirome and Ike did not seem impressed by his adeptness. These little victories added to his resistance to catching United 762 back to a life of de-smutting corn.

He'd hoped the train would be crowded and he'd be forced to be squished into Hirome, but no such luck.

In the evening darkness, John had difficulty finding the rural path but soon they reached the orchard. He flashed his light about the sacred spot.

"See, I was right. Kru's an honest shaman. Now let's go have some cold soba and hot sake. This place gives me the willies."

Ike moved around the perimeter of the willow wands. A gusty wind whipped the birch branches, dancing shadows over him: now an Ike without a head, now a torso-less Ike, now no Ike. John had no trouble seeing him as Ainu.

"John, can you remember which one you borrowed?"

John indicated the one in front of him.

"John, this one is different from the others. It is freshly carved."

"Well," John replied, "that could mean anything."

Hirome and Ike looked at him.

"I guess if this isn't the one I stole, then it hasn't been returned, it's been replaced."

Hirome traced some patterns in the dirt with a stick. Ike chewed on a piece of dried grass.

"You're wondering why the switch, when it would be so much simpler to just replace the original?"

His two friends waited under the barren fruit trees for John to figure it out.

"You know," said John, "the older original may be more valuable than its replacement. I think we need to have a discussion with Kru."

"That is a good idea," Ike and Hirome chorused.

John felt nine feet tall.

"John, what is willies?"

On the train back to Sapporo Station, the threesome first chatted and then slipped into their own thoughts. The clicketing of the train's iron wheels on the rails lulled John into a dreamy sleep.

"John, come to me," Hirome called from deep in the earth.

Her tan elm bark robe had fallen open and fox muzzled her softness. As she ran her fingers through fox's silky pelt, she turned to a nearby branch, "Sing to me, owl, as I await my lover."

John heard soft hooting and licking sounds coming from a cave. As he journeyed to the center of the world, his way was illumed by dark creatures waiting to be released. Often his branches dislodged sleeping animals and herbs. These he attended as the waiting conception need be perfect and all gods supportive.

A flying squirrel arrested his progress. "You bring us wood, now we can have a fire as only cooked foods reach our gods."

Patiently, John tolerated the crude twisting and breaking of his lower limbs. The bitter smoke of burned deer hair and hooves swirled about him. Then each of his leaves was gently rubbed, and the gods blessed his journey.

He came upon a grotto, its moist walls supporting stands of delicate maidenhair fern and dark green liverworts. In its center, diamonds dropped from above, each one splashing in a crystal pool. Supine on the lip of this pond was the goddess Hirome. Hovering about her were the craving spirits of every conceivable thing.

John gently brushed her bangs from her face, and the ocean receded from its shores exposing the marine riches that would soon be theirs: the beguiling octopus, the majestic whale, herring, kelp, sea urchins. He looked into her eyes and the moon displayed its phases and planets wove across the starlit sky. Her mouth opened and out poured song, poetry, coarse words, and a baby's cry.

She beckoned him with the hope of a perfect world. Her body yielded to John's, his every leaf kissed and aroused her. Their passion shook the earth. Lightning launched from his every branch, and shrill winds and deep thunder answered from her arching body. Heaven separated from Earth, the living from the dead, hope from despair. The Universe, Ainu Land, was born.

And Bear was pleased.

John called a meeting to discuss progress on his thesis, the politics surrounding the discovery of the scrolls and the translation of the Russian papers, topics now melded into one.

He sat on the broken chair but at his desk. Ike enjoyed the new chair, which he considered his right, given he was the one who had been knocked out. And Hirome, as usual, sat on the floor wrestling with her skirts and chewing on her writing utensils and driving John nuts.

"From what Hirome tells me, the other scrolls, while providing valuable insight into the lives of the Ainu and Japanese residents of Hokkaido during the seventeenth century, have little of political interest. I suggest we turn these scrolls over to the museum archives for safe keeping."

"John, I am sorry, but the university has not earned Ainu respect. Our ancestors were severely insulted by the University of Hokkaido anthropologists. The scrolls belong to the Ainu and, until we can properly house them, I suggest they be put in the care of Dr. Kawasaki. We hold her in high esteem."

Briefly, John felt the scrolls were his; a man died trying to save the scrolls for him. But wisdom dictated they were a national treasure. The question was, which nation—Japan or Ainu Land?

"Ike, that's a great idea. Now let's discuss the big picture, my thesis. So, what do we know?" John asked, noting his holed socks kept slipping out of his slippers.

Ike and Hirome looked at him.

That look again, he thought. When would they stop looking at him like disappointed parents? He was potty trained, after all.

"Ike, you first."

Ike was like a racehorse, realizing the race had started and he had not. "John, thank you for this opportunity. Well, we have been working for over seven months. We have established the importance of bears to aboriginal cultures everywhere, but particularly in Ainu Land. We have compared ethno-anthropomorphisms, establishing the value of these bears as a valuable cultural marker, comparable to obsidian knife-chippings."

John looked at the hole in his sock. No matter how much he trimmed his toenails, the holes keep growing.

Ike coughed. "John, I am finished."

"Yes, well done, Ike. Hirome, your turn."

She stood, did a little curtsy and, while fidgeting with the hem of her skirt, spoke. "Well, I have had an almost job with you, John. I say 'almost' because my payment is only ESL credits. I have sleuthed through mountains of moldy papers, extracting valuable information for your dissertation and, more importantly, the promise of an Ainu Land. Working with you has enriched my vocabulary. I have completed my third year of instruction in French, Mexican and American cooking. But my greatest achievement, after translating Russian texts, is beating you in kendo."

Silence settled over the office while John sought solace from the Ainu religion. *Thank you, slipper god, for cover-up.*

Hirome stomped her foot in exasperation, "John, please be with us. Give us guidance."

John carefully arranged his little army of bears, from largest to smallest, along the front of his desk. Too bad Pooh bear isn't here, he thought.

"Well, Hirome, Ike, I continue to be an almost PhD. We've accumulated a lot of notes and some neat facts. I've compared and contrasted designs and artwork. I've tried to understand the meaning of Ainu customs and artifacts, although I admit the mustache lifter has me flummoxed. I guess we will get to where we are going. There will a thesis someday. There has to be. But now I'm tired."

Ike walked behind John and kneaded his shoulders. "John, do not despair. You have accomplished some things. Look at me. I found the love of my life and got married, thanks to you. I will have a son. And because of your initiative, important people are going to worry about Ainu power and claims. And think of all the Sapporo barflies who have met a real American due to your alcoholic persistence. You have a record to be proud of."

They took a taxi to the warehouse district to meet with Kru.

"This does not seem to be a very nice place," Hirome said, peering out the taxi window at the tired, post-war relics. "Ike, are there Ainu gods here?"

"You will see," he responded cryptically.

The office door opened silently. There, sitting at the reception desk, buffing her fingernails, was John's fantasy woman of the dangling cherries. The Dragon Lady, Miss Miyabe, was dressed in a deep blue cheongsam dress, reminding John of Miss Li and the blind domino player, Koro; his first Ainu encounter.

"Miss Miyabe, nice to see you. We have an appointment to see Mr. Kru."

"Well, Mr. Fox, we wouldn't want to disappoint Mr. Kru, would we? I'll let him know you are here."

As she passed him, her stiletto heel came down on his foot. "Gomen nasai," she said with a polite bow.

John grimaced, tears stinging his eyes, and nodded. "It's nothing."

"Ouch. That must have hurt, John," said Hirome.

John thought she could show more concern.

The Dragon Lady returned and bowed, "Mr. Fox, Mr. Kru will see you and Mr. Ike now. Perhaps your assistant would like to wait here?"

"Miss Miyabe, Miss Murata translated old Japanese and Russian documents important to our business with Mr. Kru. I'm certain he'd want to hear her impressions first-hand."

The Dragon Lady responded with a chilly, "Of course."

"Welcome, my Ainu scholars," Kru greeted them, grinning. "I'm particularly pleased to meet you, Miss Murata. I understand you are making valuable translations. If we had a hundred Japanese like you supporting us, I would say Ainu victory was assured."

John stared at Kru, who was dressed today in a dark blue kimono, his hair shorter and grayer than he remembered; he could have been the Emperor's secretary.

"Mr. Fox, this afternoon I meet with executives of All Nippon Steel. My attire will flatter their nationalism and distract them from my Ainu-ness." Kru sounded like a cantering horse as he walked to the door on two-inch high wooden clogs. He asked Miss Miyabe to bring tea.

The shaman turned to his visitors. "I have an announcement to make. Since our last meeting, I have decided to shed the shallow Japanese skin I hide in. I have challenged the leading Hokkaido kendo fighter to a demonstration match. Just as the Ainu did in olden days, we will show the Japanese we are a force to be contended with. Nothing will sway us away from our dream: an independent Ainu Land. And it is going to be on national television."

With this, he sliced the air with an imaginary sword. Give him a plumed hat, and he could be Porthos, thought John.

Ike shook his head in disbelief. "You tell us to keep a low profile and now you go for theatrics. How do you know he will accept?"

"He already has. Bushido dictated he accept the challenge. Besides, he is quite open-minded . . . for a Japanese."

"This afternoon you kowtow to businessmen, wearing classic Japanese attire," said Ike. "Next you will be on national television flaunting the traditionalists."

A smooth bare arm reached around John and balanced a teacup on the arm of his chair. Her smell, freshly broken pumpkin, distracted him. On his saucer rested a card. He picked it up, turned it over and read, "Fuck you."

John looked up to see Hirome glaring at him and, startled, he spilled the tea onto his lap.

"Well Mr. Fox, you must be the ladies' man. Even my wealthiest clients get only one card."

John's thighs burned from his boiling-tea-soaked pants, his right foot throbbed and the girl of his dreams was planning his assassination. He gave a men-will-be-men-ha-ha shrug in Kru's direction.

"Well, Mr. Fox, the nature of this visit?"

"We've been to Konbu Spa. We noticed that the willow wand I sent you was not the one you placed at the orchard."

"Yes, that is correct. I switched the orchard willow wand. I would never displease our gods but, Mr. Fox, you did. It was easy to appease them. My Ainu brother, Tukkaram—yes, Mr. Ike, I have a pure Ainu brother—whittled an appropriate substitute that I sanctified. The original, I gave to a powerful petroleum executive. A sound investment for our people, Mr. Ike."

As they left, Hirome fished the card out of John's shirt pocket. She whispered, "The cherries have been plucked."

The ancient, granite-walled building that housed John's office was greasy, rain-streaked and moss infected. As he always did, he half expected to find rakes and shovels and garden snakes rather than a repository of valuable books and precious papers and sacred carved bears.

If he had hoped the inhabitants of the office would cheer him up, he was disappointed. Hirome's skirt remained frustratingly long, having reversed autumn's exquisite journey from calf to high thigh.

Ike, standing behind his desk, stuffed random items into a pillowcase. He looked shattered. "John, Miura is in labor. It is too early. I must go to my village. Please come with me."

"Ike, I've some first aid training," Hirome said. "Let me come too. I can help if needed."

"Hirome, you can't come," John interrupted. "The Ainu know me as a friend, one who provides them with resources regarding their earlier culture. They trust me to keep their secrets. If you come, they'll think I've betrayed them. It'll all be over."

"Betrayed, how betrayed?" she asked, giving John a look of disapproval.

He feared they were about to get the we-are-a-team lecture.

"John, Ike—this is about Miura, about her well-being."

Hirome seemed daunted by the narrow path that led to the village. With exaggeration, she avoided roots and holes and puddles and, to John's delight, she clung tight to his arm. Finally, their flashlights probed the village. They crossed the muddied central yard to the gathering house.

"I will go in first," said Ike. "You two wait here."

Standing next to the dripping thatch roof, listening to incomprehensible murmurings coming from within, John felt overwhelmed.

"Hirome," he whispered, "Perhaps we don't belong here. We're surrounded by good people who should hate us. Maybe we should go."

Hirome squeezed his hand and pulled him toward the door. Inside, they could hear soft moaning. The door opened noisily, but no one paid any attention.

It was darker and smokier than John remembered. There by the east window knelt Miura, her hands above her head pulling on a rope. An ancient woman gently rubbed her back as an elder supplicated the gods of fire, birth and entrances for an easy birth.

John and Hirome crouched against the wall, far from the laboring mother and low-burning fire. Miura's groans swirled about the room, pleading with all conceivable gods for deliverance. But the gods refused her.

Hirome released her grip on John's hand and made her way through the shadows to Miura's side. Kneeling she lifted her hand to wipe sweat from woman's face, but Miura hissed, "Get away!"

Stunned, Hirome backed into a dark corner. John went to her, tried to put his arm around her, but she shook him off.

For hours Miura moaned, swaying in the smoky light. Sweat poured down her face, soaking her clothes. Occasionally, her attendant gave her a drink and whispered in her ear. Miura's agony increased; her cries were gut-wrenching.

Outside they heard muttering by concerned villagers, with one authoritative, deep voice prevailing.

Hirome could take it no longer. "*Pssst*, Ike, where are you? We need a doctor," she whispered.

Ike stepped from the shadows, "Hirome, it is in the hands of the gods."

She stood, ignored Ike and went towards Miura, who used her last strength to pull herself upright from her slouched position. She faced Hirome, her eyes cloudy and unseeing, her mouth pulled into a grimace, made all the more hideous by the Ainu tattoo.

The firelight silhouetted her ponderous belly. On the ground, between her widely splayed legs, a puddle grew. Miura drew in a great breath and pushed. The midwife lifted Miura's robe, exposing the top of a hairy head. Another deep breath.

"*Oooooh*, little Ainu boy, welcome."

A deft cut, a smart smack and the future of Ainu Land lay at his mother's breast. The little bar girl had launched the Deciduous Leaf Falling clan.

Miura beckoned to Hirome, who approached and knelt, crying, beside the mother and child. Miura reached out and patted her gently on the back.

John stepped outside to thank whatever gods were available. There, crouched in an early spring shower, under the eastern window, was a lump of a human, moaning. Standing above Tukkaram and supporting his enormous head was his older brother, the shaman, Kru.

He helped his brother enter the gathering house, where the shaman presented him with the afterbirth. Tukkaram swayed and moaned, smelling and tasting the afterbirth. His head collapsed to one side; drool ran down his cheek.

Then, in a remarkably deep, clear voice, he declared, "The White Swan has given rebirth to the Ainu people. She will return to heaven when the cherry trees blossom."

The shaman lifted the child and pointed to a hole in the baby's earlobe. With a shaky voice, Kru declared, "This is a clear sign that this son bears the spirit of an Ainu ancestor, maybe the great warrior, Samkusaynu."

He bowed his head to the baby, welcoming the ancestor, "Please accept our humble hospitality and share with us your strength and wisdom."

The villagers crowded into the gathering house. They strutted around the rejuvenated fire, palmed the many gods and offered them beer; the men were fresh with the women and the children played with a long-lost savagery.

The shaman stood and the crowd became silent. He raised his arms and beckoned all the forces that dwelled in his aura.

"Witness this new beginning. Be not humble, but give these people strength with love, victory with compassion, and peace with rest."

A great roar erupted in the room, with the sounds of the animals of the earth and sky and water, the howling of winds and the cracking of branches. The fire flashed and the water turned to beer.

One hand resting on Miura's shoulder, Kru raised his arm in a salute, "Great gods-of-the-gods, protect this woman, for she has returned Ainu Land to us. Now, let us celebrate."

The ladies of the village brought out a platter of smoked salmon and a cask of beer. John and Hirome mimicked the villagers by flicking drops of beer and pieces of fish on the fire, to be devoured by protective gods.

With the first streaks of dawn in the eastern sky, Hirome and John left the village. They were a little drunk, very dirty, and pleased for their adopted tribe. John truly believed this day marked a new beginning for the oppressed Ainu and, perhaps, for him and Hirome.

Back at the office, she collapsed on the floor. "John, please make me a cup of tea." Tear streaks tracked through the dirt and soot on her face. She smelled of elm smoke and beer.

John wanted her. John wanted to lick her face clean, untangle twigs from her hair.

She wanted to talk. "I am so envious of Miura, her embracing the Ainu life, lifting herself out of ignorance to a place of pride. Giving birth must be difficult, but her own deliverance would have been no less difficult. I wish her well; her journey will be difficult."

She sighed, "Why must we Japanese put these people down, treat them like animals? I thought we were civilized."

John was about to give a speech about the inevitable conflict that exists between co-habiting races but thought better of it.

Hirome smiled at him as if to say, thank you, John.

He brought her tea, which she took and then reached up and grasped his hand.

"Sit with me."

John squatted, trying to think what to say.

"Don't say anything, John."

He didn't and it felt right.

She peered into his eyes and John wondered if he had a condom in the office. Then he remembered Lulu's gifts. The sea creatures would be a little harsh, maybe the candy bar condom?

"John, breathe."

They shared her tea and she leaned her head on his shoulder.

"I am so tired," she said, wiggling around, trying to get comfortable. As she drifted off, she muttered, "What color are your eyes, John?"

He extracted his handkerchief with the idea of cleaning a smudge from her forehead and then thought better of it. He felt cramped but didn't dare move for fear of awakening her. This slight creature, who had battered him mercilessly in the kendo tournament, now seemed so vulnerable. He fell asleep.

The pounding on the door stopped and a harsh voice demanded, "Police, open the door, gaijin, or we'll open it for you."
    John pushed Hirome into the corner and threw a blanket over her.
    "Stay still," he whispered.
    "One minute, officer," John said as he pulled on his sweater, popped a toothbrush in his mouth, and unlatched the door.
    Two men brushed past him and surveyed the room.
    "Where is she?"
    "I don't know what you're talking about. May I put my pants on, officer?"
    A fist blurred into John's face and he felt the toothbrush puncture his cheek. Another fist, a crack, but no pain. He drifted from wall to floor, from fist to boot, from ping to pong.
    This could not go on. Slowly the clenched hand arched toward John's ear. He ducked, caught the passing elbow, and shoved the man into the bathroom. He knew they wanted Little Boy. He had to attack. John grabbed the potty and smashed it into the policeman's face; pee sloshed over them.
    Damn, he'd have to get Tveit's turtleneck sweater cleaned.

A giggle rescued John. He looked down and realized he had peed his pants.

Hirome hopped up and pulled a shaky John into a standing position. Then on tiptoes, she gave him a little kiss just as Ike came in with a fist full of cigars.

"Ike, meet my new gaijin boyfriend."

They camped on the floor, in the middle of the office; old cornstalks standing in for the thatched gathering house and John's carved bears the villagers.

They, the three wise gods, smoked cigars and drank Sapporo beer from oversized tins. The more they celebrated, the more somber they became. The smoke-filled room blurred their vision and brought tears to their eyes. What future awaited the new Deciduous Leaf Falling boy?

John got off the subway at the North 24th Street Station and made his way through a half-hearted Little Ginza. A few bar girls handed him promotion sheets—the prices were reasonable—and a smartly dressed lady pressed a pack of tissues, advertising God-knows-what, into his hand. This gift would join a growing collection at his office.

The parking lot of the North Sapporo High School was jammed with media vans sprouting antennae. Technicians were dragging communication cables into the school gym. A crowd of gawking onlookers pressed toward the school. Hawkers peddled T-shirts portraying a hairy Ainu and a noble samurai.

John had expected some media involvement, but not this carnival. As he pressed to the side door, he spotted Hirome walking briskly to join him.

"Hirome, Ike will be glad you came," he said.

She took his arm as they entered the gym through the side door. A group of his teammates were just inside the door and John could see they were impressed; he preened. Hirome stepped away and John joined his kendo club.

The west side of the gym was roped off for the media. Six television cameras with their technicians and announcers rehearsed for the coming bout. John recognized the NHK TV weatherman.

The main door to the gym opened and about a hundred fans were ushered in. This was a biased crowd—no Ainu were among them. Ushers led them to bleachers along the east wall, opposite the media section. The crowd burbled with anticipation. Their chatter ended abruptly and, as a group, their eyes turned to the main door, where a small group of Ainu filed into the brightly lit gym. Four elders, one leading the grotesque-headed Tukkaram, and Ike, carrying the broken chair from their office. John couldn't see Kru. The Ainu group moved to the south side of the gym, and knelt in a row, facing the kendo club members.

The sensei entered the gym and moved to the center of the floor. His face glowed; he exuded confidence and privilege, moving gracefully. The crowd cheered and applauded.

Then murmurs, tinged with contempt, went up from the kendo club and onlookers as Kru made his entrance. A glare from the samurai sensei, directed at the kendo club side, demanded their silence, followed by the downcasting of shamed eyes. Unlike John's instructor, who was dressed in traditional kendo garb, Kru wore a white, woven-bark Ainu robe, trimmed with a red brocade pattern. The shaman's bark headband bore a carved, glaring bear face.

Shouts and hisses filled the gym, which was suddenly plunged into darkness, and angry grumblings from the TV crews, as they realized their equipment was useless with the power blackout. Then fans of green and red light played across the large space, coming from the emergency spotlights and exit signs lining the gym walls.

The NHK TV weatherman moved to the center of the floor, between the two combatants, and called for quiet. Slowly, silence prevailed, with only the brief, desperate whispering from the frustrated cameramen in the media section.

A spotlight lit the announcer. He looked about to assure all was in order. "Ladies and Gentlemen, we are here to witness a contest unique in our times. One of our leading kendo masters has been challenged by an Ainu . . ." Hisses and stomping from the bleachers interrupted the announcement.

The announcer held up his hand, "Please, respect this occasion. The kendo contest you are about to see will be conducted not with bamboo but with steel, steel swords and daggers. The fight will be over when the first blood has been drawn. The winning prize is pride. Gentlemen."

Kru took his position facing north. On the broken chair from John's office rested an ancient mustache lifter and a small willow wand. The shaman stood still, his head bowed. His feet were solid to the floor, with no apparent instep.

The sensei faced him, then pulled a dagger from his robes and withdrew his sword, placing them on the floor in front of him; Kru did the same. It was time for the seconds to inspect the weapons.

The instructor turned and gestured to John, who thought he'd collapse, as tension like a thunderstorm rolled over him.

"Fox-san," whispered his instructor.

John straightened up, took a slow deep breath, "Hai, sensei?"

His sensei nodded toward Kru and down to the weapons on the floor.

Kru turned and faced the row of kneeling Ainu, saying nothing. Ike stood and walked across the floor to stand beside John, who looked his translator, his friend, in the eye and saw pride, and what might have been a flicker of compassion.

John looked down on a shiny ancient sword that he knew had been buried near Konbu Spa, but he had no idea for how long. The Japanese had long denied the Ainu iron and they were never permitted to possess weapons other than their miniature bows and salmon spears. The ancient dagger bore engravings of an owl and a fox.

After viewing the weapons, Ike and John conferred.

"Fox-san, are you satisfied?"

John nodded and stuttered, "*Daijobu*."

They bowed to the fighters and returned to their places.

Kru placed his headband on the broken chair and gave John a supporting smile.

The kendo instructor bowed deeply to Kru, who in turn rubbed his palms together and then rubbed his cheeks, and bowed to his opponent.

Kru and John's instructor picked up their weapons, secreting the daggers away in the folds of their robes, and then firmly held their swords with both hands.

Kru, elbows bent, cocked his sword above and slightly to the right of his head.

The sensei's stance was as he had taught John: sword pointing straight ahead, its tip aimed at the opponent's throat. With a shudder, John visualized Kru, eyes glazing over, a sword through his neck, his sword clattering harmlessly to the floor.

The combatants circled each other, feet glided smoothly across the wood. They appeared to levitate. Their bodies were erect, with the gut their centers of gravity—the gut, the source of strength. They turned in, eyes locked, and approached each other. A feint, a withdrawal, another feint, another withdrawal, and then a clash. One moment they were frozen statues and the next flying banshees. Mid-air, swords crossed, they collided, landed and stepped back with slight bows, as the ringing of the swords continued. They circled, seeking weaknesses, their swords reflecting now red, now green. Another clash, another feint, and another.

The onlookers cheered and booed. The din became overwhelming. Then a chill settled over the scene and, for John, the noise was smothered. An owl hooted, twigs snapped, a brook tinkled. The wind blew through an ancient deciduous forest, a chorus to the unfolding drama, rattled leaves, brushed cheeks, bent grass. Chants to un-listening gods; shadows waxed and waned through flickering firelight.

Kru's sword swished, then halted, its edge touching the sensei's head. They parted, and the instructor bowed deeply. A shadow squatted, shifting dead fire ashes through grotesquely elongated fingers. And Kru drew his dagger from his robe. Now they sparred, swords held in one hand, daggers in the other. Ike's baby slid from its mother's womb. The ugly man rolled the afterbirth in the still warm ashes from the central fire. An oak seed germinated in a pavement crack. Kru's dagger slashed his opponent's arm. On the gym floor, a pool of blood.

Kru drew his dagger across his forearm, stepped forward, and let his blood join that of the samurai sensei.

Two club members brought bandages to the center of the gym and bound the men's cuts.

The sensei bowed. Kru palmed.

On a nod from his instructor, John stepped forward and presented Kru with a gift wrapped in the club's scarf. He looked John in the eye, untied the cloth and took out a piece of raw konbu: the same plant the Ainu had presented the emperor over two hundred years ago.

Ike crossed the floor, knelt on one knee, and presented the kendo instructor a souvenir bear wearing a banner proclaiming, "Ainu Land."

The sensei laughed—John had never heard him laugh before—and, with tears running down his cheeks, he turned and departed.

The crowd and media folk were stunned. The contest was over, and they tried to understand what they had witnessed. Silently, they left.

As they walked away from the gym, Hirome subdued and John still unable to speak, he noticed spring's offering of a new generation of hollyhocks. This heartened him and he felt he could breathe again.

Hirome slipped her arm through his and their strides found cadence. "John, let me buy you a drink."

They entered a soba shop to be greeted by a welcoming chorus of nasal, "*Irasshaimase!*" A server approached their table, looked askance at the broken chair, then took their order: cold sake and hot soba.

"This should restore you," Hirome said.

She put a little coarse salt on the lip of his cedar box of sake and then lifted hers. "Kampai."

"Kampai, Hirome."

They ate and drank in a silence broken only by Hirome's delightful slurping sounds.

"Hirome, why did Ike bring that broken chair?"

"He told me our broken chair god might be unique. He was unaware of such a god, but then, in Ainu Land, there are many gods. In my opinion, the broken chair is better than the cornstalks and maple leaf gods. I burned them. Please pour me another sake, John."

"Marry me, Hirome."

"John, do you mean it?"

John replayed his proposal to Nursey. That hadn't worked. Would this be same? He should be cautious, but Hirome—he couldn't lose Hirome.

"John, here is my heart. Take it," she said, holding her cupped hands out to him.

He froze.

Hirome dropped her hands, "John, please take me to your place, I am a little drunk and I do not want my mother to see me like this."

Back at John's boarding house, Hirome stumbled into his room. "Do you have anything to drink, John?"

"Hirome, I don't think you should drink anymore. You look a little green. Are you all right?"

She looked at him, put her hand over her mouth, and bolted for the bathroom.

John could hear her retching. Resigned and relieved, he straightened up the bed and made himself a nest on the couch.
I hope she forgets this. How could I not have accepted her heart?
A shaky Hirome returned and apologized, "John, I am so ashamed. Please forgive me. Could I lie down, just for a little bit?" She climbed on the bed and John pulled a blanket over her. She looked so vulnerable, so desirable. He wondered if they could have a future together. In many ways, she was not that different from Nursey, and that marriage failed. He liked to think it had been inevitable that they would break up, considering the racial differences. But he knew it was his inability to relate to Nursey as a mature adult, to see her as a woman and not a trophy, his kachina doll. Looking at the sleeping Hirome, he believed he was a different man now, that he could be the partner his wife would deserve. He put on Vivaldi's *Four Seasons*, cocooned himself on the couch and dreamed.

John stripped to his shorts and crawled under the sheets. This sophisticated, unattainable woman went into the bathroom. He could see her reflection in the mirror. She slipped off her jeans and shirt. She wasn't wearing a bra. Turning this way and that, she inspected her body. She cupped her breasts, giving them little wiggles. She put her hand between her legs and looked at its mirrored image, maybe saying goodbye, and turned off the light.
"*Mr. Fox, to quote an aspiring anthropologist, 'Take what is rightfully yours.'*"
Her molecules simmered like those of a roasting marshmallow pivoting between melting sweetness and flaming passion.
John pushed her closer to the flame . . .

The next morning, he awoke to find Hirome gone. He dressed and went to the Egg Coffee Shop for breakfast. It was early and there were only a few patrons sitting at the counter. He took a table near the front window and ordered breakfast: a hard-boiled egg, toast and coffee. While waiting, he scanned the morning papers.

There were some pictures of the kendo match, but he would have to get Ike to translate the text for him.

He finished breakfast and went to his office, where he found Ike.

"Good morning, John," said Ike. "I assumed you would want me to translate the published reports on last night's spectacle."

Ike put the newspapers on John's desk and pulled his chair up next to John's.

"Here is the *Hokkaido Shimbun*'s headline: 'Leading Hokkaido Samurai Draws Ainu Blood' and in the *Nikkei Shimbun*: 'Ainu Disgrace Kendo Tradition'. And John, our esteemed *Tokyo Shimbun* leads off with 'Ainu No Match for Revered Sensei.'"

John looked at the accompanying photographs; none were complimentary of Kru or his Ainu supporters.

"Ike, is this the publicity Kru was seeking? It seems damaging to me."

"John, a lot of people will read these reports and reject the clear bigotry. Basically, I believe that most Japanese are good people. Here, let me read you this from the business section of the Tokyo paper: 'Strong Ainu support promises mutual benefits from Japanese resource development, said the CEO of All Nippon Steel. I have met Mr. Kru and found him to be a staunch and worthy supporter of the Japanese way.'"

Ike stood up, "I have to go to the ministry now. But one last thing, I heard people on the subway talking this morning, saying the North Koreans were responsible for last night's TV blackout."

John arrived at the museum early, before it opened to the public. He needed time to think. Someone had seen him slip some Ainu braid-work into his pocket while he was checking the museum's archives for items that might match sketches from the Russian curator's documents. He felt ill done by: the braid-work was not properly archived; it had no label, which would make it worthless for serious study. Unfortunately, there was an ongoing series of thefts of Ainu artifacts that had everyone upset. The director, while assuring John he was not suspect for these other crimes, had put him on notice. John appreciated the director's action, but he found it hurtful.

For John, the halls were deader and grayer than usual; the ghosts were asleep except for *Hippopotamus amphibius*—his secret confidant. John's museum river horse, a partial skull with broken canine and incisor teeth, managed to look dignified. John wanted to join him, munching submerged vegetation, feeling the hot African sun on his back. "Not today, hippo."

He strode past display cases containing relics of vanquished cultures. They screamed, Give us our lives back. One case contained a hip bone that had once belonged to an Ainu. An adjacent plaque called attention to an arrowhead projecting from the bone. John knew that several renowned scientists had investigated this specimen. He wondered who he had been, what his name was.

He beckoned John and they slipped through the silent forest. Ahead could be heard happy village sounds. They crawled amid dense ferns and boggy places. Vegetation, at various stages of decay, supplied unfamiliar textures and smells; care had to be taken not to break a dry twig. At one point John placed his hand on a snake. His body turned cold, his mind numbed. Hesitantly, he lifted his hand and the serpent moved on. A reassuring squeeze on his shoulder halted his shaking. John made no sound.

They reached the back of a small hut on the edge of the village. Firelight danced on the foliage above them, but the villagers seemed oblivious. They leaned against the thick straw thatch. It prickled and smelled moldy. John's companion tapped him on the knee and slithered away.

The forest closed in, the partially lit trees seemed animated, twisting and bending to some god's will. Somewhere an owl hooted and its echo called back. The fire slowly died and the villagers, with sleepy goodnights, turned in. His eyes wanted to close; all energy had drained from his body.

A great roar, and John fought to suppress a scream. Men rushed to the fire, which they bathed in oil. The leaping flames revealed all. A caged bear slashed his paw back and forth between two wooden poles above John. Men, armed with arrows and spears, charged in John's direction. He knew they could not see him, but that would soon change.

Just as the Ainu headman rounded the hut, he jerked short, straightened up, stumbled. Reaching behind him, he snapped off the shaft of the arrow that had pierced his hip. With a guttural curse, he collapsed on one knee. A woman, John assumed his wife, grasped the wounded man's head, looked into his eyes, and then gently laid him down. She curled up beside him.

The stunned villagers had lost their leader.

"Specimen," John muttered as he walked past other display cases. What a convenient term, so impersonal. And "Vanishing Cultures." Why were they vanishing? He started to freak out. Everything was out of place. A child's broken clay doll, a carved pipe, dishes, pottery shards, a mildewed woven basket fragment. Skulls without jaws, a femur, a tibia, ribs. A jawbone.

John ignored hippo's pleas, as campus security dragged him off to the police station.

Except for posters of wanted criminals, the office of the local constabulary was a study in drab. The gray linoleum was thoroughly worn, similarly colored paint, tinged with decades of cigarette tars, threatened to curl from the walls and ceiling.

The sergeant hunched over John's documents: passport, temporary Sapporo resident permit, social insurance card, University of Hokkaido visiting researcher's certificate, library card, and Sapporo Transit pass. John eyed the faces on the wall and tried to imagine if their crimes were worse than almost PhDs trying to rescue jawbones.

Mrs. Murata impatiently flipped through ancient magazines and the museum director alternatively fidgeted with his bow tie and checked his watch.

John was unhappy that Mrs. Murata was there and embarrassed by the director's presence.

"I'll vouch for him," Mrs. Murata had said, her hand resting on John's shoulder. "I know him to be a good man. We look on him as part of the family."

Her thumb and forefinger drew together, pinching the flesh on his upper arm, bringing tears to his eyes.

She looked down at him and whispered, "My Hirome sleeps at home, Mr. Fox."

John lifted his bandaged hand to indicate he understood the message.

"What happened to his hand?" Mrs. Murata asked the director.

"Murata-san, the guards had to force it. He would not release the valuable jawbone. You must understand."

"No, I do not understand. It was not the Emperor's jaw. And to whom is it so valuable?"

John felt like a passenger on an out-of-control subway train that's been abandoned by its berserk driver: a crash is inevitable but he and the other passengers sit frozen, conditioned to hope that someone will save them. Mrs. Murata?

"This jawbone is Ainu from northern Hokkaido, Wakkanai. The

late Edo era. Ainu no longer exist there. It is one of three that the museum salvaged from that area," explained the director.

"Salvaged? Do you mean exhumed, taken from a grave?" Mrs. Murata demanded.

Everyone looked about, trying to discover the source of the ticking: a grandfather clock sound but intense, a pendulum of doom.

"Director-san, I will need to see the paperwork relating to this jawbone. I will come to your office tomorrow. But first, please explain to this constable that the museum will not be pressing charges."

John hesitantly entered his office. There was a sign on the door that said, "John Fox, Anthropologist." Inside, everything looked different.

Ike smiled, "Do you like it, John? The university administration is concerned it could be sued for using excessive force when, ahem, 'detaining' you at the museum. These," and Ike indicated the freshly painted walls, a big shiny air conditioner, "will assure your goodwill and continued good mental health."

John looked about. Nothing felt right.

"Where's god?" he asked.

Ike explained Hirome felt it best if the chair wasn't there during the renovations.

"And the scrolls and the manuscripts and my bears?"

"The museum staff thought the bears might be valuable. There was the concern they were not cataloged, an activity they have been very diligent at as of late. I assured them they were your property and not part of the museum collection. Do not worry."

John collapsed in his chair, turning this way and that. His desk was clean, the floor litter-free, and the walls no longer bore the reminders their encounter with Meatball.

"And Ike, the scrolls and papers?"

"Dr. Kawasaki has them for now. Again, do not worry."

Hirome entered the office, looking stunning. "Gentlemen, what do you think? Mother said that as I am now a sophisticated academic researcher, I should dress like one. We had a great day shopping. You should see her new outfit."

They stared—black sheath dress, stiletto heels, pearls—a Japanese Audrey Hepburn. Hirome slowly turned, then gracefully dropped into a chair, her ankles demurely yet seductively crossed.

Stunned John and Ike looked on in silence. This was a new Hirome.

She looked around. "What have they done to my office?"

She smiled across the room at John, and re-crossed her ankles, slowly. "I can live with this."

It was a particularly nice day and Hirome had suggested they go outside for ESL. She led John to the university's famous Poplar Avenue, where they perched on the dead trunk of a fallen tree.

"Do you know the story of this dead tree, John? It was one of many along this avenue that was destroyed by a typhoon in 1959. The pleading of a schoolgirl led to this one fallen tree being left as a reminder of the lovely avenue's past."

John laid his hand on a branch, as one would on the gravestone of some famous rock star. "Hirome, about your ESL. Your English is excellent. Why don't you start studying Chinese? That's going to be the next language of commerce."

Hirome squirmed on the fallen poplar tree trunk where they perched, trying to get comfortable while retaining some degree of modesty. "John, that newspaper article said your eyes are blue, but they are not. What color do you call them?"

John watched Hirome struggle to keep her balance.

"Hazel. Why did you want to come out here for your lesson?"

"What is hazel?"

"Hazel is the color of my eyes. Now, stop being silly."

"Okay, professor. I thought it would be fun to relax with you. You always seem so serious. You worry over the scrolls, you worry over your ESL students, you worry over the Japanese language, you worry over your dissertation. I think your Miss Kawaguchi was good for you: she got you out on weekends."

John understood what she was saying, but she hadn't said it all. Where was his life going after Japan, after this fling was over? Would he be an academic, an imprisoned pilferer of worthless Ainu artifacts, a bar bum? Isn't that something to worry about, he wondered.

"John, I study English because that is what people want. Japanese think English is great, that anything American is great. English declarations mix with Japanese text in our banners and signs. English words scatter through our language, but the way we use them is meaningless to you."

She stood down from the tree, straightened the pleats in her short black skirt, cocked her head, the tip of her tongue glossing her lips. "GI Joe want pretty Japanese girl?"

John was dumbfounded. Had he heard his most sophisticated student, the person he hoped would join him on life's journey, correctly? Yes, he had.

That night, after the usual ho-hum bar hopping, John lay down, Vivaldi in the background, and considered this person, Hirome Murata. The more he knew her, the more complicated she seemed. Like Aki, but also completely unlike. Who, he wondered, is the real Hirome?

John slowly slunk into the steamy waters, his feet exploring the pool's irregular bottom. Soon the water reached his nose, his eyelashes trailed like water spiders across its surface. He was hippo; his ears flapped as he glided amongst the vegetation. The sun felt hot on his back. He looked up and saw Hirome standing on the pool's edge, one foot probing the water, and one hand modestly shielding her crotch. Hippo studied her through the vapors.

Her body pulsed, elongated, collapsed. This Japanese mirage defied definition. She approached, her body being devoured by the hungry waters. Soon her breasts were upon hippo and soundlessly she shaped the words, "I am real, John."

John stopped outside his hallway classroom. He could hear music. Quietly he opened the door and observed Hirome, hunched over a guitar, absorbed in her playing, concentrating on the chords. Sometimes she would put her head back, confident of her playing, her eyes closed; other times she coiled around the guitar, struggling with a difficult stretch of notes, often repeating the piece over and over. Even with the imperfect, hesitant playing, the haunting melody pervaded the dreary classroom. John was enchanted.

Hirome looked up, saw John, and gave the strings a frustrated swipe as she put her guitar down.

John applauded.

"Ah, John, you caught me struggling for greatness. That was Andrés Segovia's *Serenata*. I love Segovia's music and his artistry. He shows restraint at the moment of passion, he cradles you, then fondles you. He lifts me when I am troubled and leaves me breathless."

John picked up the guitar and looked questioningly at her.

"I have been playing for most of ten years, John. I cook, too."

"Very impressive, Hirome. Why have you come to ESL class today? There's a power outage and the university is closed."

"I know. I thought I might have some quiet time with my guitar. Would you like to go out for coffees?"

"Coffee sounds good. We could go to the Egg Coffee Shop."

They left the campus, silently and awkwardly trying to understand their evolving relationship. The coffee shop was quiet.

"So, this is your breakfast place. The life of a bachelor."

"Hirome, I have a little present for you. Open it."

"John, is this a present to apologize for not taking my heart?"

"Hirome, you caught me off..."

"*Shssss*, John. You had asked me to marry you, after all. But we were drunk. Now, what is in here?" She unwrapped the parcel, carefully folding and smoothing the wrapping paper. John silently urged her to hurry up.

"You would not give me some silly broken Ainu comb, or one of the other trinkets I keep finding around your office, would you?"

"What are you talking about?" exclaimed John.

"Oh, John, your office is such a little world. Do you think Ike and I do not know everything that goes on in there, or that we care? Now, what is in this box?"

She lifted out an Ainu bamboo mouth harp. "John, it is perfect."

"I bought it at the Authentic Ainu Village gift shop. They assured me it was an authentic replica made in Hong Kong. And it is made of durable plastic."

"John, thank you. You are so nice."

"You mentioned doing something together, something not ESL, but something to give us a break from all those translations. Something different and relaxing."

"Do you play an instrument, something we can play together?"

"Spoons?"

Ike and John sat at the counter of his place of rest, the Yaseragi bar. Two lovely barmaids, daughters of mama-san, kept their glasses full and served them fishy treats. John loved the swish of their stiff kimonos, their demurely lowered eyes, their sweet breaths and little attentions; mama hovered nearby.

Other guests had long since learned to address John in Japanese. A bar rule. Less than a year ago, he had stuck his head in this place, not knowing if it were a brothel or a television repair shop. Now it was his second home.

Ike, smoking a rare cigarette, had them in stitches with his attempts to blow smoke rings. John thought about his friend's formal BBC English, the American-wannabe teenagers, the English slogans on Japanese signs. He thought about how Ike had referred to himself as John's lackey, and how he, John, had treated him.

"Ike, don't you resent our messing with your life?"

"Who, John?" Ike replied, as he received a stiff scotch poured from Sakana-san's Black Nikka bottle.

"Me. I feel so intrusive. If I weren't here, things might be betterish. I'm a little like Clark, the university's founder: intrusive, and he was here for only eight months."

"John, things are not as they appear. That campus sculpture of Dr. Clark is not old. During the war, the Japanese melted the original for bullets to shoot Americans. This Japanese admiration of everything American would disappear at the drop of a lie. And Miss Murata and Miss Kawaguchi and Dragon Lady would become Cherry Blossom girls, praying for their Japanese warriors to right some imagined wrong, and to expand the Japanese Empire."

Ike straightened up on his barstool. "Miura would not. Miura is already battling the Japanese. As I should be, and Kru, the appeaser, should be. John, don't worry about the problems you make. You bring us a joy. Be happy. Kampai."

Following another frustrating day of trying to organize his research notes and finish his thesis, and after a few too many scotches at his place-of-rest bar, John stumbled homeward along a Little Ginza street where a cardboard Colonel Sanders greeted him.

"Well, who have we here?" John asked. "Would you be so kind as to hold my briefcase? You see I need both hands to punch you out." John dangled his briefcase from the Colonel's outstretched left arm. "You represent everything that is ugly about America. Don't smile at me like that. Your hydrogenated, oil-soaked rubber chickens will not suck me in. Leave these little people alone, go home and finish killing off another generation of grease guzzlers before some stupid war does."

John deftly broke off the Colonel's right arm, leaving his briefcase hanging from the left, and then systematically bashed in his head, his shoulders, his sternum and finished with a knee slam to his crotch. It felt good.

John retrieved his case and continued along West 4th Street to MaxValue for some more Black Nikka whiskey.

"Zippidy do da, zippidy day, oh wadda wonderful feeling, wadda wonderful day."

The interrogation room at the police station was as dull as ever, and its familiar grayness made John feel comfortable, kind of at home.

"Fox-san, you are one strike away from three," the sergeant said.

He was eating a snack while he talked, and John liked the way he thoughtfully rested his chopsticks on his lower lip; it reminded him of Hirome. The thought of her brought on a slight qualm of guilt.

"First, there was your assault on the display cases at the university museum, for which the director kindly did not prosecute you. And now you have destroyed Colonel Sanders, the property of Little Ginza's KFC. This is an icon of our district. What if I were to assault your Statue of Liberty?"

They both stared at the yellow pickled radish, the last morsel in the policeman's bento box.

"Would you like it?" the sergeant asked.

John nodded, tilted his head back and opened his mouth, a baby robin pleading.

It was good and so crunchy John could barely hear the sergeant's next remark, "Fox-san, we think you are calling out for help."

John thought the sergeant very perceptive. The other people in his Japanese life, the ones who should know him better, never grasped his real problems. They nitpicked small issues. They sometimes joined him in his follies, but they were never really there. They were like actors reading a boring script, waiting to exit, to go back to their own lives and not be involved in the gaijin's problems.

"Sergeant-san, may I speak frankly?"

He nodded. "Fox-san, before I joined the constabulary I was a student of psychology. I loved people and wanted to help them. But how to help them? Jungian, Freudian, shock therapy . . . it was all too confusing. So I became a policeman."

John nodded and took out his bottle of Black Nikka.

"Do you have any ice?"

John began to catalog his Japanese gripes: architecture not suited for anyone over five-foot-six, a language where the spoken word does not relate to the written symbol, food of indescribable textures, tastes, appearances. "Is there nothing you don't eat?"

The sergeant remained silent and took a long drink of scotch.

"Officer, I never accomplish anything. Once I think I've mastered something, someone politely explains, 'It is not that simple, John.' Like counting things: one, two, three, *ichi, ni, san*—pencils, boats, sheets of paper, people . . . But no, no they each have their own counting words, systems. Sir, Japan is defeating me."

The sergeant stood, removed their glasses to the sink and took a deep breath. "Fox-san, to most Japanese, you are our blue-eyed, kendo scholar."

"To most Japanese people?"
"To the readers of *Tokyo Shimbun*."

"Ike, where are the originals of Ivan's papers? Does Dr. Kawasaki have them? I've had another letter from Betty and she's threatening dire consequences."

"Tell her I lost them," replied Ike. "They are too important for the Ainu to give up. Everything else is in museums, private collections, dark archives. Where they bear numbers referring to lost notes by dead people. People who got famous and died. These we keep. And we must safeguard the scrolls, too. They were saved at the expense of a man's life. Kru's father died saving them. They belong to the Ainu. And yes, our esteemed Dr. Kawasaki keeps them safe for the Ainu."

John did not have the energy or heart to once again explain the importance of scientific inquiry for the betterment of mankind. He was tired and afraid. "I'm going home, Ike."

There was little pedestrian traffic, heavy rains having discouraged all but the bravest cyclists, and the cars seemed less aggressive. Each little shop he passed presented a pleasant ambience—the soba shop with its stringent smell of sake, lovers huddled over low tables; the tempura shop with sounds of deep frying, sweet ginger smells, and baskets of battered shrimp, their tails pointing at paper lanterns; the authentic Japanese restaurant and its grated Japanese radish, its fresh mint leaves, a line of slippers patiently beckoning; even, almost even, Colonel Sanders' KFC with its sickening smell of greasy fries—enticing him to enter.

In the end, he knew he would have a nice meal and meet some new people. But the means to the end seemed so overwhelming. Incomprehensible menus; people that refused to believe, and with reason, that he could converse even at the most basic level; and his bumping, knocking, spilling things because of an unaccommodating Japanese style, all these contributed to the exhausting ebb and flow of John's confidence, sanity.

Tonight, he would go home. He had not cleaned the place for too long. He would read a book. He would listen to laughter from the adjoining rooms, smothering his Vivaldi. He would look out the window at the bundled up little bees as they bustled through the rain. He would imagine pitchers of shitty beer, jolly friends in heated debate over tomorrow's college football game, and a friendly warm world that was clueless, but sane, conversant.

My room, home. What a peculiar description that was. As John put Little Ginza behind him, a shadow flitted behind a power pole. He paused: what a parody, he thought. Projecting out from opposite sides of the pole were a bust and a butt. The bust heaved; the butt tightened. There stood Mrs. Murata, the very sophisticated mother of the sophisticated and very desirable Hirome and, John feared, the nemesis of his courting.

"Mrs. Murata, what are you doing out on such a rainy night?"

An umbrella opened and she stepped from behind the pole. She wore dark runners, a tight body stocking that went to her chin, and, when John peeked under her umbrella, he could see a black stocking cap and, most curious, a black smudge under each eye, like he saw on the Iowa State Cyclone football players.

"Ah, Mr. Fox, what a coincidence. Do you live around here?"

He nodded in the direction of his residence and waited for her answer.

"Noh," she said. "I am performing in a Noh play about a bad boy who has the mother of a fourteen-year-old virgin worried. He seems so devious. I hope you will be able to come to see it."

"I wouldn't miss it for the world. Mrs. Murata, your figure alone will assure a grand performance."

She looked at him, tilted her head, Hirome-like, in question.

Then she laughed, folded her umbrella, took him by the elbow and nudged him into a coffee house. She ordered from a nervous waiter.

"Mr. Fox, with a little discipline you could become an attractive intellectual. Ladies would flock to you . . . in countries where English is the primary language."

She looked intently at John. *You need not call here again.*

That night he dreamed a shadow, a smothering presence, had slipped into his bed.

Spring was in full bloom. Television traced the slow northerly progression of cherry blossoming: Sakura, Sakura. Within two weeks Hokkaido would be a cheerier place. Whatever it was John had to do here seemed to be ending. He had submitted a draft of his thesis, *The Bear: Iconographic portrayals and cultural affinity among Pacific First Nations*. He was not proud of this work, too much had been left out, but prevailing wisdom dictated he bail, and with a PhD sheepskin.

Dr. Baker, pleased with his thesis and the unique artifacts John had shipped to him, assured him there was a job waiting in his department.

Why did he not feel elated? Why, when he learned of this wonderful opportunity, did he feel nauseated? Why had he not told Ike or Hirome this wonderful news, or the excitement over his essay on the probable origins of the glyphs revealed on his Sapporo manhole rubbings?

"New Mexico University Leads Nation," the *Albuquerque Journal* headline had read. The article went on to describe the surprising symbolic sophistication revealed in a series of ancient glyphs obtained by doctoral candidate, John Fox. His professor was elated, the state governor was redeemed, the university mental health clinic got a fat increase to its budget, and John got a job offer.

The whole thing started as a joke. Ike, impressed with the diligence of John's pursuit of Sapporo manhole cover rubbings, suggested he send them to New Mexico. John had finally admitted his ideas to Ike, who laughed and clapped.

"Say they hint of some unknown culture. Perhaps one that passed through Hokkaido after the pit people. Before the Ainu. The Meso-Yezo Era," chortled Ike.

"John, Ike, let us celebrate spring. We should have a barbeque. How about this weekend?" Hirome trilled.

She stood in the middle of the office, her brown jodhpur riding pants tucked into black boots and a colorful silk scarf loosely tied over a man's white shirt. She lightly whipped her thigh with a wicked little riding crop: Japanese maiden equestrian subdues American and Ainu roustabouts.

Ike responded, "Hirome, I do not know. We are planning a naming ceremony for little yet-to-be-named. It might be this weekend."

"Well, we could have the barbeque at the naming ceremony in your village. I'd love to see Miura and your son. What do you think, John?"

John pondered the whip. Something to consider in the future.

"I am not sure, Hirome," said Ike. "There have been a couple of occasions of suspicious people seen on the path to our village. Last week, some of our Ainu treasures went missing. We think they were stolen by intruders. I do not know what our village will think of a lot of outsiders coming at this time."

Hirome pleaded, "We will invite everyone in your village, Ike, and Mother and I will bring lots of food. We would be honored to celebrate spring and the newly named Deciduous Leaf Falling with our Ainu friends."

Kru came from behind his desk and joined John on the couch facing the window. He seemed relaxed and in a contemplative mood. He leaned toward John, his short-sleeved polo shirt exposing strong, tanned arms and a newly formed scar.

"Mr. Fox, do you know the meaning of the word Ainu?"

John started to expound and then stopped. He knew the answer was not in any of the books he had studied.

"Ainu means good people. It doesn't mean just us hairy ones, as everyone assumes. To us, good Japanese are Ainu and bad hairy ones are not Ainu." He leaned back, sighed and continued, "Sometimes I am Ainu and sometimes not."

"So, it's like Kleenex; we say Kleenex when we mean tissue."

Kru roared, "Mr. Fox, you have the most interesting mind. Have you considered donating your brain to science?"

John had always assumed his body would be placed intact in an anthropologists' Graceland. But now that did not seem fair. He had preached surrendering the Ainu manuscripts to scientists, at the expense of the Ainu culture, and he was not willing to depart with his brain, even after he was dead.

"You look concerned, Mr. Fox. Please relax and enjoy our conversation. Would you like some tea or coffee?"

John settled back into the leather cushions and asked if he could have a glass of Grey Goose instead. Kru smiled and glanced at the wall; John followed his gaze and saw her picture: Betty standing next to the Ainu shaman, Kru.

"She's quite the woman, Mr. Fox. By the way, you needn't worry about the Russian documents. The Ainu will take care of them."

John nodded, the vodka flowed. Outside, rain drizzled down the windows. He tried to see the apartment buildings that defined his neighborhood. Ike was right, they did look like tombstones, markers for a lost race, a lost time, a lost opportunity. And they were spaced like dominos; one flick of a finger by the Ainu god of seismics and . . .

"Mr. Fox, are you okay?"

"Oh, excuse me, Mr. Kru, this is certainly good vodka."

"Tell me, what have you concluded about the significance of the Kawai Scrolls?" Kru asked, and John was flattered. His mind raced over four years of graduate training, which were useless in formulating the right answer.

"Mr. Kru, those writings represent the first-hand verification of your oral history to the outside world. Scientists often debunk oral histories, saying they are nothing but myths, fabricated half-truths. This is very convenient for politicians who use these ill-founded opinions to support their distorted historical claims." John wanted to go on, citing the Dead Sea Scrolls, the Rosetta Stone, Jack Kerouac's diary, the voyage of the *Beagle*, but decided not to.

"Very good, Mr. Fox. We believe your research and discovery will give our cause credibility in certain important government circles. Perhaps we should arrange for you to stay on after you complete your studies. We could pay you to be a consultant."

A pod of killer whales charged John's pyloric valve. His brain froze at the thought of the five thousand kanji characters he'd be expected to know. His head throbbed in anticipation of five thousand collisions with low door frames. The thought of five thousand visits to Japanese toilets . . .

"That's an interesting idea, Mr. Kru. I'll give it some thought. Could I have another vodka?"

"John, may I call you John, Mr. Fox? I have decided I would like to learn about my father. Please tell me about him."

John remembered how, at Miura and Ike's wedding, the shaman had said he wanted nothing to do with the man. He remembered his promise to the legless bookseller and he was glad that he would now be able to fulfill it.

He accepted the refreshed vodka and made good on his vow. "I visited several Tokyo bookstores in search of literature on the Ainu. Only your father, Kei-ichi Matsuyama, was sympathetic. He provided me with some important manuscripts and books and promised to find me some old scrolls."

Kru interrupted, "My father's name was Kei-ichi?"

"Kei-ichi Matsuyama," John replied. He went on to explain Kru's father's sense of humor and deep empathy. "And he really wanted to see you and your mother before he died."

"John, as you have learned, we Ainu love hearing stories. Please tell me everything you can; leave nothing out. This is the Ainu way of relating history."

John sipped the vodka and thought back to his second day in Japan. Recalling the smell of musty books, the claustrophobic feel of the small bookshop, he described Kru's father's experiences with the Ainu at the end of the Second World War, how he had met Oma, Kru's mother, and then was removed from his family on Hokkaido to Tokyo by the authorities.

"Thank you, John, thank you for my . . . my father's story. But what of your story of my father?"

"He seemed proud and cared about his appearance. He was clean-shaven and, even though his books smelled moldy, he had a gingery scent, more like a baby's than an old man's.

"He was poor. I saw a worn plastic box with a few grains of rice and meat gristle on a lower shelf. A holey blanket, crammed into the corner, probably his bed. A bedpan, discreetly tucked under a low table, his toilet. His luxury was his book collection and the occasional beer with his blind friend. I doubt he sold much. The higher shelves were dust free; I wondered at the time how he managed that. It must have been a buddy, maybe someone he could help with reading, maybe someone who came by on lonely nights, and shared a sip of whiskey and a story with him.

"He struck me as a man of integrity: a man who would be faithful to the memory of his wife and reliable in friendship. I suspect he was like many wounded veterans: isolated from society, forced to survive on a meager pension, a reminder of some colossal government error to be tolerated, and hopefully to disappear."

John's mind slipped back to the *Golden Maru* and cynical Captain Tveit. "Mr. Kru, your father's condition was as bad as it gets, but his experiences were shared by many who returned from the war, even those who were physically intact."

Kru stretched out his legs, rested his head on the back of the couch, and stared at the ceiling, trying to understand his father.

"I always thought my father was a crazy Japanese soldier, someone who murdered helpless civilians, bayoneted babies. Mother never spoke of him. I wish we had met."

Kru stood and looked out on the distant expanse of deciduous forest that covered the slopes of Moiwayama, and spoke to the comforting landscape.

"I was raised by an Ainu mother, not knowing who my father was—for all I knew Mother was raped by the occupying Japanese to destroy pure Ainu lineages, a type of genocide. I had a hard time fitting in, being Japanese. I spent untold hours in the woodlands, avoiding awkward contact with both Japanese and Ainu. Nature entered me and I accepted the Ainu notion that everything is god. Thanks to my Japanese-ness, I could attend a lowly trade school where I discovered the power of business.

"Thank you for sharing stories with me, John. Now, is there any story I can tell you?"

John thought back to the sword fight, to the enchanted transformation of the school gym, and asked about his kendo skills.

"John, I was nervous, I will confess. We shamans are quick to impress others with bluster but rarely put ourselves on the line. In that gym, I called on the greatest Ainu warrior of all times, Samkusaynu. Samkusaynu is very important to us. He grounds us and gives us pride. He led Ainu and Japanese settlers, squeezed by Honshu merchants, and challenged shogunate authority. In the battle that followed, they pitted poison arrows against guns, and they humiliated the main-island Japanese forces. The Japanese sued for peace and then slaughtered the Ainu leaders at a friendship banquet." John explained he knew of Samkusaynu from the Kawai scrolls and Kru smiled.

"Ike believes his son is that great warrior reborn," John said.

Kru went to his shaman's cloak and removed a piece of rusty iron. "This was found with Samkusaynu's defiled body. Take it and remember us."

"Mr. Kru, I owe your father a profound debt. And not just for the texts and scrolls, but for showing me his humanity. Except for Miura, he is the only Japanese I've met who explicitly respected the Ainu."

At the door, John first extended and then retracted his hand. Kru smiled, rubbed his palms and then his naked face, and bowed. John bowed back and exited from a wondrous deciduous forest.

Ike and John lugged food hampers through the Authentic Ainu Village, past gawking tourists, down the path to Ike's village, with Hirome and her mother following.

Hirome, in the spirit of spring, wore her brother's baseball band outfit, its sleeves and pants cuffs rolled up—its bagginess forcing her to walk like Charlie Chaplin. In spite of her costume and awkwardness, she appeared at ease. Her presence at Miura's birthing, her study and translation of all the ancient scrolls and documents—evidence of which could be seen throughout the village—and her closeness to Ike, made her comfortable with things Ainu.

"Set it down here," said Mrs. Murata with authority, "and help me light this hibachi."

She jumped when a white-bearded man tapped her on the

shoulder. He smiled, his eyes mere slits and his cheeks rosy, and he led her to the communal fire pit. The elder moved like a panther, and John noticed Mrs. Murata appraising his backside.

Ike's village had grown since last fall, and John hardly recognized the place, which was a fluster of hustle. Kids teasing the dogs, women grinding herbs and scraping elm bark, men in animated conversation. Outside the east window of the gathering house, he saw a cluster of freshly carved willow wands and a tarp thrown over what could have been a bear's head.

Mrs. Murata approached John. "I can see the attraction of this life. I am always worrying about Hirome's prospects, about my son's future; seeing my husband become narrower and shallower, fearing my body is falling apart—it is frightening. But if I had spent my life digging bulbs and collecting nuts, I would not have met you, and neither would have Hirome. Thank you, John."

John gave Mrs. Murata a hug, which earned her a "Mother! What are you doing?" from her daughter.

Miura beamed as she stood in front of her new home, while yet-to-be-named slept contentedly in a miniature hammock slung between a cottonwood and cherry tree.

"John, in the past, we burned the old house when we moved out," said Ike. "This released all of the house gods so they could come with us or just take a break. But now it is against the law for Ainu to burn their old houses, so we will rent it to tourists." Then he rubbed his palms and then his beard in prayer to their new home.

"But Ike," said John, "aren't you required to live in your government designated housing?"

"John, this is just one more rebellion, as we identify ourselves. Now, enough politics."

Miura approached them—she had the sweet-sour smell of mother's milk and appeared as restless as a nursing lioness—

causing Ike to puff up to ten times his usual size. He was one proud man, family man, Ainu warrior.

"Hey, husband, come here," Miura demanded. She looked haggard, but content with her new life, her husband, her son, and now a new home.

She grabbed the hem of Ike's new robe, exposing his scrawny legs, to show Hirome the brocade.

"Miura created this pattern with help of the elders," said Ike, tugging down on his hem. "It symbolizes the dawn of the new Deciduous Leaf Falling clan."

Hirome bent in close to study the detail and gave Ike a pinch. He jumped and everyone laughed.

"Mr. Deciduous Leaf Falling, they are cooking dog on your firepit!" said Mrs. Murata.

Ike bowed and said, "You do not eat our dog on a spit and we will not eat your whale yakitori. Agreed?"

She reached for Ike and gave him a hug.

"You are smart for a savage. I love your dress."

Again, everyone laughed.

"It is really a roasted piglet," conceded Ike.

The large group knelt on an enormous blue tarp as Miura, a whirlwind of activity, continued to replenish plates with food.

"Ike, one more mouthful and I'll explode."

"Is that a metaphor, John? Because if it is not, you are in big trouble."

Miura, her lip tattoo now much larger, like the villain's in a silent film, ceremoniously presented each of them with a cube of frozen salmon on a mint leaf.

Kru played a bamboo mouth harp, accompanied by the rosy-cheeked elder who strummed a stringed instrument. The sound conjured up images of foxes and owls and bears and cranes moving through deep forests and spongy swamps.

Responding to nature and too much beer, John sought relief in a nearby copse of cottonwood trees.

"Koro was right, you are well endowed."

John looked about and, seeing no one, assumed it was a god speaking. He was becoming accustomed to such visits. John gave himself a good shake, thinking: the last three drops are for you, god of whatever. Then it struck him; God had said "Koro."

Something tugged at his pants cuff. He panicked: *Hokkaido has poisonous snakes*. Tripping on a root, he found himself face-to-face with Kru's brother, Tukkaram, the big-headed Ainu with the powerful voice. John could just make out his eyes, buried as they were in the folds of his immense face. His hand gently probed John's face, clicked his jaw, yanked his Adam's apple, and finally ran his fingers through his hair.

"Koro was wrong about your hair. It is a mess."

"You're making me nervous," said John.

The Ainu nodded in sympathy.

"I usually don't see the gods that speak to me."

Again, the Ainu nodded.

"Mostly the gods tell me to buck up, do the right thing, Sunday school stuff."

The crippled man's body language revealed nothing.

"You've said things you couldn't know, like a prophet."

Tukkaram somehow managed to reconfigure his mess of a face into something that expressed modesty.

"Oh, how sweet," said Mrs. Murata. They had gathered to look at soon-to-be-named, the guest of honor, sleeping under a cherry tree. Except for Miura, who was caught up in hosting, mothering and dithering, they felt the enormity of the moment: the smell of the earth coming to life after a cruel winter, the overhead swans heralding their return to heaven, the cherry blossoms falling, and a perfect child to be named. For most, this foretold a promising future for the Ainu, but not for all.

As they returned to the tarp by the firepit, John saw Kru's big-headed brother, muttering and pretending to shoot arrows from his small bow; he looked distraught.

Then came the spring rain.

Miura passed the baby to Ike.

"Ike, see to your son, I will get more tarps."

Hirome reached out her hand and touched Miura's shoulder, "Miura, it is okay, the rain feels good. Please relax."

But she wouldn't listen. She ran into the old house.

There was a shout and then a shot, its echo destroying their idyll. A man burst out of the building, holding a bag and a gun, which he waved at the shocked group.

Frantically, Ike shouted, "Don't move, anyone, or he might shoot. Miura!" he screamed, but no sound came from the old house.

The thief looked at the group of fierce, angry Ainu and panicked; he leaped, grabbing for the baby. Then he yelped. He dropped the bag and pulled the shaft of a small arrow from his hip, its obsidian head still buried in his flesh. A confused look came over his face, replaced with one of terror, and then he slowly collapsed.

Kru stomped on the man's wrist, kicking the gun free. They watched him twitch, and he became still as paralysis crept through him. When it finally reached his diaphragm, his gasping breath stopped.

Ike carried Miura from the old house and laid her under the cherry tree. Gently, he placed yet-to-be-named on her breast. She looked peaceful, calm, and then she coughed, spraying speckles of blood onto her robe. Ike, crying, tried to blot the blood away.

Miura grabbed his hand, "Man of mine, promise me you will

continue the Deciduous Leaf Falling line. Our child needs brothers and sisters, and the Ainu need a future."

Tukkaram pointed to a wedge of white swans flying north under the soft, low-lying clouds.

There was silence and a sparrow landed on Miura's motionless shoulder; it released a cheery note.

"She has joined our gods. The happy song of the sparrow god will be our memory of her. She will return to us with the swans," said Kru, and he closed her eyes.

"We must celebrate. We have a powerful new god whom we must welcome to heaven. Miura, you rest."

John looked at her, the tough little bar girl from Muroran; her bone-deep weary face showed peace and contentment.

The day that had begun with a picnic to celebrate spring and a naming ceremony ended with a funeral. Hirome and her mother had left with the police.

The intensely burning thatch flushed John's face as the villagers presented god Miura with her new heavenly home.

John removed his tweed jacket and hurled it on the inferno. "She might get chilly," he said.

Ike had dressed Miura in her finest: an eloquent Ainu robe whose embroidery was yet to be completed and a saucy pair of red, open-toed high heels. About her were arranged her possessions: a plastic hairbrush, a lipstick, a ticket stub from her first trip to Konbu Spa. These, the mourners had broken to release their gods that they too might journey to the afterworld.

John was instructed to place a lacquered wooden bowl of sake near the body. Others had offered millet dumplings, smoked salmon, and a large birch bark bowl of pulped lily bulbs and dried raspberries. While Miura consumed the essence of this repast, the villagers danced and sang in celebration.

"Creator of the World and Possessor of the Heavens, take charge of this spirit and lead it safely to her new home," said Kru, as he distributed the offerings to all present. Everyone in turn presented three drops of sake and three specks of food to Miura's guide, the god of fire, while Kru's brother buried his portion in the ashes.

The funeral procession left through the dense woods; only Ainu walked with Miura's body. The burial site would be secret, to ensure no intrusion by those scientifically curious or criminally inclined.

John squatted, alone, by the glowing fire. He thought of Miura confronting Ike, having risked all, to start a new life with him; of her becoming Ainu; of her announcing her motherhood to a sophisticated Hirome; of her horrendous birthing of a most beautiful child; of her standing up to the powerful shaman. More than anyone, Miura, the defiant little bar girl from Muroran, had brought pride to this tribe of Ainu.

"Miura, I am ashamed of my little dabble gifts of food and drink," John whispered. "My ridiculous toilet paper wedding present." John held up the rusty iron piece, turning it this way and that in the firelight. It seemed alive in his hand: *You're a god, too.* This was a part of the great Samkusaynu, a part that was needed to overcome the treacherous shogunate.

"Miura, take this for your son." He dropped the iron into the glowing coals. A wind arose and the clouds parted, dust whirled about him. The hooting of owls answered the barking of foxes. Barefoot, he shuffled around the fire, slowly turning and dipping. And the trees swayed, the house thatch rattled, and the gods cheered him on. Bloody footed, with aching muscles, he collapsed.

"Arigato," said Samkusaynu.

"Arigato, John-san," said Miura.

John walked among the green spears of a new corn crop, the

blades carrying the promise of a good year. He would not get lost this time.

"You see, I came back, Mr. Maize."

"That's a good sign," said the Downforth-voiced god.

John wandered on rejoicing in spring and its promise for the future: the greening of the fields, the scented fruit blossoms, the loamy soil freed from the snows of winter.

But it was sad too, for the brightest flower would not see summer. Miura had left them. Tears filled his eyes and his vision blurred. There was no focus, nothing made sense. John stood, helpless. Tears ran down his face and fell among the emerging corn plants. Small hands slipped into his hands and gently led him out of the field.

At the farmhouse, he was given tea. The farmer, his wife and two children knelt around the table, facing him. They watched John, and, with nods and smiles, they encouraged him to drink and find tranquility.

He saw hope in the young smiling faces. He saw an honest connection to the land in the farmer's gnarled hands. He saw a future in the swelling of the farmer's wife's belly. Glancing about, he saw the family's Shinto shrine celebrating those who had worked this land before them.

These were not the Japanese whom Ike so resented; these were not Ainu who once lived off this land; these were the people of today's Hokkaido—Kru's Ainu. Their ancestors too had been oppressed by the main-island Japanese. Shiro Kawai had been one of these people and his testimonial would bring hope to the Ainu, with the promise of their own land, Ainu Land.

John stood, having slipped some Chiclets under his cup, bowed and departed. No word had been exchanged, but he left richer.

He boarded the subway at Makomanai. Stop after stop the train filled. Crowded around him were not bees and faceless men. They were individuals, each with their strengths, weakness, aspirations, lusts, and dark secrets. Some felt they could rise above the herd, some felt doomed by circumstance. John felt they, everyone, were shaped by invisible forces, much as iron fillings respond to unseen magnets, or a host of conniving gods.

He looked closely at his companions: the unfaithful husbands, the mahjong addicted wives, the lusting grandfathers, the dreamers, surly youths, future Einsteins, murderers. Are the forces that shape them natural laws or man's laws? Of whom are they pawns—other more powerful pawns, chaos, gods or God? Are their narcissisms, hedonisms, mysticisms, sadisms, psychopathisms, ism-isms, the way of a godless world or a world where everything is god?

A pretty girl checked her lipstick and the subway train pulled into Sapporo Station.

"Ike, you cannot do that," scolded Hirome, pointing at the little bamboo cage with its restless sparrow.

"And what is with this outfit?" she said, flicking his red tie. "Are you planning on running for Prime Minister?"

Ike smiled, wiped his palms, his bearded face, and with a little bow, walked to the cage where, after repeating the greeting, he released the bird. "I am sorry, Miura; you never were meant for a cage. I will see you when the swans return. I love you, first wife."

The sparrow landed on John's ivory Vladivostok bear, released a sweet note and shat into the carved, gaping mouth.

"Miura!" Ike scolded. And she flew away.

John turned to Ike, "Well . . . ?"

"Well, ex-boss, gomen nasai. I work for Kru now. My job is to shake hands, smile and, through the massaging of Japanese guilt, extract promises and cash. My assistant is," and here he hesitated for effect, "Mrs. Murata. She picked out the suit. Do you like it?"

Hirome crumpled into the broken chair god which, giving up a leg, dumped her.

"We are going to Sakhalin to negotiate an international Ainu treaty," Ike announced.

Hirome sat in John's chair, wearing the same outfit that had so exasperated Aki, and translated the coroner's report. "The autopsy determined the cause of death to be asphyxiation brought on by a paralytic poison. A small arrowhead was removed from the victim's hip. It had a hollow tip that contained pine resin and a trace of aconite. This poison is known to have been used by the Ainu, until it was banned for their own protection and for the protection of the general population."

Hirome leaned her head back and rubbed her temples. "No charges will be laid, John. The report says that the victim, a hoodlum from Osaka, was known to police but that no connection with other criminals can be made at this time. They say it was a single-handed burglary gone wrong. There was some question about the stolen contents of the bag. There was nothing of value, just some old artifacts and papers."

"No mention of Kru's brother, Tukkaram?" John asked.

"No," replied Hirome, "but according to my mother," and here she rolled her eyes, "who involved herself in the investigation, the police were loath to interview him. He was so ugly and would only speak Ainu and, as they had no record he even existed, they decided it would be too awkward and complicated."

Hirome stood, and modestly tugged at her shorts. "Well, John, I must go. This afternoon is Italian cooking."

"Hirome, you're still my . . . ?"

"Say it, John."

The word, like a bat in an unfamiliar house, flew about his brain hunting for an exit. John looked down and saw a young corn blade stuck to his shoe. He stared at it, waiting for wisdom, finally, "Fiancée... sort of," he sputtered.

She lifted her hands, turned them from front to back, and asked, "What is missing, John? I do not think a plastic bamboo mouth harp will do."

And then to save him further embarrassment, she continued, "Are you willing to spend your life with me and my mother here in Japan, forever? To stop staring at, as you say, every little bee that buzzes by? Chopsticks, packed subways, cars that drive on the wrong side of the street, a language of which you have yet to pronounce one word correctly? Rice and no potatoes, noodles and no bread, tea and no coffee? Oh, and I must mention getting a good job, a nine-to-niner that makes us lots of money. My lessons will continue, of course, and my wardrobe embellishments."

Hirome was making this too easy. He was about to say that interracial marriages were difficult; that, considering everything, they had best go separate ways, painful as that would be. Then John thought of all the women he had encountered, none of whom compared to Hirome. Near-sex, adventures, frustrations, solemn moments, sharing life's secrets, grieving, fighting, being silly—she beat them all, hands down.

John cupped his hands, swept them over his chest and extended them to her. "Take my heart, Hirome, and marry me."

"I will, John, if you take me to New Mexico or anywhere far from lessons and Mother, and . . ."

Confident Hirome, at a loss for words? John couldn't believe it.

He prompted her, "And . . . ?"

" . . . and we can launch the Murata Fox dynasty. Mucho arigato, John-san."

July 15, 1997
Annapolis Valley, Nova Scotia, Canada

Dear Deciduous Leaf Falling,

Congratulations on the May 1997 passage of the Law for the Promotion of the Ainu Culture and for the Dissemination and Advocacy for the Traditions of the Ainu and the Ainu Culture. We can only imagine this is a major step to the establishment of Ainu Land.

About our Canadian address. Once we settled in New Mexico, we were overwhelmed by circumstances. Hirome couldn't cope with the desert, and being amongst Navajo and Hopi—for whom she was often mistaken—truly upset her. For me, I bit the bullet, defended my thesis and received embarrassing accolades. I was given a grand office, only slightly smaller than my professor's. My students displayed total lack of interest in anything and everything I tried to teach them. They did find it funny when I ducked every time I went through a doorway and when I bowed to inanimate objects.

When I tried to envision my future, clutching my Sapporo manhole cover rubbings, struggling for an original idea, I only saw my professor and his fraudulent hash pipe. This didn't fit with my memories of doing kendo on wet morning grass, wordless communication in Little Ginza bars and my Egg Coffee Shop. In Japan, I had thrust myself into the human streams of subways and department stores, pushed my way through blue curtains into places unknown, but always delightful. I couldn't accept a New Mexico life.

Hirome suggested we try something different, new to both of us. And here we are, in Canada, farming grapes. And, a bonus, we have Siberian winters and Congo summers, just like Sapporo.

Well, that is all. Hirome says it's time to roast marshmallows.

Warm regards,

John

P.S. Please flick three drops of beer for Miura for me.